CATCH
A KILLER...

Praise the King! Elli had been found. He had one
fewer body to worry about this morning. Dubric followed close behind as the kitchen workers tried to make
room. Lars slipped between a pair of scullery maids and
disappeared into the breakfast crowd milling in the great
hall. Above them all, as if separate from the noise and
rabble, flags of the Lands of Lagiern hung from the
beams; their colors gleamed bright in the golden light of
dawn. Faldorrah's flag, white sheep and golden grain on
a field of rich, vivid green, shone brightest of all.
Brighter even than the King's purple standard. Dubric
closed his eyes for a moment. Murder had come to his
castle. He would do everything within his power to bring
justice back, ghosts be damned. Ignoring the hungry
crowd, he turned to the left, toward the carved bulk of
the main castle doors. He opened them to light snow
and a beautiful sunrise.

Both ghosts followed him.

The news of the murder drifted through the castle
like a swirl of falling snow. Before Dubric arrived, at
least fifteen people had touched the body or contaminated evidence, damaging his chance to track Elli's
killer. He guessed the actual number of gawkers to be
close to forty, if the crowd the pages held at bay was any
indication, and fresh footprints ran hither and yon in the
mud and snow. Elli had been rolled onto her back and
her dress trampled into the mud until it tattered. Some
caring, idiotic soul had wiped the worst of the muck

from her face and had covered her body with a rough wool blanket, as if to protect her from the snow. Every likely clue had either been trodden into the mud or cleaned off the body. He was cold, wet, well on his way to furious, and had forgotten about his love of the Faldorrahn flag.

GHOSTS
IN THE
SNOW

†

Tamara Siler Jones

Bantam Books

GHOSTS IN THE SNOW
A Bantam Spectra Book / November 2004

Published by
Bantam Dell
A Division of Random House, Inc.
New York, New York

ISBN 0-553-58709-9

Printed in the United States of America
Published simultaneously in Canada
OPM 10 9 8 7 6 5 4 3 2 1

ACKNOWLEDGMENTS

Writing is a lonely pursuit, a long foray into the dark unknown, but without the insight, insistence, and unfailing support of the following people, Dubric and his ghosts would have remained forever on my hard drive.

First, a thank you to my writer buddies, without whom I would have lost my way. Joshua Rode, Heather Nagey, Johnny B. Drako, J.M. Blumer, Cat Darensbourg, and Gemma Godwin. I love you all.

I'd also like to thank my agent, William Reiss, for taking a chance on Dubric and I. Bill, it's been a fabulous journey and I can't thank you enough for your guidance and insight. Another thank you to my editor, the brilliant Juliet Ulman, for seeing the potential story lurking in the shadows of my original draft and for not canceling my contract when she read the final murder. Instead of recoiling in horror, she happily told me I was a wicked woman. It doesn't get any better than that.

To Sam Godwin, proofreader and plot dissector extraordinaire, I'd like to say that without your diligence Dubric never would have found his soul. You were ruthless and wonderfully pedantic in your exhaustive critiques. You have taught me more than you can ever imagine. Thank you, Sammie! You're the best!

Next I'd like to thank my family: my parents and siblings for encouraging me, but especially my daughter for understanding that Mom had to do this, and for being a great inspiration along the way. Always be yourself, punkin, and pursue your dreams.

Last I'd like to thank my husband, Bill. Without his support, love, understanding, and patience, this would never have come to pass. Few men would encourage their wives to kill people on paper every day. With you I am truly blessed, and perhaps we, too, share one soul. I love you, babe.

It is to him that I dedicate this book.

For Bill
In your eyes anything is possible.

CHAPTER

I

✝

Dubric Byerly, Castellan of Faldorrah, sat alone at a small table in the castle kitchen, his mangled breakfast congealing before him. He sipped his tea and frowned as he poked a chunk of sausage with his fork. Having spent the past half bell toying with the food on his plate, he worried he had wasted too much time pretending to eat. The beginning of an inquiry always seemed disjointed to him. Finding the first clue, the first mistake, the first hint of guilt.

Responsible for the safety and well-being of Lord Brushgar's demesne, Dubric tried to make his presence felt on a regular basis in all areas of the castle. But as he glanced up from his plate, he wondered if he had eaten too many breakfasts alone in the kitchen. The staff gave him a wide and respectful berth as they hurried through their labors, but none gave him a second glance. Could they be too used to him? Was that the problem? Maybe so, but he had to start somewhere.

Dubric contemplated the uneaten food on his plate, he watched the kitchen staff, and he glanced out the window at the blossoming dawn. He looked anywhere but at the ghost that stared at him, silently wailing.

He had woken before dawn to find the slashed

horror of a scullery maid's corpse standing beside his bed. Her gaping spirit still stood before him in a uniform drenched and dripping with blood. He could not recall her name and had no idea where her body might be. He only knew that she had been murdered, in his castle, and that he would see her pained and tortured apparition until he put the matter to rest. Cursed by the Goddess Malanna after his wife's murder forty-three summers before, Dubric had long struggled to ignore the horrid images of wrongful death.

The ghosts came to him in the darkest part of night, in the brightest days of high summer, whenever they happened to die. The spirits would stare at him, their glazed eyes pleading, knowing he alone saw them, saw their torment, and would do his best to avenge them. A praying man would thank the Goddess that he saw only those murdered within the range of his responsibility and no others. But Dubric had denounced religion the day Oriana died and had never looked back.

The scullery maid was his fourteenth ghost, and he had ultimately solved all of their deaths, except one. He thought of his one failure for a moment, then pushed the guilt away. She had been dead for so long, more than thirty summers, and her ghost would likely walk the castle halls for all eternity.

Dubric sighed and toyed with his eggs, the fork clutched in his burn-scarred hand. In his sixty-eight summers he had found most murders to be violent yet simple affairs. Drunken fights gone awry. Spouses who erred in judgment. Lapses of reason while in the throes of extreme anger. Revenge. Uncomplicated crimes of passion, hate, or greed. Hundreds of people lived in and around the castle and occasional bloodshed was to be expected. He had solved the murders quickly, brought the killers to face justice, and continued with happier aspects of his work. But he hated the ghosts. He often wondered if he solved their murders to find justice for their deaths, or merely to get the spirits out of his sight. He hoped it was for justice, insisted in his heart it was for justice, but on this blustery morning in late winter he was far from certain.

He watched the kitchen bustle with activity as scores of folks scurried through their work. A butcher lugged in the third freshly slaughtered ewe of the morning. The herbmonger from the village argued over the price of his spices. Servitors grabbed breakfast trays and dashed away in their hurry to feed their masters. Cooks stirred, fried, and chopped. Scullery maids scrubbed. Bakers baked. Dubric watched them all for signs of stress, of nervousness, of someone stealing glances his way. None did. All seemed as oblivious to him and the scullery maid's demise as they were to her ghost.

He glanced at the ghost and wondered what to try next. She had been murdered, that much was obvious, but was not *missing*. Yet. He did not want to appear crazy, paranoid, or—King forbid—*guilty*, so ordering a castlewide search was out of the question until someone noticed her absence. Besides, for all he knew, her body had been dumped in a privy or destroyed. She was a scullery maid, he was certain of that, and logically his search should begin in the kitchen. If no one from the kitchen was to blame, then who?

The thought died in an instant and he paused, his fork poised over mangled eggs, as a sharp, cold pain behind his eyes signaled the arrival of a new responsibility. Another ghost, this one a milkmaid, flickered into view beside the scullery maid. Both screamed at him in silent terror. *Oh no, not two.* He swallowed and tightened his fist around the fork to keep it from trembling as he looked at the new arrival. The second ghost was Elli Cunliffe, an orphan who had been left on the stoop fifteen summers before.

He set his fork beside his plate and wiped his mouth with a fine linen napkin. *What a mess.*

"Leavin' already, m'lord?" Pitta, the herald's wife and morning kitchen master, looked at him with eyes as soft as her plump body.

He forced what he hoped was a calm smile. "That I am. I have much to do today."

She gathered up his mess and smiled as well. "You've never been one to shirk, sir. Hope you have a pleasant day."

"As do I," he said, knowing it was impossible. He took one last sip of his tea. The dairy barns were on the other side of the castle, outside the west tower. If he hurried, and had any luck at all, the other milkmaids would have overslept and Elli's killer might still be there with the scullery maid tucked under his arm.

Keep on dreaming, you old goat. About as much chance of that as the cows becoming excellent witnesses.

He set aside his tea, straightened his tunic, and tried not to appear to hurry across the kitchen.

He walked past the butcher, dodged a lackey carrying a sack of potatoes, and paused near the baker's ovens to allow a trio of scullery maids to hurry by with trays of dirty dishes. "Mornin', sir!" a voice called from beside him.

Dubric turned and hid the cringe he felt at the

delay. Everyone knew the baker's assistant loved to chat while he kneaded bread. But he was a decent fellow. What could a greeting hurt? "Good morning, Bacstair. How are you this fine day?"

"Doing fine, sir," he said as he raised his forearm to wipe a sheen of sweat from his brow. The mound of dough flexed, stretched, and rolled under Bacstair's expert pounding. "Otlee tells me you've passed him in history and mathematics. He's hoping to make senior page soon."

Dubric's ghosts looked on as he replied. "He is a smart boy, but he is only twelve summers. He will be a senior page soon enough. Tell him to be patient. It will happen in its own time."

Bacstair massaged the dough with his fingers. "Tis what I tell him, sir, but he works so hard at his studies."

Dubric said, "His marks are excellent."

Bacstair smiled proudly and sifted a handful of flour over the dough. "Thank you, sir. The missus and I were talkin' about it just the other day. Neither of us had a lick of education past the primers. We can write our names, read the signs in the village, not much more . . ."

Dubric nodded despite his urge to hurry. Basic education was available, and encouraged, for the common folk of Faldorrah. Few continued past the primers, though; their families desired income more than knowledge. Even with the certain realization that wisdom had freed the people from the dark's oppression, children were rarely educated beyond their eighth or ninth summer.

". . . but Otlee, sir, he was always eager to learn." Bacstair chuckled and shook his head. "'Scuse my blabberin', sir, but we know you had'ta stick your neck out to get Lord Brushgar to approve his posting. Us bein' commoners and all."

"It was no hardship, Bacstair. Really. He is a smart boy. That is all that mattered to me."

Bacstair lifted the dough and slammed it down. A billow of flour coughed into the air around him, dusting his arms and his apron. "You've given our boy a grand gift. In a summer or two he'll make senior page. When he's sixteen summers he can squire. At twenty he can be knighted, become a noble. Maybe he'll even be a lord someday. You've opened the world to him, sir." He flipped the dough over itself, pummeling it with his fists.

Dubric chuckled and shook his head as he remembered. The youngest knighting of a squire had happened nearly fifty summers ago. Tunkek Romlin, the man who would later become King, had led a group of squires and pages, including Dubric, to wrestle the land from the dark mages. All had returned to Waterford alive. If anyone had ever deserved to be knighted, Tunkek had. Dubric's hand fell to the hilt of his soldier's sword and his fingertips traced along the pommel. Despite the horror, his sharpest memories of the War of Shadows were good ones. They had been so young then. Seven friends, all squires or pages, on a noble quest to save the world. But after Tunkek's knighthood, after summers of slogging through blood and death and fire as if they were immune to it all, his friends had begun to die.

Dubric pulled his hand from his sword. Certainly they had been young. Young, idealistic, and stupid. But that was then, times had changed, and the world had moved on. Otlee might be young and idealistic, but he was far from stupid. His knighthood would reasonably wait until his midtwenties, or later. With luck, Otlee would never have to test his mettle in war or watch someone he loved die on a battlefield. "Twenty is a long way from twelve," Dubric said. "Tell him to enjoy where he is right now and not worry so much about the future."

The head baker rushed past, tapping Bacstair on the back of the head. "Bacstair, quit jabbering with his lordship! Ye've got work to do!"

Bacstair dropped his eyes, his exuberance gone like smoke on a bitter wind. He selected a long thin dough knife and sliced the mound of dough into sections, braving a glance at Dubric. "I will tell him that, sir. But thank you. Thank you for what you've done for my boy. For my family."

Dubric tilted his head in a friendly bow despite the dreadful stares from the pair of ghosts. "You are quite welcome. He is a good lad and does a fine job."

Bacstair rolled the sections into neat balls. "Thank you again, sir, but I'd best be gettin' back to work."

Dubric turned to go. His ghosts followed as he pushed through the crowded kitchen.

Moments later, a sharp-eyed, blond-haired senior page ran into the kitchen, scattering the workers like dandelion seeds. Dubric smiled at the sight of him. The son of a neighboring lord, Lars was a vital member of Dubric's personal staff, and the only page to ever achieve that questionable honor. Although jarring to the workflow in the kitchen, Lars's sudden arrival brought Dubric hope. Perhaps a body had been found.

Dubric brushed past a lackey dragging a sack of flour and hurried across the kitchen while his ghosts trailed behind him. Lars tilted his head toward the door and slipped out to the hall. Dubric followed a moment later.

The service hall was crowded with serving girls carrying trays of hot food to the great hall and scullery maids lugging dirty dishes back to the kitchen. They looked hot, sweaty, and tired. Their hair had plastered to their damp brows and their uniforms hung stained and limp from their sagging shoulders. Food-spattered lackeys dodged among them with other supplies and tools. Past the congestion of the kitchen staff, Lars waited in a side hall that led to the kitchen storage rooms. Dubric saw the pale shine of his hair in the torchlight and he pushed through to the relative quiet of the hall.

They walked a few steps away, out of earshot. A moon or two shy of fifteen summers, Lars had nearly reached Dubric's height and he leaned close as he delivered his news. "We've found a milkmaid, sir, outside of the west tower. Murdered."

Praise the King! Elli had been found. He had one fewer body to worry about this morning. Dubric smoothed his tunic and hid his relief behind the urgency in his voice. "Fetch my cloak and meet me there."

"Yes, sir!" Lars said, and hurried to the great hall. Dubric followed close behind as the kitchen workers tried to make room. Lars slipped between a pair of scullery maids and disappeared into the breakfast crowd milling in the great hall. Above them all, as if separate from the noise and rabble, flags of the Lands of Lagiern hung from the beams; their colors gleamed bright in the golden light of dawn. Faldorrah's flag, white sheep and golden grain on a field of rich, vivid green, shone brightest of all. Brighter even than the

King's purple standard. Dubric looked to the flags and smiled despite himself.

Dubric closed his eyes for a moment. Murder had come to his castle. He would do everything within his power to bring justice back, ghosts be damned. He ignored the hungry crowd and turned to the left, toward the carved bulk of the main castle doors, and opened them to light snow and a beautiful sunrise. Both ghosts followed him.

* * *

The news of the murder drifted through the castle like a swirl of falling snow. Before Dubric arrived, at least fifteen people had touched the body or contaminated evidence, damaging his chance to track Elli's killer. He guessed the actual number of gawkers to be close to forty, if the crowd the pages held at bay was any indication, and fresh footprints ran hither and yon in the mud and snow. He stood beside the corpse, his heart thumping in his chest from his early morning run across the courtyard, and he wanted to scream. Elli had been rolled onto her back and her dress trampled into the mud until it tattered. Some caring, idiotic soul had wiped the worst of the muck from her face and had covered her body with a rough wool blanket, as if to protect her from the snow. Every likely clue had either been trodden into the mud or cleaned off the body. He was cold, wet, well on his way to infuriated, and had forgotten about his love of the Faldorrahn flag.

"Watch it, you fool!" someone in the crowd behind him yelled, and Dubric snapped his head back to glare at the complainer.

Lars shoved through the crowd, a heavy wool cloak in his hands, and the bellyacher, a groundskeeper named Ord, mumbled his apologies and stepped aside. Six more onlookers burst from the west tower as Lars ran to Dubric.

Dubric took his cloak from Lars. If he had not taken time to chat with Bacstair, some of this bedlam would have been avoided.

"I take full responsibility for the damage, sir," Lars said. "We should have been quicker. Two milkmaids found her. By the time Otlee and I arrived, they'd already botched it."

"Them and the gawkers. Curse our luck." Dubric brushed off Lars's regret. Disturbed murder scenes were common and expected. He fastened his cloak, looking to the growing crowd and the six pages who held them back. "Otlee!" he yelled.

A slender boy ran up, snowflakes dousing his fiery hair. "Yes, sir," he said, standing a little taller as he glanced at Lars.

"Log witnesses and disperse these crowds. They have done enough damage already."

"Yes, sir," Otlee bobbed a quick bow and ran back to the crowd. He pulled a roll of paper and an inexpensive pressed-coal stick from his pocket, then began taking names.

While Otlee gathered names, Dubric knelt beside Elli and examined her face. Smoky, snow-dusted blue eyes stared at the sky, and smears of mud had congealed beneath her lids. Snowflakes on her eyes flickered like life before they melted to tears on her cheeks. He had always thought Elli had pretty eyes, and he sighed as he closed them. Ever alert, Lars stood beside him and watched the crowd with his hand on the hilt of his short sword.

Dubric checked her hands. Her fingernails were

intact, although filthy and worn from regular use. He found no bruising on her mud-smeared face or neck. He nodded to himself and yanked back the blanket.

Gasps rose around him like sparrows taking flight.

Dubric had no time for niceties. "Get them out of here!" he barked to the pages. Lars remained stoic yet observant and Dubric nodded his approval. Few grown men would contemplate a dead bare-chested woman so calmly, let alone a boy Lars's age.

Dubric resumed his work, his hands gliding swift and sure over her body. Despite the covering of mud, he found no injuries on her throat, chest, or belly. She still wore underdrawers, so rape was doubtful. Her legs seemed fine. He checked her armpits for temperature, her breasts for bruising, her belly, and her knees. She was still warm, considering the cold weather, and he found no apparent bruises or injuries.

"Feel here," he whispered, and Lars knelt beside him.

Lars pushed his fingers into her armpit and pressed in to gauge her temperature. "Still warm. Dead maybe a half bell?"

"Perhaps. This cold, I would guess a quarter bell."

"Cause of death, sir?"

"I am not yet certain."

They rolled her over, onto the blanket, and Dubric paused to wipe his hands before he reached for a slim leather-bound book and pencil he kept handy in his pocket. He refused to endure his duties without paper and pencil, and he had insisted that his personal staff be adequately outfitted, regardless of historical precedent. For centuries the dark mages had crushed literacy on the mainland, wiping out all traces of science and learning, but the island city of Waterford had stood alone against the shadows and kept knowledge alive. Even after the war, they continued to create the finest papers and writing implements in the world.

Beside him, Lars stood and snarled, "So help me, Ulldel, you step past that line again and I'll drag you to the gaol myself."

The crowd grumbled in response, then fell silent.

As Lars knelt beside him again, Dubric said, "Ulldel is an idiot."

"He's a drunkard, an ass, and was stealing a scrap of her dress when we arrived. He's already on my witness list."

Dubric returned his attention to Elli. Her cause of death was obvious, even through the mud. Someone had slashed her back open from her ribs to her hips; the huge gaping hole had filled with muck when she was rolled onto her back. Tapping the pencil on the page as he considered the information, he scratched a few quick notes, drew a rough sketch, and rubbed his aching eyes while Lars efficiently scooped mud from the wound.

While Lars watched the crowd, Dubric tucked the book back into his pocket and felt along Elli's upper back and legs. He found no other wounds. Expecting to find her skull caved, Dubric examined her head last and found the back of it coated in thick, cloying mud. He brushed the muck away and paused before tapping Lars's leg.

"Oh, peg," Lars whispered.

Most of her hair and scalp were gone. Her bloody skull gleamed from her crown to her nape and the skin behind her ears was tattered in muddy hair and blood-clotted flaps.

"Inform the physician," Dubric said.

"Aye, sir." Lars bounced to his feet and ran to the castle.

As Dubric stood, he glanced at the crowd. He knew all the faces, and also knew it was likely that one had murdered Elli. Fifty, perhaps sixty people to interview in the hope one would say something useful. He wrapped her in the filthy blanket, wiped his hands, and rubbed his eyes. The ghosts flickered but did not leave. He felt too old to deal with this. Too old and too tired. But there was no one else, and it was his job.

He hefted his burden and set off to the castle, ignoring the curious stares from the crowd and his ghosts trailing behind him. He felt the loose weight of her body in his arms. She was so young. So much had been taken from her.

* * *

Dubric left Elli's corpse with the physician and hurried to Lord Brushgar's office without bothering to clean the muck and blood off his clothes. Unlike the eager onlookers in the courtyard, the people in the great hall seemed quieted by the news. Breakfast ended amid the hesitant clatter of dirty dishes, people with frightened eyes hurried to work, and the herald announced a visitor for Friar Bonne, but few people talked. Except for the herald whose jittery prattle clattered around the hall, those who spoke, whispered. Dubric felt their fear in the silence and he lengthened his stride as nearly every eye turned to stare at him. Someone in the crowd dropped a goblet or a plate and the crash shattered the subdued fear. Several women screamed and part of the crowd surged forward, swarming around him.

"What 'appened, Dubric?" an old seamstress asked, her tongue flicking between her rotted teeth.

Helgith, the head linen maid, tugged on his arm. "Did he lop off her head?"

"Her head? I heard he sliced open her guts," one of the butlers whispered.

Dubric shook his head and pushed his way through. "I cannot divulge details—"

"Pah on that, Dubric. We've a right to know."

Dubric snapped his head toward the last speaker, a hulk of a man named Dulte, and said, "You have a right to know what I decide to tell you. As of this point, you have a right to know nothing. Once I speak to Lord Brushgar I will begin an investigation, and I will take comments from all witnesses. Did you witness anything, Dulte?" Dubric pulled out his notebook and raised a single questioning eyebrow.

Dulte shook his head and stepped back, his clay-stained hands held before him. His eyes flicked from Dubric's face to the notebook. "Not me. I didn't see a thing. I swear! I've been inside all mornin'. I haven't even been outside the west wing all winter!" He backed into a pair of timid privy maids who squealed and skittered away.

Dubric shoved the notebook back into his pocket. "Then get out of my way and let me do my job!"

The nervous crowd parted before him and he strode across the hall to the dais. Lord Brushgar's oak throne had stood on the platform overlooking the great hall since Nigel Brushgar had claimed Faldorrah at the end of the War of Shadows. A sparkling clean and lovingly maintained Faldorrahn flag hung on the white granite wall behind the throne like a bright and glowing tapestry; beside the flag stood a carved oak door. A cleaning maid polished the sleek woods as she did every morning, even though no one sat in the throne anymore. She glanced at Dubric, then stood, fixing her eyes straight ahead with a polishing rag clutched in her hand.

Dubric climbed the carpeted stairs. "Good morning, Josceline. How are you today?" She, and her mother before her, had been entrusted with the all but impossible task of ensuring that the trappings of Brushgar's lordship, and the rambling suite he lived in, remained immaculate.

She smiled, her attention still focused straight ahead. "Fine, milord. Thank you. How are you, sir?"

"I have seen better mornings, but my health is good."

Josceline stole a glance. He saw in her dark eyes that she had heard the news and felt sorry for the task before him. "Then everything else will manage, sir. Tis only work and there's always plenty of that."

He laughed then and the ghosts behind him wavered. At nearly thirty summers of age and the mother of four boys, Josceline was a hard worker, dependable, and not prone to gossip. Sadly, she had no daughters to carry on her work when she retired. "I suppose that is true," Dubric said. "Is he in his office yet?"

"He arrived before I did, sir. The accountants are upset about some thing or another. They're in there with him."

Josceline began her labors before dawn, so Brushgar must be unaware of the murders, unless the accountants had mentioned it. Dubric almost released a rueful sigh. If it did not concern numbers, it did not concern the accountants.

He stepped past her and reached for the gleaming brass door latch. Josceline returned to her polishing.

ubric entered the cluttered office without knock-
Startled, the junior accountant behind the door
jumped away and knocked a pile of papers, scrolls, and
books onto the dusty wooden floor, then shot a nasty
glare at Dubric. When he tried to control the ava-
lanche, he only made the problem worse.

Dubric hid a smile as he stepped inside. After fifteen summers of fruitless struggle, Josceline's mother
had admitted defeat when faced with the ever-
expanding mess of the office. Dubric doubted if anyone
had cleaned it for two decades or more. The chaos of
written records scattered among piles of antique gears
and levers barely left room to stand. Jelke, the head accountant, gave Dubric a grim nod and continued his
diatribe.

Nigel Brushgar slouched behind the mountain of
papers on his desk, which were weighed down with a
rusted, tubular bit of archaic machinery. He had always
shown an interest in the mechanisms and accoutre-
ments of the ancients, preferring collecting over actual
use and research. Wire spectacles twirled in his thick
fingers, and he sighed and waved Dubric in while Jelke
warbled numbers and pointed to marks in his ledger.

Jelke's voice trembled against the papers on the
desk. "I tell you, we have to raise taxes! Now. We're
forty thousand crowns behind expected levels—"

"We've had a harsh winter, and are running low on
supplies as it is," Brushgar muttered as he examined a
speck on his lenses. "I'm *not* raising taxes in the middle
of a harsh winter."

"Spring's only six, maybe eight phases away," the accountant by the door said as he shoved the pile of papers under the chair. "The winter will be over by the
time the people pay."

Brushgar slammed his fist on the table and the papers tottered but did not fall. "When will you get it through your skulls that *I'm not raising taxes!*"

Jelke fluttered his hands near his face and leaned forward. "You haven't raised taxes in *five summers,* my lord. We are falling behind in income projections. Even Pyrinn has more income than we do and our land is much more prosperous."

Brushgar lifted his paperweight and absently opened and closed the rear lever with his thumb while embracing the crumbling grip in his palm. "Egeslic taxes his people to death. They're starving, for Goddess's sake! Starving and dying, all for taxes and fees. I will not do that to my people, projections be damned. Haenpar taxes *less* than we do and Lord Romlin manages just fine. If we need more money, find a way for me to breed meatier sheep or harvest more grain. Malanna's blood, find more uses for granite or wool; Goddess knows we've got plenty of both around here. I don't care what you do, but *do not under any circumstances* raise taxes." He waved the mechanism toward the door, shooing the accountants like geese. "Now get out of my sight. Dubric needs to speak to me."

Brushgar dropped the artifact on his desk and lumbered to Dubric. "A problem?" Brushgar asked as the accountants gathered their ledgers and closed the door behind them.

Dubric stared forward and he snapped to attention with his feet spaced apart and his back straight. His hand rested on the hilt of his sword and he noticed Brushgar glance at it. Knowing that Brushgar would read trouble in his deliberate stance, he had hoped to brace his lord for what was to come. The last murder, nearly five summers ago, had been a simple domestic problem. Dubric had handled it quietly, with minimal fuss. It had not required this level of notification. A possible repeat murderer was a different matter entirely, and the victims were members of the castle staff. "Yes, milord," he said, his voice calm and steady. "Murder."

Brushgar stopped. His right hand reached for a sword he had stopped carrying forty summers ago. He drew in a breath, his eyes wide and startled.

Dubric knew Brushgar was not the only one who had preferred to live under the belief that nothing bad ever happened in Faldorrah. "In the courtyard. A milkmaid. Elli Cunliffe."

Brushgar took a breath and gathered his bulk as if for a fight. "That's not all, is it?"

Dubric took a breath, considering his answer. "No, milord. He cut her up. Butchered her. I have never seen such base brutality, such vicious anger and disregard for life, and I fear he will kill again. This is not a common domestic problem or drunken brawl, milord, but a rabid beast. The staff will be terrified and we must take drastic steps to keep them calm. We have a problem I cannot begin to describe." *And one girl still missing,* he said to himself.

Brushgar lumbered back to his chair. "I suppose you have no suspects?"

"Not yet, milord. But I will."

Brushgar contemplated Dubric for a moment and nodded. "If you're looking for blanket approval, it's yours. You have my full authority to catch the bastard any way you can. Do whatever you need. Take whatever you need. I cannot allow this to happen in my castle."

"Thank you, milord." Dubric bowed and turned to leave, closing his eyes to the images of the two dead girls. With his eyes closed, he stepped between them and felt them follow, silent and pleading. He did not look at Josceline as he descended the dais.

He hurried across the subdued great hall. Although many looked at him, thankfully none dared to speak.

CHAPTER

2

✝

Nella dropped the armful of dirty sheets into the laundry cart and stretched until her back popped. She stood in the outer hall of two-east, known as The Ladies' Wing to most of the castle's people. The cleaning staff, however, referred to two-east as The Bitches' Wing, or The Bitches, at least privately. Nella had to agree. She had never imagined a handful of women could be such a pain in the behind. If they weren't demanding that the staff run silly errands and boost their already oversized egos, they seemed to spend every waking moment of their lives creating work for others.

Nella shrugged and pulled a clean set of sheets from the cart. She needed the work if she was ever going to repay her debt. The ladies on two-east guaranteed her as much work as she could stomach, and Nella could stomach a great deal. Making beds, replacing bath linen, and fetching silken pillows all day was nothing compared to mixing clay and working brick ovens sunup till sundown, not to mention the threat of death or worse if quantities were inadequate.

She hummed as she carried the sheets into Lady Thremayne's suite. Like most of the ladies' suites, the single room was large and open with a private bath in one corner. The floors were polished wood with thick warm carpets, the outer walls were white stone while the rest were cheerily painted plaster. A single window faced east and the morning sun filtered through lace curtains to glisten on beautiful shining trinkets. Every day Nella wanted to touch the baubles, to see them up close and hold them in her hand, but she never did. They weren't hers to touch or admire, except from a distance. Her job was to change bedding and replace towels, not pretend she could ever be more than she was.

Nella thought Lady Thremayne's suite was the prettiest room in the castle, at least that she'd cleaned so far. She smiled and drew in a deep breath between hummed verses. Lady Thremayne used the nicest smelling perfumes. Soft infusions or tinctures that smelled like flowers and spring rain. Happily distracted, Nella dropped the sheets on an overstuffed chair beside the bed and tossed the pillow shams to Dari.

Dari never worried about looking at Lady Thremayne's trinkets. Dari never worried about much of anything. She stood before Lady Thremayne's tall mirror and fluffed her hair, as she did most mornings. She caught the pillow shams in one hand with barely a glance, and grinned. "Think I should let it grow out?" she asked, tilting her head. She pouted into the mirror and cocked her narrow hips to the side with the pillow shams fluffed out behind her like a lady's skirt.

"I think you need to get back to work before you get us into trouble," Nella said, laughter sparkling in her voice.

Dari ran to the bed, her feet a whisper on the carpets. Laughing, she belly flopped onto the feather-stuffed mattress and giggled. "I don't want to work. I want to do something fun! I haven't taken a day off in over a moon, and all this work is boring." She rolled onto her back with her feet hanging off the edge, and her eyes gleamed at Nella. "I know! Let's take your horse for a ride."

"Oh, Dari." Nella shook her head but her smile refused to hide. Button was a plow horse, big and brown and regular, but Risley had bought him. Bought him just for her.

Groaning dramatically at Nella's reluctance, Dari stretched on the wide, soft mattress. Nella could not begin to imagine how wonderful it must feel, but Dari didn't seem to think about that at all as she wiggled with gleeful anticipation. "We can ride into the village and look at dresses. Maybe we can even flirt with some nice-looking young farmers. What do you think?"

Nella shook her head. "He's not my horse yet. I still have to finish paying for him."

Dari bounced her feet against the side of the bed. "Let's take him for a ride anyway. It'll be fun!"

Nella shook her head again. "I still owe Risley twenty-one crown and change. I can't ride Button until he's paid for, even if I could take time off."

Dari reached for a pillow. As she stuffed it into the sham she said, "Nella, I'm absolutely *positive* Lord Risley would be happy to let you ride your horse. Besides, an afternoon of play never killed anyone."

"Still wouldn't be right." Nella shooed Dari off the bed and pulled the crisp sheet across the mattress. Risley would let her, all right. He'd probably saddle Button and offer to come along and pay for everything. She refused to think about it. As fun as it sounded, she did not want more debt.

Dari continued on undaunted, reaching for a fresh pillow and tucking it under her narrow chin. "I don't understand. Surely you see he doesn't want you to pay him back. He likes you." She winked at Nella and stuffed the second pillow in its sham. A giggle later, she dropped the pillow on the floor, then tucked the corner of the sheet under and tied it tight.

Nella unfolded the top sheet with a flick of her wrists while Dari tied corners. "He likes lots of girls. I'm the one who owes him money."

"So you won't allow yourself a few simple pleasures because of a little debt?" She finished tying the bottom sheet's corners and helped Nella smooth the top sheet. "You've been here almost three moons and haven't spent a penny on yourself, or taken a single moment to rest. Pigs' wallow, Nella, you even hunt for *more* work. What are you so afraid of?"

This was not a subject Nella wanted to discuss, so she reverted to the tried and true. "I have to pay the debt." She reached for the first blanket and shook the folds out.

Dari grabbed one end of the thick wool blanket and walked to the other side of the bed, her eyes rolling. "So you slave all day in The Bitches, then mend clothes and polish candlesticks half the night? All for a few more pence Lord Risley doesn't even want? You're going to kill yourself."

Nella knew what working to death was like, and making beds in perfumed rooms was nowhere close. "No, I'm not. I promise. Can we talk about something else, please?"

Dari smoothed the wool blanket while Nella unfolded the cotton one. "Avoid it all you like, it's still there. He likes you. You like him . . ."

Nella sighed and lowered her eyes. "Dari, you know that's not true."

Dari took the blanket from her and flicked it over

the bed. "Oh, don't even try to deny it. I've seen what happens. You work and slave all phase to make what? Eight crown? Ten? You count it, get all happy, tuck it in a tidy little package and give it to Lord Risley. You're so giddy you can't hold still. He's so smitten he has to wipe his drool off the floor, and all for what? A few moments of flirting followed by eight days of misery? It's crazy."

Nella picked the pillows off the floor. "It's not like that."

"Horse piss. It's exactly like that." Dari turned to Nella and leaned forward, gesticulating in aggravation. "You know what you should do? Instead of taking me and that plow horse of yours into the village, you should ask Lord Risley if *he'd* take you to town. I'm sure he'd leap at the chance to see you." She grinned again. "Besides, his horses are much prettier."

Nella shook her head and arranged the pillows on the bed. "You've forgotten a couple of things."

Dari leaned back, her hands on her hips. "Oh no, here come the excuses."

Nella ignored the last comment and said, "Not only do I owe him money, but I'm a commoner. A servant. No one."

Dari's hands moved off her hips and gestured in the air, fingers spread wide and straight. "And he's the King's grandson. I don't understand why you won't even try. What have you got to lose?"

Nella turned to her friend and said, "I don't have anything to lose. That's the point. And I've caused him enough trouble." She looked at Dari for a moment, then walked to the privy room to collect dirty towels.

The privy room was small, with barely enough room for a tub, a chamber pot, and a washbasin set on a tall narrow table. The walls were white stone, the floor bare wood. A narrow cupboard stood in the corner to hold bath linens and soaps. A small mirror hung on the wall and a bottle of perfume waited beside the washbasin, nearly lost within a tangle of soapy cloths.

While servants used rough, plain-woven wool to wash and dry themselves, the castle nobility were provided with finely woven cottons that were soft to the touch and a pleasure to behold. The delicately embroidered washing cloths were perhaps twice the size of a man's palm, and the big drying towels Lady Thremayne somehow left lying about every morning were larger, and cozier, than Nella's sleeping blanket. Nella had never understood how one woman could get so wet, or create such mess in the process of bathing.

She lifted a dripping towel from the basin, another from the middle of the floor, and knelt to retrieve one wedged beneath the tub while her mind wandered. *How can I explain Risley to Dari when I don't understand it myself,* she thought as she pulled. The towel was good and stuck—how had Lady Thremayne managed that?—and she put her weight behind it and tugged. She thought about Risley, how his eyes glimmered in sunlight, the sound of his voice, his laugh, his scent, and she shook her head and tried to shove the meanderings away. *Best not to go there, Nell,* she scolded herself. *You know better.*

From the main room, Dari squealed, "No. Here?"

The towel slid free, and Nella's head snapped up, banging against the cupboard door. All pleasant thoughts of Risley faded away.

Drenched bath linen in one hand, the other rubbing the back of her head, Nella hurried from the privy room. Her roommate, Plien, relaxed against the hall doorway as if it fondled her, and her eyes glistened with worldly ease. Her linen maid uniform had been partially unbuttoned and her golden hair framed her face like a lover's caress, extending just long enough to curl against the exposed curves of her breasts.

Dari stood quivering beside the bed and her face had paled as white as the stone wall behind her. She crushed a toss pillow in her hands, denting the silken fabric.

"What happened?" Nella asked, her throat clenching.

"You'll never believe this!" Dari said, glancing between Plien and Nella. She looked like she might rip the pillow apart.

Nella's voice hitched as she spoke. "Believe what?"

"A milkmaid was murdered," Plien said as if she were explaining a stain on her uniform. Flicking her hair from her eyes with one hand, she added, "I heard her legs were cut off."

Towels fell to the carpet beside Nella's feet with a wet *schlopp*ing sound. Her hands flew up to cover her mouth and her knees felt loose and quivery. The memory of her sister's death flared in her mind. The bastards had broken Camm's legs when they raped her. Snapped them loose from her hips before abandoning her naked corpse on the stoop. Life had never been the same. "Oh, Goddess!" she said and sat on the edge of the bed before she fell to the floor. She had never sat down on the job before. When Dari stared at her, surprised, Nella tried to stand but couldn't. She couldn't shove away the memory of Camm.

Plien examined her fingernails and smiled, the gleeful bearer of bad news. "Word is Dubric puked all over her, she was so messed up."

Dari turned away from Nella and snapped, "Take your nasty story and go. Can't you see she's upset?"

"I'm all right," Nella whispered and staggered to her feet. *Plien must be lying, creating the story to scare us,* she thought. *She's tried to frighten us before.* Nella didn't think Lord Dubric would ever vomit at the sight of death. He seemed too strong for that. She nodded, reassuring herself, and tottered to the wet towels, dropping to her knees to retrieve them before her legs gave out. Dari dropped the pillow and hurried to Nella's side.

With a toss of her head, Plien left Lady Thremayne's suite, presumably to spread more good cheer.

Nella's shoulders shook as she smelled the perfumed air and tried to calm herself. She was in Faldorrah now, not Pyrinn, and no one was raped or murdered because of debt. Ever. Risley had *promised.* Dari helped her with the puddle and she wished she could sop the memory of her sister from her mind as easily as the mess on the carpet.

* * *

Dubric was halfway to the physician's office when a scream ripped through the great hall. Far ahead of him, three scullery maids with terrified faces ran from the ale room as if Taiel'dar himself slathered on their heels. People near the ale room surged to their feet and stampeded away.

A sick feeling blossomed in the pit of Dubric's stomach as he and several others pushed through the panicked crowd. He was ashamed of the relief he felt. "Stop," he said, grabbing the only person to reach the door before he did. It was a tall, skinny kitchen lackey, perhaps ten summers old, with flour-and-grease-spattered hair and a filthy tunic. "Let me go first."

The boy nodded and Dubric pulled his sword as he pushed open the door. The crowd huddled far behind him, as silent as the ghosts.

The ale room was dark, cold, the shadows of the stacked kegs like lumbering giants in the dim light. Dubric pulled a torch off the wall and held it as he entered the room. Sword in one hand, torch in the other, he walked between rows of kegs. Something pale lay on the floor, gleaming in the torchlight as if it flowed from a tipped keg. He raised the torch higher and hissed out a breath. The hand and arm of the victim extended between the kegs.

He turned to the boy and two men who followed him. Torchlight reflected red in their eyes, like blood. "Everyone out. This room is off-limits for the time being." He looked at the boy. "And you. Hort, is it? Can you fetch two of my pages? Tell them to knock when they get here."

"Aye, milord." The boy ran off.

"What is it?" Lander Beckwith, the herald, asked. Tall, lanky, and timid, he hesitated as he looked through the door. The white feather in his herald's cap seemed to mimic the deflated and shocked look in his pale eyes. The other man was a no-account noble named Talmil. His eyes flashed eagerly and he reached for the edge of the door.

"Nothing for you to worry about yet," Dubric replied, then pulled the door from Talmil and locked himself inside the ale room.

He approached the body slowly. Two similar deaths. Could it be a demented brute on the loose or a lovers' triangle gone awry? If the unthinkable stalked his castle, could he catch the beast? Could he survive more ghosts?

He ignored his worry and resumed his examination. No idiot do-gooders had ruined the scene; the scullery maid's body waited untouched, the way the killer had left her. She lay on her side on the stone floor and faced a tipped keg covered in blood. One hand extended above her head and the other lay curled against her face. He jammed the handle of the torch between two kegs and knelt near the body, wondering what, if anything, connected the girls.

Unlike Elli, the cause of the scullery maid's death was apparent at first look.

Her throat gaped open, slashed nearly from ear to ear. Her uniform slumped loose from her shoulders with the back slit from the neck to the hips and the front sopped with gore. One shoe leaned discarded against the bloody barrel, probably kicked off during the death throes. He touched her extended hand with one finger and began taking notes. She was as cold as the floor she lay on.

He examined the body and scene as the ghosts watched him work. The scullery maid had been slashed open on either side of her spine below the ribs, leaving the remainder of her back intact. A single blue curl of intestine slumped onto the floor behind her. Dubric measured the two gashes. Neither had bled, although both were slightly longer than the width of his hand. They were as clean and straight as any cut of meat he had seen on the butcher's block. Most of the blood had pooled in front of her, indicating she had likely died before the killer sliced open her back. "He had privacy," Dubric muttered as his pencil hurried across a page in his notebook. "Privacy and time."

He looked to the back of her head next. Her head bore no wound. Her bobbed, light brown hair fluffed curly and clean; little wisps of it danced on the floor beside his knees. He picked up a few strands and put them into the crease of his book. If the details of Elli's murder had not given him cause to look, he might not have noticed her cut hair. The killer had removed a bit here, a bit there, snippets hidden by the curls.

Dubric tilted her stiff head gently. He found no bruising on her face or neck. Her eyes stared forward, surprised and cloudy; blood from her throat had splashed over her face. She had been a pretty girl. Except for her open dress, her clothes remained intact. She still wore knee stockings and one shabby shoe. Her underdrawers had not been moved. He doubted she had been raped.

He sketched her body, made a few notes, and examined the scene in which she lay.

He found a single bloody handprint on a keg behind her, where he wanted to place his own hand as he rose from kneeling to standing. Moving the torch for better light, he examined the bloody smear and saw nothing of note. Big enough to be a man's hand, four fingers and a thumb, all straight and true. It could have belonged to anyone. The blood was dry and impossible to transfer directly to parchment, but traceable. He made a note in his book as a reminder to acquire transparent parchment. He found no hairs on the floor but the victim's, no dropped clues, no bloody footprints.

When the two pages knocked, he returned to the door, looking from keg to keg as he walked through the ale room. Not a print to be seen. He did, however, find three drops of dried blood on the floor near the door. The vertical bar of the door latch was a smeared bloody mess, with fingerprints on the left, thumbprint on top, and a palm smear on the right. The killer was right-handed, or had used his right hand to open the door.

After writing a few more notes, Dubric stood again

and reached into his pocket for a kerchief. Taking care to not smear the blood, he opened the door for his pages. Both were junior pages and sons of castle nobles. Neither was terribly bright. A crowd of people huddled far behind the boys.

He glowered at them and said, "Gilby, fetch me a clean blanket. Second-floor-east storage room will do fine. Norbert, run to the mapmakers'. Tell Eamonn I need a piece of tracing parchment. If he gripes about his supplies, you tell him that is not my concern. If he refuses to give you one, fetch a squire and have him thrown in gaol. Just get me the blasted parchment. Any questions?"

They looked at each other and Norbert whined, "Why do I have to argue with Eamonn? He smells bad, and he's always grouchy. Can't you send Gilby instead?"

Gilby punched Norbert on the shoulder. "Quit griping. We'll be polishing armor for a whole phase!"

Norbert rolled his eyes and punched Gilby back. "You've got the easy job. Pilfering a blanket from the ladies' storage roo—"

Dubric towered over them. "If you two do not get your backsides moving right this instant, you will never get the armor polish out of your fingernails."

"Yes, Milord Dubric," Norbert muttered, and both boys ran off.

"What did you find?" a lady asked from the murmuring crowd, a kerchief crushed in her hand. Around her, the crowd eagerly leaned closer.

Pitta stood beside her husband. The herald's feather still drooped and he stroked his wife's arm with a shaking hand as she spoke. "I heard it from the girls, Dubric. Another one dead. Is it true?"

Dubric nodded and focused all of his attention on Pitta. "Yes. When were kegs last brought out?"

She paled. "Every night the kitchen is supposed to restock for the following morning, but we ran out of ale during breakfast. The keg should have been full, but it wasn't! I never should have sent them. I never should have needed to!"

Pitta sobbed and Beckwith drew her close to press her face against his narrow chest.

Dubric wrote, *Were the kegs emptied on purpose, or did chance bring the victim to the room?*

"What would you have us do?" Beckwith asked, his voice trembling as he stroked Pitta's hair.

"List the girls' names for me. That is all I need for now."

Beckwith held his wife closer. The crowd whispered around him and for a moment Dubric considered the pair. Although shorter than her husband, Pitta's bulk seemed to soak his lean frame into her like a dab of jelly onto a fresh-baked roll, her ruddiness nearly obscuring the horror on his face.

Dubric closed the door before he had to answer any more questions. He took a deep breath, locked the latch, and turned back to the ale room.

He examined the rest of the room step-by-step and found no more blood. He noted nothing more than thirty-two wine kegs, sixty-one ale kegs, a half-dried puddle of vinegary sludge from a leaking keg, a dusting of pipe ash in one corner of the room, and a silhouette of a man's bootprint within the ash. He knelt before the pipe ash and sketched the shape and angle of the print. The killer had found a perfect, dark hiding spot; three stacked ale kegs hid the corner from the door. *A smoker perhaps,* he noted in his book. *Likely male. Might have dropped some ash on his boot while he waited for her. Patient.*

Many Faldorrahn men smoked and most people were right-handed. Both clues were inconclusive and ruled out few possibilities. He stood and peeked through a gap near the edge of the kegs. The door was easy to see, even in the dim light.

He scratched another note, rubbed his eyes, and sighed. The ghosts flickered then appeared again, forever screaming, forever silent. He wondered if this morning would ever end.

He left the hiding spot and knelt before the dead girl one last time. He lifted the back collar of her uniform. A name was written there in shaking print, the handwriting like a child's, and he added her name to his notebook. The second victim, as the castle would call her despite her being the first to die, was named Fytte. He could not remember ever meeting her. *What a waste*, he thought, closing her eyes. They were hazel, he noted in his book.

* * *

While the castle folk fell into hearsay and rabid speculation, Dubric carried Fytte to the physician's. Lars, guarding the door, frowned as Dubric approached. Down the hall, a crowd clamored and grumbled, but they would be dealt with soon enough.

"Another one?" Lars asked as he opened the door for Dubric. "I wondered where you were."

Dubric carried her into the clove-scented air of the physician's domain. Lars followed, grimacing at the smell. Cloves and death were not a pleasant mix, but better than death alone. A soft, plump physician in a bloodstained white tunic and wood-framed spectacles looked up from Elli's corpse. Surprised, he pointed to an empty table and washed his hands.

Dubric laid her on the table. "Has Dien returned from visiting his in-laws yet?"

Lars stood straighter as he answered. "No, sir. The baby's only four days old. You told him to take a whole phase."

Only four days? It seemed like a whole summer just this morning. "He can take the rest some other time. Send someone to fetch him. We are going to need the extra set of hands."

"I can send Otlee or Trumble. Both ride well."

"Send Trumble. I want Otlee to help with witnesses."

"Yes, sir." Lars turned to go.

The physician hurried to them, drying his hands on a towel. "Twice in one morning, Dubric. Business like yours I don't need."

Dubric did not need the business, either. "No mud on this one, Halld."

Halld pulled back the blanket. "Thank the Goddess for that." He looked her over and nodded once. "Can you give me a couple of bells or so? Maybe early afternoon?"

Dubric agreed and left, closing the door behind him. He wished the ghosts would stay with the dead, but they never did. He sighed and straightened his shoulders. His office was three doors down the hall and a line of witnesses waited, their eyes full of worry.

* * *

Dubric leaned back in his chair and watched the fifth witness, a vapid milkmaid named Charli. He had met weevils more intelligent, let alone helpful. She slumped in her chair, face blotchy from crying, and clutched a ratty kerchief in her fist. Both ghosts ignored her, preferring as always to stare at Dubric and drip spectral blood on his floor. At the table beside her, Otlee tapped his quill pen on Charli's deposition paper and tilted his head, his bright hair gleaming like fire in the lamplight.

"What do you have so far?" Dubric asked him. Never in all his summers had he found anyone who took better notes than Otlee. An amazing boy. Especially for the son of an uneducated baker.

The milkmaid sniffled as Otlee reviewed the notes.

"Charli Mottle, seventeen summers, milkmaid. Identity confirmed and initialed by the witness. Stated, 'We opened the door, outta the west wing, right at dawn, just like always. Elli lay there an' I guess I screamed. I think I did, anyway. We ran to her, me an' Olita. She . . . she were all muddy, m'lord. Muddy an' covered in blood. We called fer help, an' a couple other girls came runnin' from the door. Meliss and Ingi, I think.'"

Charli sniffled again and dabbed her eyes as she nodded. "That's what I said, all right."

Otlee scratched his pen across the paper, and Dubric smiled. The boy never missed a single word.

Otlee continued, "Castellan Dubric asked, 'Did you see anyone, any man, in the area?' Witness replied, 'Nay, sir, just Elli. She were dead, sir. I ain't never seen a dead person before, don't wanna see one again.'" Otlee looked up. "Witness cried for several minutes."

"Nothin' wrong wit cryin'," Charli sniffed. "She got blood all over me. Did I tell ye that?"

Otlee added her comments, the pen tip little more than a blur. "Three times now. Want me to keep going, sir?"

Dubric looked up. Lars's voice barked and grumbled, muffled and blurred through the door. The witnesses must be getting restless. "No, I think that is enough. Unless you have anything to add, Miss Charli?"

She shook her head and glanced at Otlee as he made more marks. "Nay, m'lord. Told ye all I knew. But I would like to know who's gonna get all this blood offa my uniform? Scares the cows, it does."

Dubric wrote a few notes of his own on a square scrap of parchment. He handed the note to her. "Give this to the laundry. They will remove the blood and not charge you."

Charli tucked the note in her pocket. "Thank ye, m'lord. So yer done wit me?"

Otlee dipped his pen in an inkwell and added to his notes.

Dubric said, "If you think of anything else, tell a page you need another meeting. All right?"

She nodded and opened the door. Otlee sighed, signed the bottom of the page, and added it to a pile on the shelf behind him. As he shifted, his feet nudged a pair of books and Dubric smiled. Ever since Otlee had been approved for a library token, he always had a book or two tucked away somewhere.

The token allowed him to borrow up to two books at a time, a privilege Otlee had grasped with great relish. Clintte, the librarian, had balked at loaning such valuable treasures to a commoner—the printing presses in Waterford were far away and their recent volumes quite expensive—but Dubric had insisted moons ago Otlee be allowed to peruse at will. He would not discourage or limit a natural reader, regardless of Clintte's obsessions.

The outer office was crowded with people, and most waved their hands before their hot, red faces. Outside of Dubric's line of sight one said, "Dammit, Lars! We've been waitin' fer bells! How come the tramp gets to go first? She just got 'ere!"

Wearing his mud-spattered uniform as if his mere presence should assure compliance, Lars said, "I told you once to shut your foolish yap. I decide who goes in and when."

A comely linen maid stood beside the door, watching Lars with wide dark eyes. She held folded cloth in her hands and she looked smaller than her already tiny stature. "I can wait," she said. "I still have half a bell of lunch left."

"Spend it wit yer lover an' get outta here," another angry voice snarled from somewhere in the crowd.

The linen maid's lower lip curled in for a moment, but she made no other sign she had noticed the insult. She wore her pressed and starched uniform like a badge of honor, and she took a deep breath and raised her pert chin a little higher, like a queen among the rabble.

Dubric smiled at her even as Lars barked at another complainer. "Come on in, Miss Nella. Never mind them."

Relief shone in her eyes before it, too, was hidden behind her ever present pride. She nodded and said, "I don't want to be a bother, milord. Really. But you said to come."

"Today, during lunch. I know." He looked at Lars and nodded, ushering her inside—between the pair of ghosts, how he wished they would wander off for a while—and closed the door. The curses and complaints of the crowd were muffled. "Miss Nella, this is Otlee, one of my pages. Otlee, this is Miss Nella. She does my mending."

Otlee stood and bowed before her, gesturing politely with his thin, ink-stained hands. "Nice to meet you, Miss Nella."

She dropped into a quick curtsy. "Thank you. Nice to meet you, as well."

Otlee blushed and blustered in reply.

Away from the angry comments of the crowd, her face brightened and she smiled. Dubric leaned a hip against his desk and accepted the pair of shirts. "How much do I owe you?" he asked.

"You might want to check the collar of this one first. It was tricky, but I think I hid the repair."

He pulled the collar of the white shirt open. A drunk had ripped the collar half off and he had feared the shirt was ruined. Made of silk, it had cost him forty-seven crown to purchase the last time he was in Waterford. He loved that shirt. He smiled as he saw her handiwork. Her stitches were tiny, precise, and almost invisible. Better than the original tailor's.

"The collar's fine, Miss Nella. How much?" He knew before she spoke it would not be enough. It never was.

She smiled and shifted her feet as if she was embarrassed to be paid. "Crown and a quarter for the collar. Three pence for the buttons. I was lucky. I found perfect matches."

He shook his head and reached into a pocket. "You need to raise your prices." Any tailor would charge five times the amount and do half as good a job. He counted money into his palm and smiled at her.

"Wouldn't be right," she replied.

He dropped the coins in her hand, all pence and

scepters, and she looked at him and shook her head. She counted change almost as fast as Otlee took notes. "Overpaid me again," she said, laughing. She pulled two scepters and seven pence from her palm and set them on his desk.

"You should take it, Miss Nella. Please. It is merely a quarter crown or so." She had done his mending for seven phases and had never taken a single penny extra. It still amazed him.

She shook her head and pocketed the payment. "I can't do that. Any other mending this phase?"

He shook his head. "Sadly, no."

She nodded and the hope in her eyes faded a notch. "That's all right. Thank you, and keep me in mind for next time?"

"I will."

She smiled at him, nodded good-bye to Otlee, and took a breath before she opened the door. Her back straight, her head held high, she strode into the angry crowd and closed the door behind her.

"That's Nella Brickerman?" Otlee asked, shaking his head.

Dubric scooped up his change and slipped behind his desk, ignoring the vacant stares of his ghosts. "Not like you expected?"

Otlee sat and pulled a clean sheet of paper from the pile. "Nothing. The way folks talk about her and Lord Risley . . ." he shrugged. "I expected, I dunno . . . Not *that*, I guess. She seemed nice." He smoothed the paper and readied his quill with ink.

"She is nice." *And one amazing seamstress.*

Otlee tilted his head and his brow wrinkled. "But I heard she was Lord Risley's commoner whore. That she's only after his money."

Dubric hoped his eyes were kind even if his voice was stern. "I have had the displeasure of hearing that sentiment, and I have never believed it. Remember, Otlee, the opinion of the masses is usually wrong. Use your own judgment." He looked to the door and rubbed his eyes. Only fifty-two witnesses to go.

CHAPTER

3

†

Having delegated the afternoon witnesses to Lars, Dubric arrived at the physicians' offices at precisely two bell. Elli lay covered on one table with nothing more than the top of her head visible from beneath the blanket. Fytte lay uncovered and naked on another.

Halld probed a gash on Fytte's back with a shaking finger. He glanced up at Dubric's approach and smiled. "I've found something."

Praise the King! A clue! Dubric hurried to the exam table and nodded a greeting.

"There are similarities between them, milord," Halld said. "Do you suppose they've been killed by the same man?"

"What sort of similarities?" Dubric asked, opening his notebook.

Halld's hands seemed unable to remain still. He tugged at his white tunic, tapped the exam table, and laced his fingers together. "He took something. Look!"

Dubric leaned closer. Besides the lack of clothing, Fytte was little different than he remembered her. Her skin was blue and cool, a greenish bruise graced her hip, and her soles were calloused as if she seldom wore shoes. The slashes on her back were straight and clean.

Halld looked at him with anticipation. "What is it?" Dubric asked. He hated guessing games.

Halld straightened his back, his soft brown eyes sparkling. "First of all, I noticed it in the milkmaid, what was her name?"

"Elli," Dubric said, his voice bland.

"Elli, yes. I noticed it in her first, but didn't think much of it. Half her back is gone, probably out there in the mud somewhere . . ."

Or stolen as a souvenir by a gawker, Dubric thought.

". . . but this other one . . ." Halld turned and looked at her.

"Fytte," Dubric said, shifting his weight and narrowing his eyes. "Her name was Fytte."

Halld shook his head, clearing the thrill of discovery from his eyes. "Fytte. What an unusual name."

Dubric tried to remain patient despite the excitement of the physician. "What did you find? How are they connected?"

Halld smiled. "I noticed it while probing the wounds on her back. With your permission, I'd like to expand one of them, to see how he did what he did."

If it is a man at all.

"What exactly did he *do*?"

Somehow, despite his trembling, Halld stayed rooted to the ground. "He took her kidneys. Both of them. Or, perhaps I should say, all four of them. The milkma—er, Elli's kidneys are also missing."

Dubric stared at Halld a moment as he considered the information and tried to understand what it meant. Both of the girls' backs had been slashed open for a reason, and perhaps, to the killer, taking kidneys made sense or served a purpose. "Why would he want their kidneys?"

Halld's crestfallen face flushed. "I wish I could tell you, sir, but I have absolutely no idea. Not yet, anyway."

Dubric returned his gaze to his notebook. "Can you tell me anything about the victims?"

Halld nodded and flipped through his own notes. "Neither was raped. Both were in adequate health, but the milkmaid had an abscessed tooth and a rash. The other . . ." he flipped forward a page and said, "she had a bruise, an old one, on her hip. Probably ran into something a phase or so ago."

Dubric made his notes. "And the wounds?"

Halld shook his head. "Just the obvious ones. But he killed the girls differently."

Halld took a deep, shaking breath and flipped to the next page in his notes. "The milkmaid's back was first slashed low, above her hips, and she either fell or was shoved into the mud before he opened her up. He cut out a chunk of her and it's missing. Regardless, she may have tried to scream but couldn't, and either bled to death or suffocated. Maybe a combination of the two." He looked at Dubric, tucked his notes under his arm, took off his spectacles and wiped the lenses clean. His shaking hands calmed as he wiped.

Dubric almost dropped his notebook in his surprise. *For King's sake, half of her back is gone!* "She was still alive?"

Halld nodded. "Not for very long. Not with that rate of blood loss." He shrugged. "She clawed the mud. It's crammed into her nails, breathed into her nose and throat. There are small, round bruises along the side of her head, perhaps from the pressure of his fingers. I think he held her head down, maybe to quiet her screams." He returned his spectacles to his nose. "The attack against the milkmaid was much more brutal than the one against the scullery maid. The slashes were rougher, the damage greater. Maybe he was angry. Or in a hurry."

"Did he leave anything behind?"

Halld shook his head. "Sorry, sir. He ripped out what he wanted and left her there. Anything he might have left on her was lost in the mud." He moved on to Fytte while Dubric continued his notes.

Fytte was different, a cleaner, more precise kill, and Dubric noticed Halld tracing his fingertip along a gash on her back. "He killed this one, waiting for her to die before taking the kidneys. The back wounds were very clean, but her throat was a mess."

Dubric scratched more notes while the ghosts seemed to contemplate their own corpses. "Can you tell me anything about the knife?"

"Some. With luck I can tell you more after I open her up. I do know the knife was small. A dirk, maybe, smaller than a dagger. None of the wounds are deeper than, say, the width of four, maybe five fingers."

Dubric's head tilted as he continued his notes. "But why would he make the cuts on Fytte's back so small? Surely he would need more room."

Halld shook his head. "They're big enough, if the weapon was very small. Look." He pushed his hand into the narrow wound and her cold flesh welcomed the intrusion, molding close to Halld's hand. "Once past the muscles of the back, the internal organs are flexible enough to make room." Halld turned his hand over, inside her back, and pulled it out again. The sound his movement made was little different than the sound of a baker kneading bread.

Halld wiped his hands on a towel. "But we can't tell how he cut it or if he damaged anything else, not unless we open her up. What did he sever? What did he tear?"

"Will you be able to tell me more about the weapon?"

"I think so. If he damaged other tissue in the area, we should be able to see exactly how big the blade was. Or if he took anything else."

Dubric looked at the dead girl and nodded. "I guess we had better have a look."

Beside him, Halld reached for a surgical knife.

* * *

Blustery afternoon gave way to sleety evening and Nella huddled with Dari in the pay line at the servants' wing door. The chaos of other castle workers hurt her ears and she wished she could grab her money and run away. She shivered, goose bumps flecking her arms even though the wide hall was hot and packed with scores of people. She clenched her rattling teeth and stared at Plien's back, refusing to look at anyone else. To her left, milkmaids compared notes about the first murder, each claiming some glory in the discovery of the body. Nella found them gruesome but tolerable. To her right, a pair of privy maids commented and speculated on Nella's supposed love life. They were far worse than the glory seekers to her left. But Nella held her ground and her tongue, and focused on Plien's back.

"So, Little Miss Nose-in-the-Air," one said, leaning over as if to share a sweet secret, "does he sneak you off to his suite or just find a dark hallway?" She was a head taller than Nella and her crooked teeth gave a wisping lilt to her voice.

"I bet it's the hallway," her partner said, lewdly shaking her wide backside. "No noble worth his spit would take a Pyrinnian bug like her into his own bed. Sometimes at night, I can hear her in the back halls! Oh, Lord Romlin! Ride me like that big black horse of yours!"

"Why don't you leave her alone?" Dari asked, her hands on her hips as she stepped between Nella and the two privy maids.

"Why don't she associate with her own kind?" one replied, air whistling through her teeth.

"Yeah," the other answered, "and why don't you mind your own business?"

Dari's voice grew dangerously low. "I'm trying to mind my business, but you two piss pots keep messing with it."

"Shut the peg up, all of you," Plien snapped. "We're all gonna get double duty if you don't quit it."

"Bet Lord Romlin gives her double duty!" someone from the crowd cackled.

Both privy maids snickered. Nella tried not to blush and failed miserably.

The linen maid line lurched forward a moment later and Nella felt Dari flick her hand toward the privy maids. Nella didn't look. Knowing Dari, it was probably a gesture she didn't want to see, anyway.

The privy maids muttered a comment lost to the cacophony of the crowd, and Nella felt thankful for the small respite.

"Don't let them get to you," Plien said as she glanced over her shoulder. "They're just jealous."

Nella flashed her an apologetic smile. "Nothing to be jealous of."

"Sure. Whatever you say. But if I could snag a noble, I'd do it. Commoner men don't have any money, don't give you anything at all. All they want is a toss.

With a noble, at least you can get something for your trouble."

"I'm trying to pay him back, not take more money from him. Besides, we haven't done anything." The line lurched forward again as other linen maids collected their money.

Plien laughed and shook her head. "Sure, Nella. Everyone's seen you together. If you two haven't done anything, then I'm a nun." She glanced back and winked. "And we all know I'm no nun."

Before Nella could retort, Plien accepted her wage and hurried back through the crowd, leaving Nella to stare at Helgith.

The head linen maid tapped her foot, glowering as she counted out coins for Nella. "This happens every phase! I don't allow my girls to associate with the nobility. If I hadn't received orders from Dubric hisself, I'd have your ass in a fire, missy. Folks'er saying all my maids are a bunch of money-hungry whores because of you. You'd better put a stop to it."

Nella had heard essentially the same speech every phase, and just like every other wage day she replied, "As soon as my debt's done, we'll have no reason to see each other anymore."

Helgith leaned forward, shaking her finger. "Mind that you don't, 'cause once that's done, things're gonna change."

Nella counted her money. Helgith had paid her correctly for once. "Thank you," she said and pushed through the crowd while Helgith griped about her impertinence. Six people besides Dubric had hired her for odd jobs the past phase, and she needed to find them before they wasted her money in the gambling shacks or alehouses.

She ignored the stares and comments, ignored the little voice in her head warning her to beware of both deadbeats and overpayers, and set forth to collect what was owed to her.

* * *

"Thank the Goddess you're here," Lars said as a hulking bear of a man shoved to the front of the crowd packed in Dubric's offices, knocking aside bystanders like they were empty tankards on an alehouse table.

Dien's common clothes were filthy, spattered with mud and grime from the road, rumpled from the damp weather, and torn from the hard ride. His worried eyes were brilliant blue over a day's growth of stubbly beard, and he ran a massive hand through damp, short-shorn hair, his thick fingers shaking in relief. "Goddess damned son of a whore, pup!" He looked Lars over top to bottom and shook his head. "I leave for a few frigging days and all I can do is worry. Trumble said we'd had a couple of murdered serving girls. But you're all right. Praise the pegging Goddess for that. Dubric? He all right, too?"

"We're both fine," Lars said, glancing at his witness list and notes. "Just glad you're here. Otlee and I are struggling to take testimonies and control the crowd."

Beside Lars, Otlee sagged with obvious relief. They had finished interviewing seventeen witnesses; all seemed to be a waste of time. The end of the witness list was nowhere in sight and the office had become loud and unruly as the afternoon gave way to evening. By size alone, Dubric's squire would ensure compliance, Lars was certain of that. He handed the notes to Dien and squared his shoulders. "We can handle it a little longer if you'd like to clean up and get in your uniform."

"Work before pleasure, you know," Dien muttered.

"Little bit of dirt never hurt no one." He accepted the papers from Lars.

Around them the crowd grumbled. Otlee opened and closed his ink-spattered fingers. After all the writing he'd done, sore fingers were expected, and he was only twelve summers old.

"How's the baby?" Lars took a deep breath and glanced at the crowd. He felt a pang of guilt at having taken Dien from his family.

"Quit the damned small talk and get us outta here!" a voice grumbled from Lars's left.

Dien didn't seem to notice the grumbler as he skimmed through Otlee's notes. The complaints rolled off his back like rainwater on a bear. "She's fine. Healthy as a horse and looks just like her mother. I'm actually glad to get away from Sarea's parents, though. Her father aggravates me to no frigging end." He flipped through a couple of pages and said, "Dubric left you in charge? Where is he?"

"Still with the physicians." *Goddess only knows what that means,* Lars thought. *Probably more witnesses.*

Dien nodded and looked at Lars, scratching a day's growth of beard. "This isn't as simple as Trumble said, is it?"

Lars shook his head and Dien glanced at the inner office door. "We need to talk privately," Dien said.

Lars stretched to his full height, about the same level as Dien's shoulder, but he could do nothing to compare to Dien's girth. "Gilby, get your ass down to the kitchen and have food for forty brought here *right now.* Norbert, I need a keg of cider and forty tankards here before the next bell rings."

"But, *Lars,*" Norbert whined.

"Move it," Lars growled. "You heard the order. Don't make me punish you."

Both boys pursed their lips and disappeared into the crowd. The rest of the pages looked at Lars but did not move.

"'Bout time you fed us," someone griped. "Been here all day."

"You're lucky I don't conduct this in the gaol," Lars snapped. "Shut your yap before I change my mind."

"Can you believe this rude little bastard?" a potter said. "Acting like he's the lord hisself or somethin'."

Dien shrugged. He continued to look at the papers, and remained calm and unflustered. "Lars is in charge here, and I recommend you pay close frigging attention to what he says."

Most of the people in the room glanced at the broadsword strapped to Dien's hip and retreated a step.

Otlee looked at Lars with adoring respect. "What shall I do?"

Lars opened the door to Dubric's private office and motioned Dien inside. "Take a break, get a drink, and grab something to eat. Be back in half a bell, all right?"

As Otlee left, Dien lumbered into the office and Lars followed.

* * *

Nella finished her collections with minimal fuss. This phase had gleaned her an extra six crown three scepters from her odd jobs. She smiled. It had been a productive phase, and she'd had no deadbeats. She found a quiet, cold table near a sleet-spattered window in the great hall and ignored the people around her. While most gossiped about the murders and ate their supper, Nella stacked and sorted the coins, counted them twice, and tallied the numbers against last phase's total, just as her father had taught her. Smiling at the money, she pushed a wayward strand of dark brown hair behind her ear. She'd netted over eleven crown this phase. Perhaps, if she was lucky, she had only one more phase of debt ahead of her. Only one more phase until freedom. She sighed and watched the sleet for a moment.

She arranged and folded the money in a scrap of cloth, tied it tight, and slipped the whole bundle into her pocket. A bounce in her step and a smile on her face, she pressed through the crowded hall again and went in search of Risley.

She found him on the third floor of the west wing. Risley was tall, dark-haired, and self-assured, understandably popular among the ladies. He headed to the main hall for supper and grinned as soon as he saw her. She smiled back and hurried toward him. She only met him on wage day, and only in public. The comments and gossip were bad enough without adding private meetings to the fire.

Clotting the flow of traffic, they stood facing each other in a crowded hall and the angry glances and comments of the crowd disappeared.

"I have the payment," she said, holding out her parcel.

He accepted the money, slipping it into the pocket of his cloak without giving it a second glance. "Can you join me for dinner in the great hall?"

"No, I can't. Not tonight. I have a huge pile of mending I need to finish before bed." She had agreed several phases ago to meet him for dinner once her debt was done, after she was truly free. She often wondered whether it was anticipation of freedom or the dinner feeding her hurry to pay him back. In her heart she knew it was the dinner. Just him, just her.

"Are you certain?" he asked and eased closer to her. A cook glared at them then hurried on, shaking her head.

Nella lowered her eyes and blushed, fighting the urge to back away. "Yes, I'm sure. I'll finish paying in another phase or two. Surely you can wait that long." His familiar scent, of horses and leather and pipe smoke, made her heart dance.

"I don't want to wait," he whispered in her ear. "Dine with me. Tonight." His breath warmed her cheek. Two young ladies shot dagger glances at Nella and raised their noses in the air, then they, too, were lost to the crowd.

"Oh, Risley," she laughed. "You do this every phase."

"I keep hoping you'll accept," he replied, grinning.

She smiled back. "I will, when my debt's done."

"Promise?"

"I promise. But I have to get this done, really."

"All right." Risley started to take her hand, then seemed to change his mind. "I guess I'll see you next wage day, then, right?"

Nothing could keep her from meeting him again. "Yes."

This time he did take her hand. "I need you to do something for me," he said as he stroked her fingers. It was the first time he had touched her since the journey from Pyrinn.

"What?" she asked, still oblivious to the unpleasant glances and mumbled comments. She could see nothing but him, and that was fine with her.

His fingers stroked hers. They were warm and gentle. Just like she remembered. "Be careful. Please. *Extra* careful."

Everyone had heard about the two dead girls. "I will be careful, don't worry. I promise." As much as she wanted to stay, she had to leave before she added more wood to the rumor fire. "I'll see you next phase, all right?"

He dropped her hand and she smiled her good-bye, then hurried into the crowd.

* * *

Mirri glanced up as a man passing through the dinner crowd bumped her chair. Fluffing her dark curly hair, she smiled at him and turned back to Nella with a happy sigh as he walked away. "How much do you have left?"

"About twelve crown," Nella said and forked up some beans. "Maybe only one more phase, surely no longer than two. *If* I can find enough mending."

Plien winked at her. "I'll be glad when the mending's done. You stay up half the night and I need my beauty sleep."

Nella shook her head and sipped her cider as she tried not to laugh.

Around a mouthful of poultry, Dari said, "She has to sit in the hall to do it, you dingle. Helgith took our light away. If you were ever in the room, you'd know."

"Polishing is worse than mending," Stef said, grumbling into her mug of cider. A thin girl with dull hair and angry eyes, she leaned back and glowered. "Mending is quiet, at least. Polish stinks."

"No polishing this phase," Nella said. "I promise."

Mirri giggled, her round cheeks turning pink. "There's nothing left to polish! I walked by the ballroom the other day and every candlestick gleamed like magic in there."

"They better," Stef muttered, *thunk*ing her mug on the table. "She polished one hundred and thirty-two of the damned things."

"One fifty-six," Nella said. "Josceline gave me two whole crown to polish the two dozen in Lord Brushgar's suite. I couldn't bring those back to our room."

"Be still my heart," Stef said, rolling her eyes and crossing her arms over her chest. "Two whole crown!"

"Oh, shut up," Dari said, giving Stef an evil glare. "At least she's trying. All you do in your spare time is sleep."

"It's all right," Nella said. "I know I'm a bother."

Dari shook her head. "You're nothing of the kind."

"I sure don't mind," Mirri said, batting her eyes and resting her chin on her hand. "I think it's romantic."

Plien shrugged and sipped her cider, her eyes seeking out interested men, as always. Beside her, Stef glowered.

Nella glanced across the table to Ker. Small, shrinking, and quiet, she stared at her plate, fiddled with her steel bracelet, and grunted. Ker rarely said more than a single word or two.

"Ker don't care, either," Dari said. "Looks like you're odd one out again, Stef."

Stef pushed her plate away and stood. "Fine. I'll be odd one out. Nothing new there. But when Helgith jumps all our asses because Little Miss Perfect broke curfew to do extra work, or falls asleep on the job, don't come crying to me."

"We won't," Dari said, her voice as sweet as apple blossoms in a spring breeze, and her eyes as hard as Faldorrahn granite.

Nella shook her head and sighed, returning to her supper.

* * *

Grandfather's old cloak works perfectly, he thought as he chewed a mouthful of bread and contemplated the supper crowd.

A relic from the war, his grandfather had stripped

the warm, woolen cloak off a dying mage and had kept it secret, spiriting it home. Not only was it prone to repelling rainwater and shedding stains—once dried, most fell off as dust or were easily brushed away—it provided a unique perspective on living things.

They glowed.

While wearing the cloak he could see any detail he wanted: bare skin behind clothing, internal organs, the flutter of a frightened heart. No one knew, no one noticed. Who would give a man in a humble woolen cloak a second thought, or glance?

Grandfather had enjoyed entertaining the children by using the cloak to tell what trinkets they had in their pockets or how many fingers they held behind their backs. His best trick though, the one that made the children clap with glee, was when grandfather, and everything he held, disappeared.

Grandfather had been a fool. A kindly, shortsighted fool. Such tricks were not meant for entertaining children.

Such glorious colors, he thought with a smile, *all because of the cloak.*

While wearing it, he saw every blue-tinged bone, every crimson muscle, even the flow of golden blood through their veins. Perfectly lovely, all these beings wandering through their meaningless lives. The things he could see! Not ten lengths from him, Lady Ellianne Thremayne talked with Lady Melline Jespert over dinner and brandy. Lady Thremayne was perhaps three or four moons pregnant. An unmarried lady—such a scandal! He hoped she wasn't drinking the brandy on purpose. Brandy did such unfortunate things to babies.

He smiled and resumed eating. Despite the scandal, ladies and their problems did not interest him; they were simply not worth his trouble. Servant girls, however, were perfectly wonderful to behold. A pair of serving wenches walked by and he watched them. One had lost three back teeth on the left side, above her cracked jaw bone. Likely the fault of her easy-to-anger suitor, the damaged jaw surely made speaking painful. He wondered how well she could scream and he smiled as he added her name to the list in his head. He sought out other girls, adding names as he saw fit, and smiled at a group of linen maids who had settled around a table not far away.

He knew the six girls of this group quite well. One was already prominently featured on his list, and another, a dark-haired morsel and surely the prettiest girl in the castle, had captivated his attention and desire since he first saw her. He licked his lips as he looked at her, then drew his attention to other servant girls before she noticed his amorous stare.

They glowed beautifully in their youth—the power of their organs pulsating in their bodies, their bones straight and strong. Nella laughed over her meager supper tray, her face golden with all the blood rushing to it. The plump, giggly girl at the end of the table pretended to swoon, fanning her face, and he felt a flash of sadness that she would not be on his list in the foreseeable future. Surely a plump girl would be tasty. Sweet and tender, not salty.

He watched them as he ate, and sought other girls just as delightful. What a pleasant supper in the great hall. Such perfect variety. Such succulent morsels. He looked all around him, adding this girl and that to his evolving list until he finished his supper and could linger no longer. Before he stood, he glanced at his feet.

A shadow of stain from two drops of blood on the toe of his left boot remained, even though he had wiped them off before coming to supper. They glimmered gold and dim against the green boot leather. That snot-nosed page Lars had missed them during questioning, but they had been there, plain as day. Two spots. Fytte's blood. Dubric wouldn't have missed them. The bastard might be old, but he was a long way from dumb.

He shrugged as he stood, and looked at the perfectly delightful banquet of girls in the great hall. He smiled and ran his tongue over his lips. Dubric had left the questioning to Lars, and Lars had not noticed. All the more perfect luck for him, and for the girls on his list.

* * *

The night spread out before him, cold and blue-purple, no different than daylight with the cloak. The horse beneath his backside glowed golden and red and its breath plumed green. The cottage lay ahead, a deli-cious blackness peeking between blue trees.

The horse shied, tossing its head, but he didn't care. "Get a move on!" he said, slamming his heels into the beast's flanks. The horse jumped, took a few awkward steps, then whinnied in fear. "Damn wretched beast!" He cursed and kicked it again, gaining three more steps toward his goal.

Near to panic, the horse refused to go farther de-spite the beating, so he slid off with the reins clutched in his hands. Cursing under his breath, he tied the use-less beast to a tree and set off on foot. Only a couple of hundred lengths to go, all of it sloppy with mud and half-melted sleet. Explaining the mess might prove bothersome, but no matter. He could not stay away, not tonight.

The blackness of the cottage blossomed gloriously and he smiled. He opened the door and peered inside, the stench like perfume. He paused long enough to light a lamp, delaying his visit by moments, then strode to her.

He had met her on the road, a thief, a strumpet, a gypsy, sweet and dark and comely. She had showcased her wares, then refused to deliver on their promise. A mistake she would never make again.

She lay among the desiccated corpses of a few dogs, a rabbit, a suckling pig—creatures he barely remembered—her once beckoning body graying and cold. Since she resembled the castle's prettiest girl, he had granted her request for a ride to town. But he did not offer rides for free, not even to a shining smile, and he had demanded a trade. A ride for a ride. Laughing, she had refused him. Her, a worthless road whore! He licked his lips as he remembered the spasm in her throat. She had fought while he took her payment, until he showed her the knife. Then she had screamed.

"I had to choke you," he muttered, kneeling beside her. "You left me no choice."

She made no reply, just continued to stare at the ceiling with her one remaining eye. The other was long gone. It had tasted delightful, like a candied pecan.

He stood again and stretched. All those summers of watching girls like her, disgusting, cheap whores, and then the excitement he'd felt when he finally dared to make her pay. But she had ruined the moment. She had fought, and died, far too quickly.

And he, lost in his passion, had missed it.

Her death had not made him whole, but instead had left him wanting, starving. The filthy whore.

He pulled his blade from his pocket and peered at it for a moment, the blood-crusted steel brightening in the lamplight. His gaze moved to the sagging, ashen skin of her face, to her bruised and crushed throat. "I am improving, despite your failings."

The death of the road whore and the shame of his failure flavoring his mind, he had spent a few days in a fugue before deciding to try again. Nervous and excited, he had waited for the next, having chosen the hiding place in the ale room long ago. She had died quietly, her throat's blood bursting over the kegs. She had not seen him coming, had not suspected a thing, and he had looked into her eyes before taking a bit of her sin from her. A tasty and delightful bit to be sure. He had barely cut her, three simple slashes, yet he held her piss-filled filth in his hands. Not a perfect atonement, but a definite improvement over the road whore.

He had sat on the stone floor of the ale room for a bell or longer admiring his work, then, not sure what to do with the kidneys, he had wandered to the courtyard and fed them to the hogs.

A trembling quiver ran through him when they ate her filthy flesh, a sweet release like love's first kiss. The hogs had fought over the fresh, pissy meat, snorting and shoving, but her sin disappeared quickly, devoured and purified by the beasts.

He had walked the castle and courtyard alone for a time, hidden in the cloak and at one with the dark, while he thought about the hogs and the sin they consumed. The power of their hunger and their glee at sating it.

While he walked, the tower door had opened unexpectedly, startling him. A milkmaid, yawning and half asleep, trudged to the barns. He had smelled her lusts on the air like bitter spice and it filled his mouth with yearning and an unexpected hunger. He went up behind her. One slash across her back and she had gone down, yelping in surprise.

"I did not want another screamer," he said to the gypsy's corpse, "so I held her face in the snow and cut her open. The tower door opened and I had to hurry. It's all your fault, bitch! Why did you have to scream? Did you use your magics to curse me?"

He jabbed his blade into the gypsy's throat, but she didn't flinch, didn't bleed. She lay there like a discarded doll, both a disappointing failure and a taste of the perfection he might yet attain.

"I'll find another, you'll see! And if she's not enough, I'll find another and another. Until I'm perfect. Until I'm clean."

Grinning, he stood and glared at the thing at his feet. "And then, when I'm worthy, when I'm perfect, I'll claim the one I want most of all." He walked away and blew out the lamp, leaving the cottage and the perfect stench of death behind.

CHAPTER

4

†

The traffic in the narrow servants' hall ebbed and flowed, but Nella ignored the distraction while she finished her mending. She sat on the floor directly beneath the only working lamp in her section of hall, the best light she could find without taking her chores to another part of the castle. Most of the other servant girls had grown accustomed to her place beneath the light phases ago and no one seemed to mind.

"Last one," she sighed, reaching into her basket and pulling out a torn pair of boys' trousers. She examined the tear for a moment, then rummaged in her scrap bag for a patch.

She hummed as she turned the edges of the patch under and meticulously sewed it on while girls scampered through the normal chaos of their lives. Maybe, she thought, in another phase or two, she too could fret over her hair or giggle with her friends over a handsome mill worker. Perhaps even spend an evening in the unimaginable luxury of a nap.

From far down the hall she thought she heard her name and she glanced up. She saw no one looking at her and none of her friends had wandered near, so she returned to the patch.

"Where would I find Nella?" she clearly heard a

voice say a short time later and she looked up again. Whomever it was, she could not see them from her accustomed place on the floor. She set her mending in the basket and stood.

"Down the hall, by the light," a different voice said.

The first voice said, "Thank you," but she still could not see who it was.

An opening in the crowd granted her a glimpse of a page as he slipped between the girls and ambled toward her. He looked harried and frustrated. "Are *you* Nella?"

"Yes. Is there a problem?"

His face brightened in relief. "Not that I know of. I'm supposed to give you a message."

She had absolutely no idea why a page would deliver a message to her, and she tried not to clench her hands in worry. "All right. What's the message?"

He cleared his throat and squinted at the ceiling as if struggling to remember the exact message. He said, "There is mending to be done and you are supposed to be the best mender. It's incredibly urgent, and you must come with me right away."

Urgent mending? Was there such a thing? "Who has this urgent mending?"

He frowned and whispered, "I am not allowed to say. They swore me to secrecy."

Her hands did clench for a moment as she thought of the two dead girls, but she forced them open again. Whoever wanted her mending services had ensured a witness and an escort; Elli and Fytte had died alone. Surely, with a page delivering the message, this summons was nothing to worry over, and she certainly would not turn down an opportunity to work. Even if her benefactor wanted to remain mysterious. "They have?"

"Yes, ma'am. And I'm supposed to hurry. Tis most urgent, ma'am."

At last she nodded. Even a few small pence helped ease her debt. "Let me drop off my things."

The boy shrugged and followed her to her room.

"Did they say if it was a simple repair or a patching?" she asked.

"No, ma'am. Just that it was urgent."

Nella collected her basic sewing supplies and wondered who would summon her like this. The only noble she had mended for was Dubric, and he had already told her he had no work for her this phase. Besides, it was almost nine bell and nearly time for the castle to settle down for the night. Who would possibly need mending at this late hour?

The page led her from the servants' wing to the main stairs and up to the second floor. At first Nella thought perhaps one of the ladies had torn a slip or chemise—Goddess knew nearly everything was urgent to a lady—but instead of turning right toward the ladies' wing, they turned left toward the noble families' wing.

Her mind churning, she followed the page to a large alcove near the west tower. Cushioned benches stood in groups and clusters around low tables, giving people a place to sit and talk. The shadows in the alcove loomed thick to encourage privacy, but she saw the shape of a man sitting on a bench. He stood as she approached.

"Thank you, Deorsa," the man said, and Nella smiled.

The page nodded and ran off, leaving her standing in the otherwise quiet hallway.

"You have urgent mending?" she asked.

"Very urgent," he said as he approached her. "A life-or-death matter, I'm certain of it."

She laughed softly and shook her head. "I thought we had an agreement to avoid situations like these. You know I shouldn't be here with you."

He strode out of the shadows, but she would have recognized his well-proportioned form anywhere. He wore his fine brocaded garments with unselfconscious ease, heedless of their expense. Risley spoke to her as an equal, not as a servant. "Why not? I have mending. I do. Really."

She laughed again and wondered why the hall seemed so deserted. Maybe nobles went to bed early because they had no work to do, but Risley was definitely awake and watching her expectantly. "What mending do you have?"

He smiled and offered his arm. "Let me show you."

She shook her head with a smile, but did not take his arm. "You never give up, do you?"

He reached for her hand and placed it carefully on his forearm. "Not with you," he said. "And I do have mending."

"Really?" Despite herself, she ran a finger along the exquisite fabric of his shirt, finding it soft and sleek to her touch. The firm muscle of his forearm warmed her hand.

"Of course. Do you really think I'd lure you here on false pretenses?" When she raised an eyebrow he cleared his throat and rolled his eyes innocently toward the ceiling. "Um, how much do you charge to sew on buttons?"

"Half pence apiece, but for you they'd be free. How many do you have?"

He smiled wistfully then shook his head as if loosening cobwebs. "Uh, let me check." He looked down, then grabbed a shiny button on the pocket of his Haenparan-blue jerkin and popped it off. He held it between his fingers like a coin. "One. I have one. Can I pay you say, twenty or thirty crown to sew it back on?"

She could not help smiling. Only Risley would remove a gilded button so carelessly, as if it were a piece of lint. Even homemade buttons fashioned of baked clay or rough pine were valued by the poor. "It doesn't work that way."

He grasped the button in his fist and put it in his pocket. "I know, but I'm getting desperate. I want to see you."

"Risley . . ."

"Please, can we just . . . talk?" He touched her hand on his arm. "And I have something for you."

"Oh, Risley. No gifts. Please."

He smiled and stroked her fingers. "It's not a gift. Honest." He lowered his head and looked at her as if he was slightly embarrassed. "Actually, I went for a walk after I saw you earlier. I found myself in the village, and I stopped by the bakery." He shrugged and chuckled as if berating himself. "I bought a pie and I can't eat it alone. I have a pot of tea, and I thought we could just . . ." his voice trailed off and he watched her hopefully.

"A pie? You bought a pie?" The castle cooks made some sort of meat pie almost every day. She could not imagine Risley become so determined over something so dull.

He grinned. "Pecan. You do like nuts, don't you?"

A pie made from nuts? She had never heard of such a thing. "I've never tasted pecans. They're imported and were always too expensive."

His face fell. "Maybe I should've bought apple instead."

She touched his hand. "Oh, Risley, I'm sure pecan is fine."

"The pie doesn't really matter. Talk with me for a while. Please. I miss you."

"I miss you, too," she whispered. "It has been a long time, hasn't it?"

"Almost three moons."

As much as she worried over the trouble spending time with him would bring, she hated to disappoint him. "I suppose we could talk while I sew that button back on. And I suppose I could try pecan pie."

His smile lit up his whole face. "Thank you." He led her into the alcove and said, "You know, I can yank all the buttons off if it would encourage you to stay longer."

She laughed. "I need to be back before ten bell. I can stay until then."

He did not say a word, merely looked into her eyes and smiled. He led her to a padded bench that curved into a secluded corner. A polished wood table awaited them with a wooden box, two plates, an assortment of utensils, and tea for two.

"What if I couldn't stay?" she asked as he helped her sit.

"I refused to accept that possibility," he replied. "I could not imagine you'd let a perfectly good pie go to waste." Before she pulled her hand away, he kissed her fingers and turned to open the box. "I hope you like it."

"Here, let me do that." She tried to control the tremor in her just-kissed hand as she leaned forward and reached for the knife. "You don't need to serve me."

He gently took the knife from her hand. "Yes, I do. You relax and let me do this." As he cut the pie, he asked, "Are you still liking your job?"

Her hands gripped the edge of the cushion and she marveled at its softness. She could not remember sitting on a cushion before, and she found the whole experience nice. Inviting. And the dim light made the alcove seem almost romantic. "I like it fine," she said. "And it pays well."

He presented her with a brownish wedge of pie on a fine china plate edged in shimmering gold. "I'm glad," he said.

Goddess, don't let me break this plate, she thought as Risley handed her a shining golden fork, as well. The pie smelled wonderful and her mouth watered in anticipation. Sweets of any kind were a rare indulgence and an unaccustomed treat. But to have Risley serve her pie on a fine plate in private circumstances was almost too much for her to bear. In her nervousness she dropped the fork and it clattered to the floor. "Oh, Risley," she gasped, "I'm so sorry!"

He retrieved the fork and handed her another one. "Don't be," he said. "There is nothing to be sorry about. Relax. We're just having pie."

She nodded and grasped the fork, determined not to drop it again. "Is this something nobles do? Have pie?"

He poured their tea and sat beside her, their knees not quite touching. "I don't think so. I thought it was something two people could do to spend time together. Have pie and talk."

He glanced out toward the hallway. A nobleman walked by without noticing them. Risley sighed and turned his attention back to her. "Are you going to try the pie?"

She nodded and portioned off a bite, the fork rattling on the plate.

"If this is too much for you, we don't have to do this."

"It's not too much, not really. I don't know why I'm so nervous." She flashed him what she hoped was a self-assured smile and popped the bit of pie into her mouth.

A small happy sound escaped her throat and she sighed with utter bliss.

He smiled. "I guess you like pecan pie, and there's no reason to be nervous."

She nodded and some of her jitters fell away. "I know there isn't." She glanced out to the hall as a lackey trudged by with bathwater. "Maybe it's because anyone could walk by and stare at us."

He ate a bite of his pie. "Would you rather go somewhere more private?"

She took another bite as she contemplated her answer. "No," she said at last. "People talk enough as it is. If we were to meet somewhere private . . ." She shrugged and closed her eyes as the taste of the pie rolled over her tongue.

Risley said, "What people say doesn't matter to me, but I don't want to sneak around. Not with you." When she looked at him again he added, "But private, ah . . . meetings would probably be more acceptable to the gossipers than public ones."

"Because I'm a commoner?"

"No, because you're a woman. If I repeatedly met a wrinkled old countess, the rumors would fly. What people don't know, they can't speculate about."

She paused and took a quick sip of tea. "But everyone knows you brought me here. And besides, I'm almost done with the debt. After that you won't want to see me anymore."

He set aside his plate and gave her his full attention. "What ever gave you that idea?"

She lowered her eyes and shook her head. "It doesn't matter. Really."

"Yes, it does. Why do you think I won't want to see you?"

She stared at her half-eaten pie and said, "Lots of reasons." She drew in a breath and closed her eyes for a moment. "Mostly because it will be done then. Whatever it was that brought you to Pyrinn will be finished and you'll be sent out to do something else. Not only am I a commoner, I worry I'm the last loose thread or something." She raised her gaze to him and said, "You've rescued the helpless maiden, and soon you'll be done with the debt you were ordered to accept. After that, you'll be free of me and you'll . . ." She chewed her lip and shook her head.

He looked out to the hall again and a muscle in his cheek twitched. Three ladies walked by, talking. One noticed the pair in the shadows, paused, then hurried to join her companions as they moved off. Once the ladies were gone, he said, "You're not the 'last loose' anything and I'm sorry if I haven't been clear in my intentions. There's always an element of secrecy in my life, I suppose, whether I like it or not, and it tends to become a habit. I don't want to keep secrets from you, and I'm sorry that I have."

He sighed and toyed with his pie. "I should have told you about my mission to Pyrinn before, but I'm not supposed to talk about such things. I'm sorry about that, too. You've every right and reason to know how we came to be in this position, and how I hope we can get past it."

"You don't need to tell me. I mean, I don't want you to get in trouble with either of your grandfathers, and your missions are really none of my business. It's all right."

"No, it's not all right," he said. "I dragged you all the way here without telling you hardly anything at all beyond my name and that my father is the King's son. I not only frightened you, but placed you in debt to me. The very least I can do is offer an explanation and answer your questions. I'll tell you what I can."

He paused and looked earnestly into her eyes. "I was supposed to go to Pyrinn with my brother Aswin, but higher duty called him away and I had to go alone."

"Aswin's older than you, right?"

Risley nodded. "Almost two summers older."

Nella set her fork on her plate. She had so many questions, but one had been tugging especially hard. "You're Lord Apparent for Haenpar. Why you instead of him?"

Risley ate a bite of pie and smiled. "When my parents married they had to make certain . . . shall we say, sacrifices to appease my grandfathers. One was that their firstborn, Aswin, would inherit Faldorrah. Haenpar fell to me."

"'Sacrifices'?"

He glanced toward the hall and leaned closer as his voice softened. "This castle was my mother's childhood home, and my Grandda Brushgar was less than thrilled when his only daughter wanted to marry a Romlin. You see, my mother was the sole heir to Faldorrah, my father was the Crown Prince for all of Lagiern, and my grandfathers hated each other. I hear the argument between them became quite heated, nearly leading to a war. But my parents were determined to marry. The best solution they found, the one that appeased the most protests and kept my grandfathers from slaying each other, was to give their firstborn Faldorrah, and the second Haenpar. After my father gave up the crown, of course."

"What about your sister?"

"Torrent?" He chuckled and shook his head. "She gets all the good stuff. My gram's dishes, my other gram's lyre, the secret recipe for my da's wine, her own life to live, her own choices to make. Things like that."

"So you don't want Haenpar?" Nella asked, her voice sounding timid in her ears.

"I want Haenpar," he said. "It's a beautiful place, hills and trees and clear sparkling streams. But I'm not in a hurry to get it. My da's still got plenty of time left to rule before the burden falls to me."

"'Burden'?"

He shrugged. "It's a good deal of work to run a province properly, and not as simple as tax the poor and beat the life out of them. There's a delicate balance between the needs of the people and the needs of the government, and when that balance tips, it must tip toward the people, not away from them. My father works very hard to ensure our people live without fear or poverty and have a chance to improve their lives. When the harvests are meager or the winter runs long, it weighs heavily on my father's soul, as it should. Lord Egeslic has it all wrong, Nella. What he does to the people of Pyrinn is incomprehensible to me."

His words tugged at her heart, the impossibility of them, the hope. "But you went there anyway, to Pyrinn. Why?"

He turned his whole body to face her and sat cross-legged on the cushions. "It started out as just another mission. I'd never been to Pyrinn before, and I wasn't prepared for what I ran into."

"What happened?"

"The King had heard rumors Lord Egeslic sought illegal items in an effort to increase his power. Aswin and I were sent to meet with a spy my grandfather had established there summers ago. We were supposed to find out how much power Egeslic had acquired and what his true intentions were."

He sighed harshly. "I didn't know anything about Pyrinn, not a damn thing, and that was entirely my fault. I should have researched the customs before I left, but I didn't. I expected Pyrinn to be like most any other province where I could move around essentially unnoticed. But before I knew what happened, I had broken some law, Goddess only knows what one. All I did was try to pay a bridge toll with a gold crown. I mean, dangit, Nella, *everyone* takes crowns! The toll cost a scepter and I had no smaller change on me, but I had to pay the exact toll or be arrested, and the toll man could not give me change."

She sipped her tea. "The toll boxes are locked and only the retainers have the keys. Toll roads are horrible. They're an excuse to capture people for the work camps. Even nobles."

"Exactly. It was ludicrous. The toll man rang a bell and a handful of soldiers came to arrest me. They took my sword and started to drag me off! Since I was on a mission, I couldn't tell them who I was, but they probably wouldn't have cared anyway. All for a lousy scepter I would have gladly paid."

It all made perfect sense to her, but she knew Risley found Pyrinnian money laws difficult to understand.

"I escaped from them, but I was late for my meeting with the spy and he had gone. Soldiers were after me and I got on the first coach I saw to get as far away from there as possible."

"And when you got in the coach, you met me."

"Yes. I had ruined the whole meeting, lost my horse and my sword, and then the coach was attacked! Never had I failed a mission so badly. In many, many ways it was one of the worst days of my life."

He paused as she lowered her head. "But it was one of the best, too," he said, reaching for her hand. "If I had paid the correct toll, if I had not been arrested, then sought shelter on that particular coach, I never would have met you."

She raised her eyes and smiled. "Really? Do you mean that?"

He grinned. "Of course I mean it. Now I'm not saying that our flight from Pyrinn was an especially enjoyable experience. I hope to never fight bandits unarmed or charge a terrified horse down a collapsing gully ever again. But I wouldn't trade those five days with you for anything in the world. We should have discussed this before. I shouldn't have left you wondering."

He looked deep into her eyes and said, "I'm not going anywhere, and you'll likely see a lot more of me once the debt is paid. It doesn't matter to me if you're a commoner or a princess. I swear on my life that is the Goddess's truth, and I hope with all of my heart it doesn't matter to you that I'm a noble. I want to spend time with you. As much as you'll allow me."

She blushed and took another bite of the pie.

* * *

"Sir?" Otlee called from near the door.

"What is it?" Dubric replied. He stood between head physician Rolle and Halld, and Fytte's opened corpse lay exposed before him. They tallied measurements while the ghosts looked on. No wound cut deeper than a fingerlength and every slice was precise and measured, the damage minimal. *What kind of weapon would do such a thing?*

"Dien's back," Otlee said. "He's handling the crowd while Lars questions witnesses. We've got thirty-two left. Can we send some to bed?"

Dubric turned to look at him. "What time is it?"

"Almost nine bell," Otlee replied. The lad looked pale and tired, almost gaunt. Had he taken time to eat? Ink spots stained his worn, secondhand uniform, ruining it. Dubric wondered how the boy's family would ever afford another.

Where did the time go? "Have Dien or Lars list who is left and we will track them down tomorrow. No reason to have them stand around all day again. And get something to eat. Lars, too."

Otlee nodded and was gone.

"So, what do we have?" Dubric asked as he reviewed his notes. "Blade a fingerlength long. Also thin and light. Single-edged."

Halld and Rolle examined the collection of cut marks inside Fytte.

"Still no ideas?"

"I'm certain it's too small for a dagger or a dirk," Rolle said. He lifted a cut piece of intestine; the curved slash on it was delicate and crisp, made when the killer twisted his hand inside her. "It fit completely in his hand, Dubric. I'm sure of it."

"And the back of the blade is blunt." Halld pointed to a scrape on the back of her liver. A scrape they had measured time and time again. Flat and no thicker than half a dozen pieces of parchment. The blade had bumped the liver when the killer pulled his hand away from the kidney. Bumped it hard, but not cut it.

Dubric rubbed his eyes. "But what kind of blade fits this description? Small and single-edged? A ladies' knife? A page's first dagger? Why the kidneys?" He needed a real clue, something to follow, to look for. Something stronger than speculation.

Both physicians shook their heads and Dubric frowned. The killer had wanted only her kidneys and her hair, and he had taken nothing more, barely damaging anything else. But why? And how?

"All right," Dubric said for the millionth time that evening, "let us suppose he has a weapon, a blade of some sort, about a fingerlength long. Let us also suppose, for the sake of argument, he only needed kidneys. How could he see them well enough to remove just them, especially through that small hole, not to mention in the dead of night? I would have assumed he would cause massive damage to her insides getting the blasted things out. Tell me why I am wrong."

Halld stammered and Rolle looked at the floor and frowned. Fytte's ghost leaned forward to scream in her corpse's ear. Dubric rubbed his eyes and she flickered and disappeared. Elli, however, remained.

"We can't," Halld said, his eyes no longer eager. "It makes no sense."

"No sense at all," Rolle whispered.

It was long after midnight when Dubric gave up and headed to bed.

* * *

Risley felt rather pleased with himself as he walked back to his suite. He had enjoyed a whole bell of Nella's company—she had even forgotten the button—and it had only cost him a pie.

Well, a pie and a teapot and some tea, but the rewards were worth far more than the insignificant expense. He smiled and wondered if he should have bought candles.

"No," he mumbled to himself as he balanced the box of leftover pie and dishes with one hand and opened his suite door with the other. "Candles would have been too obvious. They would have made her suspicious."

He set the box on a table near the door and kicked off his boots. Had he ever seen her eyes in candlelight? He stopped for a moment, lost in his thoughts. He decided he hadn't and wondered how long he would have to wait. He shrugged. It would happen when it happened.

But the pie had worked, praise the Goddess!

Smiling, he padded down the carpeted hall to the bath chamber. *Ah, what a lovely night!*

"Nella, Nella," he whispered as he washed his face and prepared for bed. He sighed happily as he tossed ideas around in his head. Tea and pie tonight. Maybe he could convince her to take a walk tomorrow, just a little stroll, or perhaps they could ride down to the village and see the minstrels performing at the alehouse. She'd be hesitant, of course, but would there be any harm in an innocent stroll?

Nothing serious, nothing to raise too many eyebrows. Just two friends enjoying each other's company. He sighed her name again as he finished in the bath chamber. He'd be on his absolute best behavior, the consummate gentleman, and not even try to kiss her. Not until the debt was done, at least.

He stopped in the middle of the hallway and closed his eyes. "Goddess," he whispered, "give me the strength to control myself. Just another phase or so." He opened his eyes again. "I think I can manage after that."

He stepped into his office. As he blew out the lamp, he noticed the doodles dancing across the blotter between the scorch marks and tools. Small flowing sketches of the face that had been haunting his dreams these past couple of moons graced the surface. Work had proven difficult, but daydreaming had come easy, and he smiled before he turned away. *Nella, Nella,* he thought as he moved through the suite blowing out lamps and lights. *Only another phase or so and I can start courting her!*

As he opened the door to his bedroom, he thought about the sound of her laugh, the shine of torchlight on her hair, and how the perfect curve of her hips would feel beneath his hands—

"Julianne! Perri! What are you doing here?" Risley came to an abrupt stop in the doorway.

Two ladies, one short and plump, the other tall and sleek, lay on their bellies on his bed, their heads toward the door. Both were not-quite naked.

"We've been waiting a long time, Risley," Julianne, the plump one, said. She rolled onto her back, wiggled, and grinned at him.

"Rather late for you to be heading in, isn't it?" Perri asked. She stretched and held out a long manicured hand.

Risley stumbled back as his hopeful imaginings faded. "Wh-what are you doing here?" he asked again.

Perri raised onto her knees. "Is that all you can say?"

"Now, Risley," Julianne added, "you've been in Faldorrah all this time and have never stopped by to visit."

He took a breath and shook his head, yanking his gaze away from their more desirable assets. "I'm not interested," he choked. "You need to leave."

"Uh-huh, sure you're not," one of them said. He thought it might have been Perri. "You haven't visited any of us since you came back this last time."

The bed creaked and he stumbled back another step. He felt trapped. Ensnared. He knew Perri was exceptionally limber and energetic, while Julianne had an extremely talented tongue. The pair together would be nothing short of exhausting, and he groaned as he felt a familiar tightening in his groin. He heard the whisper of fabric falling to the floor.

"We checked," Julianne added with a giggle. "Not us or Ellianne, or Danne, or Suphpe."

"No one," Perri said. "And you always come to one of us."

"Oh, you might miss a night now and then," Julianne purred, "but since you haven't visited us, we thought we'd visit you."

He ignored the urgent pleas from his lower regions. He had more important things to worry about now, and only a phase or so to wait. "Thanks for the offer, really, but I'm afraid I must—"

One of them touched him, traced her fingers over his belly, and his eyes bolted open.

Both stood close before him, as bare as the day the Goddess gave them life. Perri reached for the buttons of his jerkin and started to undo them.

"Now, Risley," Perri said, "this playing hard to get is so unlike you."

"We've missed you so much," Julianne said, her eyes growing dark and smoky.

"Since you've turned shy on us, we thought maybe it would take something special to pique your interest." Perri leaned forward, her bare chest brushing against him, and she licked his chin. Her hand slipped downward and she said, "We want to have you back again. Let's play. All three of us."

He closed his eyes and took a shaky breath, even as he gently pushed her away. "I don't do that anymore," he muttered and opened his eyes again.

Julianne pouted and crossed her arms under her

ample breasts. "Now, Risley, if you're not careful, folks are going to start confusing you with Aswin."

Perri nodded gravely and reached for him again. "Aswin never wants to play." She hooked her fingers in the front of his pants and tried to pull him forward, but he stood his ground.

Anger simmered in his forehead and he clenched his jaw. He had said "no," dammit. In all his summers, with all his women, he had never, ever persisted past a "no." The eager flex in his groin faded to nothing as he tasted disgust in the back of his mouth. "I told you I don't do that anymore." He shoved Perri away and she stumbled back, slamming against the wall. "I'm not interested."

"Oh, that tears it!" she snapped. "What more can we do? Did you go off and get gelded or something?"

"C'mon, Risley," Julianne coaxed as she moved closer. "We only want to have a little fun, that's all. Whatever the problem is, we'll work around it. You're not the first guy to have—"

He rolled his eyes. "There is nothing wrong with me. I work fine."

Perri glanced at Julianne. "We could probably talk Ellianne into joining us. Do you think that would help?"

He ground his teeth and snapped, "No. I'm not interested. Get your stuff and go. Now."

Julianne cocked her wide hip to the side. "Yep, he's gelded."

He threw his hands in the air, walked toward the entry door, and yanked it open. "Fine. I'm gelded. Now get out."

Both girls stared at him. "It's that little servant you're slobbering after, isn't it?" Julianne asked.

Perri threw her head back and laughed, her breasts jiggling fetchingly, but Risley was not the least bit fetched. "She makes my bed, Risley. The same one you've crawled into so many times. She's not worth your time. We all know you've lain with commoners, but a servant? Surely even you have some standards."

He said nothing, only tilted his head toward the door.

Perri walked up to him and asked, "So what happens when you tire of her? Are we going to be your seconds? Is that it? Seconds to a filthy servant?"

He wanted to rip the smirk from her face, but he held his temper in check despite the pounding in his head. "Get out. And don't come back."

Julianne tossed her head and retreated to the bedroom while Perri stared at him. "You stupid son of a bitch," she whispered, then she, too, stomped off.

When they finally left, Risley slumped onto a divan and tried to control his shaking hands and knees. He had just turned down two naked and willing women, both of whom were well versed in the more pleasurable aspects of life. Three moons ago—Malanna's blood, a bell ago—he wouldn't have thought it possible.

His delightful evening forgotten, he looked out into the night and wished the throbbing pain in his head would fade so he could sleep.

* * *

Long before dawn, Dubric hurried down the main stairs, yawning as he clipped on his cloak. As he strode into the great hall he paused and smiled despite himself. Dien and Lars waited near the outer doors, sipping from steaming mugs.

"I thought I told both of you to get some sleep," Dubric said, approaching them.

Lars shrugged and Dien grumbled, "After all these summers I just can't sleep without Sarea beside me."

He pressed a warm mug into Dubric's hand. "What's the plan?"

Dubric sipped the tea and choked back a cough. "Brandy? For King's sake, it is early morning!"

Dien downed his in a gulp, his broad face turning red for a moment. "Whiskey. And not only is it the middle of the frigging night, it's colder than a witch's left tit out there."

All three glanced at the tall windows along the southern wall and shivered. "Looks like sleet," Lars said, sighing.

Dubric and Dien sighed, as well, then finished their drinks. They left the castle, pulling their cloaks close against the chill.

They walked to the east first, past the kitchen entrance and along the row of shops and buildings used by artisans. As they worked their way north, Dubric squinted at the castle wall from time to time, looking for lights. All clear, everyone asleep. Ignoring the ghosts, he led his men through the patrols and tried to stay warm.

Perhaps half a bell later, as they rounded the west tower for the third time, he stopped and Lars took a hesitant step forward. Several lights shone from the third floor.

"The four bell just rang," Dien said, squinting through the sleet. "Who but us sinners is crazy enough to be up this early?"

Lars rubbed his hands together to warm them. "That's Risley's suite. He has the first set of rooms past the tower."

Grumbling under his breath, Dubric reminded himself to ask Risley about his late-night activities. As if he had heard their thoughts, the lights blinked off, one by one. The three stood ankle-deep in slush, gaping at the wall as each light disappeared, leaving the castle dark once again.

"What the peg?" Dien asked. "Why have all those frigging lights on, then blow them out again?"

"I intend to ask him that," Dubric said. They resumed their patrol and he wondered if he were about to step into a political nest of snakes by even considering Risley, one of the most powerful men in all of Lagiern. *Maybe no one will die tonight,* he thought, *and all of my worries will be for naught.* He continued on, slopping through sleet and mud until he felt frozen to the bone.

They walked through the night and into the predawn morning, while Dubric stretched and bent his freezing fingers. His joints ached, flaring with rheumatic pain, but he tried to keep them flexible. Beside him, Dien lumbered on, never slowing, never faltering from the same steady pace, and his breath pluming with every word. The squire had spent the past quarter bell voicing his worry over his family. "Sarea's gonna insist on coming home, I know she will," Dien grumbled. "I just hope to high heaven that she leaves the girls at her mother's."

"Maybe she'll decide it's better that they all stay there," Lars offered. Still energetic and somehow warm, he meandered along behind them, checking each door they passed.

"Don't bet on it, pup. She's not afraid of a frigging thing, and she'll fret herself into consumption worrying about me if she doesn't come home." He covered his yawn with his hand. "Women. Too damn opinionated and not a lick of sense to back it up."

Dubric continued to trudge forward and flex his aching hands while Lars and Dien bantered.

"And to think you've got all daughters," Lars teased,

grinning. "Think they'd like to hear they have no sense? I'm happy to tell them for you."

Dien laughed. "I'm just talking about women in general. My girls are a different matter entirely."

Lars started to say something, but he paused, turning and sniffing the air. "Do you smell that?"

All three stopped. Dubric breathed deeply but he sensed nothing with his frozen nose. "What do you smell?"

Lars turned around, still sniffing. "Tobacco. Someone's smoking." He stopped then took a step, defiantly staring the darkness in the eye. "It's like it's right here."

Turning, Dien lifted his lantern and looked into the night. "Ain't no one there, pup. Nothing but the wind."

"You can't smell it? For Goddess's sake . . ." Wincing at his own words, Lars glanced toward Dubric as his voice faded away.

Dien shrugged and squinted into the dark. "I'm too clogged up to smell a thing. How about you, sir?"

"No, nothing," Dubric said. He rubbed his eyes with bluish hands, the joints glowing a creaky yellow-green.

Why, the old fart has rheumatism, the killer thought, grinning. *Cold damp weather like this must hurt terribly.* Beside Dubric, Dien's bulk gleamed brilliant crimson-gold, while the boy, still growing, shone brightest of all, the ends of his long bones a shiny green instead of the usual blue.

Lars's hand fell to the hilt of his sword, his golden eyes searching, while his companions shrugged and continued on.

Grinning, the killer reached into his pocket. His fingers closed around the handle of his blade, caressing it before he pulled it free. The blade left a black trail in its wake as he slashed it just out of reach of Lars's throat.

Not yet, boy, he thought, watching the blood course through Lars's veins and the steady beating of his young heart. *So naive, so trusting. I could kill you in a moment, but you're not what I need.*

He slashed with the blade again, the streak of black floating in front of Lars's throat like a gash. *Begone, boy, before I lose my patience,* he thought, his fingers tightening on the blade's handle. *Your companions won't even hear you scream.*

Lars blinked, frowning, then he turned and followed the others, leaving the black gash and its wielder behind.

* * *

She struggled to pull herself to the kitchen door. Her fingers clutched in the ice-crusted mud once . . . twice . . . and her legs stretched uselessly behind her. She felt no pain, only a sense of weakening, but she saw the castle glow in the pink of dawn. Somehow she would get to it.

Behind her, the thing she could not see tugged at her back and yanked her to it again. She gagged at the onslaught of mud and slush in her mouth but had no strength to fight. "I don't want to die," she whimpered, her breath slowing. The cold mud drew away her strength even as it absorbed her blood.

The thing that had grabbed her shoved her face into the muck so she could speak no more. Its fingers dug into her skull. "You have been chosen to feed my purpose," the thing said. "And you will feed it *perfectly.*"

She felt a tug at her head, sharp bright pain, and the pressure lifted.

The thing left her and she raised her head to look at

the kitchen door one last time. She reached forward again and clutched her cold fingers into the slush. *That voice,* she thought. *I know that voice from somewhere.*

Ahead of her, the kitchen door burst open. Six boys, lackeys, hurried into the morning to fetch firewood, their laughter bubbling warm on the bitter wind. She reached for them and spat mud from her mouth. "Help me!" she cried, her voice lost to the wind, if it was ever there at all. "Help—" The light left her eyes and her face fell into the ice again.

All six boys hollered. Two ran forward, and the rest froze where they stood.

Behind them, the kitchen door opened and closed. One lackey turned to look, but no one was there. Nothing but swirling snow.

CHAPTER

5

†

Pitta said Ennea had left the castle before dawn to fetch a bundle of dried mint from the shed. The mint and the basket waited in a slump of sleet beside the shed door, remaining pristine, perfect, and unspattered by blood or mud. Ennea, however, lay facedown in a freezing puddle of slush and gore with her back slashed open and her scalp removed. This morning's crowd numbered seventy-three, and Dien kept them far from the body. Two lackeys had touched her; all six waited with Otlee in the office. No one else had come near.

Besides those left by Ennea and the two lackeys, only one set of footprints dimpled the slush and mud near the body. The killer had knelt beside her, toes of his boots digging into the mud. Dubric touched the gentle curves cut into the slush by a heavy cloak. No threads, no scraps, no bits of fur to be seen, merely a single smear of blood in a shallow groove, as if the edge of the cloak had been stained by the gore. Dubric fumbled for his notebook, frowning. *There must be a clue here, somewhere.*

Finishing his preliminary notes, he stood, gazing along the trail. The killer's tracks walked through her blood puddle, proceeded to a kitchen door, and continued into the hustle and bustle of the kitchen.

After measuring the bootprints and killer's stride, Dubric knelt beside Ennea. Her ghost had flickered before his eyes moments after the first glints of sun broke over the horizon. She had been dead mere minutes when he arrived.

Slashed down both sides of her spine, then above her hip bones in hard arcs like wings, she had been partially eviscerated. A steaming lump of internal organs lay pulled over her right leg and hip, blood soaked her skirt, and her blouse was gone. Her hands clenched into the ice, fingers gripping the slush; it seemed as if she had tried to pull forward even as she was butchered. A fingerlength or two of distance, perhaps, but she had struggled to get away. A deep groove in the slush led to her chin and Dubric measured it. Perhaps the killer had pulled her back, toward him. Dubric scratched a few notes and looked up. Someone was coming.

Halld hurried through the slush. "Another one?"

A page handed Dubric a blanket and Dubric passed it on to Halld. "Get her inside. I want to know every single thing you can tell me. Is it the same weapon? The same killer? Why did he pull half of her guts out? Is *anything* missing?"

Halld nodded and knelt beside her.

Dubric glanced at Lars. "Take everything else to my office." Dubric turned away before Lars could nod and stomped into the castle, ghosts trailing, as always, behind him.

The kitchen staff huddled against one wall while four senior pages paced in front of them. No one worked, nothing cooked, nothing baked, and hundreds of people would be screaming for breakfast soon. He did not want to add dealing with hungry, scared people to this morning's duties—plain scared was going to be bad enough—but Dubric had never seen the kitchen quiet before. He took a deep breath and looked around the huge room. It smelled of grease, raw food, spices, and sweaty bodies; the walls were smoke-stained and spattered, the floors dark and filthy with mud, eggshells, flour, and sausage makings.

He rubbed his eyes. *Two scullery maids murdered. If the killer does not work in the kitchen, he has to be familiar with it.*

He looked at the head cook, a huge woman named Ruggie, who stood trembling beside Pitta. She seemed to shrink under his gaze. "Did you work with Fytte or Ennea?" He pursed his lips and waited for her expected answer.

She did not fail him. "Yes, sir. Both of them."

His attention snapped hard and fast to the closest page. "Moergan, take her to my office. Now."

Moergan nodded and reached for Ruggie's arm. "Yes, sir."

"I don't know anything, I swear!" Ruggie wailed as Moergan escorted her from the kitchen. The other kitchen workers watched her departure, then turned fear-filled eyes to Dubric. He had shaken them. Good. Now he hoped to get the answer he needed. The killer had walked through the blasted kitchen. Someone in this room had seen him.

His voice was hard, clear, and impatient. He pointed to the door behind him. "Did anyone see someone come through that door?"

No one answered. Several women cried, their faces covered with aprons and towels, but none looked nervous or secretive.

He pointed at the door again and tried not to scream. "No one saw a man, a *bloody* man with a *knife,* come through that door? No one saw this door open at all?"

A few people shook their heads. None responded with either their mouths or their eyes.

He stomped to the door and pointed at a blood-flecked puddle of water as his rage and his heartbeat slammed in his ears. "There are bloody bootprints here. Someone saw this. Someone!"

The wall of terrified workers quivered but did not offer any answers. Furious, Dubric stared at the floor for a moment, at the flecks of blood in the melting slush. *This is impossible! Someone has to have seen something.*

The service-hall door banged open as a pair of serving girls ran into the kitchen. One yelled, "What's keeping the eggs? We've got—" Both skidded to a stop, frozen where they stood.

"All right," Dubric said, returning his attention to the crowd. His fists shook as he struggled not to curse. He tried to keep his voice steady; he would accomplish nothing by getting angry. "I know you have work to do. Answer me this: Which of you are roommates or close friends of Fytte or Ennea? *Anyone?*"

Eight girls blabbered and tried to back into the crowd as Dubric stepped toward the pages. "Serian, Jorst, take names of everyone in this room and note who is wearing boots. Cottle, get the name of every serving wench, lackey, and anyone else from the kitchen who happens to be in the great hall." The three pages nodded and one ran for the door. Dubric stood before the crowd. "Once the pages have taken your name, you can go back to work. Except you eight. You come with me."

The girls wailed and Bacstair mumbled, his flour-dusted head lowered, "Sir, that's all but two o' the morning scullery maids. We can't run the kitchen without—"

"You will have to make do." Dubric flicked his hands to the main door and the girls stumbled forward as if going to the gallows.

* * *

Dubric questioned Ruggie first and received no useful answers, as expected. Her testimony was brief. Next were the scullery maids. Again no answers. Otlee's fingers flew as Dubric barked questions, but over and over again the best answers did not go beyond "I don't know." None knew a single blasted thing about either of the dead girls—their enemies, lovers, or opinions. Nothing. They were all as ignorant and noncommittal as a pile of rocks. Dubric processed the witnesses quickly, threatening each time to haul them back if more information was required. Every maid left in tears. Dien sat beside Otlee during the interviews but did not say a word. Lars leaned in the corner and stared at each witness, the ghosts flickering beside him.

When the last of the eight girls finished, Otlee flexed his fingers and asked, "What do we do now?"

"We question the lackeys," Dien said.

Otlee stretched and reached for a clean sheet of paper.

"I still can't believe no one saw a man walk through that door," Lars muttered as he shifted his weight. "He must have been drenched in blood."

Dubric opened the door. Two pages guarded the six lackeys. They sat hunched and crowded on the same bench; no one else waited in the outer office. "Who touched her?" Dubric barked.

Two lackeys shrank in their seats, the other four pointed.

"All right. You first." He looked at the closest boy, one who had not touched Ennea.

"Yessir," he muttered and scrambled to his feet.

The boy was named Lopa, and he was nine summers old. Otlee repeated his personal information and the boy nodded but could not sign his name. He barely knew how to hold a pen.

"Any mark will do," Dubric said. "We will witness you made it."

Lopa drew a lopsided circle. Otlee and Dien initialed it.

"Am I in trouble?" Lopa asked as Otlee began the notes.

Dubric shook his head and took a deep breath to calm his nerves. Children required a gentler touch. "No. We want to know what you saw and what you heard. Anything you remember."

Lopa nodded and stared at the floor. "I saw Ennie lyin' in the snow, sir. That's all."

"That is fine," Dubric said. "But we will start before you found Ennea, all right? Before you went outside, what were you doing?"

"Shovelin' ashes from the ovens, sir. Been doin' that since a'fore sunup."

"You like shoveling ash? Is it hard work?"

Lopa looked at his filthy bare feet. "It's not so bad. Better'n haulin' butcher slop. Sheep guts stink."

Dubric smiled and stifled a yawn. He had barely slept since he first saw Fytte's ghost; neither had Lars or Dien, for that matter. "Did you notice anything different in the kitchen this morning, while you were shoveling out the ovens?"

"Nawsir," Lopa whispered, his voice cracking in his nervousness. His foot pounded against the chair leg and he fidgeted with the laces of his greasy shirt.

"Nothing at all? An extra worker? Someone who did not belong?"

He shook his head. "Nawsir, I didn't see nobody. But the ghost were there this mornin'."

Dien and Dubric stared at the boy, Lars shook his head as if he did not believe what he had heard, and Otlee almost dropped his pen. "'The ghost'?" Dubric asked, his voice steady.

Lopa blushed, nodded, and glanced at Dubric. "I ne'er seen no ghost. Honest. But when stuff happens sometimes, we blame it on the ghost." He shrugged. "Ya know? Like when somethin' you just had turns up missin', or a pile of peeled taters falls to the floor, or the door opens but no one's there?" He shrugged again. "Ghost stuff."

"'Ghost stuff,'" Dubric repeated. Despite himself he glanced at his ghosts and suppressed a sigh. They were as useless and as incapable as ever.

"Yessir."

"What 'ghost stuff' happened this morning?"

Lopa shrugged and wiggled his dirty toes. "The door open'd when we was lookin' at Ennie. It opened right b'hind me, but wern't nobody there. I figured it were the ghost."

"Does this happen often? The door opening with no one there?"

"Nawsir. Seen it once b'fore. Last summer some-time."

"And no one was there today? You are certain?"

"Nawsir. Just us."

"But you saw Ennea?"

"Yessir, in the snow. She were reaching for us, and I think she said somethin', but I sure couldn't hear her. Ever'one else was too noisy." He shuddered and looked at the floor.

Dubric watched the boy for a moment and wrote a note: *She was alive when the boys found her.* "Did she do anything else?"

"Nawsir. She just looked at us an' died. Veller an' Neffin, they ran to her. I stayed put, just like we was told to. I did what I were s'posed to. I didn't run, nawsir."

"Did you see anyone else?"

Lopa shook his grimy head. "Nawsir. Nobody was there, even when the door opened. I looked. T'were just us an' Ennie."

Dubric rubbed his eyes while the three ghosts looked on.

* * *

After the lackeys finished their testimony, Dubric sent Otlee to fetch the physicians' report.

He yawned and shook his head to clear the cobwebs as he returned to his desk. "What do you think?" he asked Dien and Lars. The ghosts stood in the corner, annoying but ignorable.

"I think that ghost stuff is a bunch of horse piss," Dien said as he picked a wad of mud from his boot and tossed it into the corner. "Just a scared boy trying to make sense of seeing a dead girl in the snow."

Lars fell into the witness chair with the awkward lankiness of a boy on the verge of becoming a man. "Maybe so. But he seemed convincing and sure of himself."

"Best witness we've had so far," Dubric said as he *thump*ed his pencil on the clean surface of his desk.

Lars's eyes widened and he tilted his head, his fingers tapping on the arm of the chair. "I'd heard that an old friend of yours made some stuff to help you against the dark mages. Did anything he made—"

Dubric had already considered the same question himself. "Turn someone invisible? No. Nuobir made things to either kill the mages or protect us. Weapons and armor, for the most part. He never dabbled with worthless enchantments."

Lars's brow furrowed. "How is invisibility worthless?"

Dubric's stomach growled. "The mages could see magic. Being invisible would be useless against them, a waste of time and energy."

Dien nodded. "It'd be no better than a jester's trick."

"But, sir, what about magic spells?"

"Not likely." Dubric sipped his tea. "Only the most powerful mages could create such an effect, and they would not waste the spell's energy to murder a servant girl. I would be more apt to suspect Wraith Rot or other diseases before a mage."

Lars turned to Dien. "We have any gypsies wintering here?"

Dien shook his head. "No, not a one."

Dubric suggested, "Perhaps we should consider the herbmonger. Has Inek caused any trouble lately?"

The summer before, they had discovered Inek using his herbs to make people sick so they would then seek his expertise to cure them. He had received a dozen lashes for his crime, tight price restrictions, and a moon in gaol. It was not his first incarceration, or first whipping. A few moons before the poisoning incident he had started a brawl in the local alehouse and had injured several patrons. He had once attempted to molest the ropemaker's wife, and had also visited the gaol for theft and general disorderliness.

Inek was hateful and rude, but was he a murderer?

"No, sir, not lately. Want me to have him watched, just in case?" Dien asked, a vicious gleam in his eyes. Inek had set Dien's boots afire during the pursuit last summer and had burnt his feet. Dien tended to harbor grudges.

Dubric contemplated the polished surface of his desk. Inek was a pain in the backside, an angry and vile man. Although the herbmonger seemed to prefer brawls over blood, he would certainly bear one night's observation, even though there were few men to spare. "Certainly. Send a pair of archers to watch him overnight. And order more lamp oil. We are going to need it for patrols."

"Yes, sir," Dien replied.

Lars leaned forward. "What if someone's corrupted by magic? Do we have any old magic stuff here? Could someone have found it? What happened to it all?"

"What we have is locked in a metal-lined cabinet in my suite. We destroyed what dark magic we found, and Nuobir did not make as much as people think," Dubric said. "I have my old sword, Nigel's axe and shield . . ." he cleared his throat and frowned. "And Oriana's dagger."

"Sorry," Lars whispered as he shifted on his seat.

Dubric shrugged. Dien and Lars both knew the wounds were old yet festering. "That is essentially all I have. Tunkek has some, and Kyl Romlin, too, I hear. A few older things made before the war are around; useless personal items, for the most part. The mages destroyed anything that could be used against them. During and after the war, we scoured the land, looking for the mages' artifacts. Not much from those days survives at all and only the rare magical item exists outside official records."

Dubric looked at Lars for a moment and hesitated before asking, "Do you know what items Kyl has?" Lars was the only lad Dubric knew who called the Lord and Lady of Haenpar by their first names; his father was

Bostra Hargrove, Kyl Romlin's castellan and a good
friend of Dubric's. But Dubric hated mentioning Lars's
family in his presence; the tension between father and
son was obvious. Neither had explained Lars's abrupt
arrival in Faldorrah, and Dubric did not want to push
the lad. Whatever misunderstanding had happened between the two was none of his business.

Shifting uncomfortably, Lars looked at the ceiling
as he called forth the memories. "My father has
Byreleah Grennere's arrows, if I remember correctly,
five of them, anyway. Kyl has Siddael Marrick's sword,
but it's dead. Doesn't protect anymore, he said."

Dubric leaned back in his chair. Nuobir had told
them that although the daggers were eternal, the magic
in the bigger weapons would die when their bloodline
ceased to flow. The Marrick line had been gone for
some twenty summers now, and Siddael's sword was a
relic of a best forgotten time, nothing more. The Darril
family, however, had continued through Albin's sister
Brinna Brushgar to her daughter, Lady Heather
Romlin of Haenpar. She had been fourteen summers
when Albin died, and as the last of the Darril line had
accepted responsibility for the weapon. "What about
Albin's sword? I thought Kyl and Heather had it?"

"Not anymore. They gave it to Risley. He showed it
to me a couple of summers ago."

Dubric tapped his pencil on the desk. *Risley has
Albin Darril's sword,* he thought. *Is it here? In
Faldorrah? And if so, does Risley know it can do more
than protect him?* He made a note in his book. "Do either of you have any other ideas?"

Dien scratched his two-day growth of beard. "I have
a question. How can it be that none of those girls we in-
terviewed today knew a blasted thing about the dead

'uns? Girls talk, don't they? By the seven hells, I can't shut my daughters up most days."

Dubric had not associated with young girls for summers. Not since Heather Brushgar grew up, married Kylton Romlin, and moved away. He looked at Dien for a moment and said, "I think you are right. See if you can find someone they did talk to. They had to have something in common. A suitor, perhaps?"

Dien pulled his notebook from his pocket. "Yes, sir. I'll track them down."

Lars yawned and blinked a couple of times. "They did have something in common. Their names started with similar letters. E and F."

Dien laughed and looked up from his notebook. "I doubt that means anything, pup, but you never know."

Dubric noted Lars's comment in his book. Even odd-sounding leads played out sometimes. "Any other ideas?"

Lars said, "Yes. A couple of things. Who would be likely to be out and about before dawn, and why is he killing servant girls?"

"Well, pup," Dien said, "we don't know for sure it's a 'he' who's doing this, and lots of folks have to work before dawn."

Dubric leaned back in his chair. "Remember, it is only servant girls so far. Maybe it is because they are easier to find alone, or maybe because they are working before dawn. It might also be due to a reason we have not yet discovered. The killer might have ladies in his sights, too. We have no way of knowing. But after finding two sets of men's boot prints, I am fairly confident that we seek a man."

A moment later, Otlee knocked then entered, the green-sealed physicians' report in his hands. He looked as tired as Dubric felt. "They say it's the same weapon, sir," he said as he covered a yawn with his hand. "Just her kidneys and hair missing."

Dubric stood and said, "Enough talk of killers and death. It is time for dinner."

* * *

Instead of eating in the great hall with the others, Dubric decided to get a bowl of soup for dinner and eat at his desk. He entered the kitchen and immediately noticed that most of the female staff were keeping to one side of the room and the men to the other. Both sides shared uneasy glances and the air was thick with far more than the aroma of roasting rabbits. Dubric ignored the cautious and angry stares and pulled a bowl from one of the many dish cupboards along the east wall.

Three scullery maids scurried away, shooting worried glances at him even as they ran. He had invaded their territory, insecure as it was. He felt truly sorry for scaring them, but he had not eaten since the middle of the night and his stomach protested any further delay.

He dodged a pair of lackeys running past with steaming buckets of water, ducked beneath a servitor's high-piled food tray, avoided stepping through the argument between the meat carver and the swine herder, and finally reached an aromatic pot of soup bubbling in the hearth.

Pitta supervised the afternoon and evening cooking that day. She barked instructions to three meat maids, then turned to Dubric with a huge soup ladle in her hand. "Afternoon, sir," she said. Her wide earnest face was flushed from heat and steam, and she wiped sweat off her forehead with her sleeve.

"Afternoon," he replied, sniffing the air. "Chicken?"

"Not today. Tis quail and carrot. We had some left from last night."

Last night's quail had been tasty, even cold from his pocket at three bells in the morning. "Mind if I take a bowl?" he asked.

"Help yourself," she replied. She glanced at the outer door with a slight frown and handed Dubric the ladle. "If you'll 'scuse me, sir, the herb merchant just arrived."

Dubric nodded and stirred the soup a couple of times before dipping a portion for his bowl. He hung the ladle on its nail above the hearth and was about to locate some fresh bread when Pitta walked by with a bag of anise seed. He smiled. Anise seed today meant anise cookies or quick breads tomorrow.

The bakers had piles of rolls and small loaves cooling on the racks and he selected one, slipping the welcome ball of warmth into his jerkin pocket. Finished with his hurried visit, he turned from the bakers and nearly knocked over the herbmonger from the village. Hot quail-and-carrot soup sloshed over the front of Dubric's jerkin and pants with a clear bright flash of pain. He held the bowl away from him and looked over the damage before turning his attention to the herb-monger. "What are you doing here?" he snapped.

"What?" the herbmonger said, his hands on his grimy hips. "You banning me from the kitchen now?"

"I did not see you," Dubric muttered. Inek the herb-monger was stocky and muscular, built more like a blacksmith than a merchant, with dark hair thinning over a blemished pate and an unwashed odor lingering around him. Someone had cut off one nostril and part of his ear, likely in a tavern brawl. Dubric often struggled to avoid looking at the greenish bubble where the left half of Inek's nose used to be, and he often failed.

They stared at each other. "You are not banned from the kitchen," Dubric said from between clenched teeth, trying desperately not to stare at the bubble of snot expanding and contracting with each breath. "I hear you have been doing honest business these past few moons."

"You don't give me a chance to do honest business!" Several members of the kitchen staff turned to look, but Inek did not seem to notice, or care. "You've forced me to cut my prices so much it's barely worth the walk."

"Then stop coming," Dubric muttered as he flicked a slice of carrot off his jerkin.

Inek shook his greasy head. "If you think you can push me around, you're sadly mistaken."

"If you think you can cheat and poison my people, you will feel my whip again." Dubric took a deep breath, stared at the wretch for a moment, and said, "Did you want something?"

Inek grinned, the bubble on his nose expanding in his glee. "Actually, I did. I wanted to see what you looked like when someone pushed *you* around. How do you like the boot being on the other foot?"

Dubric's eyes narrowed. "No one is pushing me around."

Inek laughed again. "You sure? I'd heard you've had three dead girls 'round here."

"Do you know something about that?"

Inek shook his head. "You think I'm stupid enough to get within sight of you if I knew anything? You even thought I had something to do with it you'd kill me and ask my corpse questions. I'm no fool. All I know is what I've heard. Past two nights a girl's died." He looked Dubric in the eye and nodded. "Yup. You're scared. 'Bout damned time. How do you like it?"

"Get out," Dubric snapped.

Inek shrugged and walked away, his rolling, wide-armed gait throwing the smooth workflow of the kitchen off kilter. Dubric watched him go, then cast aside his soup along with his warm loaf of bread onto a nearby table. Suddenly, he was not hungry.

* * *

"Excuse me, Miss Nella?" a man's voice said from behind her.

She turned, startled, and a pile of towels fell to the floor at her feet. She saw only the herald, and he looked every bit as surprised as she felt.

"You have my sincerest apologies, Miss Nella," the herald said as he knelt to help her. "I didn't mean to scare you."

She smiled and blushed, shrugging as she knelt beside him. "That's all right, Mister Beckwith. We're all a little jumpy these days." She and her three friends had spent the last half bell restocking the east-wing storage closets with freshly laundered linens while Plien and Stef, who were in trouble, had to change the sheets and bath linens by themselves. Restocking was a brainless job and her mind had been wandering to when she would get to see Risley again.

The white feather in Beckwith's green herald's cap bounced as he handed her the towels. "My wife is a wreck. She's lost two scullery maids, you know. At least the children aren't here to see this madness."

Nella tried not to look at the ridiculous feather. While she spent an afternoon peeling turnips a phase or so ago for a hard-earned half crown, Pitta had mentioned their children were going north to visit their grandmother. Since that afternoon, Nella had completed five tasks for the Beckwiths; work and money she was glad to have. "Hopefully Dubric will catch the killer soon," she said as she stood again and turned to put the towels away. She flashed a reassuring smile at Mirri, who had backed against the next closet to watch the conversation, and turned back to the herald.

He rooted through the various pockets of his ruffled tunic while the feather in his cap jiggled. "I don't mean to be a bother, Miss Nella, truly I do not, but Pitta wanted me to ask if you could take a look at this. Now if I could only find the wretched thing."

Nella covered her mouth with her hand so she wouldn't laugh; she found feathers utterly hysterical. In Pyrinn only jesters wore the silly things, and in Faldorrah none but the herald wore them. Thank the Goddess he only had the one. Full, frothy, white, and prone to bouncing. She struggled with the giggles every time she saw it. His foppish, ruffled attire didn't help, either. Ker came to stand beside Mirri and she gave Beckwith a wan smile.

Beckwith didn't seem to notice the mirth bubbling in Nella's eyes. He emptied several pockets of rumpled bits of paper, a stub of green wax, various personal trinkets, and writing tools before producing a folded bit of lace. "There we go. Silly me, I spilled jam on this last evening and Pitta is about to have my hide. Her grandmother made it, you see, and I've gone and ruined it all." He looked at her and blushed as he handed her the lace. "Can you perchance get the stain out?"

She took it from his hand and unfolded it. A tatted doily made of fine cream-colored thread, it was about a length across and felt soft and sleek in her hands. A wide purple stain splotched near one side. She turned the doily over and squinted at the threads. "Do you know what it's made of? Surely not wool."

He shrugged and the feather bounced. "Spun cotton,

I think. It may be silk, but I doubt it. Pitta's family certainly never . . ." He shrugged again and started putting things back in his pockets.

Since arriving in Faldorrah, she'd cleaned several fine cotton items. "If it's cotton, I can get it out."

Relief shined on his meek face. "Do you know when or how much?" He smiled hopefully.

She looked at the doily again before returning her attention to the herald. "How does late tomorrow sound?"

All the breath left him in a rush as he stood. "Tomorrow sounds perfectly wonderful. Thank you."

"You're welcome. Probably cost about two scepters."

Absentmindedly tapping and checking his pockets, he said, "If I get it before supper tomorrow, I'll gladly pay five times that."

She laughed and shook her head. "Two scepters. That's all."

He smiled. "Two scepters it is."

She nodded, accepting the deal. "A bargain well struck. I'll have it to you before supper tomorrow."

"Thank you, Miss Nella," he said, then bowed to her friends, gracing both of them with a smile. Bidding the three "Good day," he turned to go, the feather bouncing with every step.

As Nella folded the doily and slipped it into her pocket, Dari walked by.

"You're hopeless," Dari said, shaking her head. "Have you no greed?"

Nella grinned. "None."

"You should have taken the full crown."

Nella laughed. "For ten or twelve minutes of scrubbing and rinsing with a quarter pence of soda? It's not worth a full crown."

Dari gestured to the ceiling before pulling another stack of towels from the laundry cart. "It was worth it to him. You shoulda let him pay it."

"Nella," Mirri said softly from the other cabinet, "I know you wanna pay back Lord Risley and all, but do you really need to meet with . . . well . . . *men*? I mean, with all that's going on, perhaps it would be better for us all if . . ."

Dari rolled her eyes. "You have got to be kidding me! How can she make any money if she doesn't talk to people?"

Mirri blushed and lowered her head. "I don't mean I don't want her to make money, it's just that anyone could be the killer."

"No," Dari said, balancing the towels on her hip. "It's not anyone. It's one particular son-of-a-whore. And I for one am not gonna jump at shadows because one guy has it in for us."

"But it could be anybody," Mirri said, tears welling in her eyes. "Even Mister Beckwith."

Ker coughed a short laugh, covering her mouth with her fingers.

"It's not anybody," Dari's free hand flicked the thought away. "It's surely some unmarried guy. A loner. Someone nasty."

Ker nodded. "Mister Beckwith's nice. Real nice."

"Yeah, he's nice, but how can we be sure about anyone?" Mirri asked. "Maybe Stef's right. Maybe it's Dubric. He's not married, like you said."

Nella finished with her towels and turned to the other girls. "It's not Dubric," she said as she closed the closet door, "and it's not Risley. We can trust both of them."

"I know you like Lord Risley and all, Nella," Mirri said, "but you can't be sure."

"Yes, I can," she said, smiling. "We traveled together, alone, for five days. If he was a killer he had plenty of time, and plenty of opportunity, to kill me. He was nothing but nice to me, and he saved my life. I know in my heart it's not him." She shrugged. "Beyond that, I can't say. It could be almost anyone else, but Dari's right, too. We can't be afraid of everyone. We have to keep our wits about us and stick together. Besides, he's only killing at night. It's still daytime." She smiled at Mirri and reached for a pile of linens in the next laundry cart.

Mirri and Dari looked at each other, and all the girls resumed their duties.

* * *

Lars hurried down the main stairs with a fresh bag of tea from Dubric's suite tucked under his arm. Dubric had already drank all that the office storage room contained. Goddess forbid the old castellan manage an afternoon without his tea.

Lars had just reached the second floor when a single threatening phrase caught his attention.

"What's the matter, Beckwith? You get a stain on your hankie and forget your manners?"

His errand forgotten, Lars stopped in mid-step and turned to see Risley leaning against the wall, smoking, beside the entrance to The Bitches.

The herald winced and peeked back toward the ladies' hall, smoothing his flouncy tunic with shaking hands. "There is no crime in hiring a maid to clean."

"I saw you look at her." Risley nodded once, slowly, and took another drag on his pipe before reaching over to close the door.

"That, too, milord, is no crime," Beckwith said, backing away.

Risley puffed smoke from his mouth and the cloud encircled Beckwith's head. "Stay away from her. I'm warning you."

Beckwith paled. "But I have to retrieve the doily tomorrow. I promised—"

Risley leaned close to poke Beckwith with the pipe and Lars had to strain to hear. "You've made the wrong promises."

"Please, milord," Beckwith said, cowering away. "There's nothing to be jealous about. You're getting upset over nothing."

Risley's face reddened. "Nella is not nothing."

"Stop it!" Lars scrambled up the stairs, but Risley pushed Beckwith against the wall.

"Stay away from my Nella." Risley grabbed Beckwith by the arm and shoved him aside. "I'm only going to warn you this one time before I lose my patience."

"Risley," Lars hollered as he ran to them. "Let him go."

One more shove, then Risley backed away. "So help me, I'll pluck your eyes from your fool head if you look at her like that again."

Beckwith gasped for air, fanning his face as he struggled to breathe. "Did you see, Master Hargrove? He assaulted me. I must lodge an official complaint."

Sweat beaded on Risley's brow and he tried to brush Lars aside. "I saw how you ogled her. Lecherous shit. Complain all you want. I ought to have you gelded."

Beckwith shook his head. "I did no such thing. You're wrong."

Lars skidded backward, struggling to keep Risley from reaching Beckwith. "Stop it, both of you."

"I saw what I saw. She's not some trollop, so keep your eyes to yourself, you hear?"

Beckwith cowered and hurried away, tripping as he glanced over his shoulder.

"Will you look at him?" Risley said, pointing toward the herald. "The bastard looks at Nella like she's a piece of meat, then acts like it's my fault he's a condescending puke."

Lars let Risley go. "What about your temper? And look at you. You're red in the face, sweating. What's wrong with you?"

Risley stopped glaring at Beckwith's retreating back and stared at Lars, his mouth dropping open. "I . . . I don't know." He wiped at his brow and looked at the dampness on his hand as if he'd never seen it before. "I am sweating, aren't I?"

He seemed to sag as he bent to pick up the pipe and Lars noticed a tremor in his hand. "I saw how he looked at her, and something snapped, I guess." He stood straight again and glanced at Lars, rubbing his forehead with his free hand. "Goddess, my head hurts."

"Go on and see physician Rolle. He'll have something for your headache. I'd better get back to work."

"Yeah. Thanks, Lars."

Risley gave Lars one last confused glance, then he walked down the hall, muttering.

Lars took a moment to note the incident in his notebook before hurrying on with Dubric's tea.

* * *

Throughout the castle, speculation ran wild as afternoon gave way to evening. Panic and fear led to anger. Fistfights broke out over meaningless disagreements. The herald and the head accountant came to blows over a message. Marital spats flared in public hallways. Girls of the staff clustered in nervous groups and few strayed from their friends. Flighty and afraid, many deemed every man in the castle a potential killer. Dubric received so many reports of suspicious men that afternoon that he dedicated ten pages to check the details and question all accused. He wondered how he would keep up with the flood of testimonies.

None of the men seemed guilty in any way, but Dubric added each name to a dedicated page in his book. He posted pages as sentries, assigned squires to guard the main entrances, and archers to patrol dark halls. He insisted the entire staff be re-assigned so no woman had to work alone. He did all he could to ensure their safety, but as he sat down to his late supper with Dien, Lars, and Otlee in the great hall, he wished with all his heart he could do more.

* * *

After dinner, Dubric sent Lars to catch a couple of bells of sleep and walked with Dien to his rooms.

"How many men do you trust right now?" Dubric asked as they meandered down a quiet stretch of hallway. A pair of privy maids ran past, their hands locked together and their eyes wide and watchful.

"Besides us? Not a single frigging one," Dien said.

Dubric agreed. "How many can you trust by tomorrow? And which ones would they be?"

Dien stopped and shook his head as if he had heard wrong. "Sir?"

"The army is wintering with their families until the equinox. If I send a page to fetch them in the dead of winter with a killer on the loose, the castle nobility will have me gutted. We have exactly six archers and three squires, including you, to use as guards. I cannot cover all the doors with nine men, and we have sent two of those to the village. The castle nobles are useless, foppish fools, and we have had dead girls two nights in a row. Even if the murders have stopped, which I doubt, we are going to need some help."

Dien grumbled and scratched his bristly chin, glancing at the herald who hurried by with a message in hand. "I see your point, sir, but any man we choose could be our killer. Any of the squires or archers could be our killer, too."

At this point, that worry did not matter to Dubric. Trustworthy men mattered. "Who would be your top three choices?"

Dien thought for a moment, then said, "Olibe Meiks, Bacstair Arc, and Flavin Hlink."

A gardener, a baker, and the stable master. All big men, and all calm and dependable. Only Flavin did not have a family. "Good choices, all three. One with me, one with you, one with Lars tonight. If we have no murders, then it could be one of the three and our presence may have stopped them. All three will go to gaol until we sort it out. If another girl dies and the three have been with us constantly, we can be certain that we have three trustworthy sets of eyes."

Dien reached for his notebook. "Want me to tell them?"

"No, that is my responsibility. You take Olibe tonight. I will tell him to meet you in the great hall. Lars can meet Flavin at the stable."

Dien smiled. "Bacstair'll talk your ear off."

"I am hoping he will keep me awake." Dubric smiled at Dien, then hurried to inform his new helpers.

* * *

Nella looked at the few worshipers and shook her head as she knelt in the temple. This evening's service seemed small; only twenty-two souls knelt before the altar instead of the usual thirty to forty. Most were families and married couples from the village. As far as she could tell, she was the only woman alone, and the only servant. *Folks must be afraid,* she thought as she lowered her head, closed her eyes, and breathed slowly through her mouth, calming herself. For the first time since she'd arrived in Faldorrah, she wished the commoners worshiped first instead of after the nobles. It was late and the sermon was almost over, but she was in no hurry to return to the servants' wing by herself. Walking back had never bothered her before, but it was past sundown, the halls were long and dark, and lone girls died.

Friar Bonne lifted the candle, offering its heat, its brightness, to the gods. The flickering candlelight glowed on his face as if he commanded enough power to change the course of time. He recited his often heard plea for piety, for purity in the pursuit of Holy Perfection, imploring his worshipers to do their best and then do more, all in the service of Malanna.

Nella felt the beat of her heart with each word he spoke. For as far back as memory could take her, she had tried to be good, to always do the right thing, and to work. Even after Camm had been taken, during those dark days when her father and mother both hovered close to death, Nella had worked to keep her family alive. At fourteen summers of age, she had supported her parents, kept them fed, and never used a single penny for herself. Since she had learned how to walk, she had worked every day of her life, toiled until she was too tired to stand, and then continued to work anyway. She knew serving Malanna was like that kind of work, though it was work of your heart, not of your back, and sometimes that work came harder. But the

Word of Malanna said perfection was to be rewarded, and it always gave Nella hope. Still, all hope aside, she had a dark walk ahead of her, and she whispered her own pleading prayer.

Friar Bonne's round body glided down the altar steps as he spoke the final prayers for his flock. He lowered the candle and placed it on the silver stand before the altar. "Praise the Goddess!" he said, his voice rumbling and soothing to Nella's ears as she finished her little prayer.

"Gracious Malanna, Bringer of Life!" Nella and the others answered. Far behind her, the door to the castle creaked open, then closed.

"Watch over my flock, I beg of thee," Friar Bonne said as he walked among them. "Keep them from harm. Give them strength for the work awaiting them on the morrow, and the wisdom and patience to see them through the day." Nella felt his gentle hand on the back of her head and he said, "And please, Goddess, see them safely home."

She raised her eyes from the floor and he smiled at her. Malanna's fire still flickered in his eyes and he nodded to her as if he knew a secret. A breath later, he turned from Nella and bade everyone to rise.

The comforting essence of cheese and wine hung around him and she smiled. It was a nice smell, of safety, happiness, and peace; simple things unheard of in Pyrinn. She breathed in the idea and held it close within her heart. *Oh, Goddess,* she whispered to herself, *if you can, let me know safety and happiness. And, please, I beg of you, do not let me die in the dark.* Nella closed her eyes and stood. Her heart felt free and light, better than it had for a long time, and, for some reason she could not fathom, she no longer felt afraid.

The families, the married couples, all but Nella,

found their wrappers, cloaks, and coats and hurried into the night with barely a thank you for the service. As had become her usual habit, Nella helped Friar Bonne blow out candles and clean up what little clutter the worshipers had left behind.

A pew creaked near the castle door, and Nella glanced back to it but saw no more than shadows. She continued to extinguish and gather candles, glancing from time to time into the darkness by the door. The pew remained silent while she finished her simple labor and carried the candles to Friar Bonne.

He took the candles from her and began sorting them into a box. "Such a small cluster tonight. People should come to the temple when they are afraid, not stray further from it."

"Yes, Friar," she whispered as she folded a shimmering piece of white velvet over silver candlesticks. Once wrapped, she lay them in a box and handed it to Friar Bonne.

He paused and looked at her, his wide face concerned. "Will someone come to escort you? I can walk with you, if you—"

"That's all right, Friar," a voice said from the dark pews. "I came to take her home."

Nella turned, her heart thudding. *"Risley?"*

Friar Bonne beamed. "Lord Risley! I thought it was you."

Risley stood, rising from the shadows. He slipped between the pews and walked up the aisle to them. Like Friar Bonne's prayers, she felt him as if he were a source of heat and light. "May I escort you safely home?" he asked, bowing before her.

She wanted to say "yes"—*oh, yes!*—but the debt chewed at her mind, as did the trouble she would face if anyone saw them. Instead of answering, she could only stammer. Helgith would have her hide for being seen with him two nights in a row, and the girls, especially the privy maids, would be even more horrid.

He smiled and held his hand out for her. "It's all right, Nella," he said. "I won't buy a thing. I promise. Not even a pie. I want to be sure you're safe."

"People will talk. And I've caused you enough trouble."

He stepped closer, close enough for her to breathe in the essence of him, close enough for him to pull her into his arms, and still he held his hand out for her. "They're only words, nothing more. And you've never caused me a bit of trouble. I promise."

She didn't know what to say, what to do. She was torn between her yearning for him and the crushing understanding of her position in life, even though he had tried to convince her that her status didn't matter. She was no one, he was everything, but he stood before her with his hand extended and his face glimmering in the candlelight. "Risley," she whispered, afraid to say more. She wanted to fall into his arms, wanted to run away in shame, but more than anything else she wanted to look into his eyes.

He smiled and took her hand, raising her fingertips to his lips before placing them on his arm. "Let's get you home."

She nodded, her eyes locked on his, and somehow her feet stayed beneath her. They had taken only a few steps when she glanced back to the candle cabinet. "Thank you for the wonderful service, Friar—"

The candle cabinet stood open, half of the candles put away, but Friar Bonne was nowhere to be seen. Far to her right she heard the rectory door close.

"Why would he leave?" she asked.

Risley chuckled beside her and his fingers stroked her hand on his arm. "I think he wanted to give us some privacy."

She blushed and shook her head. "I . . . I'm not sure privacy would be a good idea."

He stopped and turned to look at her. They stood in murky darkness near the middle of the temple, far beyond the light of the single lamp illuminating the altar. He lifted her hand, taking it within his own. "Why? Are you still afraid of me?" he asked, his voice soft and worried. "Because I'm a noble?"

She had been terrified of all nobles when she had met Risley. She had feared and hated him and the life he had been born into. But, Goddess, that seemed a lifetime ago. Her life in Pyrinn was like a memory of a bad dream. "No, of course not," she said, her eyes rising to search his in the dim light. She squeezed the warm strength of his hand. "I'm not good enough for you, is all."

He smiled then and leaned close, their foreheads touching. "You let me worry about that. All right?" His eyes looked deep into hers and his hand returned to her face; his fingers felt warm against the line of her jaw. "None of that matters to me. It never has."

She nodded, reluctant to pull her eyes away.

He watched her for a moment more and brought her hand to his lips again. "I can't stop thinking about you. I pray each day to get a glimpse of you, to hear your laughter in the crowd, to be brave enough to touch your cheek."

His fingers glided along the fragile bones of her face and she sighed, closing her eyes at the flickers of delight his touch gave her. She whispered his name and turned her face toward his palm, into the delicious scent of his skin.

"Can you forget the debt, Nella? Please?" His voice cracked and she opened her eyes. "I gave my word to you, to my Grandda, that I would wait."

"Until the debt was done, until I was free," she whispered.

His voice grew trembling and urgent. "Yes, but I don't know if I can. I can't get you out of my mind. I need to hold you, touch you, *kiss* you. Please, it's only money. It means nothing to me, but you mean everything. Please."

"I can't. I *have* to pay. Your grandfather ordered me to. If you won't take money, that only leaves flesh or death."

He shook his head and pulled away from her. "No. I won't. Not those. Not *either* of those."

"I'm not afraid. You wouldn't have to rape me."

He shook his head and his hands flashed out, away from him, as if cutting the idea in half. He paced along the aisle. "No, Nella. It's wrong."

"Where I come from it's the law, wrong or not," she said, her voice small in the dark. "We could finish the debt, tonight, and it would be gone. And tomorrow I'd be free. *We'd* be free."

He stopped and looked at her, his face full of burden, worry, and helpless shining need. "Do you have any idea how wonderful that sounds? To take you to my suite and make love with you again and again? To feel your skin against mine? To sleep curled beside you?" He raked his hands through his hair and shook his head. "Dammit, Nella, do you have any idea?"

She nodded, her hands clasped before her and her heart beating so loud she could hear it. "Yes."

He stepped toward her. "Cancel the debt."

"I can't. If I cancel it, if I lay with you without calling the debt, I have to *die*." She bit her lip and watched him, her hands shaking. "Please, I'll do whatever you say, but I don't want to die. I'm so close. Please. Just a little longer."

He shook his head and stared at the floor, his hands clenching into fists. "So help me, next time I see Lord Egeslic at Council I'm going to beat the life out of him," he snarled.

He sounded so serious, so angry, but she found the idea of Risley pummeling Lord Egeslic hysterical. A laugh broke free, then another, and she stumbled to a pew as she tried to control the giggles.

He gasped and started laughing, reaching for her before she could sit. He found her hand and pulled her close, into his arms, and held her while their half-crazed laughter bubbled free.

"I would, you know," he said, his voice soft as he struggled to control it. "I'd beat the bastard to a pulp for what he did to your family, for what he's still doing to you."

"I know you would," she replied, her giggles subsiding. Her hair hung to her waist, and his fingers gliding through it felt like heaven. She snuggled against his chest, breathed him in, and smiled. She always felt safe with Risley, safer than she could ever remember.

He held her close for a time, his hands on her back, his lips brushing against her brow, and she leaned in his arms to look at him, into his eyes.

His hands slid from her back, up her arms, his touch gentle and warm, and he looked deep into her as if searching for an answer to a question he was afraid to ask. She moistened her lips, holding his eyes with her own.

"I'd better get you home," he said. He kissed her fingers and led her from the temple.

* * *

Dubric decided to patrol the grounds and the castle from midnight until dawn. Every time they passed someone, Bacstair fumbled awkwardly for the sword at his hip, staring as if he expected to see a knife at any moment. Although Bacstair's mild paranoia did not bother him, Dubric was astounded to see so many people, a score or more, wandering the courtyard. Folks went to the privies or the well, sat on the steps and smoked, or even wandered aimlessly. He wondered if they were trying to help catch the killer, cause trouble, or if they suffered from an odd combination of insanity and stupidity. A killer stalked the courtyard. Surely everyone realized that?

He noted the name of every person he met, man or woman, and worried he would waste the next day questioning a pile of fools. After four bell, while he and Bacstair searched the row of servant privies on the north side of the castle, the ghost of a blonde girl in a laundry uniform flickered before his eyes. She fell forward and howled a silent wail, slipping out of the dark from beside Bacstair. Her eyes bulged with horror and she seemed to stumble. Helpless, he watched her throat slash open in a rush of blood, drenching her as if she had bathed in it, and spattering his cloak and trousers. The other ghosts moved aside to make room.

Dubric continued his search, trying to ignore the added responsibility tugging at him. Less than half a bell later, Flavin the stable master hollered for him. Bacstair jumped.

Flavin galumphed through the mud with far less grace than any of his horses. "We found one, sir! By the wall."

"By the Goddess!" Bacstair gasped, his face pale in the lantern light as a privy door slammed on his fingers. He snatched the fingers back, popped them into his mouth, and mumbled around them, "Are you sure?"

"Where is she?" Dubric refused to look at Bacstair for fear he would either laugh or curse.

Flavin's arms flailed as he gestured toward the vast area behind him. "Southeast corner, sir. Near the wells."

They ran to the southeast corner of the courtyard and Dubric saw Lars kneeling beside the body with his sword in hand. There had been no snow that night. A fingernail moon peeked from behind clouds and the courtyard was dense with dark shadows. The stink of damp mud and blood floated unmistakably on the cold air.

"He almost decapitated her, sir," Lars said as he stood. Behind him, a wide, black splatter stained the stone wall.

Dubric and the others slid to a halt in the muck. The girl lay faceup, her head at an impossible angle, and her dead eyes reflecting the moonlight. A stub of a blonde braid sprouted beside one ear and her intestines slumped beside her, oozing and dark, like snakes trying to crawl into the mud. She wore bleach-speckled shoes but no other clothes, only a shroud of blood covering her from her throat to her knees.

"Who is she?" Dubric asked as he knelt beside her. Flavin and Bacstair kept a wide-eyed distance, both drawing the mark of the Goddess on their chests, a circle within a circle. Dubric turned his head away. He hated Malanna's symbol almost as much as he hated the ghosts. *Damn wife-killing whore Goddess!* He closed his eyes and willed the anger away. Lack of sleep made him prone to resentful musings and he had no time for such indulgences.

"Not sure," Lars said, "but did you notice her shoes?"

Dubric nodded, even though the uniform her ghost wore proclaimed her job as brightly as the bleach stains. "Laundry worker?"

"That was my guess," Lars said. He stretched and looked at the courtyard. No one else was near, but folks were coming. "You two stay together the whole time?"

Bacstair nodded and Dubric asked Flavin, "How about the two of you?"

"Yessir," Flavin said. "We never left each other's sight, not till we found her." Lars nodded his confirmation.

Dubric glanced up from her body and looked around the courtyard; he heard people yelling as they ran toward him. *It is the middle of the night, for King's sake! Why are folks up and about at this hour?*

"Why don't you do your damned job and catch the bastard?" a harpy screeched as if from the depths of the seven hells. Twinges danced down Dubric's spine at the voice. The three men and the page turned to look.

A pair of floor maids ran through the dark, with broken mop handles clutched in their hands and the sharp, snapped ends pointed at Dubric. With curly red hair that seemed black in the moonlight, they were the same height, similar-featured, and both were furious. He had never seen Allin and Gaelin Mugain angry before—he had always regarded the sisters as nice, pleasant girls—and he fumbled for a moment.

Then he stood, his knees creaking. "We are doing all we—"

"Bull piss," Allin, the shy one, said. "You're doing nothing!"

The small crowd assembling behind them growled their agreement.

Dubric held his hands before him, hoping to calm their anger. "I suggest you all go back inside. It is dangerous to be—"

"It wouldn't be dangerous if you did your damned job!" a man's voice hollered from somewhere in the mob.

"Have you people lost all sense?" Bacstair said. "You could get killed out here!"

"Shut your yap," Allin said. "Dubric needs to pull his head outta his ass before we—"

Dubric didn't hear the rest of her rant, losing it to the icy weight in his head. The ghost of an egg maid appeared before him, with blood streaming from her belly and throat. Beside him, Flavin mumbled a retort, and he did not hear that, either. King be damned, he hated ghosts, and the wretched things just kept coming! Every girl thus far had been found where she worked, in one way or another, long after the killer had gone. But if he hurried, for King's sake, if he *hurried*, got to the coops in time . . .

He looked at Lars. Young, fast, smart, eager Lars. He could look, he could listen. Find out who the bastard was, for King's sake. "Son-of-a-whore," he snarled and grabbed Lars's arm, leaving Flavin and Bacstair to deal with the unruly mob.

"Sir?" Lars looked at Dubric in surprise, as Dubric yanked him away from the crowd.

Despite his heartbeat slamming in his ears, and the doubt surging through him, he leaned in close and whispered in Lars's ear. "Listen to me, and do not ask any questions, all right?"

Lars nodded.

"I am going to tell you to go to the castle and get Dien, but instead I want you to go to the coops."

Lars's eyes narrowed, confusion still written on his face.

"When you get there, I want you to look for 'ghost stuff.' Understand?"

"Yes, sir."

"And if you find *anything,* hide and stay put until I find you. No matter what, stay safe. If you do not find anything, come back. Either way, pull your sword before you get there. For King's sake, *listen,* and use your ears not your eyes. And do not, under any circumstances, do anything stupid."

Lars nodded one last time and they turned toward the loud group of eight angry citizens. Gaelin screeched an obscenity at Flavin, who seemed unable to comprehend the insult. Bacstair screamed at a short, half-drunk man while the rest of the mob encouraged a fight. Tempers had flared, and everyone had forgotten the dead girl. *What in the King's name was going on?*

Dubric shook his head and barked, "Lars, get to the castle, and find Dien." Lars ran toward the castle, but the mob barely noticed. If he had told Lars to stand on his head and moo, no one would have cared. He muttered to himself as he jotted a list of names in his book.

As soon as Lars disappeared into the darkness, Dubric stomped toward the mob. He had reached his limit of tolerance for insanity. "Enough is enough! You are all interfering in an official investigation. Get back inside or I am throwing the lot of you in the gaol!"

"Ha," the drunk said as he shoved Bacstair. "Eight of us, three of you."

"Yeah! Go ahead and try," Allin screeched, her voice cracking in rage.

Dubric pulled his sword. "Flavin, you stay here and guard the body. Anyone tries to touch her before I get back, you have my permission to make them wish they had not."

Flavin stepped over her with one foot on each side of her head, then pulled a borrowed sword from the sheath at his hip.

The mob's eyes grew wide and a few stumbled backward. Dubric stepped closer. "Bacstair, think of that sword as a heavy dough knife. All right?"

"Yes, sir." Bacstair pulled his sword, as well, and it trembled for a moment before it settled steady in his hands.

The drunk babbled and almost fell in his hurry to get away from the long blade.

Dubric drew a calming breath and let it out. "I am only going to say this once. March directly to the east-tower door. We are going to the gaol. Anyone who runs off, I will find you and drag you there later this morning. Trust me, you will wish you had walked there on your own. Now move!"

Allin screamed and lunged at him, broken mop handle in her hands. He flexed—he might be old, but he was still strong—and his elbow slammed hard into her nose. A loud snap cracked through the air and blood shot down the front of her coat. She fell like a sack of manure into the mud and screamed. The fight went out of the mob just as fast.

"Get back on your feet," he snarled as he grabbed her by the hair and dragged her upright. "I said march and I mean march!" He shoved her toward the humbled mob.

Gaelin screeched and turned toward him, her hands curling into fists as she dropped her mop handle. "You—"

His sword flashed up and he whispered, "Do not tempt me. One more body will not make a bit of difference."

That stopped her. She glared at him and turned back to the mob with a toss of her head before helping her sister to her feet.

* * *

Lars hurried toward the main castle doors, but passed them and kept on running, his feet almost silent in the mud. Dubric knew something, but what? Was this "ghost stuff" more than just the imaginings of a scared boy?

In his heart he knew the lackey had spoken the truth. He'd seen it in the boy's eyes. And Dubric believed him.

He slid to a stop at the southwest corner of the castle and took a moment to catch his breath. The stable loomed ahead and to his left; the dairy barns were to the right but still hidden behind the castle. Past the barns, near the northwest corner of the castle, were the coops. He glanced at the slim line of crescent moon shining near the constellation of the Great Ship plowing through waves of clouds—Malanna's light guiding the way in troubled seas. He said a quick prayer as he pulled his sword.

"Guide my hand, O Gracious One, and allow me to harm no innocents. But if I find that damned ghost, let me send him to the seven hells." Lars drew the mark on his chest, a circle within a circle, the four blessed phases of the moon—Dubric wasn't here to see and roll his eyes—and he took one breath and stepped around the corner.

Dark buildings, mud, and everything looking dim and hazy in the thin moonlight. Nothing more. Smelled like manure.

He cursed, remembering he was supposed to *listen*, not look, and ran across to the stable, hugging the deep shadows.

Through the dark, quiet and sleek, he moved north along the west side of the stable, then the barn, the side away from the castle, listening, always listening with his heart as well as his ears. The horses sounded nervous and restless in their stalls, as did the cows in their pens, and he felt nervous, too, long before he got within sight of the coops. At the far corner of the last barn, where the smell of chicken dung and cow manure blended into one nasty stench, he took a breath and listened. After a moment, he heard something, a faint sound, crisp and metallic in the air. His breath fell shallow and silent and his eyes closed halfway as he listened. *What is it? A cool metallic flick, like a knife dragging on a table?* No, that wasn't quite right, but he'd heard that sound before. Somewhere. He switched his sword to his left hand, wiped his right palm dry on his pants, and returned the sword to his stronger hand. Still listening, he slipped behind the first coop.

Yes, that was better. He heard a grunt, a mumbled curse, and a rustle of cloth. No more cow manure, everything stunk of chicken dung now, but he ignored the stench and listened. Another curse, muttered, low, hard to hear. He slipped to the next coop, closer, closer, and there was that metallic sound again, somewhere between this coop and the next. The slick metallic sound, then a soft, fleshy one, and his belly clenched. Had the killer found another? Was he cutting her? He closed his eyes, took a breath, and opened them again. *Quit being a runny-nosed kid. Be a man. Take one look. That's all. Just one. See the damned ghost.*

Moonlight flickered in the space between the two

coops, leaving long shadows and crevasses of dark within the edges of dim illumination, but he saw nothing. No one was there. No body. No killer. Nothing but the dark.

Relieved, Lars let his breath out in a rush and he heard a rustle and a curse as something in the dark moved, as if whatever waited between the coops turned to look right at him.

Lars froze. Dubric had warned him not to be stupid, not to take chances, just to listen and wait and hide.

There was nothing there but shadows and darkness, but, oh Goddess, it was moving this way!

The moonlit shape of a body appeared on the ground as if by magic. There was only mud, then—blink!—a girl lay between the coops, on her belly, her back opened like a book, and her arms splayed wide and dimly blue in the moonlight. The ghost moved, ever closer, one with the darkness, its shape flowing and becoming part of the night. The glimmer of moon slipped behind a cloud as if it, too, were afraid, the Great Ship became lost in the obscuring waves, and the dark became endless and overwhelming.

Lars held his sword in shaking hands, and his feet had taken root in the mud. His eyes searched the dark for movement, but *everything* was black and his mind refused to accept the impossibility of what his eyes were not seeing. He heard nothing but the beat of his heart in his ears, the terrified *whoosh* of his breath, and the heavy footfalls of death advancing toward him. He was stupid; he had disobeyed, and this time the price due for his inadequacy was far higher than banishment. Soon he'd be dead, like the girls, his kidneys taken for—

He smelled blood, smelled death and guts and rotting evil. Although his eyes searched the dark, he saw nothing but the endless blackness of the night, tainted with the stench of death.

The breath on his cheek was hot and rancid, and the killer laughed in his ear, even as he turned.

He felt cold metal against his throat and he stumbled, falling backward onto the mud.

CHAPTER
6

✝

Dubric shoved all eight troublemakers into the same dank cell and slammed the door. Olibe Meiks, Bacstair, and Dien stood behind him and the ghosts flickered just beyond his sight. "Meiks, make sure these idiots do not get into mischief. Bacstair, go help Flavin get the body to the physicians'. Dien, you come with me."

The men nodded and Dubric turned, walking between the ghosts with his eyes closed.

They had climbed the east tower, up the stairs to the great hall, and had walked halfway across to the west tower when Dubric heard a woman call, "Lord Byerly! Please wait."

Cursing, Dubric turned. A short, round woman huffed down the main stairs, lifting her frilly nightdress and showing her thick calves and dimpled knees. She was barefoot and her eyes glimmered with tears. "Sir! One of my egg maids is missing!"

"Calm down, Altaira. What happened?"

He strode back to the stairs as Altaira covered her heart with one hand and fanned her face with the other. "It were Rianne, sir! She's gone from her room."

Dubric did not bother to ask any more questions. He ran for the servants' wing, ignoring the pain in his chest and knees.

The main door to the servants' wing stood open and Dubric ran through, Dien beside him. The hall for unmarried men forked to the left, supervisors straight ahead, and unmarried women to the right. The five bell rang from the temple as Dubric hurried down the women's hall. A few faces peeked through the doors and six linen maids cowered against the wall to give him room. Three privy maids took one look at him and dashed away. Other maids scattered. Far ahead, he heard the low rumble of many voices.

The hall turned and he slowed his breakneck pace. Milkmaids and egg maids clustered in the hall and stared at an open door. They parted for him; some seemed angry, most merely frightened.

Dubric looked through the door to see three girls huddled together on one bed. Their faces were blotchy from crying and the pair on the outside comforted the girl in the middle.

"It is all right," he said, approaching them slowly with his hands held before him.

One blew her nose. The middle girl clutched a ragged blanket to her and pulled it over her knees.

"What happened?" he whispered as he knelt before them. All three girls trembled and shook their heads.

"Please. Tell me what happened."

"The slasher got her," someone in the hall said, and Dubric glanced at Dien.

Dien closed the door, blocking out the sight of the crowd, and stood before it with his arms crossed.

"Did someone come in here?" Dubric asked the girls. He tried to keep his voice soft despite the urgency he felt.

The two on the ends shrugged, but the one with the blanket cowered away.

"Did she depart on her own free will?"

Again a pair of shrugs, but the center girl nodded.

He glanced at Dien, then asked the girls, "Do you know where she went?"

Two shook their heads; the one with the blanket stared at her knees.

He looked at her. "Where did she go?"

She shuddered and drew her knees closer.

"Please. I cannot catch him if I do not know why she left. What do you know?"

She shook her head again, glancing at the other two girls before covering her face.

Dubric took a calming breath. "Did either of you hear where she was going or who she intended to see?"

"No," the girl on the left said. "We weren't here."

"Maybe we shoulda been," the girl on the right said, sniffling, "but, see, Clemeth and I, we . . ." She blushed.

"And Mathern, he was getting upset, not seeing me and all," the left girl said. "So we went together to meet our fellas."

"Down at the Dancing Sheep," right added.

Left nodded. "And when we came back first thing this morning, Rianne was gone and Zur was hiding in the corner."

Dubric touched the middle girl's arm. "What happened? Why did Rianne leave you here alone?"

She took a deep breath, clutching the blanket close, and raised her eyes to look at Dubric. They were clear and blue, the color of cornflowers. She swallowed, flinched, and whispered, "She said she was meeting someone."

"Did she say who it was?"

"A man. I told her not to go, that it was dangerous, but she wouldn't listen."

"Was she seeing anyone specific? Did he come get her?"

She shook her head and said, her voice cracking as her hysteria broke, "I begged her not to go. She left me here all alone, in the dark." She took a deep panting breath and her shaking lessened. She took another breath, squeezed the blanket, and seemed to calm herself.

"Is that what scared you? Being alone?"

She nodded. "Rianne didn't care; she just left anyway."

Dubric looked at the three girls. "Did Rianne talk about her suitors? Did she mention any names?"

The girl on the left rolled her eyes. "Ri? Maybe to Zur. She barely talked to us at all. She saw lots of fellas, though. Too many, if you ask me."

"Definitely," Right said. "She sometimes teased us about sticking with one guy, but I *know* Clemeth would never hurt me."

"Neither would Mathern."

Clemeth and Mathern were apprentices of the village miller and were well-regarded young men. They often brought flour to the castle kitchens and Dubric noted their names in his book. "You were with Clemeth and Mathern all night?"

"We *are* betrothed," Left said, raising her chin. "We've stayed at the Dancing Sheep before."

Right nodded. "We're not allowed to bring fellas to our room, even if we're betrothed. They have to wait in the hall."

"Is that where most young women go to meet suitors? The Dancing Sheep?"

Left shrugged. "It depends. Some do, some don't."

"What about Rianne?"

Right clamped her mouth closed, but Left said, "She went there, yeah, but not with a steady. We'd see her there sometimes."

"Did you see here there last night?"

Right blushed and Left stammered before saying, "We weren't exactly in the tavern, milord. She was here when we left and I don't know where she went after that."

Visible from behind her fingers, the middle girl's face had turned a deep vermillion. Dubric looked back at Dien. The ghosts stood all around him; five servant girls drenched in blood. Slashes covered his latest ghost, and each cut oozed splatters onto the floor. Through the ghosts, Dien nodded and reached for the latch, his hand slipping through Fytte's belly. Dubric's stomach lurched.

Before he shuddered, Dubric turned his eyes away and returned his attention to the girls. "I'd like the two of you to wait in the hall," Dubric said.

Left gaped. "But why?"

"What did we do? Why do we have to go to the hall?"

Dubric smiled reassuringly and said, "Please. For a few moments. Mister Saworth will be more than happy to escort you."

They both shook their heads. Dien opened the door and said, "C'mon girls. Let's go."

"But—"

Dien seemed to grow more imposing as he grumbled his uncompromising words. "You weren't here when your friend left and you said you barely talked to her. Your testimony is finished." He pointed to the door. The girls looked at each other, shrugged, and rose to their feet.

Dubric watched the girl with the blanket, feeling the ghosts remain in the room with them as a constant reminder of his duty. As soon as the door closed, he asked his witness, "What is your name?"

"Zurinn, sir."

He scratched a note and looked around the little room. Deep in the bowels of the castle, it was no more than ten lengths on a side, windowless, and cold. Four beds, little better than cots, with frames of ancient iron pipes and strung with oft-patched cloth, were bunked in pairs against the stone walls. The girls stored their belongings in crude wooden boxes on the rough stone floor. The servants' quarters were spartan, crowded, and dreary; this room seemed typical. "Just the four of you?" Dubric asked in an attempt to loosen her tongue.

She shivered beneath her blanket. "Yes, sir."

"Where do you work?"

"With the chickens, sir. We care for them and gather eggs, mostly."

He nodded as if he understood anything at all about chickens. "Do you like your job?"

She shrugged. "It's money."

"How about Rianne? Did she like her job?"

She looked at him for a moment and shrugged. "I don't know. Not really, I guess. Who wants to work around chickens all day?"

He added to his notes. "Did she complain often?"

"No more than anyone else, I suppose."

"What do you think about the other two going to the Dancing Sheep last night?"

She blinked and lifted her head. "It's all right. I told them to go. They've been courting for a long time—Bet and Mathern nearly two summers now. Sometimes I wish I could go, too, maybe listen to a minstrel or have a tonic, but it wouldn't be right."

"Why?"

The girl blushed. "Because Edgew isn't here. I can't go without him."

"Edgew?"

She smiled, her fear forgotten. "He's back home, in Oakfield. He comes up to the castle to see me every moon or so when the weather's decent. We're hoping to get married this autumn, once he's a journeyman."

"Why, child, are you here when he is a half-day's walk away?"

"Money, milord. My father died last spring from consumption and my brother lost his sight from a fever when he was small. My mother takes care of him, but she can't do that and earn a wage. Edgew doesn't make enough yet to feed and shelter everyone, but once he's a journeyman, I can go back home."

Dubric rubbed his eyes. "How old are you?"

"Fifteen summers, milord." She shrugged. "That's what I kept thinking in the dark. I'm too darn young to die and have too much to live for."

"What about Rianne? Did she have a lot to live for?"

She chewed her lip. "I don't know, milord. Not as much as some. More than others, I guess. She was always looking for the easy way, but that doesn't get you anywhere."

"'The easy way'? What does that mean?"

Zurinn sighed. "She was nice enough, truly she was, milord, but sometimes she expected other people, especially men, to do things for her or pay attention to her. She thought she deserved it, and the less she had to do, the better."

"Of these men, was there one she met frequently?"

Zurinn bit her lower lip as she considered his question. "No. I'm sorry, milord, but they were right. She saw lots of fellas and some weren't very nice."

He took a deep breath and watched her cornflower eyes. "Who? Do you have any names at all?"

She frowned, leaning back. "I tried not to know, milord, truly. It wasn't any of my business, but sometimes she'd come back with bruises or her clothes ruined. She'd have some coin or a shiny ribbon in her hair, so that must have made it all right. Twice she went to the village midwife. I went with her the second time, trying to be her friend even though I didn't think it was right, but her screaming . . . It was horrible, milord, hearing the midwife cut the baby from her.

"After that last time, she found a man to help her stop the babies from growing. He's the only one I ever knew of for sure. I guess they made a trade. I don't know his name, but I know she laid with him from time to time, when she couldn't find anyone else. He was nasty, though."

"Who?" Dubric asked, his pencil poised over the page.

She shuddered. "I saw him once when we went to the village to get the packet of poison. Disgusting man, filthy and oozing. Like a warty toad. He kept looking at me and offering me his medicines. Said they'd relax me or make me feel 'like a woman.' Ri laughed and teased me, offering to share him, all three of us together." She shuddered, shaking her head. "I left and never went to the village with her again."

"Who?" Dubric asked again. "Have you any more details?"

"I was only there a few minutes, milord, but I've seen him in the castle now and then, so you might know him. He's about my height, broad and strong-looking, but scarred and dirty. Scabby. He's missing part of his nose and it's—"

Dubric lurched to his feet and laid his finger on his nose. "The nostril is gone? On this side?"

"Yes, with snot dripping out. You know him?"

"I am afraid that I do." Dubric closed his notebook and bowed slightly. "Thank you, miss, for your help."

Grimacing as he reached through Fytte, Dubric opened the door and looked at Dien. "Have you finished? I want to check with the physicians before we ride to the village."

"Of course, sir," Dien said, walking with Dubric down the hall. "Why the village?"

Dubric glanced at Dien. "Inek knew the missing girl. Intimately."

"Why am I not surprised?" Dien muttered a low curse and held the door open for Dubric.

* * *

"Mirri, calm down!" Nella said, stroking the other girl's hair. Her friends had all run back to their room after Dubric flew past, and they were going to be late for work if they didn't hurry. Nella felt time slip by and the instinct to get moving slammed in her veins. Tardiness was unimaginable. In Pyrinn, being noticeably late meant a whipping or a broken arm. She did not want to find out what it meant in Faldorrah. Mirri, however, was too scared to do more than tremble and frantically babble.

Mirri blubbered and tugged at her curly hair, her hands shaking and damp with tears. "But what if . . ."

Nella tried to keep her voice calm and sure. "There's nothing to worry about. Dubric is going to catch him and everything will be fine."

"Goat piss, Nella," Stef muttered. She sat on her bunk beside Ker and frowned. "Dubric isn't doing a thing and you know it as well as I do."

Nella stroked Mirri's hair. "He's doing everything he can."

Stef rolled her eyes. "I still think it's Dubric himself."

Mirri made a small, terrified squeak and her dark eyes flicked to Nella.

"I'm all for staying in here all day." Plien lay on her bunk above Stef and Ker, buffing her fingernails with a scrap of bark.

Stef nodded. Ker shrugged.

"You're willing to lie about every day," Dari said, frowning with disgust. She leaned in the open door and watched the others. "Some of us need to work so we'll get paid."

Nella smiled at Dari. Dari smiled back.

"Just because I'm not supporting a house full of brats back home doesn't mean I don't need money, too," Plien said as she examined her fingertips. "I'd rather be breathing tomorrow than risk my life out there today. Whether it's Dubric or not."

"But what about tomorrow?" Nella asked. "Or the day after? Or next phase or next moon? When will it be safe to work?"

Plien shrugged, buffing out a rough spot and examining her nails again. "Don't know. Don't care. I'm staying right here."

"Do we hafta go? I don't wanna die," Mirri said.

"None of us want to," Nella said, "but if we hide, he wins." She wrapped an arm over Mirri's soft shoulders and said, "I won't let anyone come near you, all right? Dari won't, either."

Stef snickered and kicked Nella's bed. "Look at you! You're barely as tall as my shoulder and skinny as a twig. How are you going to protect yourself, let alone anyone else?"

Nella gave her a warning glare, but before she could respond, Dari snapped, "Oh, shut your yap. You know she escaped Pyrinn. She's much tougher than she looks." Dari motioned toward the hall. "Let's get our butts to work while we still have jobs."

Stef kicked the bed again, shifting it on the floor. "Lord Risley dragged her here to keep her as a pet. She didn't escape."

"Believe whatever you want." Nella stood, ignoring Stef's attempts at goading her into an argument. "You coming, Mirri?"

"We'll make the beds, you can do the towels," Dari offered.

At last Mirri nodded. She took a deep, shaking breath and the three girls left the room. Ker followed them.

Dari closed the door. "All four of us, then?"

Hands locked together, they hurried from the servants' wing.

* * *

After he turned the corner, Dubric blinked at what he saw written in blood on the outer wall of his office. He froze for a moment, his head hammering, until, beside him, Dien slumped against the wall. Dubric read the message again and a cry bubbled and grew from within him, finally breaking free. Screaming, he spun around and ran through the back hall to the west tower, sword clenched in his hands. Noble and commoner alike fled at the sight of him. Dien followed, his sword also drawn. They ran from the office hallway, past the servants' wing, past the northern doors of the great hall, past the workshops, accountants, seamstresses, storage, past even the entrance to the temple wing, the one place in the castle Dubric avoided. Dubric screamed a long mournful wail as if his heart

would burst, and a group of altar boys and nuns froze
where they stood.

Dubric shoved through the horde of astonished altar boys, ignored the startled gasp of the nuns, and the
shocked stare of Friar Bonne. Still screaming, in his
heart, his mind, he ran. He dared not look at his ghosts,
not yet, not ever, not when the message said: *NEVER
send a boy.*

* * *

The first glints of sunrise flickered on the crenella-
tions of the west tower as Lars staggered through the
mud with his bloody hands tied in front of him. His
face and his chest were covered in blood, as if he had
rolled in it, and he repeatedly tried to spit away the foul
taste polluting his blood-smeared mouth.

He was relieved he hadn't puked over whatever putrid thing had been used to gag him. It lay discarded
somewhere beneath the coop, surely a horror that he
did not want to contemplate or see. After facing the
thing in the dark, and finally managing to spit the noxious gag away, he had decided that his life was truly a
miracle, even if it was over.

He fell to his knees beside the body of the egg maid,
and he muttered a curse as his shoulders slumped in
shame. His shortsword had been thrust into the back of
her head and it stood there jauntily, the hilt dripping
with blood. Dubric was going to have his ass, that was
as sure as the coming dawn, and not only because he'd
let himself be seen.

Whoever had killed the egg maid had hacked apart
her body with Lars's sword, shot her with a bolt from
his small crossbow, and stolen his dagger. Lars had ruined the murder scene, ruined it by his presence, and
any clue the killer might have left had been compro-

mised. He was covered in her blood, with the stink of her death, and he was in deep trouble.

"Oh, dammit!" he cried, his face turned to the brightening sky. He prayed for a moment and looked back at the body. At least he was still tied, with a length of intestine that had been knotted and cut. Dubric would know he did not kill her and he would not be found guilty of murder. Stupidity, perhaps, but not murder. He breathed easier and settled his backside into the cold mud to wait for Dubric.

Moments later, a group of milkmaids opened the west tower door and he cursed again. He should have stayed stuffed beneath the coop.

One girl screamed, and all five pairs of eyes lit upon him, each flickering with murderous fire in the dawn. They ran toward him. "You bastard!" one screeched.

They had him outnumbered. "Oh, curse it!" His bound hands fumbled to his thighs as he tried to shove himself to his feet, but his balance was off and they would be upon him before he—

His eyes darted to his sword and he lunged for it, stretched over it. "Forgive me," he whispered as he ripped his hands toward the blade and pulled, slicing through the slimy binds like a hot knife through soft cheese. In a blink he ruined both the scene and his alibi, again, but what choice did he have?

The sections of intestine fell into trampled mud and he pulled his sword and stood, all in one fluid movement. "Back off!" he snarled. "This is an official investigation!"

"You sneaky, lying bastard!" a milkmaid snarled. "You did this! Dubric's horse-raping page!"

The girls surrounded him as he stood over the dismembered torso of the egg maid with his bloody sword in his hands. "Go to work, go back to bed—I don't really give a damn—just get away from here!"

"He's just a boy. We can take him," one milkmaid said, her eyes flickering fire.

"I didn't kill her! Now go away before I drag you all to the gaol." He stumbled over a severed arm but didn't fall.

"Little pissant boy. Think you're a hot bastard now?"

"You like cutting us up?" Two girls slipped behind him while the other three still paced in front.

Oh, Goddess, this was bad. "I didn't cut her up! Now, please, go on before I—"

The girls moved closer and Lars braced himself, his eyes resting on one girl who stayed in front of him. He didn't want to hurt them, but he had no intention of dying, either.

"If we move together, we can take him, sword or not," the one directly in front of him whispered. She stood over a hand and a hunk of meat that might have once been part of a thigh. Her face was hard and deadly. The other girls looked at her and nodded. Lars swallowed and blinked as he tightened the grip on his sword. He'd drop her first.

"Perhaps, but I wouldn't recommend it," a man's voice said to Lars's right, and all the girls turned to look.

Lars watched the girl in front of him. He knew better than to get distracted.

The girls jumped back, startled, murder fading into uncertainty in their eyes. Risley stood beside the next coop with his gloved hand on the hilt of his sword and his cloak fluttering in the chilly morning wind. "You all right, Lars?"

"I'm fine." He glanced at the girls behind him; both had retreated a few steps. He looked back to the girl in front of him. "Just a mess."

Risley nodded. "So I see. You causing all this trouble?"

"No. Not me. I swear." Still watching the lead girl, Lars shook his head and stood his ground.

Risley shifted his hand on his sword and tilted his head toward the castle. "You heard him, ladies. Why don't you return to your duties? I'll hold him here until Dubric arrives."

"He did it," the leader said. "We saw him!"

"That's not for us to determine," Risley said. "You can take it up with Dubric later. Right now, you need to leave. No one else needs to die."

The girls looked at one another, looked at Lars, and looked at Risley. After a few moments they nodded. Grumbling all the while, they stomped through the mud toward the cow barns.

Risley moved toward Lars, his hand remaining on his sword. "Tell me what happened, and it had better be good."

Lars forced his eyes from Risley's hand to his face. Lars had known Risley for his whole life and could not ever remember seeing his eyes so hard before. "Dubric sent me here, to watch and guard, and I was stupid. The killer saw me, dragged me to her." He looked at the girl, at her dismembered body. "He tied me up with her guts, took my weapons, and shoved me under a coop. By the time I crawled out, he'd gone."

The threat in Risley's stance lessened, but most of the hardness remained. "He set you up."

Lars nodded. "Thank the Goddess you came when you did."

"Five to one odds aren't fair," Risley said. Smiling, he approached and moved his hand away from the sword as the hardness faded another notch, closer to the friendliness Lars was used to. "Three of them you could've taken." He picked a chunk of meat out of Lars's hair. "You sure you're all right?"

Lars relaxed and tried to wipe his sword clean on his sleeve. "Yeah, I'll be fine. After a bath and about six phases of sleep."

"You knew Dubric would work you to death. We just never thought . . ." Risley shrugged and looked at the pieces of the egg maid scattered hither and yon between the coops. "Goddess, what a mess. Here, give me that."

Lars was too coated in blood to wipe the sword and he gladly handed over the weapon. "Thanks," he said with a smile, but his expression dried and faded on his face. A thin line of fresh blood was streaked across Risley's cheek, right above his jawline. Lars pulled his eyes away before Risley noticed the stare.

Beside him, Risley wiped the sword clean with a handkerchief and returned it. He looked at the body again, rubbing at his forehead as if he had a headache. "I hope you solve this soon."

"Me, too." Lars stared at the dismembered corpse and wondered what to do.

CHAPTER

7

✝

Bells later, Lars sat in the witness chair. Otlee slouched beside him, pen tapping on a piece of paper void of ink as he read from a tattered book. Dien had gone to the physicians' offices for the day's reports and Lars hoped he'd get back soon. At least Dien didn't look like he was about to explode.

Lars shifted uneasily in his chair as he remembered the morning. Dubric had burst wailing from the tower door moments after Risley arrived. Both Lars and Risley had jumped, and the group of milkmaids had squealed and run for their barn. Dubric's scream had stopped, he had stumbled and commanded Lars to get his ass inside, in the office, right that instant!

No questions of what he'd seen, no questions of what he'd done. Just the command to leave.

He'd left, as commanded. He always did his best to follow orders. Women had screamed at the sight of him, and children had fled as he walked across the castle. He'd wanted to crawl into a hole and die of embarrassment, but he had reached the office hall in one piece. Then he saw the bloody writing, though Otlee and Trumble were busy trying to scrub it off the wall.

From the few details he'd heard, the egg maid, Rianne, had been completely eviscerated as well as dismembered. Dien had found her intestines beneath the coop where the killer had stuffed Lars, as well as smaller organs like her spleen, pancreas, and heart. Lars did not want to know what piece or part had been crammed into his mouth as a gag. Whatever it was, it had tasted horrid. Her liver had been stuck to the wall outside Dubric's office with Lars's missing dagger.

The killer had scrawled a message on that wall, a message Lars didn't want to think about—he had enough bad stuff clattering around in his mind to last him a lifetime—but it kept slamming into his brain anyway.

NEVER send a boy!

It had been written in blood and bile over the length of the wall and the liver stabbed at the end like a misshapen exclamation point.

He had no idea who had first found the message, that had not been mentioned during the meetings, but he feared the reprimand brewing and festering on the other side of Dubric's desk.

So he sat in the witness chair in blood-soaked clothes that had long since dried stiff, the smell of death hanging heavy in the air, and Dubric either stared at him or rubbed his eyes.

The noon bell rang and Otlee looked up from his book. "Sir, perhaps we should—"

"Shut up," Dubric snapped, his attention leaving Lars for the first time in what seemed like forever.

Otlee shrank and put his book away.

Lars hadn't slept much the past few days, but he doubted if Dubric had slept at all. He looked tired. Gray puffiness surrounded his eyes, his normally healthy old-man's skin seemed transparent, and his bald head no longer gleamed. Was Dubric getting sick?

Feeling his age? Something else? None of them had been eating well. Every time he saw meat it smelled like death. But what about Dubric? Something was wrong, something more than the search for a killer. Dubric had seen lots of dead bodies and solved several murders. Why was this different?

Before Lars could contemplate more questions, a quick knock rapped on the door and Dien stepped inside with an unsealed report in his hands.

Dubric looked up. "Well?"

"Same bastard, both times. Same weapon on the laundress, not sure about the egg maid." He glanced at Lars and shrugged. "Kidneys and hair missing on both. The egg maid is also missing about five lengths of small intestine, her stomach, and bladder. Everything else is accounted for. I went over both murder scenes like you said, sir. Piddling step by piddling step. Got a few pebbles, a couple of coppers, broken crow feather . . . Nothing at all interesting except a couple of loose bits of flesh and skin, which I've given to the physicians. There are too many hairs to count, sir, from all sorts of people."

An intensive search would possibly glean a clue, but they had held little hope. "Anything else?"

"Yes. Couple of things. The laundress was Celese Harper, and she works the overnight shift in the laundry. We've also got verification that the egg maid fought back. She has three broken fingernails on her right hand and one drew blood. They think it's the killer's 'cause it had been blocked under her nail by mud."

Dubric's attention returned to Lars. "Dien, you and Otlee go on to lunch. I want to talk to Lars alone."

"Yes, sir," Dien and Otlee said together. Moments

later, Lars was alone with Dubric's anger simmering across the desk.

They stared at each other. Lars wanted to apologize for his stupidity, but he held his tongue and waited.

An eternity later, Dubric took a shaking breath and said, "I should not have sent you."

"I tried to do my job, sir."

Dubric looked at his desk. "You always do a fine job and I forget how young you are."

"Sir?"

Dubric's hands clenched on his desk and they looked old, skeletal. "You could have died, and it would have been my fault."

"Sir, if you will pardon my impertinence, when I accepted this position I understood that—"

"You don't understand a damned thing," Dubric said as he rubbed his eyes.

Lars clenched his fingers over the arms of the witness chair.

Dubric sighed. "Relax. You are not in trouble. I cannot believe I risked you like I did."

Still clenching the chair, Lars took a deep breath and said, "May I ask a question, sir?"

Dubric took a deep breath himself. "All right."

"How did you know, sir? About the killer being near the coops?" Lars leaned forward, the chair creaking. "It's bothered me all morning. Somehow, you knew, but I don't see how."

Dubric sat rigidly straight, his palms on his desk. After a long moment, he said, "This is between us, Lars. You and me. No one else."

"Yes, sir."

"It is complicated, but have you heard how Aswin Romlin can see into people's hearts?"

Lars felt his fingertips tremble against the hard

wood. He'd known Aswin for all of his life. Of course
he'd seen the curse firsthand, how Aswin could see
into some people's minds, their hearts. How the burden pulled on Aswin's soul. "Yes, sir. He hates it,
knowing things he has no right to know. He calls it his
curse."

Dubric's hands clenched. "In many ways I am responsible for the life and well-being of every person living within these walls." He took a deep breath and
tilted his head toward the corner. "I also am responsible for their deaths, their murders, and their ghosts. No
matter how much I don't want to be. Like Aswin, I, too,
have been cursed. But my curse is seeing death. They
stand there now, watching me. Five bleeding girls.
They give me no peace, and will not let me rest, not until I have avenged them. I took a chance that, like the
others, the egg maid would be found near her work.
Evidently I guessed correctly."

Lars shuddered at the shiver slithering down his
spine and loosened his grip on the chair. "You know
when people die, sir? See their ghosts?"

"Today I feared I would see yours, that you would
stand among them. I could not bear for that to happen." He wiped his eyes with his fingertips and shook
his head in shame. "How could I look myself in the mirror knowing I sent you to your death because I felt too
damned old to run across the castle grounds? How
could I live with the guilt?"

"It's all right, sir. You were doing your job."

"No, it is not all right. It is reprehensible I would
send a boy to do a man's job, that I am so beleaguered
by these damned ghosts that I cannot think straight. I
was willing to risk the life of someone I trust above all
others just to save me some blasted time!"

As Dubric pounded his fist on the desk, Lars whispered, "It is my job, too, sir, the job I agreed to do. The job I love. I am at your disposal to save you time, sir, to run errands, to gather evidence, question witnesses, even be the first at a scene, if need be. I was foolish, stupid, and the killer saw me. That was my fault. I was hidden, but I broke cover and he saw me. I am old enough to take responsibility for my mistake, sir."

Dubric sighed and Lars sat straight in his chair, his heart skipping and light sweat beading on his brow. "I will not make the same mistake again, sir. You have my word. You tell me to hide, I'll hide. You tell me to kill, I'll kill. You send me to die, I'll die. I am yours to use as you see fit."

Dubric waved his hand as if brushing away Lars's pledge. "Did you see him?"

"No, sir. Not really. It was too dark to see anything but shadows."

Dubric's chair creaked as he leaned forward. "'Shadows'?"

"Yes, sir. I never saw him, not exactly, but he blocked out starlight when he dragged me from behind the coop. He wore a dark cloak. I could not see anything but a cloak-shaped void. I felt his hands, his breath. He was living flesh, sir, not a ghost, but I could not see him. It was just too dark."

"Did he speak?"

"No, sir. Not a word. But he did laugh." Lars repressed a shudder.

"Was the laugh familiar?"

"No, sir."

"Did you glean anything else?"

"Yes. He was reasonably tall, as tall as you or a little more. Strong. He dragged me as if I were a toy. Hot, like a fever. He wore gloves." Lars paused a moment and whispered, "And his breath smelled like death."

Dubric reached for his notebook. "Could it have been Inek?"

"I wouldn't say so, sir. He was too tall and the smell was all wrong. His breath stank, but he didn't. And he was thinner than Inek, not as bulky. Quick movements. Finesse, not power."

Dubric noted the information.

Before Dubric began the list of standard questions, Lars said, "There is something else, sir. Something you should know before we go any further."

Lars gripped the chair arm again. *My family*, he thought. *I'm about to testify against my family and my home.* But he knew his duty and the oath he had taken to protect Faldorrah over everything else. Even family. He nodded to himself and took a deep breath. "This morning, when he saved me from the milkmaids, Risley had fresh blood on his cheek from a scratch of some kind. He was wearing gloves. And he carried Albin Darril's sword."

Dubric dropped his pencil and muttered a curse.

* * *

After sending Lars to bathe and get a bit of rest, Dubric and Dien rode to the village south of the castle.

"I know the boy doesn't think it's Inek," Dien said as they approached the herbmonger's shop, "but in the fear of the moment, in the dark, he could have been wrong about the killer's size or the origin of the smell."

Dubric dismounted. "Even trained observers like Lars make mistakes." Looking toward Inek's door, Dubric released the peace bond on his sword. A disheveled young man came from the herb shop, glanced at them and hurried away, tucking a parcel in his coat pocket.

Dien tied the horses and watched the man scurry

down the road. "Inek selling contraband concoctions again?"

"It would not surprise me." Dubric strode to the shop door and shoved it open while a bell on the hinge announced their arrival.

Bundles of dried plants hung from the rafters, bags and boxes of assorted materials sat on shelves, and pots bubbled in the corner fire. The room reeked of the pungent scent of herbs, flavorings, and medicines blurring together. One breath smelled of sweet cooking spices, the next a bilious stench of a vomit inducer. Inek came from the back room, bringing his own special aroma with him, and he grinned at the sight of Dubric.

"M'lord Dubric! What brings you to my humble store? Been pissing your pants lately? Old bastards like you often have trouble holding their water. It must chap your ass to have to change trousers every half bell or so."

Dubric ignored the taunt. "I hear you are removing pregnancies. Would you care to elaborate?"

Inek laughed and strode to a locked cupboard. "Karalelle's got her unders in a bunch, eh? Thinks I'm stealing all her business. You just tell that crotch-probing witch I'm—"

"The midwife has nothing to do with this. Are you removing pregnancies or are you not?"

"Not," Inek said as he opened the cupboard. "Once they've started, it's not my problem." He pulled a block of pressed leaves from a wrapper, snapped off a corner, then held it out for Dubric. "Here. This should settle your bladder. Hate to think of you pissing all over yourself and ruining your fine silks."

Dubric ignored the offering. "Pregnancies. Who has been using your services?"

Inek shrugged and slammed the cupboard door. "I already told you. I don't kill babies. That's Karalelle's domain, and I don't want her hacking me up like she does her customers."

Dien loomed behind Dubric's shoulder. "Enough stalling, dung hole. We know you're giving medicine to pregnant girls."

Inek crossed his arms over his wide chest. "Like hell I am, unless you're worried about the ones who don't want to puke their way through the first three moons, or to ease backache when the little bastard's been kicking them in the kidneys. Those, my friends, are valued and long-standing medicinal standards."

Dubric stared at him. "Rianne, an egg maid, came here to stop a pregnancy."

Inek took a step back, startled. "Ri? Peg, no. She came to not get knocked up. She's one of my better customers, I must say. Fine girl." Inek turned and started to walk away. "Give her my love, will you?"

"We can't," Dien said. "She's dead."

Inek stopped, turning abruptly to face them. "What? Ri? It's not possible."

"When did you last see her?"

Inek shook his head. "Yesterday. Well, last night. She was fine, I swear."

Dubric tapped his pencil on the notebook. "Of course she was. When did you part?"

"About eight, maybe nine bell. She said she had to make curfew and she went back to the castle." He blinked and his face reddened. "The pegging slasher got her, didn't he? You worthless, conceited old bastard! You let her die!"

"And you were quite possibly the last person to see her alive."

"No, she left with Celese. Talk to her. She'll tell you."

"Celese Harper?" Dubric flipped back through his notes.

"How the peg should I know? Girls like Ri and Celese don't use their after names, for Goddess's sake. Celese works in your laundry, probably washes the piss from your pants."

Dien reached for Inek's arm. "Amazing coincidence, that. Celese died last night, too."

"No! Hey, wait! Let go of me, you bastard," Inek snapped, wrenching his arm free. "I never hurt those girls. We were just friends."

"What's the matter?" Dien backed Inek toward a corner. "The girls not pay for their medicine?"

"They always paid! Always. One way or another."

"Why did you kill them?" Dien shoved Inek against the wall, knocking some parcels from nearby shelves.

The bubble on Inek's nose expanded and popped, sending a string of greenish fluid across his cheek. "I didn't! Piss! I swear! I was home all night, and I had company. Ask her!"

Dubric took a single step toward them. "Who?"

Inek looked back and forth between them, wiping his snot on his grimy sleeve. "Gal named Vertea. She works at the Sheep. I never killed anybody! Least of all Ri and Celese! I swear!"

Dien shoved him one more time and followed Dubric from the store.

* * *

Marlee, the head bar matron at the Dancing Sheep, filled a mug with ale and set it before Dien. "Yeah, Inek was stinking up the place last night, along with a couple of castle girlies." She took a drag from her pipe then filled another mug, sliding it down the bar. "What'd he do this time?"

Dubric sipped his cup of tea. "We are not certain yet. What time did he leave?"

"'Bout midnight, give or take. Was after the minstrel finished. The castle girlies were long gone before that."

"And Vertea?" Dien asked.

"She worked till close. Why?"

"Inek says they were together last night."

"Damn," Marlee muttered. She dropped her pipe in the ash bowl and stomped to the kitchen door. "Vertea! Get your ass out here!"

A scrawny, tangle-haired girl staggered through the open door. "What? Can'tcha see I'm sleeping?"

Marlee's fists gouged into her hips. "Inek? Last night? Have you lost all sense?"

Vertea scratched her backside and yawned. "He offered me some good smoke in trade for a gobble. What's it hurt? Hells, I fell asleep in the middle of it, anyways."

"It hurts because he's a customer! I don't run a damned brothel!"

Dien sipped his ale and glanced at Dubric. He set the mug on the bar and said, "Guess Inek wasn't pulling our chain."

"Apparently not, but if she fell asleep, how strong of an alibi is she? He could have been long gone by the time she awoke." Dubric listened to the tongue-lashing for a moment more, then fished a few crown from his purse. Marlee was still yelling when they left the Dancing Sheep.

* * *

Dubric sat alone in the great hall as the dwindling midday crowd finished eating. His plate of boiled vegetables and roast lamb sat untouched before him, but he had refilled his teacup twice as he reviewed his notes.

The archers Almund and Werian had been sent to watch over Inek the night before. Both had just confirmed that he had returned from the Dancing Sheep after midnight, with a girl, and had not left again that night. Inek, for once, had told the truth. It did not confirm his innocence—he had admitted to knowing the dead girls and could have snuck away without the archers seeing, especially with the tavern wench asleep—but could he have entered and exited the castle grounds without being noticed? What if the killer lived here, in the castle? That would simplify movements and make it easier to hide.

Dubric ignored the angry mumbling of the crowd around him as he flipped through his notebook, page after page of tiny script, and added names to a list. Names of castle men who had the skills and fortitude to murder five women. Names of men who were known to be armed. Sadly, all were men he thought he could trust.

His own name headed the list. Next came the three squires, his and Lord Brushgar's: Dien, Fultin, and Borlt. He rubbed his tired eyes—the ghosts flickered but refused to leave, damned things—and he added the six archers: Derre, Egger, Quentin, Ghet, Almund, and Werian. Then, after a few moments of deliberation, he added Lars. No one else was permitted to walk about the castle while armed. At the end of this list he added a single name. Risley Romlin. He had been in the courtyard with a sword that very morning.

Dubric looked at his list and frowned. Other men had swords, mementos from the war and heirlooms from dead relatives, especially the castle nobility. He added these names to a new list. Risley, Sir Talmil, Sir Knud, Sir Berde . . . When he finished, he had twenty-two nobles listed. While not all of them were pleasant fellows or popular members of the household, most were loath to get their hands dirty or let raindrops muss their hair. They were as useless as the puppies carried as living decorations by the ladies in King Tunkek's Court. Only one noble on the list had squired, under Lord Bhruic of Rotherwood during the three-moon bloodbath of the Pirate War, no less. Only one had the training to be a killer. Dubric circled his name and sighed. Once again, Risley Romlin.

Referring to names compiled by Lars and Otlee, he listed every member of the staff, man or woman, who used a knife as part of their duties. This list included almost every member of the kitchen staff, the potters, the glaziers, stable workers, physicians, and others. He smiled and nodded to himself. Risley was not on this list, praise the King! But Risley's primary function was to spy for the King and run other sordid errands. A job requiring talent, patience, knowledge of a variety of weapons, and other unsavory skills. Frowning, he added Risley's name to the third list. He shuddered to think of how many villagers could be included.

Deciding that the culprit likely lived within the castle, he contemplated all three lists, took a sip of his tea, and started drawing single lines through names.

Two archers had been in the village watching Inek. A line went through their names. He, Dien, Lars, Bacstair, Flavin, and Meiks received lines, as well. These eight names he added to a fourth list, the clean list. Men he knew he could trust. He frowned. The clean list seemed so small when compared to the others.

He looked at the rest of the names, nearly one hundred souls on three lists, and sighed. He began drawing lines through names again, fainter lines, for men and women who had missing or malformed fingers on their right hands, who had poor health, who were old,

squeamish, physically weak, or were otherwise un-
likely to be able to commit the crimes. He knew none
were unable—anyone could kill if properly moti-
vated—but the faint lines shortened the list of the
most likely suspects. He also marked out the eight angry souls he had dragged to gaol. As he drew the faint
lines the list clarified.

The two bell rang and he lifted his attention from
his notes and sighed. Whose leg was he pulling?
Certainly not his own. One man had a scratched and
bloody cheek this morning, reported officially by six different pages, not to mention the angry gossipers in the
great hall this very afternoon. No one else in the whole
damned castle was apparently scratched. One man had
been seen in the courtyard with an unapproved
weapon, a weapon Dubric knew was more than it
seemed. One man had the training, the time, and the
health, to commit these crimes.

Dubric stood. One man. One man with a known
taste for young women, commoners as well as ladies.
One man who happened to be Lord Brushgar's grandson as well as the King's. The son of good friends. The
future Lord of Haenpar. A young man he hated to accuse. Damn the Goddess to the seven hells. Why did
Inek have to have an alibi?

Dubric grabbed his notebook, slapped it closed,
took a last sip of tea, and walked through his ghosts to
the main stairs, grumbling all the while.

* * *

Dubric stood before Risley's door for a long time
while passersby regarded him with apprehensive
glances. He closed his eyes and rubbed them, but the
tug of the ghosts did not dissipate. *I have no real evi-*

dence, he thought, *nothing set in stone. Only specula-tion and worry and circumstance.*

He opened his eyes again. *And five dead girls. Mutilated dead girls. I had best keep that in mind as I add the son of a good friend to my suspect list.*

Gritting his teeth, he knocked on the door with a shaking hand. Unlocked and unlatched, it opened a crack. *May the King give me strength,* he thought, hearing Risley moving inside the suite.

The door flew fully open and Risley stood before him, smoothing his hair and tucking in his unfastened shirt. His feet were bare and embarrassment shone on his face, like a boy who had been caught with his hand in the honeypots.

When Dubric's eyes passed over him, pausing at his feet, Risley curled his toes and took a quick step back. He shrugged and smiled, holding the door open. "Hello," he said with forced cordiality. "How's the investigation going?"

"It is not going particularly well," Dubric replied as he stepped inside Risley's suite. The entry room was cluttered with books, the casual regard for their value giving silent testament to Risley's personal wealth. Two chairs and a small table stood near a window and three books had been piled on the floor beside one chair. There were other chairs, but all had books on the seats. A ledger with a broken seal of Haenparan-blue lay upon the floor with loose papers spilling out. *Does the boy allow cleaning staff in here?* he thought, noting the mess.

Risley frowned and closed the door. "That's why you're here, though," he said.

"Yes."

Risley paled as he picked the three books off the floor and tucked the papers back into the ledger. "Is

Nella all right?" he asked, his voice shaking. He clutched the books in his hands, denting a cover.

Still five ghosts. "She is fine."

"Thank the Goddess," Risley replied. "You're sure?" He set the books with some others on a shelf, knocking aside a lovely mechanical antique of pitted and tarnished brass.

"Yes. Mind if I sit down?"

Risley's eyes narrowed briefly. He grabbed a discarded pair of shoes from beside the door and yanked them on. "Please make yourself comfortable. Can I get you anything? A drink?"

Dubric sat on a well-stuffed chair near the window and he looked out to the western courtyard, to the milk barns and the coops. *Does he watch the girls come and go?* "Water would be fine, thank you."

Risley disappeared into the suite, then returned with a pitcher of water and two goblets. His hands shook as he poured the water clumsily.

Dubric politely took a drink before pulling his book out of his pocket. "I need to ask you a few questions." He knew the King's family did not have to submit to preliminary questioning, but surely Risley realized that refusing to cooperate would cause greater suspicion. *His response should prove interesting.*

Risley looked at Dubric and nodded slowly, as if attempting to gauge the threat the older man posed. "Certainly. Anything. Ask away." Risley sat across the table from Dubric and held his goblet of water in both hands.

Dubric opened his book and licked the tip of his pencil. "Where were you three nights ago?"

"Night of the first murders? I was here, sleeping. I heard about them at breakfast."

Dubric made a note. "Was anyone here with you?"

"No," Risley answered, his fingertips paling on the goblet.

"And the night before last? What about then?"

"Same thing." Risley took a gulp of his water and slopped a drip onto his shirt.

Dubric leaned forward. "No one was with you? Come now, Risley, I know you. There had to be someone."

Risley shook his head and stared at the water. The white fingertips turned pink again. "No. I stopped doing that. No one was here but me."

"Are you sure?"

Risley looked up, a quick burst of startled anger in his eyes. "Of course I'm sure."

"What about last night?"

"I was here. Alone. Again."

"What were you doing, all of these nights alone?"

Risley shrugged and his fingertips paled again. "Working on my receipts and cargo papers, mostly. I'd brought some with me, and Pritchard just sent another batch. They're here, if you want to look at them."

He is lying. "Maybe later. Were you doing anything else?"

Risley swallowed his water and smiled. "As a matter of fact, yes. I was trying to figure out if I could bribe some people to give Nella odd jobs so she could pay me off sooner. But I decided she'd find out about it and be mad at me."

Dubric looked up from his notebook and stared at the young man, holding his nervous gaze. "Do you need money?"

Risley laughed and seemed to relax a notch. "Absolutely not. I just want her debt done."

Dubric added to his notes. *Risley is not worried*

about money. "Did you do anything else these past three nights?"

"I didn't kill them."

"Did you do anything else?" Dubric's tone remained hard and insistent.

Risley sighed and leaned forward to put his goblet on the table. "You want the truth? Fine. All I've done these past three nights is think about her. For Goddess's sake, Dubric, it's all I've done since I brought her here. I can't eat. I can't sleep. I can't get my books balanced." He pointed to his cheek. "I can't even shave anymore, and that's probably why you're here. I know Lars noticed the cut this morning. I have no alibi; I have no witnesses. I spend every moment I can in this castle so I can be close to her, even if I can't see her. I've canceled all my other romantic endeavors, told Grandda Rom no, I can't go hither and yon at his whim anymore, even if he is the King, and have barely spoken to anyone in my family since I brought her here."

He shrugged and stared into Dubric's eyes with steady forthrightness. "If falling in love with a commoner from Pyrinn is a crime, then I am truly guilty. But I haven't murdered anyone. I've done nothing wrong. I'm obeying my Grandda's orders as best I can. Not pursuing her is one of the hardest things I've ever done, but so far I've been able to keep myself from groveling at her feet by barely leaving these rooms."

"You expect me to believe you have forsaken all other women for this one, and that is why you spend all your time in here? That you are so enamored you can barely function? That not only are you sleeping alone, you are choosing to do so? All for her?"

"Yes. Crazy, isn't it?"

Dubric smiled, hoping Risley spoke the truth, and he made a note. "Not crazy, Risley. Not crazy at all. It is welcome news to me."

Risley relaxed back into his chair. "Tell you what, in a phase or two, when her debts are all paid, I'm sure I'll have plenty of alibi. All right? Malanna willing, everyone will know where I am and what I'm doing."

Dubric nodded and he paused before shifting his tack. "Fair enough. Your love life is your own business. But unauthorized people loitering at murder scenes is mine."

"You mean this morning?"

Dubric said nothing.

"I already told you I can't sleep. I was awake before dawn, staring out the window, my mind on, well . . ." Risley shrugged and picked up his glass of water again. "I saw Lars stagger out from behind the coops. He looked like he was in trouble, so I hurried out to help him. I didn't see the body until I got there."

"He mentioned you arrived rather abruptly this morning. Would you care to explain that?"

Risley muttered into his water, "My suite is right beside the tower stairs. Generally speaking, it doesn't take much time to get from here to the courtyard."

"Now is not the time for belligerency."

Sighing harshly, Risley rolled his eyes. "How else would I get there? Fly?"

"I seem to recall a young man with a penchant for crawling into young ladies' windows late at night after their parents had gone to bed."

Risley laughed, shaking his head. "That was summers ago! Goddess, I was maybe sixteen the last time I did that!"

"And, if I remember correctly, the same young man

purportedly snuck into Lord Bhruic's castle and killed a group of pirates who had held the castle hostage. Rumor is, a shadowy assassin climbed through a tower window in the dead of night to slit the pirates' throats."

"Something like that, yes."

Dubric rubbed his aching eyes. "Have you been climbing through windows again?"

"This castle is made of granite and it's the dead of winter, Dubric. That's a silly question."

"I notice you are not answering it."

"Of course I might be stupid enough to try and climb rough-polished granite that's potentially coated in ice. If I had a death wish, or if my Grandda Rom had run out of other options and ordered me to." He sipped his water and winked. "But I don't, and he hasn't, so I'd have to say your answer is 'no.'"

"This is not a joke, Risley. Someone is slipping past my guards."

"It's not me. Check my windows if you'd like. They're all sealed for the winter."

"Swords are supposed to be sealed away, as well, or have you forgotten?"

"I haven't forgotten. I'm perfectly aware of the rules. I just choose to ignore some of them."

"You are not allowed to run around armed."

Risley sipped the water and stared at Dubric, his eyes growing hard and cold as a muscle in his cheek twitched. "Try to pegging stop me. Unlike the sheep you herd through this castle, I won't count on your false security or hide from the unknown. You've got a lunatic on the loose and anything and everything I can do to protect these girls I'll do. Anyone even thinks about looking at Nella and I'll hack them into little bits, I'll guarantee you that."

Dubric ground his teeth. "We have the situation under control."

"Horse piss. You've got five dead girls, that's what you've got, and you nearly had a dead page, to boot. How would you have explained to Bostra that you let his son get killed by a lunatic?" Dubric remained silent and Risley said, "I've worn my sword several times during the past couple of days, in case I happen to bump into the son-of-a-whore who's doing this, and I'm going to continue to wear my sword."

"You are not a member of the security staff, nor a member of the Faldorrahn Army, and cannot—"

Risley knocked the pitcher aside and it smashed against the wall in a burst of glass and water. "Oh, peg that frigging 'not a member' line! I'm trying to help, for Goddess's sake. I'm trying to catch the bastard."

But can you control your temper? "That is not your job. It is mine. Your job is to—"

Risley leaned forward and slapped the table as he interrupted. "My job, for at least the next phase, is to ensure that I don't grovel at Nella's feet and make a total fool of myself in her presence. My duty is to kill anyone who tries to harm innocent people, especially servant girls, and particularly Nella. Do not tread on my job or my duty, Dubric."

Dubric blinked, raising an eyebrow. "Is that a threat?"

"Take it however you want." Risley stared at Dubric as sweat beaded upon his reddening face. He drained his glass of water in a gulp, then rubbed his forehead as his skin returned to its normal hue. "Goddess, I'm thirsty."

He reached for where the pitcher had stood but a moment ago, then, paling, he stared at the broken glass and wet spot. Risley looked at Dubric then back to the wall, setting aside his water glass as if it were diseased. He mumbled something Dubric could not hear and rubbed his forehead again.

"How did you cut your cheek?" Dubric asked, pausing in his notations. "One of the victims scratched her attacker."

Risley braved a nervous glance. "Shaving, this morning. I started drifting and thinking about Nella. I wasn't paying attention to what I was doing and I cut myself. That's all." He tilted his cheek toward Dubric. "Take a look. It's not a deep cut, but it bled like a bastard."

Dubric examined the cut and had his hopes dashed almost instantly. The single cut was shallow, about half the length of a finger, just above and following the jawline. It was clean, straight, and unscabbed. Definitely a cut, not a scratch, and certainly not made by fingernails. The razor was very sharp and Risley had given himself a common shaving cut, nothing more.

Dubric's eyes widened as sudden implications danced in his head. *The blade! Blunt back, the perfect size.* He swallowed before he said, "May I see your razor?"

Risley hesitated before rising from the chair. "All right." He paused, then disappeared into the bath chamber down the hall. A few moments later he came back with a razor and a bloody towel. He handed both to Dubric. "I fished the towel out of the laundry bin. The blood's all mine."

Dubric glanced at the towel and handed it back. There were a few blotches of blood, but not many. It had merely been a shaving cut after all, barely worth notice. The razor, however, interested him a great deal.

Dubric turned the folding razor over in his hands, marveling at his luck. He traced his finger along the back of the steel blade, over the sleek ivory casing that protected the blade and whoever handled it, and the shining brass hinge. Grinning, he slipped it into his pocket and pulled it back out.

"How do you open it?" he asked.

Risley pointed to a raised panel on the side. "Press here. It will lift right out."

"Like this?" Dubric asked, and the razor slid open with a soft metallic *click*.

"There's a little spring in there, and a latch," Risley said. "Pressing the side releases the latch."

"And activates the spring. Ingenious." Dubric examined the razor and hefted it in his hand as he gauged its weight. He measured the engraved blade alongside his finger. Tracing along the seal of Haenpar and Risley's name carved into the ivory handle, he noted that the entire piece was immaculately clean. It was a solid, well-maintained razor. "How do you close it?"

Risley pulled his attention away from the broken pitcher. "Just press it closed. All there is to it."

Dubric did, pushing against the slight resistance. The latch chirped a sharp faint click and Dubric grinned, feeling like a child with a new toy. He had always found working mechanisms fascinating, but had encountered so very few. "Where did you get it?" He opened and closed the razor a couple of times.

"There's a smith in Aberville who makes them. My da gave it to me when I turned seventeen summers."

Dubric paused to make a note in his book. "Aberville is three days' travel to the south, right?" When Risley nodded, he asked, "Is this the only one you have?"

"I have another, not as fancy, that's in my travel pack."

"May I see it?"

"I'll see if I can find it."

He rummaged somewhere Dubric could not see and returned with another razor, wadded up in a small towel with other shaving supplies. It was somewhat humble, with a handle of polished cherry instead of carved ivory and the blade clear of engraving.

Dubric hefted it in his hand. The cherry razor was as clean as the ivory one but lighter, and the casing was splintered, worn, and battered from use. "Do you mind if I ask what this cost?"

Risley shrugged and his eyes rolled toward the ceiling. "About thirty-two crown, I think. It was middle of the road in price, more or less. Some were rather expensive, but most were under fifty."

Dubric nodded, opening and closing the second razor as well. "Do you know of anyone else around here with a razor like this?"

Risley gaped. "You think they used a shaving razor? Goddess, no wonder the murders are so messy."

Dubric shrugged, resisting the urge to look at the ghosts. "'Messy' is as good a word for it as any."

After a moment, Risley shook his head. "No one specific, but any of the squires or officials could have one, I suppose. I'd doubt the commoners would travel all the way to Aberville for a folding razor when there's a steel smith in town."

Dubric added the information to his notebook. "Have you seen these for sale anywhere but Aberville?"

"No. Never seen one at all till Da gave one to Aswin. I've never seen any others here, but I'm sure they're around. The smith does a good business."

Dubric thanked Risley and returned the razors. He added another note, closed his book, and stood. He said, "I have set an order that no woman is to be alone under any circumstances and that they are to be in groups of at least two at all times. Guards will be posted at all entrances and men moving about alone will be stopped and questioned."

"Will it help?"

"I hope so, but I doubt it. The staff are shaken, but he is still out there, watching. Surely, he will catch another."

"It's not me. I swear."

With that temper? We shall see. You're up to something late at night, and I intend to find out what. Dubric strode toward the door, his thoughts churning. *Perhaps I should assign the boy to guard duty. It would quickly eliminate or confirm him as a suspect.*

Risley held the door open and Dubric nodded his thanks as he walked through. "Oh, one more thing," he said, turning. "Would you be able to serve a guard—"

The door slammed and latched, ending the conversation.

Dubric took a startled step backward, feeling the cold of a ghost slip against his spine. He stared at the door for a long moment before adding a comment to his notebook. Sighing, he turned and walked away while the ghosts dragged along in his wake.

CHAPTER

8

†

I can't go to Haenpar," Nella said, throwing used towels into the laundry cart.

Risley's face was flushed from running. "I want you somewhere safe. The farther from here the better."

She drew him toward an alcove while her terrified friends watched. "I understand your concern and I have the same worries. But I can't leave. I have a job, and I have to finish my debt."

"I don't care about the debt," he snarled as he grasped her arms. His touch was urgent, firm, and painless as he held her before him. "To the seven hells with the debt. I want you safe."

She shook her head, feeling the debt lying heavily in her heart. "No. I'll be careful. I'll—"

"Girls are dying, Nella."

"Don't you think I know that?" she whispered. "The staff is so scared barely anything is getting done. We're all jumping at shadows."

"All the more reason for you to get out of here." He released her arms. "Please. I can protect you in Haenpar."

"But what about them?" she asked, gesturing back to the girls from her sleeping room. They huddled together in the hall like sheep. "You can't possibly take every female servant to Haenpar."

He nodded as if accepting her proposal without a second thought. "I will if I have to. If that's what it takes to—"

"No. You can't. You step within ten lengths of any of them and they'll start screaming."

He looked at the girls and most of them flinched and took a step back. "They've never been afraid of me before."

"They're afraid of everyone. You. Dubric. Lord Brushgar. Everyone. Every man in this castle is suspect."

"But I'd never hurt them."

"I know that. But someone is doing this. It has to be someone familiar. Someone who doesn't scare us, at least not until they get close. Rianne knew to be afraid, and she's dead. Celese did, too. Trust is in pretty short supply right now."

Risley took a hesitant breath and asked, "Do you trust me?"

"Yes." She grasped and squeezed his hand. "I trust you. I tell them they can, too, that if you were a butcher you had more than enough time to kill me before we got here."

"You're not serious!"

"Of course I'm serious. There has to be someone we can turn to, someone we can trust, and most of the girls need reasons for that trust."

"But anyone could be judged trustworthy in the right light."

"I know," she whispered. "But there has to be someone to trust. I think it should be you."

"Thank you." He glanced at the girls again. "What do they think?"

"Everyone has a different opinion. Some trust no one; others think it's a stranger. Stef insists it's Dubric."

He frowned and shook his head. "It's not Dubric."

She asked him a question she'd been asking herself. "Are you willing to stake my life on that?"

He stared at her for a moment, then he nodded. "Yes, I think so."

She nodded back. "I think I would, too. But I'd still be nervous if left alone with him. I'd want others to know where I was. Just in case. Same with Lord Brushgar. If anyone else came near me while I was alone, I'd start screaming, or run."

"But you wouldn't be nervous with me? Or scared? If we were alone?"

"No. I'd feel safe with you."

"Thank you," he said, his eyes growing deep and dark, and she thought for sure he was going to kiss her.

"You're welcome," she whispered and smiled, her heart thudding. "I'd love to go to Haenpar with you. Really. But I can't leave them. Someone has to keep their head around here or more girls are going to die." Her voice turned hard. "I'm not going to let that happen to my friends, if I can help it."

Risley muttered a curse and slammed the side of his fist against the wall. "Can I at least have you guarded, have you moved to my suite, *something*?"

She considered her reply, weighing the assurance of her personal safety against the responsibility she felt for her friends' lives. "I'm not sure how you could manage it," she said at last. "I think there are too many of us to watch over."

"Maybe so, but my main concern is you. Whatever it takes to keep you safe, I'll gladly do."

Her eyes searched his and she felt a blush creep onto her cheeks. "Thank you."

He squeezed her hand. "Even if I can't protect everyone, I'll protect you. Somehow. I promise."

She smiled and then he was gone, stopping once to look back at her.

She hurried back to the group and continued through the day, wishing in the secret depths of her heart she'd agreed to go to Haenpar.

* * *

"Piss in a cart, Dubric! Arrest him, already. We've all seen the mark on his face."

"Yer playin' fav'rits!"

"Five girls dead! Do yer job and hang 'im."

"Gut 'im like the swine 'e is!"

Dubric ignored the angry demands of the crowd assembled outside his office. He pushed through them and slammed the outer door in their faces, cutting the noise to little more than a nuisance. He fished the key from his pocket and locked it. His ghosts passed unseen through the crowd and through the thick wooden door. Turning his back to them, he barked, "Dien! Lars!"

Otlee sat on a bench in the outer office. He had piles of notes on both sides of him, a notebook much like Dubric's on his lap, and an expensive new pencil in his hand. Startled, he turned toward Dubric and a few sheets of paper slipped to the floor. "Sir?"

Lars hurried through the office door, his hand over his mouth to hide a yawn. Dien followed, lumbering, his hands full of papers. "We're here, sir," Dien said.

Dubric nodded. "Everyone in my office. Otlee, bring a chair."

"Yes, sir," Otlee said and leapt to his feet.

Dubric waited until all three were in his office, then he locked the door. He looked to Otlee first. "You have taken most of the testimonies, and although they are private, witnesses have been known to talk."

Dien suppressed a snicker and Lars rolled his eyes.

Witnesses were certain to talk, and both knew it. Otlee did not seem to notice their sarcasm.

"I've never said a word about the testimonies, sir," Otlee said. His brown eyes were earnest and sure. "Not to anyone but the three of—"

Dubric waved his hand to cut short the boy's comments. "I know you have not. But today we are doing something different, and this must remain private. No matter what."

"Sir?"

"We are about to discuss possible suspects and murder weapons, and everything pertaining to them is to be held in the strictest confidence."

"I thought only staff—" Lars started.

"I think our Otlee is deserving of a promotion," Dubric said.

Otlee paled and looked to the others.

Dien's chair creaked under his weight as he leaned forward. "Isn't he kinda young, sir?"

Dubric nodded, his eyes resting on Otlee. "Yes, but he is four or five moons older than Lars was."

Dien shifted in his seat. "Yes, sir, but Lars came from a ruling house. His father's a castellan. The responsibility might be too much for Otlee."

"I considered that, but he has done quite well so far," Dubric said. "Remarkably well for a lad."

Dien said, "He is a quick learner. I guess we could watch over him for a while."

Lars shrugged. "I think he'll do fine."

Dubric leaned a hip against his desk. "Otlee," he said, "what we are about to discuss cannot leave this room. Do you understand?"

Otlee looked at Dien and Lars, then back to Dubric. "Yes, sir."

"Can you promise to uphold the laws and safety of

Faldorrah above all else? Above your family? Above your own life?"

"Yes, sir."

"Can you promise to give your honest opinion, even if I or anyone else in authority does not agree or see things the way you see them?"

Otlee tilted his head. "Sir? You want me to promise to disagree with you?"

Dien said, "No. He wants you to promise to speak up if you do."

Lars leaned over and said, "It's to ensure no one man makes all the rules and forces others to follow blindly. We need to know all the risks and all sides of the story as best we can."

Otlee looked at Dubric, then Dien and Lars. "You really want me to have a say in this?"

Dubric said, "In my opinion, you have a unique perspective on this entire situation. Can you promise to speak frankly, no matter what I think?"

Otlee swallowed and sat a little taller. "Yes, sir. I promise to speak my mind."

"One last thing. Can you promise to take a life if need be, or give your own, to protect Faldorrah and its people?"

"Yes, sir."

"Until death takes you from your duty?"

"Until death, sir."

Dubric bowed slightly as he accepted the boy's pledge. "Welcome to my staff, Otlee. After we are finished here today, Lars will take you to the armory and fit you with a sword."

Otlee let his breath out in a rush and relaxed. "Yes, sir. Thank you, sir." Dien and Lars both patted him on the back.

Dubric walked behind his desk. "Do not thank me

yet. We have five dead girls, no hard suspects, and it will be nighttime in less than four bells." He sat and looked at the others. "I think I have discovered the murder weapon today, and we need to start eliminating suspects. We also need to choose another batch of men to help patrol the grounds. I had considered asking Risley, and I would like to hear everyone's input on that particular idea. I am not certain if we possess enough trustworthy men to watch over him at this point, or if he would even agree." Dubric paused to rub his eyes. "Damn, what a mess."

He cleared his throat and pulled his notebook from his pocket. "We had best get to work. Otlee, you take notes."

When Otlee nodded and reached for the pile of clean papers, Lars said, "Don't forget to speak up. It's all right to ask questions."

"I have a feeling I'm going to have plenty of those." Otlee grasped his pencil and Dubric opened his notebook to Risley's testimony.

* * *

"He's gonna get us in trouble," Stef mumbled, glancing to the hall. She stuffed a pillow into a sham and glared at Nella.

"No, he's not," Nella said with a smile and gathered an armful of dirty linen. Two rooms to go and they'd be done for the day.

Dari hurried from the bath chamber with dirty towels. "Besides, last I knew, you were already in trouble."

Stef muttered a low curse as Nella and Dari walked to the hall. Both girls smiled at Risley when they dropped the dirties in the laundry cart. He leaned a hip against the balcony railing and nodded a return greeting. He had stood no closer than fifteen lengths from the girls since arriving not long before three bell. He had not said a word to any of them, not even to Nella, had not tried to touch them, or done a single thing to upset the flow of their work. He only stood and waited and watched.

Mirri came from the next suite with dirty towels in her hands. "Oh, darn it all," she whispered, her face flushed.

"What's wrong now?" Dari had dropped her towels into the cart and knelt to grab a fresh stack from the shelf below. "Did you break something again?"

"I gotta pee," Mirri whispered.

Dari shook her head and stomped toward the suite. "Great. It's after dark. Couldn't you have gone during our midday meal? When it was still light out?"

"We've only got two more suites," Nella said. "Can you wait a little longer? We can all go when we're done."

Mirri blushed and bobbed on one foot. "I'm sorry, Nella, but I can't. I've already waited too long."

"So go already," Stef said from the doorway. "What's stopping you?"

"It's dark out there!"

"I'll escort you to the privies," Risley said from his place at the balcony.

Mirri took a quick step back, her eyes wide. "Uh, that's all right, I, uh . . ."

Nella sighed. "He's not going to hurt you. I promise."

Mirri looked back and forth between them, and resumed bobbing on the one foot. "I'll be fine," she said. "I can wait a little longer. I think."

"Oh, bother," Nella muttered and stepped toward the suite door, ignoring Stef's disgusted sneer. "Dari! I'm taking Mirri outside for a minute. I'll hurry back."

Dari looked up from the fresh sheets she was tying onto the bed. "Be careful."

Muttering, Stef shoved past her with an armload of towels.

"I will." Nella turned back to the hall. "Does anyone else have to go to the privy?" she called out.

Ker exited her room, as did two floor maids and a window maid from down the hall. They huddled together, worried eyes watching Risley.

Nella smiled and said, "Let's go."

Mirri glanced at Risley and chewed her lip. "But . . . but . . ."

Nella looked at Mirri, shook her head, and grabbed Mirri's arm to get her moving. They hurried down the hall, all six girls clustered together. Risley followed them with his hand resting on the hilt of his sword.

* * *

Dubric reviewed the list of that night's suggested volunteers one last time. Again, every name belonged to a family man; two were nobles. "Dien, I will let you notify tonight's batch. If anyone seems hesitant or refuses—"

"I'll throw their butts in the gaol and worry about it tomorrow," Dien said as he yawned.

"Lars? Do you know what you're supposed to do?"

Lars looked up from the slim scrap of paper he had been writing on. "Yes, sir. I'm finishing the note now. My father should be able to send someone to Aberville to question the steel smith. He'll get our message by morning. With luck, we'll get his response day after tomorrow."

Dubric nodded and noted the expected reply date in his notebook. Messenger birds flew frequently between Faldorrah and Haenpar, and this afternoon there had

been one Haenparan bird left. Praise the King! Perhaps
he would get a break in this investigation after all.

"Otlee?"

"I'm supposed to go with Lars to the birds, to the armory to choose a sword, and start research in the library. We're going to find a reason why he's taking the
kidneys and hair, if we can. After that, we're to make a
chart comparing the victims."

"Very good." Dubric ignored the reluctance in
Lars's eyes. Both boys had been delegated to safe duty,
and both had been instructed to go to bed by midnight.
Dubric did not want to take another chance with Lars's
life, or Otlee's. Not after this morning.

"And you, sir?" Dien asked as the boys gathered up
their papers and turned to go.

"Questioning victims' friends and acquaintances.
Most likely a waste of my time, if past interviews are
any indication."

His three assistants nodded their sad agreement
and left the office. Dubric spent a few moments glaring
at his ghosts, then he left, as well.

* * *

A few people turned to look at their odd procession,
but Nella didn't mind. She had learned long ago the
truth of safety in numbers. Every time she passed a
cluster of servant girls, she said, "We're all going to the
privies." More often than not, their group would grow.
By the time they reached the rows of privies behind the
castle, seventeen servant girls had come along. All were
members of the cleaning staff.

The night was clear and cold and the stars sparkled
like hard glints of ice in the sky. As soon as he stepped
out into the chill, Risley removed his cloak and handed
it to the shivering girls. "Try to stay warm," he said.

Some of the girls looked at him nervously, while others babbled their thanks. His cloak was wide and flowing and the girls soon discovered if they huddled close together, many could be protected from the wind.

The castle loomed above them as they hurried to the privies. Many of the windowed rooms were lit by candles or lamps, and dim light flowed into the courtyard. The courtyard was dark, but not pitch-black, and Nella could make out the shapes of the privies, the potters' sheds, and the leather shop.

Ten privies waited in one long row, and Risley checked each one in the line before he let a girl enter. After deciding to use three at one end, Risley and the huddle of girls waited outside the middle privy's door. The girls had merely half a dozen steps to any of the three privies. The warmth, and the protection, remained close.

Nella snuggled into Risley's cloak, her face pressed against the woolen fabric so she could breathe in his scent, and she watched him as best she could in the dark. He seemed so sure of himself, so invincible.

Almost half of the girls had gone to the privy when they heard a pair of men walking toward them. The men chatted with each other and did not seem to notice the huddle of girls wrapped in the cloak. Not until Risley spoke.

"Halt there," Risley said and took a couple of steps to stand between the two men and the girls. "These privies are in use."

"Eh, wot? I's got to use the shitter," one said.

"We always use the end 'uns," the other said. "They're the closest."

"Not this time." Around Nella, several girls gasped when Risley pulled his sword and his voice dropped to a venomous snarl. "You've been warned. Halt now and go around to the other end."

Even Nella knew openly displayed weapons were forbidden, and she winced at the threat.

Both men stopped, their shapes dim shadows in the dark. "An who be tellin' us ta go 'round? Ye ain't Castellan Dubric, that's as sure as me ass."

"Risley Romlin. Now get the peg out of here." His sword winked in the dim light from the castle and both men jumped back.

One of the men blabbered, "Curse it, Sawllt! 'E's got hisself a sword! We ain't gotta go dat bad." Both ran back into the dark, until only the sound of their footsteps remained.

Risley turned back to the girls as he sheathed the sword. "Everyone all right?"

Seventeen dimly lit faces watched him, fourteen in the huddle, the other three peeking from the privies. Some of the faces nodded, but most cowered away.

Nella said, "We're all fine."

He rubbed his hands together as if to warm them and said, "Good. Everyone keeping warm?"

All seventeen nodded.

Everyone but you, Nella thought. *You've got to be freezing*. But before she could say anything to him, it was her turn. Risley watched her open the privy door, and he was still watching her door when she stepped out a few moments later.

* * *

Dien burst into the outer office and startled three laundry workers waiting on the bench. He did not glance their way; he hurried to the inner office door and knocked.

"Come in," Dubric said and rubbed his eyes. A

plump girl with limp, mouse-brown hair sat before him. Her hands were red and blotchy from bleach and the rest of her was pale and mealy-looking. She had spent the past quarter bell complaining about her back and Dubric was ready to toss her out the door.

"Ah, Dien!" Dubric stood and motioned Dien in. "This is Grentche and she was just finishing her testimony."

Dien grumbled a greeting but barely glanced at the witness. "We have a problem, sir," he said.

Dubric hurried around his desk and held the door open for Grentche. As soon as she shuffled out, he closed the door and said, "What happened?"

"We've had an incident in the north courtyard. I've got two potters, both on our hopeful list for tonight, who are mighty upset over being threatened at sword point."

"Risley?"

"Yes, sir. But that's not all."

Dubric's sigh was harsh. "What else has he done?"

"Sent the last frigging bird to Haenpar this afternoon. A message to his father is all I know. We won't receive new birds for at least three days."

"Fetch Trumble," Dubric said as he stomped out of his office.

* * *

Dubric found Risley easily enough. A cluster of cleaning girls wrapped in a nobleman's cloak and walking through the north door would have been hard to miss. The fact Nella Brickerman called for more made it harder still. The dozens of other servant girls milling around the entrance made it downright impossible to ignore.

Nella slipped out from the cloak and said loudly

enough for all to hear, "Anyone else need to go to the privy?"

At least twenty hands shot up.

Risley accepted his cloak from the last batch of girls as Nella said, "We can even keep you warm out there. Warm and safe."

Dubric pushed through the assembled crowd; most of the girls scuttled away from him but a few gave him scathing looks. "What do you think you are doing?" he asked Risley.

Risley held his cloak open while Nella herded the girls inside its folds. "I'm making privy runs. If you'll excuse us?" He opened the door and the bundle of girls stepped into the cold.

Dubric followed. He had to jog to keep up and his breath billowed white with every word he spoke. "I informed you earlier today that this is not your concern."

Risley shook his head and said, "And I told you it was. Did you know these girls are officially allowed only one trip to the privy during the workday? One damn trip, preferably over their lunchtime, along with the rest of the staff. It's a wonder they don't burst open. And, to make matters worse, by the time they get done working it's dark. How would you like to face death every time you were allowed to take a leak? I'm just glad Nella's duties are finished for today. Without her here to assure them that I'm harmless, the others would be on their own." He looked back to the girls and said, "We're using the three on the left, ladies. Since we've been in the castle for a while, let me check them before we get started, all right?"

Dubric fumed while Risley checked the three privies. Once deemed safe, the girls started in.

Risley stood behind the group, his hand resting on the hilt of his sword.

Dubric shivered and wished he had grabbed his cloak. "There are other privies."

Risley's attention remained on the girls. "Not for the servants. There's the privy beside the barn, for stable hands, pig masters, and so on, a few privies for the kitchen staff—far too few for all of them, by the way—and another three for the accountants and office workers. Most of the female staff, especially the cleaning maids, have to use these."

From the bundled group before him, Dubric heard someone say, "Yeah. Not only do we hafta go outside, we gotta share with the men. We need our own privies!"

A chorus of angry agreement floated through the cold air.

Dubric could not believe what he was hearing. "But they work in the living quarters! Every large suite, and every floor, has privies."

A girl turned to look at Dubric. "Pah! It's against policy to let us use the floor privies, let alone the private ones. Automatic dismissal, they tell us. Those privies are for the nobles and families. Not us poor girls." She turned away and muttered, "Bastards."

Dubric pursed his lips. No wonder the killer found girls outside alone. The staff supervisors were not supposed to limit privy access, especially in the winter!

Risley watched the girls enter and leave the privies, and the tone of his voice was merely curious. "Are you after me for making privy runs or have I stepped on someone's toes?"

Dubric sighed and rubbed his eyes. All he needed was to add privy usage complaints to his already full plate of problems. He would worry about the privy mess tomorrow, since Risley's flagrant disregard for policy was a more immediate concern. "I hear you unsheathed your sword tonight."

"Of course I did. Two men approached and refused to stop, and I had seventeen girls to protect. They're both lucky they're still breathing."

Dubric stomped his feet in a vain effort to keep warm. "Give me your sword."

"No."

Excuse me? Dubric thought, and when he spoke again his voice growled. "I will throw you in gaol if I have to."

Without taking his eyes off the girls, Risley retrieved something from a pocket and smacked his palm against Dubric's chest. "No, you won't. Not this time."

As Risley's hand moved away, a piece of parchment fluttered into Dubric's hands. "What is this?" he asked, clutching at it.

Risley watched a tall, thin floor maid enter a privy. He seemed utterly unconcerned with Dubric. "King's Writ."

King's Writs guaranteed full weapon privileges, access to restricted areas, and other indulgences. They were only available from King Tunkek Romlin himself, and were almost as rare as feathers on a horse. "Bull piss. Waterford is a fortnight away. You cannot have a—"

"I have three or four of them tucked away at any given time. Never know when I might need one."

Dubric crushed the crisp parchment in his hand. If it was a King's Writ, Risley could swing his sword around in a crowd of children and pregnant women, carry it without a scabbard or peace bond, and show it to every person who walked by. As long he did not intentionally harm innocent people, Dubric could do nothing to stop him, legally. Perhaps not even then. "You son-of-a—"

"Now, now," Risley said as the last girl stepped

from her privy, "watch what you say about my mother." He flashed a grin at Dubric and called out, "Everyone finished?"

A chorus of agreement bounded through the cold air. Risley stretched to see and count the whole group, then followed the bundled girls back to the castle.

* * *

Dubric stomped to his office, crushing the writ into a tight ball. "I simply do not have time for this madness. Damn that boy."

He threw open the outer office door and startled a senior page from the bench.

"You wanted to see me, sir?" Trumble asked, bowing. Small and slender built, the lad was one of the best horsemen Dubric knew.

"Yes. I need a rider." Dubric fished a twenty-crown coin from his purse and handed it to Trumble. "In Aberville, a village about two days' ride south on the merchant's road, there is a steel smithy who makes razors. I need to know what Faldorrahns may possess them."

Trumble bowed, pocketing the coin. "Yes, sir."

"Take a bird with you," Dubric said, rubbing his eyes. "I do not want to wait four days for a reply."

"As you wish, sir." Trumble bowed again, then left, closing the door behind him.

* * *

More than a bell later, Nella stood in the supper line with a few seamstresses and a very tired-looking glazier. All of her friends had already finished supper while she continued to help with privy runs. She sighed at the thought of facing a meal alone. Risley walked beside her and watched the crowd.

"Aren't you going to eat?" she asked.

"I'll eat later." He gave her a quick wink and said, "I'm working now and I can't eat on duty."

Nella shook her head and smiled at him, then turned her attention to the thin pickings available to eat from the servants' allotted portions. Whatever had been the main meat choice was long gone; perhaps ten spoonfuls of greasy meat pie remained. Nella didn't mind the lack of meat, since she had never developed a taste for it. Shellfish and an occasional mangled fowl were the closest to meat that Pyrinnian peasants ever had. After arriving in Faldorrah, she had sampled pork, venison, and beef, and had found them all disgusting. Since fish had never appeared as an option, and chicken was available only once a phase or so, she usually looked instead to the kettles of greens or vegetables, the bowls of baked or boiled tubers, the tray of breads, and whatever fruit was available. But tonight she was over a bell later than her usual supper time and had little hope for her choices.

The fruit compote was gone and the baked tubers as well. Only dark rye bread, boiled squash, and porridge with maple syrup remained. She sighed and asked for a bowl of porridge while the seamstress in front of her griped about the meager selection.

The serving lass shrugged and slopped a ladle full of greasy-meat-goo onto a plate. "If'n ye get here late, you take yer chances," she said. The seamstress sniffed the goo and wandered into the thinning supper crowd.

The serving lass looked at Nella and at Risley, her eyes growing wide as she fumbled for the porridge spoon.

"Is there a problem?" Risley asked.

"No, sir. No problem 'ere. Just ne'er seen ye at me line b'fore. Surely ye don't want the organ-and-trimmins pie or porridge."

Risley looked at the food table as if he'd never laid eyes on it before. "Don't you have any good stew or roast pork? Perhaps some pheasant and dumplings or a nice bit of mutton?"

Nella hid a chuckle behind her hand as the serving lass answered, "They're serving roast pork t'night, I'm sure of it, at the nobles' tables, sir. And I thinks I saw dumplins in the kettle this evenin', too." She carefully spooned up a bowl of porridge and handed it to Nella.

"What about here? Don't you serve the same food over here as at the nobles' tables?"

"Oh no, sir. Not for the servants, sir. They get the seconds and whate'er's left from yesterday or from earlier. Whate'er the nobles won't eat." She shrugged.

"You can't be serious."

The serving lass reddened. "Honest and truly, sir. I wouldn't lie 'bout nothin'."

Nella giggled and shook her head, helpless to smile at Risley's surprise. "Surely you didn't think that we servants are treated the same as the nobility?"

"It simply never occurred to me that the kitchens would bother serving separate meals. Lately I'm discovering several things that I'd never considered before." Sighing, Risley looked at Nella, and at the small bowl of porridge as she poured a dollop of maple syrup on top. "Please tell me you're eating more than porridge."

Nella lifted her bowl. "I wish I could, but the tubers were all gone."

"Then let's go over to the other tables. Maybe, hells, *surely* they still have something more substantial than porridge."

She smiled and walked past him, heading to a seat. "I can't do that."

"Why not?"

She sighed and whispered, "You keep forgetting.

I'm a servant, not a noble. I'm not allowed to get food from the nobles' tables." Her eyes rose up to his and she hoped they were not ashamed. "Porridge is fine."

"Nella . . ." he whispered, but the nearby crowd had fallen almost silent and his voice rang oddly in her ears.

She shook her head and glanced at the people around them. "Not now, Risley. Please. People are staring."

He nodded, grumbled, and followed her through the crowd. "Things are going to have to change around here," he muttered.

* * *

Dubric lay in his bed, in the dark, staring at the ceiling. A scattered ring of five ghosts glowed faintly around his bed. He rolled onto his side and squeezed his eyes closed. He had to stop thinking about the case, the ghosts, everything. He had to get some sleep. Patrols started in four or five bells.

He lay there for a few moments, perhaps to the count of ten, and his eyes bolted open again. The ghost of Celese the Laundress stood before him, hazy blood dripping from her throat to forever drench her uniform. Her eyes glowed creamy green and her mouth cried out in silent anguish.

He rolled over again. Elli Cunliffe this time. Her front was clean—he knew her back was a gaping hole of gore, but he could not see that, at least not now— but her glowing eyes, once so blue and pretty, were dead and gone. Vacant, horrified, and pleading, they stared at him.

"Go away and leave me alone!" he yelled, but they did not listen. He rubbed his eyes. Still they remained. He cursed them again. Nothing happened. Fytte stood at the foot of the bed, her throat slashed and her eyes dead and glowing. The first of the ghosts, her specter was the brightest, the strongest. Fytte alone could move her limbs, but he suspected Elli would start moving soon, then Ennea. What then? Would they reach for him? Drag him to their bloody bosoms? As each one grew stronger, would they become more of a nuisance than they already were? Was that even possible?

He sat up and stared at Fytte. At her slashed throat, her dead yet aware eyes, the blood-drenched apron, the short curling hair. She moved her mouth, over and over again, repeating the same message until he thought it would drive him mad. She had been saying the same thing all day.

"Please," the movement of her mouth said, "please help us. Please, please help us. Please, please help us." Over and over again, with only a blink of her dead eyes to separate the requests for help. It was almost enough to drive a sane man back to religion.

Dubric slammed his fists on the bed and looked from one ghost to the next. Did they not understand that he was doing all he could? He had assigned patrols, questioned witnesses, and traced every possible lead, no matter how minor it might be. Why did they not understand this was different than some drunken fool beating someone to death or a woman who could take no more of her cheating man and bashed his head in? Why did these ghosts have to be so blasted complicated? Why did they have no apparent connection other than their status? Their killer had left no clues and no reason for their deaths. Besides, it was a killer no one had seen, and every murder scene save one had been severely compromised, leaving him no way to track the beast. How in the seven hells was he supposed to catch a killer he could not see or follow? Maybe when he was younger, maybe back when his mind and reflexes were quicker and stronger, he could have thought his way around this problem. Did these damn ghosts not understand that he was an old man, not smart enough, or creative enough, to catch the bastard?

"I'm an old man. Leave me alone and find someone else to bother." Dubric closed his eyes, growled his anguish, and threw himself back onto the bed.

His ghosts, however, remained.

* * *

Nella sat between a chattering pair of privy maids and a nervous group of old women and felt utterly alone. She had always enjoyed the company of her friends during meals, but tonight they were gone and no one at the crowded table talked to her. She wondered if it was because they didn't know or like her, because they were either shy or standoffish, or if it was because Risley stood behind her and watched the crowd.

As much as she hated to admit it, even to herself, she'd have waged money on it being Risley. If he wasn't there, the privy maids would be commenting about her at least.

She sighed and forced down another spoonful of porridge. If he would sit she could talk to him, but no, he had to watch over her. He had to stand and not eat. Goddess, didn't he realize no one was going to bother her in a crowded—

"Stop there," Risley said, and she almost dropped her spoon.

"I've got work for your girlie," a grumbling man's voice said. She turned to smile at a villager named Inek. He stood an arm's reach from Risley, with his glittering eyes focused on the sword. "I'm not looking for trouble, Nell, but I went to your room first—"

"Excuse me?" Risley said as he leaned forward, his

fingers flipping loose the strap over the hilt of his sword.

Nella wiped her mouth and stood. "It's all right. I patch the knees in his trousers. Two pair a phase for an eighth crown."

Inek nodded. "My woman left a while back and I need someone to patch my clothes. Nell here needs money. It's a fair swap."

Risley grimaced. Nella was sure he could smell the reek of unwashed skin every bit as much as she could, and she was thankful Risley's hand moved away from the sword. "I'd be happy to patch them for you," she said with a relieved smile. "Did you bring them here or leave them at my room?"

"Damn, woman, of course I brought them with me." Inek thrust a ragged, burlap sack tied with twine at her. "Last two pairs of trousers. Still have plenty of shirts. Then we can start on bedding."

Nella took the sack from him. "Thank you kindly. I should have them finished tomorrow."

"Thanks, Nell." Inek winked his thanks and swaggered back into the crowd.

Risley turned to look at her. His mouth worked for a moment as he struggled not to voice whatever thought he did not want to say aloud. At last he sighed and said, "Go ahead and finish eating."

She returned to her meager meal. Beside her, a privy maid snickered and resumed her gleeful gossip.

CHAPTER

9

✝

Dubric did not move when he heard the knock on his door. He merely blinked at his reflection in the faintly glowing mirror and sighed. "It is open," he called out.

Far behind him, Dien opened the door and light spilled into the otherwise dark room. "Sir?" he said. "We're almost ready to start patrols."

"All right. I will be in my office in a few minutes," Dubric said. Long since having given up on sleep, he sat—fully clothed and ready to work, no less—on a chair before a tall oval mirror. Its oak frame was old and chipped and the silver had flaked off the back of the glass in several places. Despite the age, and the wear and tear, the mirror still worked fine. *Just like me,* he thought with a slight, sad smile. Nuobir had made the mirror as an experiment when they were still in University, before the death and blood of the war had overrun their lives. He had created it as a way of keeping in touch with far-flung friends and relatives. You merely had to gaze into the mirror and hold something that belonged to the person you wanted to see. The mirror would show you where they were and what they were doing.

Nuobir had intended the mirror to be used for good;

to check on aged and ailing family, make certain everything was all right at home, or be sure the children were safe while out playing. But life was never simple, and good ideas did not always achieve their potential. Days after its creation, the news of the mirror had spread across Waterford and visitors to Nuobir's workshop were not the least bit interested in seeing Grandma gnaw her mashed tubers to goo or a child study for exams. Oh no. Folks wanted to spy on the secret, sordid details of their lives. Was the innocent daughter remaining virginal while being courted by Sir So-and-So? Was the husband out gambling or whoring? Was the sweet little wife stealing money from the sock under the bed?

Less than a phase after its creation, Nuobir announced at Council he had smashed the mirror. Destroyed it and all the sick desires along with it. Nuobir had never been one for folly and evil indulgence. He had also been a hesitant and terrible liar. Dubric sighed. *I miss you, old friend,* he thought.

Dien entered the suite, his shadow reaching forward as if to draw Dubric into the light. "Are you all right, sir?"

"I am fine," Dubric replied. "Just visiting with my memories." He stood and looked at the mirror one last time, Oriana's shining silver dagger still clutched in his hand. The reflection of Oriana stood beside his chair, her rich dark hair loose and flowing down the back of her bard's doublet. She was young and sweet, forever untouched by the ravages of age. For a few moments he had felt her fingers along his scarred cheeks, smelled her delicate perfume, and he had wept with joy. He missed her so. If only he had been cursed before her death, he could see all of her he wanted. If only she had never died at all.

Dien's faintly glowing reflection nodded. "How is she, sir?"

"Still waiting for me." Dubric touched the glowing surface. Oriana smiled and seemed to nuzzle into his palm, and he could imagine her warmth against the cool glass. He almost added that she scared away the ghosts, but he held his tongue instead. Dien worried enough over the occasional indulgence of the mirror and dagger without adding bothersome ghosts to his headaches.

As if on cue, Dien said, "Sir, you are still being careful with that damned thing, aren't you?" His eyes were narrow and watchful. Suspicious. Dien had never touched a Mage Killer's dagger; few men had. An understandable phobia.

Dubric said, "It is merely a dagger, after all. It will not harm me if I am careful. Even if I am not, what difference would it make now?" He looked one last time at his beloved Oriana, then put the dagger in its sheath before he did hurt himself. Mage Killer's daggers were dangerous to men, even dried up old buzzards like him. The slightest attack, a threatening twist, even scraping mud off boots would forever unman the strongest and fiercest of men. Although Dubric had not lain with a woman since Oriana's death, he had no desire to lose the ability. He always handled the dagger with reverence and respect.

Sighing at the return of the ghosts, he glanced at Dien, covered the mirror, and placed the dagger carefully in its drawer.

"I heard Inek was in the castle, sir. Caused a bit of a stir at supper by talking to Risley's girl, but he and Risley didn't come to blows. After that, he apparently left. Shall I have him watched again tonight?"

"No. We cannot afford to waste the men." Dubric

closed the drawer and turned back to Dien. "Are there any other developments this evening?"

Dien flipped open his notebook. "The lads have finished their research and they're waiting in your office. We've got every common exit guarded, and all entrances to the servants' wing. All unnecessary exits from the castle have been locked and barred. With luck, the staff will sleep soundly tonight."

Dien paused and took a breath as if he were reluctant to continue. "The only bug in the works, so far, is our resident troublemaker."

Dubric sighed and grabbed his cloak. "What has Risley done now?"

"The bastard's camped out in the middle of the female servants' wing, sitting on the floor with his sword across his lap. Insists he's not moving. Half the girls are hiding, the other half are furious, sir."

"At Nella Brickerman's room?"

"Yes, sir."

It was not surprising. "Tell him his writ does not allow him to lurk around the women's quarters like a lecher, then drag him to my office."

"Yes, sir." Dien turned and left.

Dubric departed a few moments later.

* * *

"You found nothing?" Dubric leaned back in his chair and rubbed his eyes. The ghosts had taken to wandering around the room instead of languishing in one place. Elli's ghost had started tugging at her own hair, while Fytte's pleaded incessantly. Dubric struggled to keep his attention on the boys.

Otlee shook his head and glanced at Lars before looking at his notes. "Sorry, sir, but we even went through books in the restricted section. We found no medical, or magical, connection between kidneys and hair. Nothing. But I did find something that might explain how no one is seeing him."

While Dubric waited, Otlee flipped through his notes. "There are conditions—two, actually—that I've found so far, that might explain . . ." He paused, searching the notes. "Dysodermneurpytis is my best guess, sir, but it could be a stelan-seula."

Dubric forced his hands open, suddenly aware he had clenched them together. "Let us hope it is not Wraith Rot," he said, his fists clenching again, "and the other is . . . unthinkable."

"I really don't think it's a soul-stealer, sir," Otlee said, referring to his notes again. "Surely no one here has been exposed to one. Besides, without a mage to control the remains, they'd be little more than a breathing husk. But Wraith Rot is a slight possibility. If the person in question had been to particular quarantined areas and happened to pick it up."

"What is Wraith Rot, sir?" Lars asked, frowning.

Dubric rubbed his aching eyes. "A highly contagious disease where the body and mind rot away, turning the victim into little more than haze."

"So they become a wraith," Lars said, shuddering.

"But it's not a sudden change," Otlee chirped in, running his finger down his notes. "Symptoms start with headaches and nervousness, then excitability and aggression, even memory loss and dementia. Then their skin develops sores and starts disappearing, they lose weight, and their teeth fall out. It can take moons for the rot to become permanent, and the victim might not even know what's happening to them until they're vaporous all the time. But by then it's too late to treat. I can go get the book, if you're interested. Fascinating stuff!"

"That is not necessary," Dubric said. "I have seen the effects personally. As for the other option, there are no stelan-seula beasts in Lagiern. We killed them all, decades ago."

"Yes, sir," Otlee said. "That's why I don't think it's a soul-stealer. But it's probably not Wraith Rot, either, just a remote possibility."

Dubric wrote in his notebook, struggling to keep his tired hands steady. "Nice job. What else have you found?"

Lars pointed to a map-sized piece of parchment on his lap. "We've found a few similarities between the girls, too. They're minor, but . . ," he shrugged and moved his fingers across the paper. "Not only are they commoners, but they have no other family here at the castle, no reachable next of kin. Elli Cunliffe was the only definite orphan, but the others might as well have been. All were born commoners as far as we can tell. Their ages are similar, but they're all unmarried servant girls, so this is likely coincidence. They had reputations as having loose morals. According to their supervisors, all were mild disciplinary problems, but not enough trouble to ever get fired or reassigned. They weren't shining members of the staff, but weren't the worst, either. The biggest consistency, though, was that all were found near places where they worked. Why were all but one found outside? That's what I'd like to know."

Beside him Otlee nodded. "That and why does no one seem to care about them? I mean, please excuse me, sir, but I'd think someone would be upset. Surely. The castle as a whole seems angry over the murders, but not individual people. Someone has to care about these girls."

"I am certain someone does, Otlee," Dubric said. "But folks are upset, scared, and afraid to draw attention to themselves. Sometimes it is easier to relish your own grief than to share it with everyone else."

"Witnesses don't like to come forward on their own," Lars said. "We usually have to drag information out of them."

Otlee was about to ask a question when a ruckus erupted in the previously silent outer office. Something slammed hard against the wall and both boys turned their attention to the door. Fytte and Elli turned, too. Dubric almost groaned. Ghosts paying attention. What next? A quilting bee?

"Get your filthy hands off me!" Risley said as clear as day.

"Quit your bellyaching!" Dien replied, and the door burst open. "Get your sorry ass in there!"

Risley stumbled into Dubric's office with his hands tied in front of him. His clothes hung askew and his hair had plastered to his sweaty brow. Despite being tossed through the door like a pail of discarded dishwater, his demeanor remained controlled and haughty. He had a bruise and a scrape on one cheek and ice flashing in his eyes. "Your goon here threatened me," he said calmly to Dubric. "I'd like to lodge a formal complaint."

"Complaint my pimpled ass," Dien replied through puffy, bleeding lips as he lumbered in. The knuckles on one hand had split open and blood spattered his shirt. "I found you loitering in a restricted area with a restricted weapon in plain view. You're lucky I didn't toss you in gaol and forget you ever existed." Dien dropped Risley's sword and scabbard on the desk, then pulled three daggers from his pockets. "Pretty boy here was armed to the teeth."

Risley smiled at Dien. "I have a writ."

Dien growled low in his throat and pushed Risley's chest with one thick finger, towering over the young lord. "*Had* a writ. Girly peepers don't get to have writs."

Dubric stood. "That's enough!" He stared at Risley and said, "I warned you to stay out of this. I do not want to throw you in gaol, but if you do not cease, and I mean cease right now, I will—"

"Ha! You don't have the mettle to challenge this. I've got another writ. And another and another. You're not going to stop me from protecting her. If you try again, I'll personally drag your carcass in front of the full Lord's Council and have you brought up on charges of treason."

Treason? Dubric considered, though his face remained emotionless. *How in the seven hells could he accuse me of treason? I am not threatening national security or the safety of the King's family or officially protec—It must be the girl, the damned girl!* He frowned and said, "Tunek will never allow you to do this."

"My grandfather's opinion does not matter, not this time. I've already sent word to my da and I filed the preliminary petition myself two moons ago. My da sanctioned their approval. Now untie me before I get really ticked."

If anyone knew how to get around the King, Kylton Romlin did. If he had been helping Risley, there was no limit to how far this could go. "How did you manage to have a Pyrinnian commoner placed under royal protection?"

Risley leaned forward, "You don't get it, do you? Once she's finished with the damned debt, I intend to court her. Publicly. At least until she figures out she can do far better than me or sends me packing. Either way, it's up to her, not you."

Dubric still could not believe what he was hearing. Risley had professed to being in love, but this was ridiculous. "You have really filed to have her listed at court? A *commoner*?"

"Filed and received. My initial petition and her tentative approval for court status should arrive here in a couple of days. Until that time, I'd like to commandeer a member of your *elite security staff* to aid me on my—"

Dubric's hands slashed out. "No. Absolutely not."

Behind Risley, Dien rolled his eyes and muttered, "This is frigging ridiculous."

Risley held out his bound hands and glanced at them as if to remind Dubric to untie them. "Want me to take over around here? I can do that, you know. Those writs allow more than weapon privileges, if need be."

Dubric yanked on the ropes around Risley's wrists. "I am short-staffed as it is. If you take one of my men, that leaves areas unwatched and puts the girls you are supposedly determined to protect in greater danger."

"Then I'll take Lars. I hear you've pulled him off night duty anyway."

"Me? Why me?" Lars stood and handed the piece of parchment to Otlee.

Risley turned to look at the boy. "I know you can handle yourself in a fight. I also know you don't quite trust me right now. From my position, that's an asset."

Lars stepped forward, his head shaking. "'An asset'? What the heck are you talking about now?"

Dubric had finished untying the ropes and Risley rubbed his wrists as he said to Lars, "I've traveled to a lot of places these past few summers, seen and done terrible things in the name of the King. Who's to say I haven't been touched with some dark magic? Been tainted somehow? Completely lost my senses? I know

I'm a suspect here, and I can understand that. I also know I haven't been the easiest person to deal with. Maybe it's my infatuation with Nella, maybe not, but if I'm to blame for any part of this, someone needs to stop me. Especially if I'm guarding the maids all day. What if I'm alone with one, even for a moment? I can't watch them alone. I can't take the chance."

He turned his attention to Dubric. "I'm innocent; I know it in my heart, but what if my heart is lying? For Goddess's sake, you saw what I did to that pitcher this afternoon, and I don't even remember doing it."

"Risley—" Dubric started.

Risley shook his head. "Even if you won't admit it, I'm a suspect, at least in your mind. You and Albin Darril were good friends, so you probably know that the sword can make someone dim. Not invisible, but hard to see."

Dubric hoped his face did not pale.

"It also can make them fast, *very* fast, and help them hear. Heartbeats, even, although I've never been able to hear those myself. I understand Albin was an amazing thief."

Dubric nodded. "He specialized in information and item retrieval."

"And assassination."

"Yes. He was very good at what he did." Under the dead of night, Albin had seemed to be little more than a ghost, a shadow. Fast, quiet, and deadly. Much like the killer stalking the castle.

Risley picked his sword off Dubric's desk and pulled it from the scabbard. The blade was shining and silver as if it glowed with light of its own. "And this blade is not always what it seems." Risley glided his fingers over a bluish gem at the side of the pommel and the blade wavered, then shrank. Smaller and smaller it became, until it disappeared into the hilt completely. Behind Risley, Lars, Otlee, and Dien gasped. Dubric alone nodded.

"All of Nuobir's swords do that, Risley. Even mine. It made them easier to conceal."

Risley twirled the hilt in his hands. "I'd heard that." He glanced at Lars and returned his attention to Dubric. "If I am doing this, somehow, and not remembering, someone needs to watch me. Hells, sometimes I don't trust myself these days. I can't sleep, my head pounds incessantly . . . But I need to protect Nella. Whether it's me or not."

Crossing his arms over his chest, Dien said with a grin, "The solution's easy. We lock you up for a couple of days."

"No. I can't protect her if I'm locked up."

Dubric sat in his chair and rubbed his eyes. The ghosts wandered around the room, not the least bit concerned with either Risley or his sword, but that didn't surprise him. They hadn't been interested in, or afraid of, anyone. "Is this why you've made such a public spectacle of yourself?"

Risley nodded. "If everyone is watching me, I'm not going to hurt anyone."

"I do not know what you expect me to do about it."

Risley dropped the hilt on Dubric's desk and leaned forward. "I want her safety guaranteed."

"I cannot guarantee anyone's—"

"Bull piss. I'll turn in this sword, right here and now, if you can guarantee me she'll be watched all night by someone you trust. Like the big bully behind me, perhaps?"

Dien growled. "Watch the insults. I outweigh you by a good three stone and can snap you in two without breaking a sweat."

Dubric glanced a warning at Dien. "I do not have the manpower to dedicate to one girl. We are stretched thin already and can barely cover the castle as it is."

"Either I sit outside her door or someone you consider trustworthy does. This is not negotiable."

"How about we lock both you and your little whore up?" Dien asked. "That should satisfy your frigging demands."

Risley spun with staggering speed. Before Dubric could stand, before Otlee had burst from his chair or Lars had turned and drawn his sword, Risley had grabbed and slammed Dien against the back wall. "You can say what you want about me, but never, ever, about her," Risley said, his voice low and even.

Dien looked at Risley, and his puffy lip curled in a sneer. Even held against the wall he loomed immense and threatening, dwarfing the man holding him. "Your rank means squat to me. Your family even less. You hear?"

"Perfectly."

Dubric hurried around his desk. "Risley, release him!"

Risley loosened his grip and Dien dropped to his feet and straightened his tunic. "Uppity bastard. Think you can—"

"Dien! That is enough." Dubric stood between them and glared at Dien before turning his attention to Risley. "Fine. You could indeed be a suspect and I can agree to protect Nella. I will personally guarantee her safety and I will keep the sword. Now get out of here before you cause more trouble."

Risley bowed slightly. "And I get full use of Lars during the day."

Dien stepped forward, but the movement of

Dubric's hand stopped him. "He is all yours for the next few days."

Risley nodded his agreement to the terms, then said to Lars, "Nella's shift starts at six bell. I expect to see you around five so we can escort them to breakfast."

Sheathing his sword, Lars mumbled, "I'll be there."

Risley left the office, closing the door behind him.

"Excuse me, sir," Dien said as he raked his hands through his short hair, "but what in the Seven Hells of Vartek just happened?"

Dubric frowned at the door. "He is the King's grandson; you have to remember that."

Dien grumbled low in his throat. "A spoiled pain-in-the-ass pup is what he is. Threatening to cause trouble and prancing around with his nose in the air."

Dubric ignored the last comment. "He is also the Lord Apparent of Haenpar. Personally, I would rather stay on the good side of both King Tunkek and Lord Romlin, if it is all the same to you. I certainly do not want to go to war over the safety of a linen maid."

Dien grumbled again and fell into his chair. "But, sir, we can't have folks boss us around like that. Besides, even though Lord Risley's an oozing pustule on a goat's ass, surely he wouldn't start a war over—"

"It's doubtful, but not impossible," Lars said and looked between the two men. "His father almost sent the whole country into a civil war to marry Lady Heather, remember? If he's serious about Nella, there's no telling what he might do."

"She is just the infatuation of the phase," Dubric said to reassure himself as he sat on the edge of his desk, "and he is jealously guarding her, like any spoiled child with a new toy."

"But this child has the ear of the King," Lars said.

He looked at Dien as he sat again. "And the Haenparan Army winters at the manor. Nearly a thousand men. He could have them here in a couple of days if we angered him enough."

Dien grimaced. "All right, I see your point. But dammit all, we can't let the bastard come in here and give orders."

Otlee cleared his throat. "I don't understand all the politics involved, but didn't Lord Risley say someone should watch him? He is still a suspect. I know his name's on the list. And since the murders seem to be happening at night, shouldn't someone watch him all night?" He looked at Lars as if seeking approval. "Whether he's causing trouble or not. Right?"

Lars laughed and stood. "Find someone else for that one. I'm already following him starting at five bell."

Dien rolled his eyes and leaned back, rocking the chair onto two legs. "Great. Just great."

"Who are we going to assign to guard Nella?" Dubric asked.

"How about Flavin?" Lars offered.

Dubric shook his head. "An unmarried man alone in the female servants' hall? I am not willing to upset half the staff just to appease Risley."

"I could do it," Otlee said.

"What about Bacstair or Meiks?" Dien offered. "Or maybe Werian?"

"Any of the three would be fine, but with you on the third floor, that only leaves five men besides myself to watch over the whole castle and assure the trustworthiness of tonight's volunteers."

"Aw, dammit all to the seven hells," Dien said, crossing his arms over his wide chest. "You're sticking me with the bastard."

"I could do it," Otlee said again.

Lars said, "If it's going to be someone we trust, it has to be one of the five, and only Bacstair, Meiks, and Werian are married."

Dubric grabbed the night's assignment list. "All right. If we move Bacstair to Nella's room and have Werian—"

Otlee put his narrow hands on Dubric's desk and said, "I can do it and you won't have to rearrange anything."

Dubric sighed. "Otlee, I know you want to help, but you have never served guard duty before."

"Neither did my father until last night. I've passed all my weapons classes, none of the girls are going to be upset with me hanging around, and besides, you've got guards assigned for both servants' entrances in case I have trouble."

"He's got a point," Lars said.

"You do not need to help," Dubric said.

Lars ruffled Otlee's hair. "C'mon, Dubric. It's not like he's gonna be in any danger or anything. Nella's not exactly a troublemaker or prone to wandering around the castle late at night, so he'll just be bored out of his mind and have sore feet."

Dien leaned his chair forward again. "Might be good for the boy to serve a duty shift, and it's not going to get much safer than guarding a roomful of sleeping girls. He'll be fine."

Dubric looked at Otlee's eagerness and thought of Bacstair's hope for his son. Despite the worry clenching his insides, he said, "Grab yourself a blanket and be sure and take your sword. You are guarding Miss Nella's door until dawn."

"Thanks!"

Dubric smiled at Otlee's exuberance. "Let us see

how excited you are in the morning, after the long night ahead of you. It is almost midnight and the girls will sleep until five bell or so. You should be quite bored. Just stay awake and do not let anyone through their door. No books. Pay attention." He rubbed his aching eyes. "Lars, go get some sleep. If today was any indication, Risley will keep you busy all day tomorrow.

"And you," he said to Dien, "pick a name off our roster for tonight and take him with you. If Risley wants to be watched, then watched he will be. Wake him at least four times, more if you are up to it, and search his entire suite at least twice. Seize any potentially incriminating evidence you find. Just try not to break him, all right?"

"Yeah, yeah," Dien grumbled as he took the sheet of names from Otlee.

"Maybe we could add Risley to tonight's roster instead of guarding him," Lars said.

Dien coughed. "If you think I'm going to stand for that arrogant bastard taking control and pretending he's in charge, you got your brains scrambled."

Dubric stood straight and stretched. "Risley causes enough problems on his own without us giving him explicit permission to throw his weight around. Even if he is innocent, he is not likely to follow orders and patrol his assigned area. We would spend half the night dragging him from the servants' wing."

Lars nodded reluctantly. "I see what you mean, but one night on patrol would exonerate him."

"Maybe," Dien said. "If he played nice and followed the rules. More frigging likely, though, he'd cause trouble or not be where he was assigned. We'd be no better off than we are now."

The midnight bell rang and Dubric walked around

his desk. "We have kicked a dead horse enough and it is time to get to work. Let us try to not let anyone get killed tonight, shall we?"

Everyone in the room nodded and a few moments later they hurried to their assigned posts.

As Dubric strode to his scheduled meeting with his partner, he tried to smile. One dozen men had been assigned to guard the castle and its people. Perhaps the night would pass without incident. Surely constant patrols would make any sane man think.

But Dubric doubted the killer was sane, and he doubted he would last the night without adding another damned ghost.

* * *

"Looks like Lord Sweetie isn't so sweet," Stef sniggered, yanking the tangles from her hair.

Dari snatched Stef's comb. "You complained, didn't you? Just can't leave anything alone, you jealous witch."

Stef shoved Dari, retrieving her comb. "Didn't you notice how he watched us all day? It's creepy."

"She's right," Plien said. She sat on her bed and smoothed herbal ointment on her face. "Not that I mind men hanging around, but with all that's going on, I'd rather not have some strange man lurking right outside my door."

"He's not strange or creepy," Nella said, pacing. "He's trying to protect us." She glanced at the door and chewed her lip. "I hope everything's all right."

Stef rolled her eyes and resumed combing. "He did it. He killed those girls. That's why Dubric's squire hauled him away."

Mirri lay curled on her bed with her pillow clutched

to her chest. "I don't wanna think Lord Risley hurt anyone. He followed us most of the day and if it's him . . ."
She shuddered.

"Someone did it," Stef snapped. "I bet it's Lord
Sweetie."

Dari yanked off her shoes and tossed them into the
corner. "This morning you thought it was Dubric."

Nella stopped pacing and her hands clenched. "It's
not Risley!"

Their door creaked open and all five girls gasped.
Ker slipped in with her face flushed and her hair disheveled. "Hey," she said, hurrying to her bed.

Stef tossed aside her comb. "Where have you
been?"

Ker shrugged and pulled off her uniform. "Nowhere."

Plien regarded her with an appraising smile. "You
naughty girl."

"Who was it?" Stef asked. "Anyone we'd know? You
put out?"

Ker blushed and shook her head, climbing into bed.

On the bunk below her, Mirri sighed and rolled
over. "Now Ker has a suitor. Why can't anyone notice
me? I'm going to die a spinster!"

While Stef teased and taunted Ker, Nella sat on her
bed and stared at the door, worrying about Risley and
wondering why he had been dragged away.

* * *

"That's the three bell. Let's go," Dien said to a coppersmith as he pushed away from the wall. Risley's
door had not moved during the past half bell and it was
time to spread some good cheer.

The coppersmith fidgeted with his sword, but Dien
didn't care. He stomped across the hall to Risley's door

and banged on it with the side of his fist. "Rise and shine!"

A groan, a *thud*, and footsteps before Risley yanked the door open. "Didn't you just leave?" he asked, yawning. Barefoot and nearly nude, he blinked blearily and trudged down the hall, shucking up his undershorts as he walked.

"It's time for another complete inspection," Dien said, walking through the open door.

Risley waved a hand in agreement. "Fine. Inspect away. I'm going to converse with my pillow, if you don't mind."

Dien heard a *fwupp* and looked through the open bedchamber door to see Risley lying facedown on the bed. "You, too. Full inspection."

Risley groaned and rolled to his feet, then stood beside the bed with his arms held wide. "When I volunteered to be guarded, I assumed I'd be asleep."

"Never assume anything. Let's see the teeth," Dien said.

Risley yawned, widely opening his mouth. Dien peered inside. Standard set of teeth with a few bits of pricey repairs. Sleepy breath with a hint of pipe smoke.

Dien stepped back and Risley asked, "You're not going to ask to look inside my shorts, are you?"

"Not if I have anything to say about it. Let's see the bottom of your feet." Dien saw nothing noteworthy there, either, so he turned Risley around. The same silvery scars marked Risley's back and arms, two his abdomen, and some were long enough to have warranted urgent medical attention.

Dien sighed and stepped away. Soles clean, scars healed, not a mark on him other than the last shadow of a shaving cut. Hands and fingernails clean. Damn, how much more innocent could he look?

"Can I go back to bed now?"

Dien glanced at his assistant, who strode forward to search the bed as he had five times before. "Nothing but sheets and blankets, sir."

"Enjoy your beauty sleep," Dien said. He checked Risley's closet and dressers—same stuff, different time of night—and left the bedchamber.

He and the coppersmith searched the remainder of the suite, the sitting room, library, bath chamber, and office. All rooms were cluttered but clean and he saw no blood or evidence of trouble. Dien sat at Risley's desk and looked through the drawers, again finding nothing unusual or suspect, but when the breeze from the open window blew a small pile of papers off the desk, he grinned.

On the doodle-covered blotter, partially hidden beneath loose sheets of parchment, lay a slim, leatherbound book. He opened the book and scanned the contents before handing it to the coppersmith. *Risley's ledger should prove interesting reading.* "This goes in the evidence bag," he said. "Go ahead and fetch a cup of tea. We'll do this again at four bell."

The coppersmith nodded and left the suite. Dien made a final circuit, then resumed his vigil across from the entrance door.

* * *

We might make it after all, Dubric thought. He walked through the courtyard in the quiet of predawn with a sleepy leather worker named Shartte. His ghosts still numbered five. There had been no alarms from the castle and few unauthorized people in the courtyard. All patrols and guards had kept to their schedule. Otlee had been awake at each check and Dien had reported no trouble from Risley. It had been a quiet and cold night, like it was supposed to be, and Dubric was thankful for the relief.

The five bell had not yet rung when the first lights in the castle flickered. Dubric smiled. People were rising, getting ready for work, and it had been a quiet night. A wonderfully quiet night. Praise the King.

* * *

"I don't care what Dubric told you, I have to go to work!" a raven-haired girl said, high color on her cheeks. Beside her, a plain, freckle-faced girl nodded. Both had darkly stained hands, and filthy, dye-covered aprons.

The guards, Bacstair and a yawning weaver, both glanced at the sheet of instructions Dubric had given them. "Miss . . . uh . . ." Bacstair said, his tongue fumbling.

"'Miss'? That's right. Miss one more day and I'm fired," she said with a flick of her black hair. "I've been sick fer a phase, women trouble, you see, and if I don't get the dye vats ready before Glis gets there I'm outta work!"

"Glis don't put up with no dingling," the freckled girl said earnestly.

"Only certain folks are allowed to leave the servants' wing before five bell," Bacstair said and pointed to the paper. "I have my orders."

"We're just going over there!" the black-haired girl whined as she pointed down the back hall. "We work with the weavers. Dyeing cloth. And if I don't have those vats ready by the time Glis gets there—"

"I understand what you're telling me," Bacstair said. "But my orders are my orders."

The freckled girl grinned at the weaver and giggled and poked him in the ribs with her elbow. "Tell him, Molur. Tell him we just work down the hall."

"They do, I knows that fer a fact." He swallowed and looked at the girls. "They're dyers, like they said. And Glis can be a real bastard when folks is late or if'n they mess up a color."

"See, what'd I tell you?" the first girl said.

"You know these girls?" Bacstair asked.

Molur licked his lips as his face reddened. "There's a dozen or so dyers, maybe twenty weavers. I don't know ever'one, sure as the seven hells ain't no time fer chitchat, but I've seen 'em dyein'. I know that."

Bacstair sighed and tried to read the instructions again. It all seemed like a pile of gibberish to him. Only a few words made any sense. He looked down a servants' hallway, the girls' hall, and saw Otlee standing fifty lengths or so away, not far from where the hall curved. The boy could read Dubric's paper, that was as certain as the coming sunrise. But his son was on guard duty and had been promoted. Even presented with a fine steel sword and given expensive official uniforms. Otlee was on the road·to nobility, and Bacstair would rather gouge out his own eyes than ruin Otlee's chances.

From his post, Otlee watched his father struggle with the paper and called out, "Father, do you want me to—"

Bacstair shook his head and pulled his gaze away from his son. He looked at both girls and straightened his shoulders. Might as well act official. "What are your names, please?"

The black-haired one smiled and looked him over. "Tis Cheyna. What's yours?"

"Bacstair," he muttered while he tried to write her name with the pencil Dubric had given him. The closest he could guess was "Shena."

Once he finished that struggle, he asked the other girl the same question.

"It's Claudette," she said with a giggle, her dye-stained hands coyly coming up to cover her plain face.

"Claudette," he muttered and forced "Claedect" onto the paper.

"You've got our names," Cheyna said with a knowing gleam in her eye. "What do you want us to do now?"

Claudette giggled again and batted her eyes. Molur grinned and winked at both girls. Bacstair did not notice a single thing except the marks on the paper. He pulled his attention from the gibberish he had written and said, "You're only going a few doors down the hall?"

"Um-hmm," Cheyna said. "To the dye room."

Bacstair looked down the hall and sighed. No one was nearby. The closest person he saw was the archer who had been patrolling the hall all night. He was far down, near the rectory wing, and moving farther away by the moment. "All right," Bacstair said, "but once you're there, stay put. Can you promise to do that?"

Cheyna nodded, Claudette giggled. "We'll do whatever you say," Cheyna replied with a wink.

Bacstair looked at the note one more time and returned his attention to Molur. "Walk them to the dye room and make sure they get inside safely."

"Sure thing," Molur said.

Bacstair watched the girls walk arm in arm down the hall and hoped he had done the right thing.

* * *

The door was close, fourth one on the right side, and Molur opened it and looked inside. Not a soul to be seen. Claudette sighed with relief. She had almost expected to see Glis waiting to catch them arriving late, or some fearsome stranger skulking in a corner. The room was dark and cold, empty except for the dye vats, drying racks, and kegs of dye powder. Nothing new, nothing exciting. Same old boring job.

"Let me get the light for you," Molur said and grabbed a torch from the hallway wall. While the girls followed close behind him, he lit the lamps within the room.

Claudette liked watching him walk. She liked watching all the decent-looking men walk, but Molur was especially nice. She giggled and had to cover her mouth with her hand so he wouldn't notice.

"Thank ye, kind sir," Cheyna whispered as she reached for the waistband of Molur's trousers.

Claudette's eyes narrowed for a moment, then relaxed. *Ah, what the peg*, she thought. *Cheyna was always willing to share.*

Molur sighed and pushed the hands away. "Sorry, but I can't. Dubric will have my ass, for sure."

Wish I could have it, just for a little while, Claudette thought, but instead she said, "Not to mention your wife," with a giggle in her voice. Married men were the best. They didn't want any more than a toss from time to time. Love 'em and leave 'em. No strings attached. She liked nothing better.

Molur shrugged and walked once around the room as his gaze darted into corners and under the vats. "She's not as smart as Dubric," he said with a grin.

Both girls sighed happily. There was hope after all. Cheyna said, "Maybe later, then."

Molur nodded and finished his tour of the room. He looked at the girls, touched his hat and winked. "Have a nice day, and I'll try to stop by for a sample later."

"We'll be waiting," Cheyna said.

Claudette giggled and smiled coyly.

As soon he left, Cheyna laughed out loud. "Men!

Just bat your eyes and they'll do almost anything for you."

Claudette agreed wholeheartedly, but they needed to stay focused and get to work before Glis came in. Playtime was over. "What do you think? Mix the red and yellow kegs first?" Orange was her favorite.

"Nah. Blue and yellow. Glis wanted us to start with green. Damn boring green."

Claudette sighed. Almost everything was dyed green. Stupid, boring, Faldorrahn-green. With a grunt, she pried the lid off the keg marked YELLOW, while Cheyna kicked a few hunks of wood under a vat. Claudette scooped out a can full of acrid yellow powder, poured it into the vat, and tapped the lid back on the keg. That done, she turned to the keg marked BLUE.

Cheyna poured a sack of soda into the water. "You hungry?" she asked.

Claudette shrugged. She was always hungry.

Cheyna pulled a huge, flat stick from the rack along the back wall. "Why don't you grab us a couple of quick breads or something? I can keep it stirred by myself for a while."

"Sure it will be all right?"

"Yeah. It's morning, and only what, fifteen lengths or so to the great-hall doors. Everything's guarded. We'll be fine."

Cheyna was right. There was nothing to worry about. Claudette grinned as she thought of another bonus. "Maybe I'll blow a kiss at Molur while I'm out there."

Cheyna laughed. "You've always liked Molur."

"He don't knock me around when he's done. And he's nice-looking, too." Claudette flashed a cheery smile and scurried out to the hall.

Before Bacstair could holler to stop her, she ran to the great-hall entrance and slipped through. A few people ate their breakfast, milkmaids and scullery maids mostly, and no one seemed to notice her. Sneaking to the front of the line, she grabbed a pair of muffins and half a loaf of bread, then scurried back to the hall, ignoring the disgruntled griping and muttered curses.

"Just grabbed us some breakfast!" she called out to Bacstair, and whatever he said in reply was lost to the sound of her munching. The muffin was a wee bit dry and the crust crunchy, but the flavor fine. Applesauce. Her favorite. She kicked open the door to the dye room with one foot and slipped inside.

Cheyna was nowhere to be seen and the paddle lay in a wet puddle on the floor beside the vat. Something stank, like gassy farts or rotten . . .

Claudette swallowed her bite of muffin before she puked it out instead. "Cheyna? Where are you?"

No answer.

Her heart leapt to her throat. "Quit joking around. This isn't funny, you know." Hands full of baked goods, Claudette circled the room much as Molur had. On the far side of their vat she stopped, her mouth working and her hands shaking. The bread and muffins fell at her feet and crumbled. For a moment, her vision blurred and she thought she would faint.

Dark red blood splattered the dye kegs, flowed along the floor toward the vat, and hissed in the fire. The stink was sickly sweet and repulsive. A curved chunk of raw and bleeding flesh lay on the floor near the middle of the blood and another lay not far beyond. *Oh, Cheyna!* Claudette tried to scream, but no sound came out. The lamps extinguished, one by one, plunging her into darkness. Her hands clutched at her face and her mind demanded that she *Move, dammit, move now!* but the signal somehow got misplaced and it took a few precious moments for her feet to get the message. A scream fluttering in her throat, she finally scrambled back and stumbled for the door, tracking blood with each step she took. *That Bacstair guy, he had a sword, and so did Molur. I'll be safe there*, she thought, *safe with—*

Something yanked at her hair, dragged her back toward the vat, and Claudette never had another thought. Or time to scream.

•

CHAPTER

10

Dubric considered making a detour to the kitchen, grabbing a spot of hot tea, and finishing patrols. The night was almost done, no one had died, and all the sentries remained on schedule.

"No," he muttered, wincing at the image forming in front of him.

Behind him, Shartte said, "What was that, sir?"

"Nothing." Dubric took a deep breath and stomped toward the castle as the five bell rang. Before he reached the main doors, both the sixth and seventh ghosts had joined the party.

Where the seven hells do I look? he thought. *Who are they? Where are they?* He trudged through the great hall while the early morning workers, including a few tight clusters of milkmaids and scullery maids, watched him with mixtures of alarm and wicked curiosity. He dared not look at the ghosts long, not with Shartte dogging his heels and people staring, but he had noticed that the girls were filthy, with their skin stained dark in patches, and wore lowly uniforms of unskilled, unschooled labor. Privy maids? Clay mixers? Wool dyers? Metal polishers? Barrel greasers? Manure spread—

"Sir?" Shartte asked, nearly startling Dubric out of

his skin. "Is something wrong? Is there something you need me to do?"

Dubric deliberately relaxed his jaw. "No, of course not. It has merely been a long night."

"Aye, sir," Shartte replied.

The five bell rang and most of the workers in the great hall stood, scurrying to their jobs and walking through the ghosts. A few shuddered and drew their wrappers close, but most hurried toward the back hall without a second glance. Dubric and his ghosts followed them.

He reached the back hall and watched the workers separate into groups heading to work. A few new arrivals stumbled from the servants' wing on their way to breakfast. Dubric leaned against the wall, out of the way, while his heart pounded and the ghosts shimmered near the edges of his vision.

Shartte, thankfully, stood beside him and remained silent.

Supervisors walked past, some from the servants' wing, some from their own rooms upstairs, and no one paid him any undue notice. The castle came alive around him and he wondered where the bodies could be. Inside, outside, upstairs, the main floor, or in the bowels and catacombs beneath? Lowly workers labored everywhere in all kinds of weather. Since their ghosts had appeared only moments apart, he knew both were likely killed in the same place, wherever that may be. But where, dammit, where?

A few minutes later, Lars and Risley walked down the main stairs. Dubric eyed Risley carefully, noting his immaculately pressed linen shirt, Haenparan-blue jacket, black trousers, and flowing cloak, as well as boots that had been polished to a sparkling shine. His hair was freshly combed and his hands were clean. All in all, a perfect image of a young lord about to take a public stroll. Dubric frowned. Wherever Risley had been during the past half bell, skulking around outdoors seemed doubtful. Risley gave Dubric a cordial nod, while Lars raised a single questioning eyebrow.

Casually looking away from the pair, Dubric scratched the corner of his mouth, signaling Lars that they would talk soon. Both disappeared into the ever increasing flood coming from the servants' wing.

Yawning, Otlee exited a short time later amid a rush of linen and floor maids. Dubric motioned him over. "Stay with me. I may need you."

"Yes, sir," Otlee said, stifling a yawn.

"Any incidents last night?"

"No, sir. Not for me, anyway." The boy paused and lowered his head. "My father had a problem, though. I think he had trouble reading your instructions."

Dubric felt a quick pang of guilt for putting an unschooled man through such a demeaning ordeal, but with Dien relocated to Risley's suite . . . He shook his head, dismissing it. "What sort of problem?"

Otlee yawned against the back of his hand. "Couple of girls wanted to go to work early, I think, but since they weren't milkmaids or scullery maids, he didn't want to let them through. Evidently he found their names on the list, so it turned out all right."

Dubric's heart skipped a beat. There were few female staff members on the early-workers list. "What time was this?"

"Gosh, I dunno, sir, maybe quarter before five bell."

Dubric closed his eyes and opened them slowly, hoping Otlee did not hear the urgency in his voice. "Did you happen to notice who the girls were or where they worked?"

"Sure. They walked right by me. They were dyers, but I didn't get their names."

Dubric turned to the left and hurried down the hall, Otlee and Shartte on his heels.

The door to the dyer's workroom stood ajar, offering a narrow shaft of dark shadows to peer through and a low fire crackling beneath a vat on the far side of the room. When he had walked past during his patrol, this very door, like the others along the hall, had been closed. "Get your father," Dubric said, pulling his sword, "and whoever was assigned to help him."

Otlee swallowed, backed a step away, then turned and ran.

"Oh, Goddess. Oh, good gracious," Shartte babbled.

"Quiet," Dubric snapped, his voice just a whisper. "Arm yourself and button your lip."

Shartte's voice and hands shook as he yanked the sword free. "Yessir, whatever you say, sir. I certainly will—"

"Shh!"

Otlee appeared at Dubric's elbow with Bacstair and Molur behind him. Both men remained silent, their faces the color of Bacstair's dough.

"Someone fetch me a light," Dubric said. "Otlee, you come with me. The rest of you, no one except Otlee and I comes through this door, in or out, under any circumstances. Do you understand?"

"Yessir," they replied, and Bacstair seemed to waver a moment, anguish and guilt vying for control of his face.

Dubric looked away from the three men and gave Otlee a reassuring smile. He opened the door, noting that the outer latch appeared clean.

Otlee lit the nearest light while Dubric walked slowly into the room. "Sir? We have blood here."

Dubric breathed in the scene, smelling the acrid tang of dye mixed with the sweetly metallic scent of fresh blood. "On the door or the floor?"

"Just the latch, sir."

This is the second time he has left a bloody latch. He does not bother to wipe his hands before leaving. Why? Was he not afraid his bloody hands would be noticed? "Can you lock it?"

"Sure." He heard a *click*, then the light shifted as Otlee came to stand beside him again, the lantern clutched in his hand. "Pushed it up with my pencil, and I didn't leave any marks."

"Good job. What do you notice? What do you see?"

"The smell, mostly. Doesn't smell like the others."

"That is the dye. Anything else?"

"Not yet, sir. They're not out in the open like the others."

Smart boy. Very insightful. "No, they are not. Why do you think that is?"

Otlee glanced behind him, nodding toward the door. "Because he left it unlocked on purpose, didn't he? In case someone came in. He'd know about them before they knew about *him*."

Dubric nodded. *That is why they appeared a short time apart. He killed one while waiting for the other.* "Are you ready?"

"Of course I am, sir."

Together they walked toward the huge vat, pausing at the scattered pile of baked goods beside smeared footprints that tracked into a puddle of blood. Dubric knelt beside them and began his notes. "Why are the prints bloody, yet walking into it?"

Otlee knelt as well, his knees less than a hand's width from the nearest print. "They're small and without shoes. Our killer has bigger feet and wears boots, so maybe the second girl tried to back away?"

"That is my guess, as well."

"How did you learn all these things, sir?"

Dubric grunted as he stood. "Trial and error. And more investigations than I care to count."

They walked around the puddle, noting each footprint and smear. A slab of flesh lay on the far side of the vat, near the eviscerated corpse of one dyer. She sprawled faceup on the floor with her head and right arm sizzling in the fire, her belly open, and her entrails lying over her left arm.

Sighing, Dubric pulled her from the fire and knelt beside her. He measured the gash across her abdomen, reading each measurement aloud while Otlee noted the information. Wincing at the burnt flesh, he pulled open her mouth and her charred cheek ripped apart. "Her gums are swollen but her back teeth have not appeared. Mark her age as around fifteen summers."

He continued his examination, moving downward from her head. "Possible bruising on her neck, but it may be a result of the fire. Blouse and apron cut open, right arm completely charred. Abdomen is dissected below the sternum and digestive organs removed, as are . . . What's this?"

Otlee remained silent as Dubric leaned close and probed her chest cavity. "Lobes of the lower lungs are missing. That is a new development. Heart remains intact and in place, but the aorta is mang— Ow!"

"Sir?"

Dubric pulled his hand from inside her chest and stared at the pointed strip of wood protruding from the back of his finger.

"How did that get in there, sir?"

"I do not know." Dubric pulled the sliver from his hand and leaned over the corpse again. Slowly, he reached in, mimicking his previous movement. The back of his hand rubbed against the sternum and ribcage. "I believe it was stuck against the back of the sternum, above the lower heart, unless it was already attached to me somehow. Make a note to have Rolle split her rib cage. I want to see where the sliver came from."

"Yes, sir."

Dubric turned the splinter in the light. About as long as his thumbnail and varnished on one side, the wood was coated with blood. *At last a clue! Is it oak? Maple? An exotic and traceable wood? Could it have come from the killer's hands or his clothing? Is it a clue to where he works or where he lives?* Dubric looked around the dyer's shop, at the wooden racks, the wooden paddles, shelving, and sticks. Some were varnished, some were not, but everything showed evidence of wear and splintering. *Hells, did it get in there when he dragged her to the fire?*

Once the sliver was safely tucked away, he finished examining the dyer but found nothing more of note. He stood, brushed off his hands and walked around the vat, looking for the second girl.

He found her propped in the far corner with her legs splayed out and her intestines lying on her lap. She had been cut open from her sternum to her pelvis. The flesh from her left thigh was gone, cut from the bone, and both arms were missing.

"Where is the rest of her, sir?"

Dubric walked around the vat and looked inside. The green fluid had a brownish scum on its surface. "I want this drained."

"Yes, sir." Otlee knelt before the sitting girl and sketched her position. Once finished, he started to stand, then tilted his head to the side as he knelt again. "I think I see something, sir."

Dubric leaned over, squinting to peer beneath a set of shelving. A faint brownish smear marked the floor before it, and Dubric held his breath as Otlee reached under.

The boy winced, his face contorting into a slight grimace as he retrieved the hidden treasure. Blood coated his hand, oozing thickly between his fingers. "I think it's a piece of liver, sir, but I'm not quite confident on anatomy."

Dubric rummaged through his pockets, seeking a small sack. "You are correct. It is indeed part of a liver. What can you tell me about it? Nearly every clue has a story to tell."

Otlee turned the piece over in his hand. "Still kinda warm. And it's been cut, not torn, except for . . . Horse piss! Sir!"

Dubric looked up at the horror on Otlee's face as the boy backed away, holding the bit of liver like an offering. "What? Otlee! Are you hurt?"

Gasping, Otlee stopped his retreat and stared at the dripping hunk of meat in his hand. "It's bitten, sir! He took a bite of her . . . of her . . ."

"Shh, now. Calm down." Carefully, Dubric took the piece from Otlee's hand, examining the marks along the shortest side. *Teeth, no doubt about it. What kind of monster eats people?*

Dubric reached into a pocket with his clean hand and retrieved his kerchief. "I believe your lessons are done for the time being. Fetch Rolle or Halld. Get their backsides out of bed, if need be."

"Sir, I'm sorry. It just startled me and won't happen again."

Dubric stared at the teeth marks while his stomach roiled in disgust. "No need to be sorry. You are doing a fine job." He paused and looked at Otlee. "Go get them. I will wait for you to return and we shall pick up where we left off. All right?"

"Yes, sir. Thank you, sir." Otlee bobbed a quick bow, then left the room, informing the outer guards of the change of plan before he closed the door again.

Dubric gently placed the bitten liver in his kerchief, taking care not to dislodge the bread crumbs adhering to the bitten side as he wrapped it. *The bastard made a sandwich.*

* * *

"The bastard never left, sir! I'm sure of it." Later that morning, Dien sat in the witness chair and banged his fist on the thick wooden armrest. "We woke him at four bell, checked the whole suite, checked *him* for good measure, then let him go back to bed. He sleeps in his underdrawers, and he sure as the seven hells wasn't armed at four bell, I can guarantee you that. By the time Lars got there, his lights were already burning and he had dressed. I tell you, he never left!"

Dubric shifted in his chair. "Lars admits he overslept. Not by much, maybe ten or twelve minutes. He didn't get there until almost quarter after five bell. That left Risley over a whole bell to—"

Dien shook his head. "He never left, sir. Not unless there's another way out. The damned door was in my sight the whole night except when we were inside. It never opened. Not once."

A knock rattled the door and, after Dubric's grunt,

Otlee peeked in. "We've found part of the second body in the vat," he said. "Rolle says the chewed liver came from her, and the flesh of her thigh is just gone. He says he needs to talk to you."

Dubric grunted his agreement and stood, shoving aside Risley's ledger and ship manifests Dien had seized for potential evidence. Between the records and the ghosts, he wondered if he would ever get a moment's rest again. "Dammit, Dien, who else can it be? Find someone to watch him. I do not care who, just do it! We have to solve this before other young women die!"

Dien stood. "Yes, sir. Whatever you say. But unless he's got a secret passage we don't know about, he's innocent."

"Someone is doing this. Whether it is Risley or not, I want to hear possible alternative suspects and solutions when I return." Grumbling, Dubric stomped from the office.

* * *

Lars stood beside Risley as they leaned against the wall near the storage closets of The Bitches. The screaming in Dubric's office had to be intense this morning, and Lars felt glad to be stuck on guard duty. Even with Risley. "You're in a world of trouble, you know," he said, shifting on his already aching feet.

Risley rubbed his forehead. "I'm getting used to it. Maybe you should have been on time."

Lars watched the plump girl, Mirri, gather an armload of blankets. "Would it have made a difference?"

"Maybe. Well, *probably* not. At least not to Dubric. He thinks it's me." Risley smiled at Nella. She carried a fresh armload of sheets into the room across the hall and flashed him a happy glance before she hurried inside. "But Nella still trusts me. Thank the Goddess for that."

Lars watched Nella flip a sheet over the bed, her fifteenth one of the morning. He hated to pry into personal matters, and he knew Risley's romantic interests were none of his business, but Dubric wanted answers, needed answers, about his primary suspect. Lars tried to sound nonchalant, no more than politely curious. He tilted his head toward Nella and asked, "So, what's really happening between you two? The rumors true?"

Risley laced and unlaced his fingers. "Depends on which ones you're talking about. Do we sneak away and rip off each other's clothes? No. Do I make her do unspeakable things for my pleasure? No. Is she bribing me, or me bribing her? No. Are we having a torrid love affair? No."

He paused and looked through the open door as Nella stuffed a pillow into its sham. "Is she affecting my judgment? Probably. Did I bring her here to keep track of her? Probably. Do I think about her every waking moment of my life? Yes." He smiled and said, "Definitely yes."

The quiet girl, whose name Lars hadn't caught, hesitated, then rushed to the storage closet and grabbed a stack of sheets before running away from them. After she was out of earshot, Lars said, "I suppose next you're going to tell me not only are the two of you not laying together, you've never touched her."

Risley glared at a passing nobleman, his hand falling to his sword. "I wish I could. Do you understand Pyrinnian debt?"

"Of course I do. Customs and laws of the neighboring

provinces are required reading. Dubric makes certain we know all their idiosyncrasies in case we have an official visit."

"Well, I didn't. I thought 'Customs Studies and Provincial Law' was a waste of time."

Lars nearly laughed. He could almost see Risley struggling to understand the oddities of Pyrinnian debt law. But he was on a fact-finding mission and needed to ask questions. "What happened?"

Risley frowned and he shifted his feet. "We'd been walking for two days when we came to the village. We hadn't eaten a thing except berries and the one rabbit I killed."

From what Lars had read about Pyrinn, fresh berries and rabbit would have been a feast. "So? You were hungry. What was the problem?"

"The problem was I bought us dinner at the inn. Nella asked me not to, but I bought it anyway. Two bowls of stew, a loaf of bread, and a bottle of really bad wine."

Lars turned to stare at him as the humor flipped to horror. Surely Risley was not that ignorant. "She asked you *not* to, but you bought dinner anyway?"

He nodded, shifting his weight again. "Yes. And a room."

Lars glanced at Nella and felt incredible sorrow for her. "How much did you spend?"

"Three, maybe four crown altogether. She wouldn't even look at me, and I had no idea why. As Malanna is my witness, I didn't know. I swear I didn't."

Lars's mouth had gone dry. "What happened?"

Risley smiled kindly at a maid's angry glower and waited until she had walked on. "When we got to the room, Nella . . ." he closed his eyes for a moment, then opened them again. "She . . . she insisted I call the debt."

Lars nodded, relieved. At least she had been willing and Risley hadn't raped her. "That was what she was supposed to do if she didn't have the coin right then. That's what the law required her to do. Private debts must be paid immediately, while debtors have three days to pay taxes and fees. She had no choice."

Risley looked at Lars. "I know that now, but when she started undoing her dress . . ." He paused to take a shaky breath. "I probably shouldn't be telling you this, you're too young to understand, but I was weak, Lars, for a moment I was weak, and I have never forgiven myself."

Lars looked at Nella and back to Risley. Something didn't make sense. If Risley had called the debt, surely Nella would hate him, not—

When Risley spoke and interrupted Lars's train of thought, his voice was soft and full of yearning. "I kissed her, and for a few blessed moments I held her in my arms before I regained my senses. It was the only time I've touched her improperly, just the once, no matter what anyone thinks."

But it made no sense. "You *kissed* her? What about the flesh debt?"

"I refused. She pleaded. Begged. Threatened me. Still, I refused." He laughed ruefully and shook his head as he watched her finish making the bed. "You have no idea how hard it was to refuse her, but I did."

Lars looked at Nella again and said, "But I thought debts had to be paid with flesh or life? She's obviously alive. By law she'd be required to take her own life if you refused her flesh."

"I know. But somehow in all that madness I convinced her that I could make her Faldorrahn, and she could pay her debt in coin later instead of immediate flesh or death. I thank the Goddess every day that she finally agreed."

Lars looked between them with new understanding. No wonder Nella trusted Risley. Not only had he refused to take her flesh, he had granted her life, as well. She would likely trust him forever, no matter what he did. Guilty or not.

"It sure is taking her a long time to pay you four crown," Lars said.

"I assumed it would be the original four crown. Nella, however, insisted on paying all of it back. Every penny I spent during our journey. Eighty-three crown and change altogether. Malanna's blood, Lars, I bought travel gear, horses, even clothing. But she didn't mention a thing about the full amount until my grandda insisted she pay me."

Lars whistled between his teeth, barely believing the sum. Surely it seemed an impossible amount to Nella. "No wonder she works all the time."

"Yes, but she only has a phase or so to go. Then we'll both be free of that damned debt."

"What then? Have you two talked about it?"

"No, not really. We're biding our time. Trying to play by the rules even though we're not quite sure what they are." He looked at Nella and bowed slightly, bringing a flush of pink to her cheeks as she walked to the next room. "But if she'll have me, I plan on taking her home, or anywhere else she wants to go."

Nella glanced back at Risley and their eyes locked for a moment. Lars recognized that look and he smiled. Despite what Dubric thought, Risley wasn't messing around with infatuation. Not this time. He was serious. And she was, too.

I think she'll have you, Ris, Lars thought. *Actually, I'm sure of it. I just hope she's not putting her faith in the wrong place.*

* * *

Not long after eight bell, Dubric heard a knock on his door. He yawned and scratched his belly, setting aside Oriana's dagger before answering the summons.

Lars stood in the hall, picking at the broken green seal on the note he carried. "You wanted to see me, sir?"

"Yes. Please come in."

Lars glanced at the mirror and tilted his head. "I've never seen it uncovered before, sir. Are you preparing for an official function I'm not aware of?"

Both my lads are observant, praise the King. Smiling, Dubric glanced back at the full-length mirror and felt a gentle tug at his heart. "No, no, nothing like that. Did you have any problems with Risley today?"

"No, sir. None at all." Lars accepted an offered chair and told Dubric of their conversation about Nella and the debt.

"Did you notice anything unusual about him? Anything out of place? Any changes from his usual self?"

Lars said, "It's probably nothing, but he seems absentminded. His suite door wasn't locked this afternoon and he's usually picky about things like that. And he was rather jittery. He fidgeted a lot, nervous tics, talking fast. It wasn't like he was worried or guilty, it was more like he had too much energy and nowhere for it to go. Like a high-strung horse.

"He had a headache, too, I think. He never mentioned it, but he often rubbed his forehead."

Dubric opened his notebook and noted the information. "Did he eat today?"

Startled, Lars leaned back in the chair and considered the question. "Now that you mention it, sir, I don't believe he did."

Dubric paused, his pencil trembling over the page. "Nothing? All day?"

"No, sir. We watched over Nella and her roommates through all three meals. I ate a couple of biscuits at lunch, then had a late dinner after Risley dismissed me, but I never saw him eat a single thing." He paused, closing his eyes for a moment while he thought. "He did have a drink, though, both of us did. Cider, during the afternoon."

"Did you see any blood? Any stains? Any potential evidence at all?"

"No, sir. I even made sure to look at the soles of his shoes. He was immaculately clean, top to bottom."

Once the lad had gone, Dubric returned to the mirror and Oriana while questions tumbled in his head.

* * *

By the time Nella crawled into bed that night, Risley had guarded the girls for that whole day and part of the one before. She lay awake for a while, shivering under her thin blankets and thinking about him. She knew her friends had reluctantly become accustomed to his presence, even if they still did not trust him. He seemed to be doing everything possible to ensure their safety, and surely the others would realize it soon. But, then again, he had been forbidden to guard them at night. She hadn't had a chance to ask him why, but he'd tell her if it was important. Wouldn't he?

She rolled over and looked toward the door. Of all the girls, Nella alone wondered why Otlee, instead of Risley, had been assigned to guard them while they slept. Dari had confidently insisted it was so Risley could get some sleep, but Nella was not so sure. She thought Otlee was an odd choice. He was only a child. Although none of the girls feared him, they had little faith in his ability to protect them. All six would lay awake for a time, listening, as the boy paced outside their door. The last one awake, Nella sighed quietly and worried about Risley. Sometime after the midnight bell, she, too, fell asleep.

Later, she had no idea when, Nella woke to Mirri's muffled crying. She sounded as if she were in pain.

"What's wrong?" Nella whispered through the dark. She wished Helgith would allow them a lantern so they could see, but phases ago Helgith had caught her sewing in the wee hours of the night and had taken the light away. Not long after, all but one of the lamps in the hall had been extinguished. Lamp oil had evidently become quite precious and most of the girls had become used to living in the dark. Mirri, however, was not one of them.

"Sick," Mirri answered. "My belly feels like someone is ripping it apart. I need to use the shitter, but it's death out there and I don't wanna go alone!"

Probably all that pork you ate at dinner, Nella thought. "I'll go with you." She yawned and slipped out from beneath her blanket.

"Nella, you *can't,*" Plien whispered from across the room. Normally the one to defy the rules and flaunt her independence, Plien had become increasingly paranoid as the murders continued. Before, it was a rare night for Plien to sleep in their room. Now she rarely left, much to Dari's aggravation.

"Yes, I can," Nella replied.

"But . . ."

Nella rose from the bed and found her shoes and cloak. "C'mon, Mirri. Let's go."

"She can go alone, or not go at all," Stef whispered. "Your sword-wielding lover's not here to escort us. Remember? Just the kid."

"She's got to go or she's going to mess the sheets, which will mean all of our hides once Helgith finds out." Nella's voice grew very hard. "She's not going alone."

"She's right," Ker grunted, yawning and getting out of bed herself.

Stef cursed under her breath. "You're crazy."

"No, I'm realistic," Nella said, helping Mirri to the door.

Plien and Dari crawled out of bed, too, and the five moved out to the hall.

Otlee almost jumped out of his skin when the door opened. "What the heck?" he gasped. "I thought you were all asleep! It's after three bell."

"She's sick," Nella said as she helped Mirri through the door. "We've got to go to the privies. Now."

Otlee nodded. "All right. I'm supposed to escort you." He held his head high as he led the odd procession down the servants' hall.

Holding her belly, Mirri whimpered, "I'm sorry."

Plien grumbled around a yawn, "Let's do this quick and get back to bed."

They had almost reached the outer door when they heard someone behind them. Like a terrified warren of rabbits, they turned, screams nearly escaping and Otlee pulling his sword, to see Stef scurrying up the hall.

"You dingle," Dari gasped, her hand over her heart. "You scared the breath outta us."

Stef crossed her arms over her narrow chest and rolled her eyes. "I'm not staying in that room alone."

"Then get with the group," Otlee said as he motioned her forward.

"So we're all together," Nella whispered.

They nodded to one another and stumbled into the night.

They had barely opened the doorway when a sword and a polearm were shoved into their faces. All of the girls gasped, almost screaming, as snow swirled into the hall. Otlee alone did not flinch.

Sheathing his sword, a guard snapped, "Where are you going?"

Tilting his head toward Mirri, Otlee said, "She's sick. So they're *all* going to the privy."

"Third group tonight," the other guard muttered.

The first guard glanced at Nella before looking back at Otlee. "Your group, eh? Want one of us to go with you?"

"I can handle this," Otlee said. "The privies aren't far away and the patrols are out. Shouldn't take more than a minute or two."

One guard said, "All right. The other two groups did fine all on their own. Stay together. Okay?"

The girls all set off, trembling, with Otlee guarding the rear. The night was black and swirling with blowing, falling snow. Nella wished it were Risley watching over them instead of Otlee, but at least he was armed and they weren't alone.

"I bet it's one of them," Stef whispered. "We're better off on our own out here."

"They're Dubric's guards," Nella said. "It's not one of them."

From behind her, Otlee said, "That was Olibe

Meiks and Caley Kirklan. Olibe's been on guard duty for days. You can trust him. And Caley—"

"Trust him, my ass. You can't trust anybody," Stef interrupted, squinting into the dark.

"I trust Risley. And Dubric. They're trying to protect us," Nella said. "You, too, Otlee."

Plien laughed. "Lord Risley isn't protecting us. He's tracking us. Like prey."

"No, he's not," Nella muttered.

"Yes, he is," Plien said. "He had his cheek scratched up, remember? Dubric knows he's guilty but is too old to do anything about it. I'll bet next wage day's money that your Lord Risley is a suspect. I heard they had him under guard last night. Tonight, too. Isn't that right, Otlee?"

Otlee said, "I'm not allowed to discuss who is and who is not on the suspect list. Or who is being guarded."

Nella refused to hear such nonsense. "Well, *I'm* sure he's innocent. Risley would never—"

Stef snickered. "I don't know why you insist on defending him. Even if he's not the killer, which I still think he is, he'll use you and toss you aside once he tires of you. It's what he does, Nella. Any idiot can see that. I mean, it's not like he's buying you anything or taking you anywhere."

Despite her anger, Nella held her tongue.

They reached the bank of new and half-built privies and selected one. Otlee checked it before letting Mirri go inside. The rest of the girls huddled together outside the door and tried their best not to hear Mirri's poor belly release its pain. Otlee stood before them, his hand on the hilt of his sword.

After a few minutes they heard someone approach

from the castle. "You all right?" a rumbling male voice asked. To Nella it sounded like the guard with the polearm.

Otlee answered. "We're fine, Olibe. Thanks."

"Just checking," Olibe said, then moved toward the castle.

"He's gonna get himself thrown in gaol if Dubric catches him away from his post," Otlee muttered.

"At least he could have brought us a light," Stef grumbled.

Otlee sighed. "I've already told you. We're nearing the end of winter and the oil supplies are low. We're using what little we have for patrols. There are no extra lights. Not for anyone."

"I bet Lord Sweetie could get us a damned light," Stef said. "I hate the dark."

Nella sighed. All she needed was to add the price of a lantern and oil to her debt.

Beside Nella, Plien squinted into the darkness. "What was that?" she asked, her body and voice shaking.

"Stay calm. We'll be fine." Nella reached out to calm her, but Plien leapt away, terrified.

"What?" the others asked, pressing together. Otlee grasped his sword.

"Musta been nothing. My imagination," Plien said, her voice cracking.

And the girls got very quiet.

Moments later a squeal rang through the courtyard from somewhere to the south, followed by the call of a trumpet. They heard the metallic clank of men with weapons move toward it.

"This is bad," Plien said.

"Real bad," Stef agreed.

Otlee backed toward them, his feet wide apart. "I think it's time we headed back."

A strange, terrified squeal fluttered in Plien's throat.

Oh, Goddess, she's going to run! "We'll be fine, stay calm—" Nella started.

"I can't take this," Plien gasped, then bolted.

"Plien!" they all called out. Otlee tried to grab her, but she slipped past and disappeared into the swirling dark.

"Get back here," Nella whispered, as loud as she dared. Her heart leapt from her chest, landing somewhere in her throat.

Otlee took a single step forward. "I order you to get back here this instant!"

Nella was sure she saw a shadow move through the darkness. Beside her, Ker whimpered.

Plien's voice drifted back, "Uh-uh. I'm going back to the cas—"

And then silence.

"Plien!" the girls cried.

Nella strained to hear and caught on the wind, "No, please, let me—"

Otlee backed toward them again and pulled his sword. "Stay here. Stay behind me."

"Oh, Goddess," Nella said, scrambling to the snowy pile of lumber for a new privy. Frantic, she rummaged through the scraps.

"What are you doing?" Dari asked, tugging on Nella's cloak hard enough to knock her off balance.

Otlee glanced at them and said, "Miss Nella, you need to stay with the group."

"I'm getting Plien," she said, lifting a sword-sized chunk of wood and yanking her cloak from Dari's grasp.

"You can't," Dari cried. "We have to stick together, we have—"

"Stay here with Otlee. Until the guards get here. No matter what."

"Are you crazy? You'll die out there!"

Otlee tried to herd them toward Mirri's privy. "Miss Nella, you have to stay here. I've been ordered to—"

She shook her head and slipped past him. "No. Watch them, and do not follow me. I'll be right back. I promise."

Otlee tried to grab her but she was quick and determined. "Miss Nella, you can't! You have to stay here."

But she was already gone.

She ran forward, through the frigid dark, while the girls behind her begged Otlee not to follow. Ahead, someone gasped for air. "Please, please," she heard.

"Plien?" Nella called out, slowing her blind dash. She saw something move through the snow, like an eddy through the flakes, directly in front of her. She froze. The eddy moved through the dark, moved away, and her heart stopped.

The gasping continued.

Slower, Nella moved forward, stumbling over something warm as her eyes searched the dark snow-filled air around her. She reached through the dark and touched Plien's head.

Behind her, the voices jumbled in their urgency. Otlee hollered for her to come back. Dari screeched that they needed to go and get her. From inside the privy, Mirri screamed, "Don't leave me here alone!"

Plien gasped, reaching for Nella. "Oh, dammit, it hurts."

"What? Oh, Goddess!" Nella cried, dropping to her knees, dropping the wood.

She reached for Plien and found warm repulsive wetness where her back should have been. Nella almost snatched her hands back, but didn't. "Are you hurt bad? Can you walk?"

"Cut my back. Oh, Nella." Her voice was no louder than the wind.

"Guards!" Nella called out to the dark. "I need help. Please. She's hurt!"

The other girls whimpered but stayed at the privy. Otlee, too, called for help.

Nella pulled off her cloak, wadded it up, and tried to stop the bleeding, but Plien's whole back was so dark, so wet. Nella stroked Plien's head and tried not to cry. Flakes swirled around her, threatening to find an opening, a weakness, but she saw no one. Nothing but the sparkling menace of the snow.

"It's going to be all right," Nella whispered, smoothing Plien's hair, her own heart hammering as her eyes searched the dark. "Shh. You're going to be all right."

Abruptly, the snow stopped swirling around her. It fell softly, gentle on her face like a cool caress, and clear terror entered her heart.

"We have to get back," she whispered before her voice failed her. "Right now. We have to—"

From behind her, someone snatched at Nella's hair hard enough to send white pain down her spine. She sucked in her breath and stiffened as something cold and sharp and stinking of blood pressed against her throat.

"You're where you don't belong, little girl," a harsh voice rasped in her ear. Hot breath burned her cheek and smelled like onions and blood and old ale. Rancid.

"Are you going to kill me?" Nella asked, her voice quivering as she stroked Plien's hair. Far behind her, Otlee still screamed for help. Her heart slammed in her chest. And the lovely, deadly snow fell and melted on her upturned face.

Whatever held her laughed, hot breath on her cool

skin, and worked its fingers through her braided hair like snakes crawling through weeds. "You're not on my list, little girl. Not yet. But you will be, oh yes, you will be."

The cold sharp thing at her throat—*Goddess, please don't let it be a knife!* she prayed, but she knew it was—slid lower, its hard tip gliding along her collar bone. "You're on Risley's list, for now," the voice said, scalding her cheek with each word.

"'Risley's list'?" she asked as she screamed silent prayers with her mind and stared into the falling snow.

He—Nella was sure it was a man—yanked on her hair, making her whimper. "He thinks he loves you," the horrid voice rasped, "but I know better." Dry lips kissed her ear, a hot wet tongue flicked out as if to taste her, and the knife traced up her throat, to just below her jaw. "Do you love him?"

She shivered in revulsion, whimpering. She wanted to scream, but suddenly she thought of Risley. His face, his eyes. The feel of his fingers on her skin. Calm flowed into her heart and she blinked once. If she were to die, she would die thinking of Risley, no matter how the monster cut her.

"Do you love him, bitch?" The voice snarled, impatient, and he yanked on her hair yet again, hard, lifting her chin toward the black, endless, snow-filled sky. The blade pressed against her throat, almost choking her. "Do you?"

"Yes," she said clearly, tears streaming down her face. "Yes, I love him." *Please, Goddess,* she prayed, *let him know I love him.*

Like a gift, the pressure at her throat disappeared and everything went blank.

CHAPTER

11

✝

Dien burst into Dubric's office without knocking. His nose bled freely, one eye had swollen shut, and his puffy lip had split completely open. Otlee gasped, looking up from the witness chair. Dien barely paused before saying, "We've had an incident in the servants' wing. I've got three men down, one is unconscious. Every woman in the place is screaming. He got away from us, sir."

"Son of a buck!" Dubric snarled as he stood and slammed his fists on his desk. "You had four men. Where in the seven hells did he go?"

Dien wiped at the blood on his face and looked at it, astounded. "The mouthy one, Darli or some such, told him the bodies had been taken to the phy—"

Dubric shoved past him and ran to the hall.

* * *

Dubric burst through the physicians' door to find Halld clinging to a rack of shelving and struggling to stand. Muttering a low curse, Dien skidded to a stop beside Dubric. Two bodies lay on the examination tables. They were naked and partly covered by sheets; their backs had been opened and slashed. The third victim was gone, with only a smear of blood remaining on her table.

"He wouldn't listen," Halld said as his knees buckled and he slumped to the floor again. He wiped his hand across his mouth and shook his head as if to clear his vision. "I tried to stop him but he wouldn't listen." He climbed up the shelving again and rolls of bandages tumbled onto the floor.

Dubric screamed a curse. He turned away and stomped back through the door, snarling, "I don't give a peg who he is! He can't steal my only Goddess-cursed witness!"

* * *

Nella believed for a moment she was floating. The ceiling above her had been painted frothy blue and white to resemble clouds, and whatever she lay upon was soft and comfortable. Her face felt cool and clean. She blinked, and with dizzying surreal clarity realized she lay in a finely furnished room she had never seen before.

Beyond the door, Dubric stared out of a tall sunny window with his hands clasped behind him, while Risley sat beside her on the bed with a cool rag in his hand. Worry left his eyes in an instant, replaced with relief, as he lifted her into his arms.

The back of her head throbbed mercilessly, but in his embrace she felt safe.

At the sound of her movement, Dubric turned and entered the bedchamber. He looked very tired. "Tell me what happened," he said.

"No," Risley said, his voice flat and commanding. "She needs to rest."

Where am I? she thought. *Is this a dream?* Risley held her closer, gently cradling her throbbing head. He was warm. Wonderfully warm. She sighed and relaxed against him.

Dubric's hand fell to the hilt of his sword. "I have to speak with her. She is the only real witness I have."

Nella's brow furrowed as her mind began to clear. *Witness? I didn't die? But he had a knife. And Plien. She was hurt. She . . . What happened to Plien?*

"You can talk to her later," Risley said and drew up a blanket to cover her.

"What about Plien?" Nella asked, her voice soft, muffled against Risley's shirt. "Is she all right?" She looked up at Risley. "Where am I?"

"I've brought you to my suite to keep you safe," he said, his hand gentle and warm on her head and back. "No one will come near you. No one. Never, ever again."

Despite Risley's arms around her, she suddenly felt very cold and started shaking. Her hands raked through her hair and came up short. Her hair was missing. Most of the length of it, anyway.

Panic edged into her voice. She pulled away and sat shakily beside him. "What happened to my hair? Where's Plien?"

"Enough of this. Let me talk to my witness."

Nella looked at Dubric, then back to Risley. She felt light-headed, and did not trust her voice. But she had to know. "What's going on?"

Risley grasped her hand. "You were supposed to be protected." He shot an angry glare at Dubric. "I was *assured* you'd be protected, but they found you and Plien last night in the courtyard. You were unconscious."

She shuddered. "And Plien?"

He lowered his eyes and shook his head.

Tears welled in her eyes and she shook as Risley eased her back into his arms. "No," Nella whispered, "she was still alive. She was hurt, but . . ." *Oh, Goddess, what happened?*

"I am sorry, Miss Nella, that we failed you." Dubric rubbed his eyes and sighed.

Her shaking intensified and Risley held her close, pulling a blanket up to cover her, to help her get warm again. His voice was hard. "Express your sympathies later. She needs to rest."

Dubric nodded reluctantly. "All right. But she does not leave this room until I have talked to her."

"Don't worry. She's not going anywhere."

Dubric left as Risley held her. She lay upon what she assumed was his bed and he held her close until she finished shaking. No matter how many blankets he piled on, she couldn't get warm. She thought at one time she might have fallen asleep, and she knew she cried, but Risley never left her, not for a moment. He was constant, unflinching, a steady force for her to hold on to.

When the shaking finally subsided to shivers, Risley sent a servant to fetch her some hot soup. From the nobles' table.

She curled in his arms, wrapped and bundled in the blankets. "He cut off my hair?" she asked, her voice cracking. She was still half numb, and they were the first words she had spoken since Dubric left.

"Shh. Don't worry about that now." He stroked her brow, his touch tingling and warm on her skin.

"I have to know what happened," she whispered as she buried her face against his chest.

"You should rest. Get your strength back."

"I have to know." She held herself close to him, close to his warmth. "Please."

A long pause later, he said, "I don't know much and Dubric's not talking. Before they found you, they'd found another. Daughter of a peddler. She wasn't quite dead and had crawled out of the barn. While they were trying to save her, the guards heard screams from the privy area. That's when they found your friends and Otlee. They're all right. Scared, but all right."

"All but Plien."

"They found you beside her. She was . . . like the others. You were unconscious, praise the Goddess."

"She was alive," she said, clutching at his chest. "Her back was bleeding, but she was alive."

She felt his grip tighten. "Yes. You were covered with her blood."

"But why didn't he kill me, too? Why did he cut off my hair?"

"I don't know. Maybe he's cut hair off all the girls. I don't know why."

"Risley," she asked, her voice small and trembling, "do you have a list?"

His hands on her back paused and she thought she felt a startled tremor. "'A list'? A list of what?"

"I don't know. Before I blacked out, he told me I was on your list."

"My list?"

She nodded.

"I don't have a list, at least not one that I know of."

The food arrived, brought by a kitchen boy with a tureen of soup and platter of sandwiches. Risley ate a venison sandwich, Nella ate her soup, and he never left her side. Not for a moment.

They were still eating when Dubric entered without bothering to knock. Dubric stared at her. "If she can eat, she can talk."

"Are you ready?" Risley asked. His arm slid around her shoulders.

Nella nodded and lowered her spoon, her hand shaking.

Dubric pulled a battered leather-bound book from

his jerkin pocket and licked a pencil. "Start at the be-ginning."

Nella told her tale, but when she reached the last moments in the snow, her mouth fell dry and she wished she had a drink of water. "When I found her, she was still alive, but her back was bleeding."

"Where was she cut? How badly?" Dubric asked.

Nella's stomach clenched. *Goddess, she was cut more than once?* "I don't know," she said finally. "It was dark. She seemed to have trouble breathing or talking. I . . . I could barely hear her."

He scribbled some notes. "Go on."

"I tried to stop the bleeding but couldn't. Maybe if I could have seen . . ." She wiped at her eyes. "I held her, and called for help. That's when he grabbed me."

She started to shake again, and Risley drew her close despite her fingers clutching and digging into his thigh. "He grabbed my hair, pulled it, and he held a knife to my throat."

She paused, winced, and forced herself to remem-ber. "He . . . he . . . he said I wasn't where I belonged."

"He talked to you?" Dubric's eyes lit up. "Did you recognize his voice?"

"Not exactly." She paused for a moment, trying to remember. "I think he was trying to change it, make it deeper, rougher. But it was still familiar." She frowned. "Not someone I knew, not like you or Risley, but . . ." she shrugged.

"But it was a voice you had heard before." Dubric stared into her eyes. "You are certain of that?"

"Yes. Familiar, but not real familiar. Does that make sense?"

He made a few notes in his book. "Did you notice anything else?"

"Yes. His breath was bad, like rotten meat. Just horrible. And he was hot."

"What happened after he said you were not where you belonged?"

"He called me a child . . . no, a little girl. Yes, that's right. A little girl. I asked if he was going to kill me."

"What happened then?"

"He said I wasn't on his list."

Dubric's attention flashed to her with such abruptness she jumped. "'His list'?"

She nodded, glancing at Risley. "He said I wasn't on his list, I was on Risley's. The knife was moving over my throat and I was so scared, but he said . . . he said that Risley thinks he loves me, and he asked me if I loved Risley, too."

"Oh, Nella," Risley whispered, still holding her close.

She looked up at Risley, tried to smile, and almost succeeded. "I didn't know what to do. What answer he wanted to hear. I finally realized that all I could do was tell the truth." She reached up to squeeze Risley's hand on her shoulder. "So I said 'Yes, I love him.'" She lowered her eyes as he kissed her forehead, then she turned back to Dubric. "Next thing I knew, I woke up in here."

Dubric's pencil paused. "Did you see anything? His clothes, his hands?"

"No. It was too dark. I didn't see anything at all but the snow. He was behind me."

Dubric sighed, wearily rubbing his eyes with the back of his hand. For a moment Nella thought he might slump to the floor, but he reached for a chair and fell into it. He took a long time adding to his notes, then he drew a breath and looked into her eyes. "I need to understand the dead girls. How many of them did you know?"

"Plien," she said, her fingers digging into Risley's thigh again. "She was the only one I knew, I guess, but I'd met Celese . . ." she shrugged. "I think I talked to the egg maid—Rianne, is that right?—a couple of times. We're just all so separate, Dubric, grouped together by job, we don't have much time to meet new people or make friends. At least, I don't. For the most part, we know who one another is, but beyond that . . . I'm sorry, but I didn't really talk to any of them, except for Plien."

"Please," he said, "surely someone in the servants' wing knows these girls. Someone gossips, someone has an opinion, a hunch, a fear." He glanced at Risley, then returned his attention to her. "No one likes to speak ill of the dead, but there has to be a connection between them, a reason why they were killed and you were not."

She shivered, chewing her lip, as worry skittered across her belly. "All right. I don't know how much help I'll be. I truthfully don't know much about the others, but Plien . . . well, she tended to make up excuses to get out of work, and she liked to spread rumors. Sometimes she teased people, but otherwise she was nice enough. Friendly, for the most part, willing to help."

Nella's eyes rolled up as she thought, gazing into the clouds painted above Risley's bed. "Dari told me right after I came here to always write my name on my things because, if I didn't, Plien might steal them. But, honestly, I never knew her to take anything." She returned her attention to Dubric and said, "Plien and I always got along. We weren't good friends or confidantes, but she was all right, all things considered."

"Did she ever mention anyone special that she met with? Who was her closest friend? Did she owe anyone money? Did she complain about her job?"

Nella shook her head and cringed. "No, not really. Stef is the complainer. Plien, mostly, never asked for anything or offered anything. She just . . ." Nella shrugged. "She just kept to herself, I guess. I don't think she had any really close friends, no one that she giggled with or anything."

"Did she see a lot of men? Lay with them, perhaps?"

Nella blushed, fidgeting. "I guess so. I don't think she cared who she bedded."

"Are there rumors about particular men? Whispers that all the murdered girls met this fellow or that one? Were there any men you often saw in the women's quarters?"

"Lots of us have male friends. Some are honestly courting, some not, and after a while the faces become familiar, so we stop noticing them. At least, until this started." She felt a blush creep onto her cheeks. "Some of the men are married, and we all know it, but we never talk about it. I guess it just wasn't our business."

Dubric's pencil paused as he looked at her. "Did Plien see married men?"

Risley's arm around her shoulders felt warm and comforting. "Yes," she replied, her throat clenching. "Sometimes."

"Is there any chance that the voice you heard came from one of Plien's lovers?"

"Maybe. I guess it's possible."

"What about the other murdered girls? From what you know, and what you have heard, did they have many male companions?"

Her belly burned in shame and embarrassment. "I think so. Some of them, their morals weren't the best, I guess."

"Married *and* unmarried men?"

"Yes, I suppose so. I didn't know them, though. Really. I can't say for certain, but the rumors . . ."

She looked at Risley and swallowed the bitter lump burning in her throat. *There are rumors about me, about us.*

Dubric's question turned her attention back to him. "What sort of rumors, Miss Nella?"

She laughed harshly and shook her head. "There are so many rumors, Dubric, you have no idea. Every man is suspicious. You. Lord Brushgar. Risley." She smiled into Risley's eyes before turning back to Dubric. "Every man old enough to shave is suspect. Someone looks at us wrong, he's the killer. He's lurking in every shadow. Hiding behind every door. We truly have no idea, no idea at all. I'm sorry."

He watched her, his wax-coated pencil quivering in his grasp. "But there is a particular rumor, isn't there? The one that scares you?"

"No, not really."

"Miss Nella," he said, leaning forward. "I want to catch this monster and I cannot do that if you lie to me. He cannot harm you now."

She shook her head, swallowing and trying to breathe.

"It's okay, love," Risley said. "I'm right here and you're safe. No one will harm you. I promise."

She tried to speak but no sound came out. She shook her head, clenched her fists, and tried again. "He's hunting whores," she shoved out, her voice barely above a squeak.

"Oh, Goddess, love," Risley said, drawing her closer. "But you're not, *we're* not—"

"Can you repeat that, please?" Dubric asked. "I couldn't hear."

"Maybe that's why he left me alive," she said, struggling to control her terrified heart and gasping breaths. "I'm not on his list, not yet. But he said I will be!"

"No!" Risley turned her, holding her face in his hands. "No, you won't. I won't let it happen. I will never leave the slightest doubt of my intentions, I swear I won't, and no one will accuse you—"

"What in the seven hells are you two blabbering about?"

Nella shuddered. "They say he's hunting whores, Dubric. But why didn't he kill me? Everyone thinks Risley and I . . ."

"Shh. Not everyone, love," Risley said, stroking her hair. "Not everyone." He held her close, protecting her in his embrace.

Sighing, Dubric rubbed his eyes and searched for a different page in his notes. "No one of any sense whatsoever thinks you are a whore, Miss Nella. You are a forthright, hardworking, honest, virtuous young woman. Of that there is no doubt."

"Thank you," she mumbled. *But you don't hear what they say about me, what the other girls think. Oh, Goddess, what am I going to do?*

"Do the other girls do more than dredge the deceased's questionable morals? Are there no useful insights or prevailing rumors?"

"No, Dubric, not really."

He leaned forward, staring at her. "There is no name the staff whispers? No man that seems to worry them? A place all the dead girls tended to frequent? A consistent fear I can trace?"

"I'm sorry, Dubric, but we're all just terrified, no matter how moral or immoral we are. It could be anyone. Even you."

Dubric sighed and stood. "I know that you have had a bad scare, Miss Nella, but I want you to pay close attention to any voice you hear for the next few days, to see if—"

"No," Risley said, and the arm around her shoulders suddenly felt stiff. "No."

"The bastard is in my castle, boy, and if she can identify him, she has to."

"No. He let her live once, he might not do that again. She's not going to become a target."

Dubric slammed his book shut. "She will not be a target."

"How do you know that?"

Nella mewled and curled into his arms. She started to cry.

"I'm sorry, love," Risley said, stroking her hair, "I shouldn't have said anything."

"She is my only damn witness, Risley. She has to."

Nella shook her head and clung to Risley.

"Nella," Dubric said softly, "If I do not catch him, kill him, he is going to keep on killing."

Nella wailed.

"Get out," Risley snapped. "She told you all she knows."

Frowning, Dubric looked at Nella and said, "If you think of anything else. No matter how minor you may think it is . . ."

She shivered and wished she could climb into Risley's skin where it was safe and warm.

Dubric said to Risley, "She cannot leave the castle. I will arrest you if you try to take her away. I mean it." His eyes bored into Risley, then he turned and left them to her pain.

Ever so gently, Risley carried her from the bed to a divan by the window. "Maybe sitting in the sun will help you get warm," he said. Wrapped in blankets, she curled within his arms and let him hold her.

"How did I get here?" she asked, slowly calming, her face pressed close against his chest as he held her.

"When I got to the servants' wing this morning, I knew something had happened. There were guards posted at your door and more inside your room. You'd been found in the courtyard during the night. I didn't know what to do. I . . . I hit one, maybe all of them. I went crazy . . ." He held her even closer and kissed her hair, and she noticed the bruising on his hands. "It took all of them to stop me from ripping the place apart, and Dari said you'd been taken to the physicians'.

"When I ran in, you and the others were on tables." His voice cracked, wavered. "You were covered in blood, so much blood, but you were still breathing. It looked like your throat had been slashed, but it hadn't." He kissed her head again. "Thank the Goddess, you weren't hurt. The physician told me you had no more than a bump on the head, that you'd be all right."

"But not the others," she whispered.

"No. One was just . . . the other . . . he was working on her."

"Go on," she whispered.

"I grabbed you," he said. "The physician tried to stop me, but I had to get you out of there, away from all that death and blood. I wrapped you in the blanket and carried you here."

"Thank you," she said, wondering how much sanity she'd still have if she'd woken at the physicians'.

He stroked her hair, her back. "Right after I got you here, Dubric came and screamed at me for stealing his witness. I think I punched him, too." Risley shook his head and shrugged. "Anyway, I cleaned you up as best I could, then I begged and bribed a group of maids to do the rest and gave them a shirt to dress you in. I never left the room, I swear. I never left you alone for a moment after I found you."

She felt a tingle of embarrassment as she huddled close to him, absorbing his warmth. "Thank you," she said, trying not to think about being naked and bloody in his bed.

"That's all I know. Dubric kept coming in, glaring at me, pacing the room, then leaving."

"What time is it?" she asked.

"Midafternoon," he said.

That's why the sunlight seems so odd. She looked out the window. "How long can I stay here?"

He touched her cheek, drawing her gaze back to him. "As long as you want to. As long as you'll have me."

Her eyes searched his for a long moment, then she nodded and laid her head against his chest, content to sit in the sun, wrapped in a blanket and his embrace.

* * *

The moment Dubric reached the main hall, an angry crowd swarmed him.

"It's him, Dubric. Can't you see?"

"Arrest the bastard!"

"Hang him!"

"He let his bitch live!"

"Kill them both!"

Dubric ignored them all and pressed through to his office, snatching a sealed message from the herald before the nervous prat uttered a word. He had no time to reflect upon the extreme anger of the crowd, no time to worry about why they hated Risley with such unexpected vehemence. Whether Risley was the killer or not, the misguided fury would not help him.

Alone in his office for the first time in days, he

closed the doors to the crowd's screams and sat at his desk, pencil poised over his notebook.

He had wasted much of the day holding out hope for Nella's testimony, but it had led him nowhere. The victims' moral failings had come as no surprise, nor had the staff's fear. He stared at the page containing her recollections and he frowned. A list. A possibly familiar voice. How could anyone follow those clues? While educated people might write things down, even illiterate farmers kept lists in their head.

He opened a drawer and pulled out a battered book, flipping to a page. At census last autumn four hundred and seventy-three souls lived in the castle and its grounds, and more than eleven hundred others in the village. Nella had lived in the castle for moons. How many people had she talked to in that time? How many voices would she consider familiar but not incredibly familiar? Scores? Hundreds?

He sighed, searching for an elusive clue, a connection between the victims and the survivors. Surely there was a reason why Nella and Lars lived while everyone else died, and a reason the killer removed, and—after seeing the dyer's liver—presumably ate the kidneys of his victims.

Dubric tapped his pencil on his teeth. *Could I be examining this from the wrong direction? Is it virtue he craves? Innocence and forthright honor? Is that why he did not kill Lars or Nella? Why she was not yet on his list?*

But who would care about virtue? Who would penalize those who did not meet whatever arbitrary standards they have applied? What virtue-seeking man would kill? How could that make sense?

Frowning, he returned to his notes and the evidence. Despite the light snow, the moon had been bright the night before and still Nella had seen nothing.

The kitchen lackeys had seen nothing. Lars had seen only a shadow. There had been no real witnesses at all. He made a few notes and stumbled into the luxury of wild thinking.

What about the heat? Both Lars and Nella mentioned that the killer had been hot. Shadow Followers burned of Taiel'dar's heat, but he could barely imagine such trouble had come to his lands. Surely there was another explanation. What if it had been a ghost, a specter, or a spirit? What about curses, prophecy, or magic? He grunted to himself and frowned. Oriana had indulged in such fancies, had embraced the magic of religion, and it had killed her. He would not make the same mistake, even if he had gone nearly a phase without a night's sleep and had nine ghosts following him. There had to be a logical, sensible explanation. A *person* had done this, not a ghost. He, perhaps more than anyone, knew that ghosts were annoying but harmless. Whomever it was, he would catch them and kill them, or die trying.

He smelled thyme in the air and he looked to the small table beside the door. Someone from the kitchen had left him a lunch tray. Grimacing, he turned away.

He wasn't in the mood to eat.

* * *

Stroking the prize in his pocket, he followed Nella down the stairs, admiring the gentle sway of her hips beneath her simple garments and the way they clung to her small, slender frame. He followed her like a shadow to a crowded table during the busiest part of the evening meal. He remained perfectly friendly, perfectly concerned, and perfectly polite despite the nervousness of nearby maids. As he ate, one hand would creep from time to time to his pocket and stroke the perfect braid of dark hair he had cut from her the night before. Her hair felt different from the others, and he wondered if it was because he had granted her life, or because she was still perfect and unspoiled.

He sat near her, close enough to touch her skin if he dared. Watching her, saliva filled his mouth as he ached to taste her again. She had tasted so sweet, perfectly luscious and delectable, much better than the piss-filled kidneys.

He blinked and smiled at her. She smiled back, delicately eating her vegetables as she stifled a slight tremor in her hand. He swallowed his mouthful of saliva and shared an inane bit of news with her, marveling at how quickly she had recovered from her fright the night before.

He had not meant to frighten her, goodness, no, why would he wish to frighten the object of his desire? Brave and lovely, intelligent and compassionate . . . so unlike the others. So perfect for him, now that he had changed, and such a perfect prize to win.

Telling a charming joke, he winked at her with wry amusement. She laughed softly, her hand covering her mouth and caution leaving her lovely brown eyes for a moment as he fell into them. She, of all people, had nothing to fear from him, after all, and somehow she seemed to realize how precious she was to him.

Soon, he thought as he ate with a perfectly grim smile on his face. From time to time he wondered whose flesh he would taste that night.

But mostly he stroked the slim dark braid coiled in his pocket and thought of the day she would become his.

CHAPTER

12

After dinner, Risley and Nella returned to his suite and spent a quiet evening together. Nella relaxed and explored the rooms while he trailed behind her like a shadow. Risley's suite was bigger than any she'd cleaned, with seven rooms plus a privy chamber. The stone walls had been plastered and painted lovely hues, each room tinted to match the furnishings and carpets. She opened every closet and cupboard, searching for phantoms that weren't there.

"Do you want a guard in here with us?" he asked, hesitantly taking her hand. "Or a chaperone?"

She shook her head, seeing little point in quelling rumors after what had happened. "No. I trust you."

"Are you sure? I have a reputation, you know." He reached out to touch her cheek. "And you don't need to be sullied by it."

She had heard long ago he had a girl in every castle. "Your reputation has never frightened me."

He smiled into her eyes and for the first time that day she felt truly warm.

He called for a bath and poured the water himself, setting out towels and soaps on an oak bureau for her. Once her bath was readied, he sat outside the open door, facing away from her, with his back against the wall. He remained close, protecting her yet giving her privacy.

Beside the towels stood a selection of pretty bottles and a basket of soaps. Captivated, she let her fingers glide along the bright glass. "Are all of these yours?" she asked, sniffing a smooth, floral-scented loaf. "These soaps?"

Remaining in the hall, Risley was silent for a moment, then his voice came out in a rush. "Of course, but they're yours to use if you wish, love. I didn't know what you might like, so I put out several."

Nella smiled, shaking her head at his gentle fib. Surely he did not bathe with lilac bath oil. She almost asked what they cost, then pursed her lips and shook her head. He would insist they were his and refuse payment. Sooner or later she'd go into the village and find out their price for herself, but she was too curious to let the indulgence slip her by. "They're beautiful," she said, lifting the soaps to her nose. Each had a different scent. Light, delicate, evocative. She smiled. "Thank you."

"You're perfectly welcome."

She selected a soap, hesitated, and pulled off her dress. Risley had not moved from his place outside the door. She slipped into the hot water and sighed as the heat removed any taint of shivering. "Oh, Risley, this feels nice."

"I thought it might relax you."

She smiled and closed her eyes, letting the heat soak in. "I've never had a hot bath before."

She heard the smile in his voice. "Take your time."

They chatted while she bathed, about nothing of great import. When she rose from the tub, she splashed and his voice stumbled.

Wrapped in his robe, she came from the bath chamber with her oddly short hair damp and her face fresh.

He leapt to his feet, fumbling, and she felt the heat of the blush on her cheeks. "May I borrow your shirt again? My nightgown . . ." her voice faded away and she shrugged.

He nodded. "I'll get one."

He hurried off and she trailed behind him. "They're in here." He pulled open a drawer full of crisp white shirts. "Use whatever you like."

"Thanks," she said, and glanced at her little pile of clothes folded neatly on his bedside table. Her pile wouldn't even fill half of one drawer. She suddenly felt very small.

He looked at her for a moment, then turned his eyes away. Opening a closet and removing a couple of blankets, he said, "I'll take the divan. Do you need anything else?"

She shook her head.

Blankets tucked under his arm, he reached out and lifted her chin with one finger. "Dubric's squire's been checking on me at night, so if you hear someone walking around don't worry. He'll certainly keep your reputation intact, all right? But I'll be in the next room if you need me. You're safe here. I promise."

She nodded and tried to smile.

After one last longing look, he left her to herself, not quite closing the door behind him.

She combed her hair and heard him blow out the lights throughout the suite. Through the crack in the door, she watched him settle into the divan by the window, a sword on the floor beside him and his face and body turned toward the bedroom door.

She lowered her head and turned away. As she climbed into the massive softness that was his bed, she said, "Good night, Risley."

"Good night, Nella," he replied. "Sleep well."

I'll try, she thought, pulling his pillows close against her chest and burying her face in them. Everything was too soft, too big, and she wondered if she could sleep at all.

* * *

Dubric patrolled outside the castle with an accountant named Cotter. They tried every door, gate, and window they could reach. The grounds remained secure, no unauthorized people entered or exited the castle, and the waxing moon left plenty of light to see by. Dubric tried not to get his hopes up.

Once again, the night was nearly over. Once again, no new ghosts had yet joined the group. As he walked his patrol, he contemplated what had changed within the castle during the past day. What could account for this peaceful night? He could only think of one thing.

He wondered if the presence of Nella in Risley's suite, and presumably in his bed, had quieted the beast. Were the murders a symptom of Risley's frustration and loneliness? Surely the young man had not spent more than an occasional night alone in summers. Dubric knew as well as anyone that an abrupt shift from regular, ample release to absolutely none could accentuate any man's aggression. And when the desired object of affection remained in sight but out of reach, it was quite possible that a normally sane man could snap. Especially a man who had long ago become used to getting his way. Even the similarities between the victims made sense now. Nella was a servant, so all the victims were servants. Nella was a commoner, hence the victims were commoners. Nella was young . . . Nella was alone . . . Nella worked . . .

Dubric frowned. The clues were there from the beginning, and as he examined the facts, admittedly from the benefit of hindsight, he could see them falling together. The final piece was perhaps the most important. Of all the girls that were attacked, only Nella survived. If the others were indeed lacking in moral fortitude, that piece fit, as well. They provided easy access to release, while Nella did not. A stunning contrast. Exactly the criteria Risley craved, but not the person herself, and he killed them for their lack. But no matter how angry or frustrated he was, he did not want to hurt Nella. In his frenzied, misplaced passion, he had cut her hair, but did not truly harm her.

But Nella was no longer out of reach. She was close at hand, almost property. Risley's base desires could be sated, Nella could be pursued and adored as whim demanded, and the frustration of being kept from her had come to an end. It made perfect sense. There would be no more murders simply because Risley was once again physically involved.

Dubric felt worry gnaw at his entrails. Even if Risley were guilty, no good could come from accusing him. Not only would the King be furious, Brushgar would prefer that his province collapse around his ears before admitting that Risley may have done wrong. And Kyl and Heather . . . Finding their son accused of murder would break their hearts and ruin a treasured friendship.

"Damn," Dubric muttered. He trudged on, the ghosts weighing on his soul. *What choice do I have? Do I ignore the evidence and allow him to continue, or do I truly consider his possible guilt? Do I risk all-out war with Haenpar and perhaps the King? If it came down to it, could I hang the lad? I have changed the boy's diddies, for King's sake, and witnessed his parents' wedding. I look upon the lad as a nephew. Family. Yet I have a duty to Faldorrah, a duty I cannot deny.*

They walked east along the southern wall, past the pair of men watching the main doors, then rounded the corner toward the kitchens. Dubric paused, holding out his arm to stop Cotter's steady trudge.

Something moved in the darkness, a shadow, a wraith, black against the night.

"Remain silent," Dubric whispered as he pulled his sword. He crept along the east wall, past the kitchen door and the place where Ennea had died. The ghosts hung behind him, oblivious to his quiet hurry, tainting the castle walls with their dead, green glow.

The wraith moved away, braving moonlight as it slipped toward the gardens, and Dubric followed, trying not to grin. *Bastard son-of-a-whore, I have you this time.*

He lost track of Cotter, forgot about his ghosts, and was so intent upon his quarry he barely noticed when he twisted his ankle in a hole. The man was clothed in darkness and he slipped from moonlight to shadow while Dubric dogged his heels as silently as any ghost.

The shadow reached the castle cistern—a stone well that granted access to an abundant spring—and it climbed the wall to stand upon the edge.

Is that how he's getting in? Dubric thought, easing closer. *Could someone crawl through the piping to the kitchens?*

Then he stopped, momentarily aghast, as the man opened his black trousers and urinated, polluting the castle's water supply. His backside gleamed pale and hairy in the moonlight as his pants fell about his ankles.

What in the seven hells? Dubric thought, hurrying toward him. *Has he been doing this all along? Is this the connection to the kidneys?*

Dubric's sword winked in the moonlight, but the man on the well did not move until the tip poked against his spine. "Get down. Immediately," Dubric said.

The man startled and turned, still urinating, and spattered Dubric with hot fluid. "Aw, peg!" Inek gasped, stumbling over his pants and nearly falling into the well.

"Get down," Dubric said, astounded. He had expected to see Risley.

Waggling his penis at Dubric, Inek shook the last drops free, then yanked up his pants. "Piss on you! Piss on all of you!"

Dubric pointed his sword at Inek's chest. "Get down. Now. I do not want to send your filthy corpse into our well."

"Piss off," Inek said. He spat, then walked along the well's edge. "Go ahead. Kill me."

Dubric stood his ground. "Get. Down."

Inek turned and Dubric was surprised to see tears glistening on his cheeks. "You killed Ri, you pegging bastard!"

Before Dubric could respond, another shadow moved in the dark. It leapt and lunged, knocking the herbmonger from his perch. Both men rolled to the ground.

Dubric ran to them and pulled Cotter away before Inek caught his bearings again. One foot on his prisoner's chest, Dubric held his sword to Inek's throat. "Enough of this madness. If you resist, I will run you through, but just enough to hurt and bleed. That means you will suffer, do you understand? And I can make you suffer greatly for a very long time. To save both of us needless mess and screaming, you are going to get up, slowly, and once you are restrained we will walk, calmly, to the gaol."

Inek writhed, but the sword kept him pinned to the ground. "I'm not done with you yet, you old chicken shit bastard. You'll pay. Everyone will pay."

With his free hand, Dubric ripped a small coil of rope from his hip and tossed it to Cotter. "Tie him, and place a loop around his neck. He has a tendency to slip from wrist binds."

"Yes, sir," Cotter said. He grabbed Inek's hands, wrapped his wrists, and knotted the rope before wrapping a loop of the remainder around the herbmonger's throat.

Reconsidering Risley's guilt, Dubric stepped off of Inek's chest. "Get up."

"Peg you! I'm not doing anything!"

Dubric took the rope from Cotter and yanked on it, dragging Inek off the ground. "I said to get on your feet."

Inek gasped and struggled, but Dubric had his way. He shoved, dragged, and forcibly prodded Inek down the east-tower stairs to the gaol and shoved him into a vermin-infested cell. Half-strangled and punctured in several places, Inek ultimately stumbled to the rancid cot, cursing Dubric with every breath.

Dubric slammed the door and locked it, staring at the filthy bit of refuse the night had brought him while his ghosts meandered among the cells. "Did you kill those girls?"

Inek spat, his saliva flecked with blood, and he staggered to his feet. "What if I did? What if I didn't? Who the peg cares? All you've got on me is pissing in public, but you'll make up any damned lie to peg me. Bastard." He spat again and graced Dubric with an obscene gesture before falling back onto the cot.

Dubric stared at him for a moment, then left the gaol, thinking of searching Inek's home and shop for additional evidence concerning the murders. As he climbed the east-tower stairs, he heard the five bell ring and he smiled. *Perhaps it has been Inek all along and I will have a night without another ghost. And to think I considered Risley! Sexual frustration and similarities to Nella! Pah. What a fool I can be.*

Dubric had always considered Risley to be a good lad. A bit headstrong, a bit spoiled, but with a good heart. Now that he thought about it, what young man in the early stages of romance did not get upset from time to time? When he and Oriana were first courting, when he had wanted her so badly he could taste it, the slightest incident angered him. Unless of course she were nearby, then all was right with his world.

And Inek. By the King, how many times had Inek been in trouble for fighting, fraud, or petty theft? He had admitted to having had sexual relations with at least one of the dead girls, had made a habit out of causing trouble, and showed no remorse for the loss of life. Perhaps he had finally snapped, falling into madness and murder.

Dubric looked to the brightening sky and took a deep breath. The culprit likely was in gaol, there would be no additional ghosts, and soon, with luck, justice would be served. Once again life would return to its predictable quiet and he could get a full night's sleep.

He grinned. *What a beautiful morning.*

* * *

Not long before dawn, the milkmaids began leaving the castle, each group escorted and guarded by a pair of men who had been volunteered to help protect the courtyard. One, a castle squire named Fultin, had been assigned the west-tower door. He had also been assigned a list of the maids and their appointed barns. His sole duty, at least concerning this list, was to check off the milkmaids' names and note the guards assigned to them. A group of five maids approached. All were scowling. "Names please?" Fultin asked, his pencil poised over the last set of six names.

All answered, confirming their places on the list. "What about Nansy?" he asked as he checked off the five new arrivals.

"She's running late," one said. "As usual."

He frowned. Four guards remained at the door, awaiting their charges. Two were supposed to escort the last set, the other two to patrol the barn area once all the girls were inside.

"We can wait for the straggler," the bigger of the men said, "get her where she needs to be, then patrol."

His partner shrugged and nodded.

"Are you sure about that?" Fultin asked. "We can wait for her to get here."

"We don't wanna get in trouble," one of the milkmaids said.

"She's always getting us in trouble," piped in another.

"We can handle a single milkmaid, boss," the bigger of the men said, his hand on the hilt of his very big sword. His partner nodded. He carried a chunk of wood, about the size of a sword.

"All right," Fultin said. It seemed like a reasonable solution to him.

The five milkmaids went forth with their pair of guards and disappeared into the dark. A thin line of pink glimmered on the horizon when Nansy trudged to the door, her hair half-combed, her eyes half-open.

"Mornin'," she said, yawning. Roughly half her teeth had gone missing and her breath stank.

What a charmer, Fultin thought, crossing off her name. He nodded grimly, then motioned her into the dark with her two guards.

Not long afterward, the screams began.

CHAPTER

13

✝

*N*o! Dubric thought, turning to stare at his ghosts. *It can't be! Not again! For King's sake, Inek is in the gaol!*

Olibe Meiks flickered into view before him, screaming in astounded anguish, blood coursing from his throat. Dubric wavered, holding his aching head, as Meiks's ghost seemed to solidify. Meiks's death felt heavy, so damned heavy, like a lead weight tied behind Dubric's brow.

A moment or two later, barely long enough for Dubric to realize the castle slasher was not afraid of guards or men, a milkmaid eased into view, her guts falling from her belly over and over and over. Under the burden of eleven ghosts, Dubric's knees buckled and he fell, slumping onto the muddy ground.

Cotter ran to him, trying to help him stand. A scream whispered through the air, echoing through the dawn like a frigid north wind, and he shivered.

"By the gods!" Cotter muttered, turning to the west. "Another one?"

"It would seem so." Shoving himself upright despite the pounding in his head, Dubric staggered toward the western side of the castle. A guard trumpeted an alarm, filling the air with golden sound that brutally mimicked the blossoming morning.

* * *

Trumpets echoing through the last vapors of her dream, Nella opened her eyes to a dark room, blinking at the unfamiliar surroundings. She felt strangely out of place, as if she had dreamt upon a silken cloud. She had clutched Risley's pillow to her chest while she slept, and she pressed her face against it, breathing in his scent.

Risley, she thought, smiling. *I'm in Risley's suite, in his bed, and he knows I love him.*

Still smiling, she sat and stretched, swinging her legs out from under the blankets, then she paused, staring at the door and the thin line of bluish light peeking from beneath it.

Didn't I leave that open? Frowning, she looked at the closed door then climbed from the bed, her bare toes curling against the chilly floor.

She reached for the latch and paused, her hand trembling. A trumpet warbled somewhere outside, ringing in her ears like a warning. The trumpet faded away and she wavered where she stood, caught in the echoing silence. Her heart hammering, she tapped the wooden door, leaning her ear against it. "Risley?"

Nothing. No reply, no snoring. Nothing.

Taking a breath, she pressed the latch and opened the door.

The divan Risley had slept on stood across from her. His blanket lay puddled at one end, spilling onto the floor, while a pillow had been cast aside and forgotten beside the sheathed sword. Violet sky shown through the window, giving the cluttered scene a chilly glow.

"Risley?" she called again, venturing into the hall. She looked toward the main doors and frowned. Locked.

"Well, he must be here somewhere," she mumbled, moving deeper into the suite.

The privy door stood open and she peeked inside. Empty. The book-filled room he had referred to as his library remained exactly as it had been the night before, as did the sitting room across the hall from it.

"Risley?" she called again, louder this time. *Where could he have gone? Where could he be?*

Gasping, she stumbled backward as a crash filled the air, then a muttered curse. "Nella!" Risley's voice said from down the hall. "I'll be right— Oh, damn!"

"Risley?" She hurried forward, then stopped as she heard a low *thud* followed by another curse. She swallowed, staring at the closed door to his office. She heard a key in a lock, then the door opened. Risley hurried through, closing the door behind him.

"Good morning, love," he said, smiling and rushing to her. "Did you sleep well?" He drew her gently into his arms, one hand flat and massaging her back, the other balled into a fist and held against her arm.

She nodded as he kissed her forehead. His hand on her arm felt tacky and wet, soaking through her sleeve. Her smile faded as she drew away. "You're bleeding."

He blushed, looking at his hand and absently wiping the mess onto his stained and rumpled trousers. "Oh, that. It's just a cut, nothing to worry about."

She looked from his bloody hand to his eyes, his caring, earnest eyes, and gave him a consoling sigh. "Let me look at it," she said, reaching for his hand.

"It's nothing, love, really. Just cut myself."

*Tsk-tsk*ing him, she opened his fingers and sopped the blood with the cuff of her sleeve. The shallow gash ran along the firm flesh beneath his fingers, splitting open the callus. "It's not very deep, but you'll probably need stitches. Here, let's get it cleaned up."

Grumbling good-naturedly, he let her drag him to the privy room where she continued to tend his injury and wipe up the mess.

"How did you cut your hand?" she asked, dipping a clean rag into a basin of water.

He chuckled and held his palm open flat for her. "Being clumsy. I fell asleep in my office and you startled me. I fell and tried to catch myself on a box of armor." He shrugged and looked at his hand. "I suppose I should ask Rolle to sew it up before it gets infected."

"Nonsense," she said. "I can do it. Only take a moment."

He smiled, looking deep into her eyes. "I have needle and thread in the library cabinet. Top left drawer."

She nodded, closing his fingers around the wet rag. Refusing to let fear get the best of her—Risley would never hurt her—she hurried to retrieve the needle and thread.

He accepted the stitches stoically, watching her work. Once they were in, he flexed his hand and smiled. "You've done this before."

She washed blood from her hands, struggling to keep them from shaking. "Once. But that was a long time ago."

He sighed sadly and stared at her hands. "My clumsiness has ruined it. You're afraid to stay here with me, aren't you?"

She shook her head, blinking back tears.

He took her damp hands and gently dried them. "Don't be afraid. I'm not the killer, love. I swear on my life that's the truth." He raised her hand to his lips. "I'm making something in my office. But it's a secret. A surprise."

She looked up at him quickly. "'A surprise'?"

He nodded, easing her closer and holding her eyes with his own. "I give you my word that it's not dangerous in any way, and I have harmed no one. Do you believe me?"

She searched his eyes and nodded with relief, smiling. He was Risley, her love, her protector, and he had merely fallen and cut his hand. "Yes, yes I do."

He sighed happily, kissing her forehead. "Then stay here. With me," he whispered against her brow, drawing her gently into his arms.

She snuggled against his chest, safe and warm and adored. "I can't, no matter how much I want to. I . . . I have to work. The debt—"

"Then forget the debt," he said. "For me, for us."

"I can't forget it," she said, leaning back to look at him. "I'm so close. Just a few more days."

"I . . . I can't wait a few more days," he said, lowering his head until his breath warmed her lips like a promise. "May I have one kiss, love? Just one?"

Her eyes closed slowly, opening again as she nodded. "Just one," she whispered and he smiled, pressing her close as his breath mingled with her own.

"I love you," he murmured against her mouth. "Forever and always, my love, my Nella." He held her face in his hands, then he kissed her.

A small cry escaped her throat as her arms came up to encircle his neck. His breath in her mouth grew ragged and warm, sweet with his need, and his hands moved from her face to her arms, her back, her waist. Their lips never parting, he lifted her, knocking aside the washbasin and setting her upon the bureau.

Her knees on either side of his hips, she held him close and dear, her fingers curling into his hair. An endless moment later, when every conceivable bit of her body tingled, he drew away, sighing, and looked into her eyes.

His voice sounded soft, edged with a warm rasp that made her ache low in her belly. "I've waited a long time for that."

"Me, too." Nella's fingertips trembled against his stubbly cheek and she licked her lips to ease the stinging burn.

She thought for a moment he might kiss her again, but he cleared his throat, his hands resting on her waist. Looking into her eyes, he smiled. "Since we're on, um, kissing terms now, even with the debt, a minstrel from Jhalin is playing at the alehouse in the village. Could I take you to see him? Tonight?"

"You mean . . . like courting?"

He grinned, snuggling her close. "Exactly like courting." He kissed the tip of her nose and said, "Debt or no debt, I want to court you, publicly, letting everyone know that my intentions are honorable. If you'll let me, that is."

"Risley, I . . ."

He grasped one of her hands and traced her fingers with his own. "I'll wait until your debt's done if I need to. I will. I don't want to break my word, but I don't want to miss this chance, either. I promise to be a perfect gentleman tonight, and I can find someone to chaperone, if that worries you, or we don't have to go to the alehouse at all. We can take a walk through the castle, or look at the paintings in the ballroom, or—"

Her fingertips on his lips quieted him. "Yes. I'd be honored to listen to the minstrel with you."

He grinned, his nervousness slipping away with a relieved rush of air. "You will?"

She nodded and giggled. "Yes. No chaperone necessary."

Still grinning, he lifted her from the bureau and set her back on her feet. "Then we had better get our day started, so this evening will arrive that much sooner."

Nella held his hand and smiled. She couldn't agree more.

* * *

The trumpeted alarm had long since faded away by the time Dubric staggered to the scene. Milkmaids and interested gawkers were kept at bay by a handful of volunteers while Dien stood over the body of the milkmaid, taking notes. Fultin, looking confused and out of his element, guarded Meiks. One other body lay near, tended by a pair of the night's volunteers, and Dien nodded toward it as Dubric approached.

"The herald's just bashed on the back of the head. He'll be fine."

"Like Nella," Dubric said. Unlike with the female victims, Dubric saw no passion in the way the killer attacked men. Meiks was bigger, more of a threat, so he was likely dropped first, fatally. Beckwith's survival was probably irrelevant to the murderer. Sparing Lars's life showed that he was not interested in killing men the same way he was preying upon women. *He has merely upped the ante this morning, showing me that he can kill at whim and even guarded women are not safe. With Inek in gaol, and innocent of murder, who would make such a point to taunt me?*

He approached the closest body—the milkmaid—scanning the ground and seeking stray footprints, dropped clues, drips of blood . . . anything he could discern. Layers upon layers of prints dimpled the mud and sloppy snow, most following along the same oft-trodden paths to the barns, but others moved back to the castle or crossways in all directions. Jumbled and haphazard, the prints made little sense from an investigative standpoint. The main route had been used by countless people for decades, and a score or more had traveled its familiar terrain just this morning.

Dubric knelt beside the grimy, blood- and bile-spattered body of the milkmaid. She lay upon her back, staring at the morning sky, while a puddle of blood and viscera lay congealing and oozing beside her. Her belly loomed utterly empty from her diaphragm to her uterus. Everything between had been yanked out, still attached by shiny, bluish lengths of intestine.

"Have you a name yet?" he asked Dien as he pulled a measuring string from his coat pocket. Despite himself, he wondered if she had been a whore.

"Nansy," Dien replied. "I found her faceup, but I'd lay odds she landed facedown."

Dubric measured the rounded, conical depressions on opposite sides of the intestines. She had fallen on her own viscera, landing on her elbows and knees, judging by the dents in the mud.

Her filthy uniform was flecked with bloody fluid, dark bile, mud, and smears of feces. "Where is her liver?" Dubric asked.

Dien knelt beside the pile and used his dagger to gently lift a tangle of muddy intestines. "Looks like it landed first, sir," he said. "Everything else seems to be on top of it."

Dubric added to his notes. "We have Risley's sword. If he is to blame, he has another way of becoming dim. And I tossed Inek in gaol less than a bell ago."

Dien said, "Some other bastard is prowling the courtyard, or one of the pair has an accomplice toying with us. Diddly damn great."

The west-tower door opened and both men looked up at the sound of running.

"I thought I heard a trumpet," Lars said, hurrying to them. "I'd have been here sooner, but I didn't know which door."

"You haven't missed much, pup," Dien said. "Same shit, different corpses."

Lars skidded to a stop, his mouth dropping open. "Boar piss! Is that Meiks and Beckwith?" As Dubric nodded, Beckwith moved, moaning, and Lars sighed with relief. "Left another one alive?"

"Better a hit on the head than a slash across the back or belly," Dien said, holding the measuring string for Dubric as they tallied the length of the slashes across the milkmaid's abdomen.

Dubric noted the measurements then looked up. Fultin had paled to a noxious shade. "Examine Meiks, will you, Lars? Fultin looks about ready to drop."

"Yessir," Lars said, moving to the big man's body.

Fultin staggered toward them, wiping his mouth with the back of his hand. "Sorry, milord."

Dubric waved off the apology. "Check the gaol, will you, and make certain Inek the herbmonger is still in his cell. Fourth in on the right."

"Yes, sir. Of course, sir." Fultin bowed before hurrying away.

Around them, the crowd mumbled their concern but Dubric tried to ignore the noise. Between the added ghosts and the details of the murder, he had the patience for little else. He had barely finished checking Nansy's hands for signs of struggle when Lars returned to them.

Lars knelt and leaned close. "Meiks is different," he said, his voice barely audible over the wind.

"How so, pup?" Dien asked, continuing with his own notations.

Lars swallowed and leaned even closer. "He still has his organs. I don't think the killer took a single thing from him except his life."

Dubric and Dien both looked up. "Are you sure?" Dien asked.

"Yeah. His throat's slashed once, nearly clear to his spine on the right side—a death blow, for sure—but his back . . . He's cut, but it barely reached the muscle layer."

Dien stood and Dubric followed suit, despite the fatigue trying to hold him down. *Of course. Men do not matter, so their organs do not matter. Only the girl matters, even if he has to kill a man to get her.*

They knelt beside Meiks to examine the shallow wounds, and Dubric glanced at the morning sky and frowned. The staff would be heading to work soon, and Risley had no one guarding him. Dubric shifted his gaze to Risley's windows. Someone peered through the one nearest the tower. Suddenly the curtains drew closed, leaving the window blank like the others.

Nearly snapping his pencil in his fist, Dubric looked to Dien first. "Risley has been watching us. Any incidents last night?"

"No, sir. They were as quiet as church mice. He opened the door around ten bell, showed us his girlie was sleeping, and asked us not to wake her." Dien paused and shrugged. "I saw no reason to bother them, sir. I heard the trumpet echo up the west tower and got here as fast as I could. Other than Fultin standing at the tower door, I was first to arrive. No one's touched them but us, and I sure as tits didn't see anyone here."

Lars stood. "I'm still watching him all day?"

Dubric looked up to the lad and nodded. "Keep an eye on him, and watch closely when he learns what happened this morning."

"Yessir." Lars turned to go and ran back to the castle.

"He's waking, sir!" a guard called from beside Beckwith.

Dubric shoved himself upright again and rubbed his aching eyes. *Hopefully this witness saw something useful. I do not know how many more ghosts I can survive.*

Lander Beckwith wobbled as he sat on the open ground of the courtyard and the guards stepped back to give Dubric room. "What happened?" Beckwith muttered. He rubbed the back of his head with a gloved hand and dazedly looked around him.

Dubric pounced on him, the two dead bodies forgotten for the moment. "You tell me," he said, licking his ever-present pencil.

Beckwith twisted his neck as if it were stiff. "I'm not sure. We were taking the milkmaid to her barn and it felt like the back of my head burst." He looked at the crowd of people and his dazed but hopeful expression fell. "Oh no. Her, too? What about Meiks?"

Dubric moved to stand in front of Beckwith, hoping he could block off sight of most of the crowd and lessen his witness's newfound stage fright. "Did you see anything? Anything at all before you were attacked?"

"No," Beckwith said as he glanced around. "Nothing, I'm afraid. She was chattering away about how mistreated she was, having to get up before dawn every morning, and Meiks and I followed her, just like we were supposed to. I suddenly had the strangest feeling that someone was staring at us, so I turned." He rubbed his head and winced as he drew his hand away and looked at it. "Then the bastard whacked me on the head." He stared at the smear of blood for a moment and said, "I don't know what happened after that."

"Did you hear anything? Smell anything?" *Just one damned thing*, Dubric thought. *A lead I can follow.*

While Dubric waited for an answer, Beckwith shook his head and groaned. His brow furrowed as he rubbed the back of his neck and gathered his feet beneath him. At last he said, "Nothing. It was like a phantom or something."

Dubric put away his pencil and closed his book. "If you think of anything else, no matter how minor . . . Anything."

"I'll let you know. Immediately." Beckwith dragged himself to his feet.

"Have the physician tend to your head," Dubric said, "and tell your wife that you are all right and are excused from further guard duty. That should allay some of her fears." Sighing, he turned back to the corpses. *Two more, and one a man! The killer is getting braver, taking chances, but still not making mistakes. Will this madness ever stop?* Muttering under his breath, he stomped forward and barked orders at Dien and the guards.

Dubric heard the tower door open and he turned, hoping to see Rolle or Halld coming to tend the bodies, but Risley strode to him, frowning.

Risley met Dubric's eyes. "I had Lars escort Nella to work while we talk." Sighing, he looked past Dubric to the two bodies and Beckwith, who was trying to find his balance. "Goddess, is this ever going to end?"

Dubric pointed at Risley's windows. "What did you see?"

"Just you looking things over." He stared at Nansy's eviscerated body and said, "I stood at the window while Nella dressed, saw what had happened, and turned away. I didn't want her to know. Didn't want her to see. I still don't."

Dubric looked Risley over from top to bottom, and blinked in surprise. *For King's sake, is the boy that addled?* He drew a single breath to steady his voice, keeping the tone of his remarks conversational. "You have blood on your trousers."

Risley shrugged, returning his attention to Dubric. "Cut myself." His manner remained calm yet concerned and he shoved his hands into his coat pockets. "You going to be able to catch this bastard? I can ask my da to send a few dozen soldiers, if you think it would help."

Dubric pursed his lips and said nothing.

"Dammit, Dubric, this madness has to stop. You don't trust me? Fine. I honestly couldn't care less. But girls are dying every damn night and you don't seem to be making a lick of difference. Let me help you."

Help you hide behind your soldiers, you mean. It will be a cold night in the seven hells before I allow you that particular luxury. Scowling, Dubric pocketed his notebook and took a single step toward Risley. "I do not need you or your father's assistance, and I suggest you continue on your way before I charge you with interfering in an investigation." His hand fell to his sword and he stared at Risley. "Now."

Throwing his hands into the air, Risley stomped off while Dubric let a relieved sigh slip free.

"He causing trouble, sir?" Dien asked, coming to Dubric's side as he finished the last of his notes.

"No more than usual," Dubric said. "But his clothes were bloodstained and someone had recently stitched his left hand."

"Peg my mother. Is he so arrogant he thought you wouldn't notice?"

"Perhaps. Either that or he is completely innocent."

Dien put away his notebook. "Or trying to confuse us. Damn it all to the seven hells." They watched Risley enter the tower and disappear into the castle. "How the peg can we throw Lord Romlin's son in gaol without risking war?"

Dubric sighed and rubbed his aching eyes. "By being completely certain and having the evidence to back us up."

* * *

The killer slipped a hand into the right side pocket of his leather coat. The stolen kidney remained a delightful weight, moist and still warm. It would make a perfectly lovely snack, and his mouth filled with saliva at the thought.

As expected, his rooms were quiet and empty. Once he assured himself of his solitude, he emptied his pockets onto a low table and stripped to his skin, leaving his clothes where they fell. He cleaned himself, scrubbing his fingers until they shone. That done, he rinsed the kidney, dried it, and placed it upon a shining plate edged in gold.

Humming happily, he threw his filthy, bloodstained clothes into his hearth, poking them into the coals until they caught aflame. Licking his lips, he picked up a wad of hair from the low table. He looked at Nansy's hair for a moment and crushed it in his fingers, remembering the loose weight of her head as he had cut off her hair. She had died easily, but loudly, screaming as her steaming guts fell onto the ground. But it was all over in an instant. He smiled. Perhaps her heart had burst with the surprise and shock. Not tidy, but certainly quick. An improvement to be sure, and it had brought him within sight of his goal.

He sniffed her hair and strode to his bedchamber,

pulling a pillow from its case. He unfastened the pillow's laced hem and slipped the hair inside, taking a moment to breathe in the scent of the other dead girls. He could identify each one, from the gypsy's spicy tang to the calming quality of the first milkmaid, each a distinct reminder of how he was nearly clean, nearly perfect once again.

Back to the table, he looked at the kidney waiting on his plate, then fetched himself a fork, a knife, and a lovely glass of wine. As he poured the wine his stomach grumbled.

He'd already decided how he wanted his breakfast. Raw. With a bit of salt. How perfect for such a salty girl.

And after breakfast there would be one quick errand. He was so close now, nearly purified. Dubric must be reminded of how perfect he had become. How untouchable.

Smiling, he picked up his knife and began to eat.

* * *

While Otlee and Dien tended to the examination of the newest murder scene and interrogation of any potential witnesses, Dubric dealt with the frightened, angry people of the castle, a battalion of fatigued guards, the physicians, the tenth and eleventh bodies, and Lord Brushgar.

Lord Brushgar was not happy, had not been happy for days, and Dubric had nothing new to tell him.

But Lord Brushgar did not seem to care what progress Dubric had or had not made. He only wanted resolution. "I want this stopped, *now*," he said as he loomed over his desk.

"I realize that, sir," Dubric said and rubbed his eyes. The ghosts flickered, a few faded and disappeared, but most remained standing among the chaos of the office. Dammit, he needed to get some sleep before he simply dropped dead from exhaustion.

Brushgar waved his hands in the air and knocked over a stack of rolled maps and scrolls. "Then stop it."

"It is not that simple. He is somehow finding lone women—"

"Then do not allow them to be alone."

Dubric wanted to sigh his aggravation, but he refrained. "I have tried that. They panic, they hide, they disobey. Somehow he finds them. This morning he attacked a woman with two guards. Separating the women is not helping us, sir, it seems to be helping him."

Brushgar slammed his palms on his cluttered desk. "Two guards? Who the bloody hell could attack two men like that? Who?"

Dubric pulled out his notebook and flipped through. "I considered that question myself, sir. Logically speaking, everyone has been cut from very close range, so far, so I doubt our killer is an archer. They are not prone to utilizing close combat, after all."

Brushgar rolled his eyes and spoke as if addressing a small child. "The soldiers are all wintering with their families, you fool. We only have six archers in the castle now and none of the footmen."

Why did everyone insist on reminding him of things he already knew? "I realize that, sir. With the army gone, it severely limits the possibilities of who the attacker might or might not be. If we remove the six archers from the possibility list, that reasonably only leaves us five names, myself included. Assuming the culprit lives in the castle."

"Five? That's it?" Brushgar waved his hand as if

dismissing the problem. "Arrest them all and sort it out later."

Dubric frowned and held out his book. "Perhaps you should look at the list, milord."

Brushgar took the book from Dubric's hands. The page was filled margin to margin with close compact writing, details of the crimes, but the suspect list was reasonably easy to see. It was a list of eleven names surrounded by a box and separated from the other notes.

Dubric knew Brushgar would recognize each and every name, and every man could be trusted, had been trusted, for summers. Brushgar shook the book at Dubric, his face turning red. "This is it? This is your list? Dammit, Dubric, my grandson's on here!"

"I realize that, sir. So am I, all six archers, however doubtful they are—"

Adjusting his spectacles, Brushgar read on. "*Both* of my squires? You've lost your mind."

Dubric nodded. "Yes, milord, yours and mine. Eleven names total."

Brushgar tossed the book on the desk amid the rubble. "Impossible. It's not any of these men."

Dubric snatched his notebook back and flipped it open again. "Then who the bloody hell is it? Who else can do this? I have been tracking the bastard for nearly a phase now, and have no real leads other than he is quick, clever, and apparently invisible. It has to be one of these men. By reason, it *has* to. We are on very short supply of men trained to use weapons, men trained to kill, who are young or healthy enough to spend who knows how long out in the cold, waiting for a victim to walk by. And now he is attacking men, too. If it is not one of them, who else could it be? My other possible suspect spent the latter part of the night in gaol and he was securely contained during the latest murders. His apparent innocence leads me back to the same eleven damned names."

Brushgar loomed over his desk again and his voice rumbled. "I tell you, it's someone else. It's not any of these men."

Dubric reread the list for the thousandth time. "I know that, sir. They have all been watched. All have passed."

"Good, then." His hands clasping over his ample belly, Brushgar sat and peered at Dubric.

"No, milord, it is not good. It has to be one of them. Reason demands it. But it is not, not unless they had help, someone else who is killing, as well, and that does not seem to be the case, either. I have had every one of them followed and watched, myself included, by at least three independent pairs of eyes. All accounts have come back clean. So, if it is not myself, Risley, Dien, Fultin, Derre, Borlt, Egger, Quentin, Almund, Werian, or Ghet, then who in the seven hells is it?"

He flipped back a couple of pages. "The only clues I have are that he is taking kidneys and hair, he is possibly a right-handed smoker, left Nella Brickerman and Lars Hargrove alive by choice, Lander Beckwith probably because of time constraints, might be using a shaving razor, is tall, seems to be eating what he takes, and is keeping some kind of list. No one has seen him, but one witness may have seen his shadow and claims he wears a cloak. He also is not afraid of armed men. Both Beckwith and Meiks were put down quickly, and Meiks died. I am missing something, an elusive connection, but try as I might, I cannot see it."

Brushgar leaned back in his chair. It gave off an appreciable creak. "What about the girls? Any consistencies there?"

Dubric flipped a few pages forward. "Some. All are unmarried and members of the service staff. All commoners by birth. Ages range from fourteen to nineteen summers, as far as I can tell. All shapes, sizes, hair and eye colors, although he does seem to have a slight preference for blue-eyed girls."

"Nella is brown-eyed, if I recall," Brushgar said, tugging on his beard.

Dubric nodded. "But so were Celese and Fytte."

"Who's Fytte?"

"The girl from the ale room, milord. I postulate that he is afraid of being seen and that the dark, preferably outside, suits him better. But then again, I do not know that, I am merely guessing."

Brushgar thought for a moment and asked, "Of the likely men, whose name keeps turning up most often?"

Dubric sighed and sat down. It seemed like it was the first time he had been off his feet in days. "Risley," he said, without softening the blow.

Brushgar slammed his hand on the desk again. "Risley? You have got to be joking! My grandson would never—"

"Begging your pardon, milord, but *someone's* grandson is doing this," Dubric snapped. Sighing, he flipped through his book again. "He meets the necessary criteria and then some. He has not one razor but two—that he has shown me at least—and both are collapsible and small enough to conceal. Nella Brickerman lived—damning evidence right there—and he had Albin Darril's sword. He readily admits he has no alibi for the early murders." Dubric closed his little book, putting it away. "I hate to even consider him, and I know if I arrest him it will kill Heather and Kyl. They will never forgive me. But reason and evidence insist it has to be Risley."

Brushgar's voice was soft and dry, as if he had trouble breathing. All the color had left his face. "Why haven't you arrested him, then?"

Dubric sighed and shook his head. "Because, despite the circumstances piling against him, I have no definite proof. He has been watched nearly constantly for three days. Not once has he left his suite between bedtime and breakfast. I thought perhaps there was a concealed door inside, something to give him access to the courtyard without us knowing, but that does not appear to be the case, either. For two nights I had him woken at least four times a shift, and he was always there. On the second evening he left his door propped open throughout the night so my men could enter at will to see that he slept in his own bed." Dubric paused as his fingers gripped the chair. "Now he has acquired an alibi, as well, at least for last night's victims."

Relief shone on Lord Brushgar's face like sunlight sparkling on water. "Good. What alibi is that?"

"Nella Brickerman. Risley moved her to his suite yesterday, after she was attacked. She will vouch for him even if the rest of the castle wants to hang him." Surely even Brushgar knew rumors about Risley and the linen maid had become a gossip staple. Dubric forced his fingers to relax their grip, and he flexed his aching knuckles.

Brushgar frowned. "She's one tough girl, I'll give her that. All she's been through. Stubborn little thing. My grandson seems to think he's met his match there."

Dubric agreed. "Aye, sir." And the fact that they were smitten with each other complicated matters, as well, he thought.

"But, since associating with her, Risley has become infatuated with the plight of the servants. He has demanded more privies, of all things, better rations, even improvements for their quarters. I fear she may be polluting his mind."

More likely opening his eyes, Dubric thought, but said nothing.

Brushgar pursed his lips and stared at Dubric. "So not only is my grandson falling into madness over the plight of the peasantry, you assume he's the killer. What's worse, you haven't made a lick of progress in finding another man responsible, even though you've been looking for over a phase. How do you intend to remedy these situations?"

"I am not sure yet, sir."

"That's not good enough." Brushgar leaned back in his chair and glared at Dubric.

Dubric prepared to endure his lord's wrath.

* * *

With a right proper castigation and almost no sleep, Dubric trudged through the castle to his suite. He was dog tired, his feet hurt, his brain ached, and he felt no closer to catching the monster that had been preying upon his castle. Scores of people approached him, so many that they became a blur, and most accused him of favoritism. Everyone knew it was Risley, so why was he still free? And what about the uppity commoner whore? She knew something. And why wasn't he doing his damned job?

Tired, grumpy, and just plain fed up, Dubric refused to answer.

He had nearly reached his suite when Otlee ran to him, waving urgently. "The message, sir. From Aberville."

Dubric yawned and accepted the miniscule twirl of parchment, breaking the seal.

Trumble's message was tiny but perfectly legible.

Lord Brushgar, seven razors last autumn. No other known Faldorrahns.

"Sir? Is something wrong?"

Other than that my life is collapsing around me and I fear this torture will never end? "No, of course not. Resume your duties."

Otlee gave him a concerned glance, then hurried off.

Cursing under his breath, Dubric read the message one more time before returning to Lord Brushgar's office. He did not bother to knock.

He slammed the door behind him and stared at the old man behind the desk. "Is there a reason why you neglected to mention that you purchased seven shaving razors?"

Brushgar stood, staring back. "Because my personal purchases are none of your concern."

Dubric stepped forward and knocked nearly every paper, ornament, and artifact off Brushgar's desk. He spoke slowly, struggling to control his anger. "Every damned thing pertaining to this investigation is my concern. I told you, days ago, by the seven hells, less than a bell ago, that the weapon seemed to be a collapsible razor. Today, after I sent a rider two provinces south, I discover that you bought seven of the wretched things!"

Brushgar blinked. "They were not 'wretched.' They were finely carved walnut, custom engraved with gilded inscriptions, and cost me nearly three hundred crown apiece." He sat and leaned back in his chair. "Such fine gadgets would not be used to murder servants, for Goddess's sake."

"Where are they?"

Brushgar rolled his eyes. "I have no idea. I gave them away as gifts at the conclusion of the fall festival, so I would assume the recipients have them. I certainly do not."

"Who? Damn you! Who did you give them to?"

Brushgar shrugged. "I can't recall."

"You what?"

Brushgar leaned over and grabbed a pile of papers and gadgets. "I can't recall. I gave them all away, remember? All but the one I kept."

Dubric let his breath out in a rush and staggered back, rubbing his eyes. "You expect me to believe that you dispersed nearly two-thousand-crowns' worth of custom-built razors and cannot remember who you gave them to?"

"Perhaps I gave them to Talmil, Berde . . . maybe Knude. I can't possibly remember for sure." Brushgar dropped the armload of mess on his desk. "I have more important things to do with my time than discuss this further. You will immediately cease this needless argument." He took a breath and stared Dubric in the eye. "This matter is closed. Good day." He nodded once, then leaned over to grab another armload of mess.

Dubric cursed and left Brushgar's office. *Six, perhaps seven razors*, he thought. *Damn. Who? Who would know where they were?*

He stomped past Josceline while his fatigued mind raced. Nigel would not deliver the gifts himself. That would be beneath him. Who would he assign the task to? Who would he trust with such valuables?

Frantic, he looked up the main stairs. Would Lord Brushgar's herald have any insights? Would Beckwith still be awake after this morning's drama and his injury? Dubric tried not to get his hopes up as he hurried up the stairs and to the families' wing.

Beckwith answered the door freshly washed and wrapped in a bathing robe, his head bandaged. He blinked in surprise and backed away from the door, beckoning Dubric to enter. "Milord?"

Dubric pulled out his notebook and did not bother with niceties. "Several moons ago, during the fall festival, did you happen to deliver some gifts for Lord Brushgar?"

"The razors? Of course, milord. All six, precisely as requested."

Dubric struggled to remain calm. "Do you remember whom you delivered them to?"

Beckwith paused, tapping his chin, then he turned and walked away. "I don't trust my memory after all this time, especially after today, but I do keep records of such things. One moment."

Dubric waited at the door while Beckwith opened a drawer and rooted through some papers. He returned with two bound stacks and tucked one under his arm while he slipped the twine from the other. "The fall festival, correct?" As Dubric nodded, he flipped to the lower part of the stack, then slowed his search. He frowned, shook his head, then dropped the stack on the floor.

Releasing the twine from the second stack, he searched through three sheets, then paused, smiling. "Here we are, milord. All six names, checked and initialed. They were beautiful razors, milord, and all were happy to receive them." Beaming, he handed Dubric the paper. It contained a list of names written in Brushgar's hand, each crossed out and initialed by Beckwith with a date and time beside each.

Dubric nodded his thanks and read the list:

> Sir Talmil, Sir Berde, Sir Knude, Risley Romlin,
> Friar Bonne, Head Accountant Jelke

"Has someone complained of an error in delivery?"

"No," Dubric said, looking up again. "May I keep this?"

Beckwith bowed, holding his bandaged head. "Of course, milord. I am delighted to help."

Dubric folded the list and put it in his notebook. "How is your head? Did you require stitches?"

"Oh no, milord. Apparently it is more of a scrape than a gash and doesn't require stitching." Beckwith shrugged and rubbed the back of his head. "Rather painful, though."

Dubric thanked the herald, then went to find Dien.

* * *

As Friar Bonne shoved his bulk from Lars's chair, Otlee glanced at Dubric, then initialed the friar's testimony and set aside the sheet of paper. "How many more, sir? So far their responses have been the same."

"Just one," Dubric replied. He had given Dien a list of six names, instructing him to send in each man in that particular order, preferably with his razor.

Sir Knude and Sir Berde were both of ailing health, and both had insisted that their razors were treasured gifts that had never left their possession. Bonne had used his, remarking often about how well it kept an edge, but his razor was pristine, and bore no signs of being used as a murder weapon. Jelke's razor had broken—he had inadvertently dropped it on a stone floor, popping loose the spring mechanism—and Sir Talmil's razor was coated with layers of soap scum and stubble.

One man remained on the list and Dubric stared at his name. Most of the ghosts milled about, bored, but Nansy wailed silently while her guts constantly fell from her belly and Meiks glowered, staring directly at Dubric and nowhere else.

Otlee looked up at a commotion in the outer office, but Dubric clasped his hands together and tried to smile.

Risley flung the door open and stomped through with Dien right behind him. "How many times do you have to look at my razors? By the Goddess, you've seen them. He's seen them. Peg, it's a wonder half the province hasn't seen them. But now he tells me you're not interested in *those* razors, after all? Dammit, what do you expect me to do? Create one out of thin air?"

"Do you or do you not have another?"

"Yes, I have one. It's back home, in my bath chamber."

"Not that one. The one your grandfather gave you."

Risley stared at Dubric as if he had grown a second head. "My Grandda Rom never gave me a razor."

"I am talking about a gift from Lord Brushgar. Where is it, Risley?"

"He never gave me a razor, either." He rolled his eyes and turned away, but Dien shoved him back toward Dubric's desk.

Dubric remained calm. "I have documentation proving that you received one last autumn. As a gift. Where is it?"

Risley turned, fuming. "I never received a damn razor and your silly games are keeping me from guarding Nella." He started to leave again, but Dien blocked the door. "Get out of my way."

Dubric stood. "On the third day of ten month last autumn, at ten minutes before two bell in the afternoon, you received a specially crafted wooden razor with your name engraved in gold leaf. Where is it?"

Risley turned slowly. "You've lost your mind."

Dubric set Sir Berde's razor on the desk and it

gleamed, polished and golden. "It looked just like this, except with your name. We have confirmation of its creation and delivery. I know you received it."

Risley stared at the razor, paling, but he said nothing.

Dien shoved him, and Risley stumbled forward, his hands landing on either side of the razor. They clenched, then opened, and Risley shook his head.

"Why did you kill all those girls?" Dubric asked.

Risley looked up at him, pleading with his eyes. "I didn't kill anyone. I swear." He shoved away from the desk. "I don't remember getting a razor from Grandda. Please, you have to believe me."

Dien remained rooted before the door. "A moment ago you insisted you did not have the razor, now you're saying you don't remember receiving it. Seems like your story is changing, your lordship."

Risley looked back and forth between Dubric and Dien. "I just want to protect Nella. I haven't cut anyone."

"Were you here during the fall festival, especially the third day of ten month?"

"I . . . I was here during part of the festival, I think, but I don't remember what days."

Dien pulled three slips of paper from his jacket. "I checked with the listings for contests. You participated in staff fighting, knife throwing, and pig roping on the third."

Risley backed away, rubbing his forehead. "Pig roping?"

"Came in second, too," Dien said. "You won a copper pot. Yauncy keeps track of such things."

"Where is the razor, Risley?"

"I don't know."

"You put part of a dyer in a boiling vat. Why?"

"I didn't."

"Or you can't remember?" Dien prodded.

He abruptly turned to Dien. "I absolutely do not remember putting anyone in a vat."

Dubric kept his voice low and soothing. "Do you remember nearly decapitating a young woman near the well or hacking another to bits?"

"No! I haven't hurt anyone."

Dien loomed close and snarled, "You tied Lars in intestines and shoved him under a chicken coop."

"No! I'd never hurt Lars. Never. He's like my brother."

"You didn't hurt him," Dubric said, sitting again. "You merely tied him up and shoved him aside while you had your fun."

Risley took a deep breath and another. "I am the King's grandson, for Goddess's sake, not an uneducated fool. I did not hurt anyone, nor did I receive a razor, let alone one like that. Unless you can prove, with something more than bits of paper, that I did, I am not going to listen to this madness any longer. Excuse me." He looked at Dien, then shoved past, nearly running from the offices.

Dien watched him go. "Catch all that?"

"Yes, sir," Otlee said. He initialed the papers and handed them to Dubric. "Every single word."

* * *

After discussing Risley to the point of exhaustion, Dubric decided that their suspect was not going to get into additional trouble in broad daylight while being observed by Lars and two other trustworthy men. Barely conscious, Dubric reached his own chamber door and yawned. He had to get some sleep, and he had to get away from the ghosts, murders, and frightened rabbits of the castle, at least for a little while.

Half asleep already, he located a length of red cording and tied it on the door handle as a signal not to disturb him even if the castle was burning down. He slammed and locked the door, pushed a chair in front of it, and climbed onto his bed, not bothering to remove his sword or his boots. He ignored the damned ghosts. The busy ones, the fresh ones, and the screaming ones. He closed his eyes and told them all to go to the seven hells.

He was asleep before his head had touched his pillows.

He slept past lunch, a whole three or four blessed bells, and woke feeling like a new man. He washed—even took a moment to shave—changed clothes, and readied himself for the remainder of the day. Sighing, he unbarricaded his door and opened it, wondering what had been left outside for him to deal with.

His laundry waited bright and folded in a woven basket, and a lunch tray sat atop the laundry. An envelope had been stuck into one side of the basket and a parcel from Waterford in the other. He lifted the entire basket and carried it inside. The hallway was utterly empty, but some of the ghosts watched with bland boredom.

He set the lunch tray upon his little table, the laundry basket on his bed, reached for the envelope, and broke the seal.

It was his copy of this morning's physicians' notes. Normal details with the girl, if any aspect of brutal murder was normal. Meiks had been cut on the back after his throat was slashed.

Dubric read the rest of the details with slight boredom—notes about angle and depth and body positioning—and he opened the lunch tray.

Fried chicken and potatoes. Praise the King!

Grunting happily, he grabbed a piece of chicken and ate while he read. The physicians still seemed to agree that the weapon could be a razor and that gave Dubric some satisfaction, however minor. He finished the letter, tossed the chicken bone in the wastebasket, and grabbed another piece before tending to his laundry.

Shirts put in one drawer, kerchiefs and socks in another, a chicken thigh sticking half in his mouth, he stopped and stared at the laundry basket.

There was something under the folded trousers. Something bulky. Curious, he set aside the piece of chicken and pulled a stiff brown package out of the basket. It was not quite square, about a length long, less than a hand tall, and wrapped in stiff cloth. As he lifted it, he noticed that the whole thing stank of death and rot. The cloth was an odd, mottled color of russet-brown and had been tied with a cheery green ribbon. It seemed to be the same kind of ribbon most of the cleaning girls wore as part of their uniform. He set his food tray on the floor and considered the new curiosity as he placed it on his table.

He lifted the package, turning it this way and that to examine the outside. He saw no writing of any kind on the blood-soaked cloth. Once again, he had no apparent clues. The wrapper seemed to be made of muslin or a simple weave cotton, and had definite weight. Something hard was inside; it clinked, like metal.

He set it back upon the table and examined the ribbon. Unlike the wrapper, the ribbon was pristine and clean, without a drop of blood to be seen. But there was something. On one of the tails. He turned the ribbon over and saw NB written in black ink. Tiny perfect letters.

He knew most of the girls marked their things to avoid confusion and theft. It was Nella's ribbon. He was sure of it. His heart hammering, he tugged at the ribbon and the bow opened. It had not been knotted.

He took a single breath and opened the package. Grimacing, he grabbed his notebook and desperately examined the gruesome present. He had been presented with a smorgasbord of clues, but what did they *mean*?

Minutes later he was out in the hall, hurrying to his office.

CHAPTER

14

†

L ars yawned. Risley had barely spoken a word since
returning from Dubric's office and the day had
dragged along like sludge in a creek bed. They leaned
against the wall of two east and watched the maids
work while an additional pair of guards watched them.
The girls' shift would be done in a bell or so, and he had
gathered not a single bit of useful detail. The two men
staring at Risley were not helping matters.

"So Nella stitched up your hand?" Lars asked, trying
again to encourage Risley to talk.

Risley glared at the pair down the hall. "I'm not saying anything, and your fishing for a confession isn't going to work."

Lars leaned back, bouncing his head against the
stone wall. "Don't be mad at me, Ris. I'm just doing my
job."

"I didn't kill them. I'm sure of it now." He nodded
politely to Ker and smiled at Dari. "I also know damn
well Dubric is trying to pin this on me, but he's wrong."
He paused, turning to look at Lars. "Besides an imaginary razor, what other evidence has he concocted
against me?"

"You know I'm not allowed to discuss case particu-
lars."

Risley seemed about to retort, but he raised his head and looked to the left. "Otlee's coming."

Both stood straight and Lars neatened his jerkin. "You have something for me?"

Otlee did not glance at Risley, only watched Lars. "Dubric wants everyone in his office. Immediately."

"Some new bit of make-believe evidence against me?" Risley asked, leaning against the wall again. "Or has Dubric resorted to rooting through my underdrawers and gathering my shoe lint?"

What do you expect, Ris? Lars thought. *You're certainly not doing anything to help yourself.* Frowning, he said, "I'm right behind you."

Otlee hurried away, weaving through a cluster of window maids on their way to the next set of suites.

"Go on," Risley said. "Before you get into trouble."

"You sure?"

Risley bowed to Nella, bringing a sparkle to her eyes as she walked to a linen cupboard. "Go. One of us in Dubric's bad graces is bad enough."

His mind churning, Lars left, hurrying down the hall and wondering what was important enough to pull him from his post.

He stopped, frowning, as he saw Otlee waiting in the east tower. "Thought we were supposed to meet in Dubric's office?"

Otlee waited for a nobleman to walk by, heading downstairs. "His suite," Otlee whispered, turning and running up the stairs.

"But you said—"

Otlee opened the third-floor door. "Dubric specifically said to not let Lord Risley know where our meeting is."

Lars remained beside Otlee and whispered, "What happened?"

"The killer left a clue for Dubric. But I don't know what. Just that we're supposed to meet in his suite." They turned the corner toward Dubric's suite and Otlee nodded to Fultin, who stood outside the door.

Fultin knocked, then Dien opened the door from the inside.

As soon as they entered, Lars wrinkled his nose. It smelled as if something had died and had been soaked in chicken grease. "What happened?" he asked.

"You'll know when I do," Dien said, motioning them in.

* * *

"So, what did you want to show us?" Dien asked as he stepped into Dubric's suite with the boys walking behind him. "I've noticed you've gone sloppy."

Dubric glanced around the room. He had always been particular in his neatness, but today he had left laundry tossed on the bed, a food tray lying on the floor, and the air smelled like fried chicken and decay. Perhaps he should have tidied up before fetching his team. He almost laughed at the thought.

"Never mind about that now. Lars, did Risley leave your sight for any period of time this afternoon?"

"Other than when Dien came to get him?" Lars asked. "Yes, he did. A couple of times, to go to the privy." He frowned, approaching the table. "What's going on? Otlee said you'd found a clue."

So Risley had opportunity after all. Dubric placed his hands on the top of a box, patting it. "I received a parcel today."

"You got a box?" Otlee asked, tilting his head.

Fytte and Elli both looked at Otlee and laughed. Ennea tilted her head and yawned. The rest of the ghosts loitered around the room, oblivious as always.

Dubric rubbed his eyes and the ghosts faded away for a few moments. "No, no. It is inside the box. I am merely storing it so I will not lose any part of it." He lifted the lid and tossed it aside.

Eagerness pulsed in Dubric's veins and everything within his sight seemed clearer, sharper. Was it an effect of hope? Something else? He barely contained his giddiness as he spoke. "I tied it back up, so you could see how it came, see all of it, just as I had."

"Is that fabric or paper?" Lars asked.

"Fabric. But do not touch it. It has been soaked in blood."

Lars leaned in for a closer look. "Where did you get it?"

Dubric lifted the parcel from the box and set the revolting bundle on the table. "It was in my laundry. See the ribbon? It belonged to one of the girls."

Dien glanced at Dubric before returning his attention to the package. "Which one?"

Dubric tugged at the ribbon and pulled it away from the package. "Nella, I believe. I think the fabric came from Celese. Her whole blouse was missing." He dropped the ribbon onto the table, where it puddled into a pile much like Nansy's intestines.

"What's inside?" Otlee asked.

"This," Dubric said. With the slightest touch of his fingers, the package opened like a gruesome flower. The smell that wafted out was as bad as a bloated deer corpse that had been rotting in the woods for several sunny summer days.

"Is that grass?" Otlee's eyes were huge.

Dubric shook his head. "No, it is hair. Bloody hair."

Dien swallowed as if it pained him. "And that meat . . ."

Dubric said, "Kidney? Probably, but I have to check with the physician to be sure."

Dien ran his fingers through his hair. "Taiel'dar's balls, sir. It's on a plate!"

Specifically a china plate, from Lord Brushgar's custom service, reserved for special guests and private dinners. If that was not a clue, he would eat his own boots. He pointed to the flash of gold peeking out from beneath an artful pile of curly light brown hair, most likely Fytte's. He kept his voice calm yet curious. "Cutlery, too. He took the time to arrange it like a gourmet meal."

Dien grimaced. "What kind of lunatic would do such a thing?"

"Is that all he sent, sir?" Lars asked. "A plate of kidneys and hair? Why go to all the trouble?"

"Because of this." He moved the plate from the wrapper and placed it on the table, taking great care to not dislodge a single hair.

Hidden under the plate, a long dark braid tied in a ribbon as cheery and green as the one outside the parcel lay coiled in a near-perfect circle over a piece of folded parchment. "I almost missed this," Dubric said softly. "If I had not moved the plate, I would never have seen it."

Dubric lifted the braid and it hung like a dead snake from his fingers for a moment before he dropped it on the table.

Unlike the wadded tangle of other hair, the braid was clean and unclotted by blood. Much like a surviving victim.

"It's Nella's, isn't it?" Lars asked.

"Yes, I believe so. It seems to be the right length, the right color, and perhaps half of what he cut." Dubric lifted the parchment from the bloody wrapping. "Our friend sent me a note."

The three remained quiet and watchful as Dubric opened the parchment. "As I said, I almost missed this. But I think he planned it that way. To test me, perhaps."

"What does it say?" Otlee asked.

Dubric cleared his throat and read with as little emotion as possible.

"*My Dear Castellan,*

"*I have marinated Rianne and aged her to a fine and sinful vintage. You will find her juices to have a delightful flavor: piss and corruption and lust. To welcome carnal sin back, my Lord Castellan, to consume it, is to purify oneself.*

"*You've overlooked the blood on my hands, the blood and lust cleansing my soul. You've witnessed it, yet ignored the perfect truth of my atonement. Girls are dying, my Lord Castellan, every night beneath my razor, but you are not making a lick of difference. I expected so much more of you, but you continue to disappoint me.*

"*No matter. I shall savor these wicked sheep as whim takes me and I shall no longer be constrained by darkness. Soon I shall be pious once again. I know how sin tastes, how it purifies. Do you?*

"*Enjoy your repast.*'"

Dubric looked up from the note to see the others staring at him. "That is all he wrote. No signature."

Dien blinked, then shook his head. "That's all? Pardon me, sir, but I've never frigging heard of a letter from a criminal, let alone one so damn conversational."

"Yeah," Lars said. "At best we get a crude nude drawing in a cell or a botched forgery."

Otlee asked, "Can I see it?"

Dubric handed Otlee the letter and then pulled his notebook from his pocket. "A good man died today, as did another maid. I'm eager to hear any insights you may have. This must stop. Remain impartial in your observations. It may not be Risley, after all."

"All right," Lars said, rooting through the hair on the plate with one finger. "Can I separate this?"

Dubric bowed his head in agreement but said nothing, trying to let his men come to their own conclusions.

"He's definitely educated," Otlee said. "Not only can he write, he writes well." He held the paper to the light, squinting at it. "This is parchment, not paper, right?"

Dubric nodded, checking off notes he had listed upon his initial examination of the package, and preparing to add new ones.

"Who would use parchment?" Dien asked. "We use ground wood pulp for all of our paperwork." He lifted Nella's braid and examined it, weaving it through his fingers.

"The accountants do, too," Lars muttered. "Eamonn uses parchment for some of his maps, I think."

Eamonn, Dubric noted with a slight smile. At nearly eighty summers of age and crippled, the mapmaker barely saw past his drawing boards, but he knew his papers and inks.

"Mostly lamb vellum these days," Dien said, measuring the braid against the loose bit of ribbon. "He says inks shine against it."

"This ink isn't shining," Otlee said, setting the letter

on the table. "It's cheap. Cheaper than what we use, at least. It smears and fades as he writes."

Inexpensive ink, Dubric noted.

Dien sniffed the braid. "It smells like soap, even with the decay stench." Setting the hair aside, he reached for the wrapping cloth and paused, looking back at the braid and puddle of ribbon. "Risley's girl's here twice. Her ribbon and her hair. Think that's significant?"

"Maybe the killer's infatuated with her?" Otlee offered. "She is a servant, like the rest. And we still don't know why he didn't kill her."

Dubric added more notes.

Lars fiddled with some small things in his hand. "Ten thin slices of kidney," he said, setting a roundish dark bit of dried mud onto the table, "and one hunk of dirt. The girls and Meiks?"

When everyone nodded, he pulled the next trinket from his palm, a bit of white feather. "This would represent Beckwith, I'd assume." He paused, chewing his lip before dropping a silver coin on the table. "This was mine. I think. It's an old scepter with King Byreleah Grennere on it." He glanced at Otlee and shrugged. "My great-grandfather. I hadn't seen it for a few days, but I honestly can't remember if I had it with me on patrol that night."

"You think he might have stolen it?" Dubric asked, scratching in his notebook. "From your rooms?"

"It's not impossible," Lars said. "We never lock the door, and people are coming and going all the time. Heck, I'm almost never there. I'll check with Trumble. He'd know if other things have turned up missing."

"Is there a way to find out whose parchment it is?" Otlee asked.

"I know how," Dien said, paling. He glanced over his shoulder and said, "That damned mirror."

Otlee tilted his head. "'Mirror'? What 'mirror'?"

The mirror! Dubric wrote, underlining the word. *Why, for King's sake, did I not think of that earlier?*

Leaving Dien standing near the table, Dubric walked to his mirror while the boys followed him. "Sett Nuobir made it a long time ago, intending to use it for communication, or to watch over loved ones far away." He pulled the cover off, letting it fall to the floor, and the mirror shone, polished and well-tended. "It was supposed to be destroyed, but Nuobir could not bear to smash it. I have had it ever since."

"How can it show us who this belongs to?" Otlee asked.

Dubric had the boys stand on either side of him. "Like this," he said, holding the parchment in his right hand like an offering. "Show me."

Their reflection wavered, flickering, and seemed to move backward and to the right until Lord Brushgar's image appeared. He lay on a divan with a blanket across his lap and his mouth hanging open, drooling through his snores.

Otlee grinned as he leaned toward the glass. "Who could get parchment from Lord Brushgar?"

Dubric lowered his hand and Brushgar faded away. "I have no idea. To the best of my knowledge, his parchment is in his desk, in his office."

Dien chuckled. "How can you tell he has a desk, let alone parchment? There's nothing in there but a pile of rubble."

Otlee squinted at the mirror. "Could the killer have pilfered it? Who goes into Lord Brushgar's office?"

Dubric considered the idea. "I suppose that would shorten the list considerably." He tapped his chin, thinking. "Josceline cleans for him, and of course the accountants are always there. His squires, Friar Bonne, the herald, Flavin—"

"Don't get too close, Otlee," Dien said. "It's dangerous."

Entranced, Otlee took another step forward. "Amazing! Hey, look! There's something written along the edge of the frame."

"Merely a message left by Nuobir, warning users to be careful," Dubric said.

"It might be 'amazing', but it's not fair to spy on innocent people." Reddening, Lars stuffed his hands into his pockets. "I mean, everyone needs their privacy, don't they?" He walked to the table and started rooting through the clues again.

Dubric glanced at Lars, then looked away. He remembered what it had been like to be young and healthy, and without feminine companionship. The thought of someone spying on his private time would have been embarrassing for him, too.

Turning back toward the mirror, Dubric's attention settled upon a pewter box on his shelf. He nearly stumbled as the realization hit him. *The sliver of wood! Goddess damned son-of-a-whore!*

"There may be one more thing we can use the mirror to trace." He walked to the shelf and lifted the pewter box. The sliver of wood he had found in Claudette's chest lay inside, tucked carefully in a folded bit of paper. Hope singing in his heart, he turned back to his men.

"I think I found something, too." Lars looked over his shoulder and motioned the others over.

"What is it, pup?"

"A hair," Lars said, flattening the bloody wrapper. "Just one. It's inside a crease." He met Dubric's gaze.

"And it doesn't seem to match any of the victims, or any of us."

They gathered around, examining the bloody cloth and the single nearly-black hair. Too short and too dark to be Nella's, too straight to be Ennea's or the peddler's daughter's, the hair clung to the cloth as if it wanted to hide in the coarse weave.

"Good eye, pup," Dien said, patting him on the back.

Dubric picked the hair from the cloth. It resisted for a moment, then broke free. "Two definite clues and a way to trace them. Perhaps we will finally finish this."

His men standing beside him, he held the sliver before the mirror.

"Show me."

A moment later Dien cursed and pounded the wall. Otlee sagged, shaking his head. Dubric held the hair next, but the image in the mirror did not change.

Lars took a shaking breath. "Now that we have proof, what would you have us do, sir?"

Scowling, Dubric turned away from Risley's reflection. "Capture him alive, and prepare for war."

* * *

Nella, Ker, and Mirri finished the last bed and privy room of the day and they restocked the supply cart for tomorrow. Stef walked by, sneering, with an armload of rumpled sheets, and Mirri stuck out her tongue.

"She's just jealous," Mirri said, returning to the task at hand. "It's not every day one of us gets courted, especially by someone like Lord Risley."

Ker shoved towels into the lowest shelf. "He's nice," she said, "but not as nice as . . ." She shrugged, grunting.

Mirri giggled, nudging Ker with her elbow. "When

are you going to tell us who this mystery fella is? At least we know who Nella's running away with."

Ker said nothing more, but Nella blushed as she glanced at Risley. "We're just going to hear a minstrel in the village. It's not like he's whisking me away to Waterford or anything." He smiled at her, gazing into her eyes, and she felt very warm.

Mirri babbled on, swooning at the notion of being whisked away to Waterford, but Nella barely heard. The memory of the kiss still left her giddy.

In a daze, she walked with her friends back to their room with Risley and the two new guards following them like shadows. While her friends went in and Stef sulked off to gossip and gripe with others, Risley stopped Nella outside her door and grasped her hand.

"I'll be back in about half a bell or so. Will that give you enough time?" He kissed her fingers and gazed into her eyes while passing maids gave them furious glances.

"I'll be ready," she replied.

He smiled, gently squeezed her hand, and left.

He had taken no more than four steps when someone grabbed Nella's arm and yanked her into their room.

Dari closed the door, cutting off the curious stares of the others. "You *must* tell us what happened last night."

Nella shrugged and leaned against the wall. "Nothing happened."

"I know that's not true," Mirri said, giggling. "You sat with him at dinner, slept in his suite. Something happened and we want all the juicy details."

"*All* of them," Dari said, sitting on Nella's bed. "How was it? Was it like you imagined?"

"Did it hurt?" Ker asked, leaning forward.

"Did what hurt?" Nella blinked, shuddering at the repulsive memory of hot fingers snatching at her hair. She knew her friends were just trying to remain distracted from the horror of the past days and she decided that she might as well play along even if it meant certain embarrassment. Not that she had much choice, with Dari and Mirri both badgering her.

"Sleeping with Risley, silly," Dari said. "We've seen how he's been looking at you. The fire in his eyes could burn the castle down. For Goddess's sake, he kissed your hand right outside this door, in front of everybody! The secret is definitely out, Nella. We know you've lain with him."

Mirri lay on her belly, her feet entwining in the air. "In case you hadn't heard, Ker met this guy, and they might, and we, er . . . she is curious. So tell us, um . . . her all about it." Mirri tittered her amusement, wriggling on the bed. "If we wait for Ker to explain it all, we'll never learn anything!"

Blushing, Ker smacked Mirri with a ragged pillow. Nella started brushing her hair. "Honest, there's nothing to tell."

"Oh, there's something to tell," Dari said, leaning forward. "You spent the entire day and night in his suite. Two floor maids told everyone he made them dress you in his shirt and that you were naked in his bed."

Nella stopped brushing, her breath catching in her throat. *No one was supposed to know that!*

Mirri and Dari burst out laughing. "Goddess, Nella! A goose just walk over your grave?"

She blustered and finished tidying her hair. "Nothing happened, really." Ignoring their curious stares, she slipped off her uniform and pulled on her best dress, a worn and faded garment that had seen better days. "Do you think this will be all right?"

"It'll be fine," Dari said. "And you're changing the subject."

"We didn't lie together," Nella said, fidgeting. "He slept on the divan. Honest."

Mirri giggled, "But you slept in his bed?"

Nella turned, gaping at Mirri's audacity. "I slept. Just slept. It was big and soft, like a giant pillow, and I slept. He never touched me and was a perfect gentleman the entire night."

Dari rooted through a box in the corner, searching for shoes. "But he kissed you, didn't he? At least once?"

Nella's cheeks burned and her lips throbbed for a moment before she licked them. She tied up her dress, then smoothed the skirt. "Can I borrow your cloak, Dari? Mine's rather ragged."

"Sure," Dari said, holding up a pair of shoes. "And he did kiss you. It's about time."

Mirri leapt from the bed, squealing. "He actually, really, truly *kissed* you?"

Nella shrugged, sitting on her bed to put the borrowed shoes on. "It . . . I . . . ." She shook her head and tried to compose herself. *This is getting too personal.* Clearing her throat, she pushed out, "I shouldn't say anything."

Ker sat beside her and Dari sat at her feet, grinning. "How many times? Did you keep count?"

"Just once, but really, considering all that's happened lately, with Plien and all, it's not something—"

Mirri squealed, jumping around the room. "Lord Risley kissed you!"

Dari gave her an annoyed glare, then turned back to

Nella. "Just one kiss? And now you're courting? What about the debt?"

"Musta been some kiss," Ker said.

Oh, it was, Nella thought. As she finished getting ready, she tried to fend off the blizzard of questions, pushing aside the dark memories of two nights ago.

* * *

Dubric released the peace bond on his sword. He, Dien, and Lars walked down the third-floor-west hall, fifty lengths or so behind Risley, and the ghosts paraded along behind. Their quarry hurried to his suite and seemed unusually chipper.

Lars and Dien unfastened their swords, as well. "Only one room inside has a lock," Dien said. "His office. It's mostly full of junk, though. A saddle, box of armor, things like that. There's nowhere for him to hide. One razor is in a leather bag in the lowest drawer of his armoire and the other is in the top right drawer in the privy room. He has some papers and a dagger on a bedside table, and all his swords are kept near the entrance. Those are all of his weapons. With luck, he'll be unarmed."

"So once we're in, we've got to get him quickly," Lars said. "Guilty or not, this is not going to go over well with his father, Lord Brushgar, or the King."

"Then we will keep it quiet. They will not need to know until we are ready to tell them," Dubric said, holding out his arm to stop his men. Risley opened his door and slipped inside as if everything were right in his world. He even nodded cheerfully to a passing floor maid, although the girl shied away. Still grinning, he closed the door without a backward glance.

"Bastard sure is confident," Dien said.

"Maybe he's not thinking about the murders," Lars said. "I heard some of the maids gossiping today about Risley and Nella going to hear the minstrel at the Dancing Sheep tonight."

"You think maybe that's why there were so many clues alluding to Nella?" Dien asked. "He's planning on taking her somewhere private to have his bit of fun?"

Weaving slowly between the few people walking down the hall, Dubric said, "While I would not consider the Dancing Sheep to be private, there are certainly a great deal of dark, private places between here and there."

They stood outside Risley's door for a few moments while passersby gave them angry and disgusted looks. "About time," an elderly lady said, tottering past.

Lars glanced her way, then said softly, "I'm sorry, sir, but I can't believe that Risley would harm Nella. I've seen them together. It's just not possible."

"Anything's possible, pup," Dien replied, trying the latch. Unlocked.

"Maybe so," Lars said, "but I still don't think he'd hurt her."

Dubric frowned at the small crowd forming in the hall and sighed, rubbing his eyes. Even his ghosts insisted upon remaining to watch the show. They tried to bother the other onlookers, but succeeded merely in making a few shiver. "We have delayed long enough. Let us finish this," Dubric said. "And break it down. I want to scare him."

Dien kicked open the door and bits of molding flew every which way.

"What in the seven hells?" Risley yelled from the bowels of his suite as the three rushed forward. Stripped to the waist, he burst from his bath chamber with soap on his face and a razor in his hand. His hair dripped into his eyes and he wiped it away with his free hand, standing dumbstruck in the middle of the hall.

"Drop that thing and drop it now!" Dien barked, pulling his sword.

"What? What 'thing'? For Goddess's sake, I'm just getting—"

"Now!" Dubric said, pulling his sword as well.

Risley blinked, astounded, then closed the razor, soap suds and all. "I'm shaving. Just shaving. That's not illegal, is it?" Slowly, his eyes locked on Dubric's, he set the razor on the floor and backed a step away. "Can't I prepare for my evening without you scaring the day-lights out of me?"

"Not tonight," Dien said, knocking the razor toward Dubric with the tip of his sword. "Face the wall."

Risley's eyes narrowed. "What? Is this a joke? I have plans for tonight! Can't this madness wait? For Goddess's sake, do you have any idea—?"

Dien shoved him backward, spinning him around. "No frigging joke, pretty boy! I said face the pegging wall!"

Risley's soapy cheek smeared the painted plaster. "I don't want to cause trouble. There's been a misunder-standing. No reason to get upset."

While Dien held Risley against the wall, Dubric re-trieved the razor and handed it to Lars. "You are hereby charged with murder, and we have eleven damned rea-sons to get upset."

Lars opened the razor and examined it, wiping the worst of the suds on his trousers. "It's clean."

"Of course it's clean! I've been shaving! And I haven't murdered anyone!"

Dien slammed him into the wall and Risley's ribs

creaked audibly. "We've got proof, so shut your fool yap."

Risley pursed his lips for a moment, then said, "Whatever proof you have has misled you. I never received a razor and I haven't murdered anyone. I swear."

"Somehow I don't believe you," Dien said. He leaned close, hissing in Risley's ear, "You liked sending us that disgusting package? Get your jollies off?"

"What 'package'?" Risley's eyes rolled toward Dubric, pleading for understanding. "What is he talking about?"

Dubric stared at Risley without feeling the least bit of empathy. "It is too late for these games. Take him to my office."

"Yessir!" Dien said, shoving Risley away from the wall and sending him reeling down the hall.

Risley caught his balance near his bedroom door and said, "At least let me wipe my face and put on a shirt before you parade me through the castle like a prized goat."

"Lars," Dubric said, and the boy nodded, slipping past Risley and entering the bedroom.

"Oh no," Risley sighed, suddenly deflating, as he looked through his bedroom door. "It's not what it looks like."

Lars came out a moment later with a bundle of papers tucked into a battered leather satchel and a pair of shirts clenched in his hand. One was spattered with blood. "It was laying on the bed," he said, staring at the shirt with astonishment and horror. "Right there, in plain sight."

Handing the bloody shirt to Dubric, he tossed the clean one at Risley. "And to think I've been defending you. You bastard."

Elli and Ennea laughed and pointed at the stained shirt, doubling over in their mirth.

Risley stared at Lars and yanked on his shirt. "I did not kill those girls, and I want a message sent to my father to notify him of these absurd allegations. Immediately."

"People in the seven hells want snow," Dien snarled, shoving him through the door and into the public hall.

Gawkers sneered, cheered, and threw things, pelting Risley with rotten food, tobacco juice, and vicious words. His head held high, he walked to Dubric's office without speaking.

* * *

Nella paced in her room while her friends watched.

"He's gonna come, I'm sure of it," Mirri said for the umpteenth time.

"Stop it," Dari said. "Can't you see that's not helping?"

"I'm all right," Nella said. "I just thought—"

The door burst open and Stef swung in, grinning from ear to ear. "Guess what, Miss Perfect? Lord Sweetie's been dragged, in chains, to Dubric's office."

Nella stared at Stef, who stuck out her tongue. "Told you he was the slasher."

Dari leapt forward and punched Stef, knocking her to the floor. "You said no such thing! You're just jealous and mean!"

Stef wiped at her mouth and scrambled to her feet, balling her hands into fists.

"Stop it," Nella said, taking deep breaths to slow her thudding heart. "Both of you." She lowered her head, her mind racing, then looked up to stare Stef in the eye. "Did you see it yourself, or is it just a rumor?"

Stef crossed her arms across her chest. "Everyone's talking about it. I don't have to see. Lord Sweetie's guilty of murder."

Nella shook her head, her eyes remaining locked on Stef. *It's just a rumor. Maybe he witnessed something; maybe Dubric decided to question him; maybe it's all a misunderstanding.* She swallowed her fear and said, "He hasn't murdered anyone." Gritting her teeth, she ran from the room with Dari on her heels.

* * *

Risley tried to stand, but the shackles kept his wrists attached to the chair. "Whoever put you up to this, they're wrong. I haven't killed anyone."

Dubric rubbed his eyes, but the ghosts refused to leave. Fytte and Ennea argued over Rianne's severed forearm, while Elli tied Nansy in her own intestines. Olibe Meiks, however, scowled at Dubric, his dead eyes glowing a hideous green.

Dubric flipped through his notebook and tried to ignore his aching head. "Evidence disagrees. We have you neatly corralled, Risley. You may as well admit your guilt and save everyone needless time and heartache."

"But I didn't do it," Risley said, trying to stand again. "And get these things off me! For Goddess's sake, I'm not a criminal."

"You are now," Dien said. "And those shackles are your own damn fault. You wouldn't stay where I put you." He jangled a set of keys before Risley's eyes.

"Peg you," Risley snapped. "I'm innocent and I demand that my father be notified of this insanity." He turned his gaze to Dubric and added, "And I demand to know what evidence you've concocted against me.

What? One of the girls write my name in the mud? Or did someone leave a trail of blood and body parts leading to my room?"

Lars leaned against the wall, not far from where Fytte tortured Rianne. "You're better off not talking."

"Boar piss! I have every right and reason to be upset. You've forced me to come here, got me splattered with spit and filth, and Nella's probably worried sick or thinking I've changed my mind about her! All for some mucked-up charge that's based on hearsay and wild speculation. If you've slopped up my evening for nothing, there'll be hell to pay. I don't know a damned thing about that razor or the murders and I demand to know how in the Goddess's name you've decided I'm responsible."

Dubric watched Risley closely. "Someone sent me a disgusting gift." He pulled the fabric-wrapped horror from the box and set it on his desk. Pulling the outer ribbon loose, he said, "Nella's ribbon. Her initials are on this end. See?"

Risley's eyes grew wide and he swallowed but said nothing. Dubric dropped the ribbon, letting it land in Risley's lap.

A touch of Dubric's finger and the stiff fabric opened, revealing the plate and its contents. "Your grandfather's personal china and cutlery," he said, moving the plate aside. "Not only is it filled with human kidneys and hair, someone put trinkets from each of the victims inside. Nella, incidentally, had *two* trinkets, while the others merely had one."

Risley watched, horrified, as the plate clattered onto the table and Dubric lifted Nella's braid. "Ah, here we are," he said, letting the braid hang from his fingers. "Another bit of evidence taken from your newest conquest." He tossed it onto Risley's lap, ignoring the small sound escaping Risley's throat.

"There is more," he said. "Shall I continue?"

Risley's face had turned pale and he stared at the evidence in his lap. "I'm not sure," he replied.

"Oh, but I am," Dubric said, lifting the note. "Someone educated sent me a lovely piece of gloating filth on your grandfather's parchment. 'You've overlooked the blood on my hands.' Were you referring to the literal blood and stitches I saw on your hand this morning or the figurative deaths you've taken?"

Risley stared at him, his eyes cold and hard. "You tell me."

"I will, in time," Dubric said, reading from the note again. "'Girls are dying, my Lord Castellan, every night beneath my razor, but you are not making a lick of difference.'" He met Risley's eyes and smiled. "You said almost exactly the same phrase to me this very morning. Do you remember?"

"Vaguely," Risley said, his stare not faltering.

"You have called the people of my castle 'sheep' to my face, and now this." Dubric rattled the note.

"I did not kill those girls. Someone else wrote that damned letter."

"And I suppose someone else was able to pilfer parchment and dishes from your grandfather, as well as use your phraseology. Someone else received the razor last autumn, and someone else has committed these crimes?"

Risley did not flinch or waver. "It would appear so, yes."

"And you insist you have never seen this before."

"Dammit, Dubric, I guarantee that if I'd ever seen that disgusting thing, I'd remember."

Dubric sighed and lifted a bundle of papers from his desk. "I have known you since you were an infant, Risley," he said quietly as he found his page, "and I have never known you to be unreasonable or dangerous. Even when wallowing in the headstrong tendencies of youth, you have always kept your mental faculties." He looked at the paper and leaned forward. "I want to believe you today. I do. I do not wish to think you intended to hurt anyone. That simply is not the young man I know.

"Do you remember what you said to me when Dien brought you here for lurking in the servants' wing?"

Risley blinked in reply.

Dubric read a section of Otlee's notes aloud. "'Who's to say I haven't been touched with some dark magic? Been tainted somehow? Completely lost my senses?'"

Dubric smiled at Otlee and set the note aside. *Every damned word, praise the King!* "You added, 'I'm innocent, I know it in my heart, but what if my heart is lying?' Do you remember?"

"Yes, I remember."

Dubric accepted two papers and a battered ledger from Otlee before he returned his attention to Risley, waiting a long moment before speaking again. "Been having headaches lately?"

"Some. I haven't been sleeping well. People do get headaches from time to time."

Dubric tapped a finger in the ledger. "But I believe that you are the only person in Faldorrah to have traveled to Astaria. Lars mentioned your headaches days ago, but I had not made the connection until today. Did you happen to visit Vehnliel?"

Risley's brow furrowed. "You've likely got the page in front of you, so why bother asking me?"

Dubric leaned a hip against his desk. "Surely you know travel there is forbidden."

Risley exhaled slowly, his fingers gripping the chair. "That is restricted information of a sensitive nature."

"And yet you maintained records, written in a hand that has an uncanny resemblance to the note the killer left me. We even had the scribes and herald compare parts of the two and they agreed with our assessment." Dubric tossed a page of manifest toward Risley and it floated onto his lap. "Would you care to explain what item number seventeen is?"

"No. As a courier and representative of the Lagiern Crown, I am authorized—"

"You are a murder suspect in Faldorrah! I do not care what secrets the King is hoarding. We are discussing your life and the deaths of eleven people!"

Risley grumbled within his throat and said, "Yes, I went to Vehnliel and yes, I acquired a particular rarity for which my grandfather has spent decades searching. I never touched the item in question, or spoke to it, and it certainly did not bite or inject me. After assuring its presence in the holding vessel, I sealed the jar with wax and delivered it, still sealed inside, to my grandfather for destruction."

Lars had turned nearly as ashen as the granite wall behind him. "Don't soul-stealers drink people's blood and replace it with their own urine? Goddess, you actually brought one to Lagiern?"

"Damn right I did. I killed three Pyrinnian couriers to get it, and an Astarian spy. I couldn't let it fall into Egeslic's hands. Do you have any idea what he would do with a soul-stealer? Can you imagine an army of zombies? They'd fight without fear, remorse, or even pain, obliterating everything in their path. Possibly getting a case of rot was the least of my concerns."

"You should've dropped it in the sea," Dien said, scowling.

"The little bastards don't drown. Would you have taken the chance that it could escape the jar and find land? What if it bit someone? What if it spawned?"

Dien grumbled his reply and crossed his arms over his chest.

Dubric frowned. "Headaches are a symptom of Wraith Rot, as is uncharacteristic aggression. Surely you know this."

"I considered it when this first started, I did, but I was in Astaria nearly nine moons ago. I was in a quarantine zone, yes, but I show no definitive symptoms of Wraith Rot and I don't have a single lesion, anywhere, or any other late-stage symptoms. Besides, if I'd been exposed, I'd likely be dead by now."

"Or stark raving mad trying to maintain a solid form," Dien muttered.

"I'm not dead or insane, nor has my soul been stolen and my veins filled with soul-stealer piss. I'm just tired. That's why I'm having the headaches." He took a cleansing breath and met Dubric's gaze. "You have to believe me."

"How can I when every new piece of evidence we find points to you? Every last one." Dubric slammed the ledger closed. "Either condition could lead you to brutally murder without remorse."

"It's someone else."

"Someone else who happens to have blood on their shirt?"

"I fell this morning. Ask Nella. She was there."

"Yes, Nella," Dubric said, leaning closer. "Of all the victims, only she lived. Why is that?"

"If you had kept your promise, she never would have been hurt at all."

"And two bits referring to her, instead of one, like everyone else. Why is that?"

"I don't know. But when I find out, I'm going to gut the bastard like a fish."

Dubric reached for his notebook. "We will not give you the opportunity to cheat justice. There is too much evidence to deny."

"Listen to me. Someone—I don't know who, but someone else—did this. Not me. Besides, none of this directly connects me to that disgusting thing or any of the murdered girls. It's all speculation and deduction."

"This is not," Dubric said, lifting the hair from his notebook. "We found this inside the wrapper, in a crease. Do you recognize it?"

"It's a hair. Most people have hair, or have you forgotten?" He glanced at Dubric's shining pate and raised a single mocking eyebrow. "Ow! Hey!"

"Oh, excuse me, your lordship. Thought I saw a snarl." Dien handed Dubric a single dark hair and Dubric placed them side by side. The lengths, color, and shape were comparable and Risley gasped.

"That's impossible. I never saw that horrid thing before!"

Dubric handed the second hair back to Dien and returned the original to his notebook. "It is a fact, Lord Romlin, not speculation or deduction. An irrefutable fact. We found your hair *inside* the nest of clues because you assembled them, you gathered them, and you killed for them."

"One hair? You're basing this on one damned hair? Goddess, how many people in this castle have hair like mine? Scores, surely."

Dubric lifted Risley's wooden razor and contemplated the dents and scratches. "I had first thought that this was battered from travel. Surely being jostled in saddlebags and packs would wear such a fine piece of wood. But look here, do you see this strip missing? This narrow sliver? Do you know where the missing piece is?"

"I've had the thing for summers. It's most likely in the bottom of my travel pack, but it could be anywhere."

"Are you so certain?" Dubric asked, opening a small paper packet. He pulled out the sliver of wood and held it before Risley's eyes. He had not cleaned away the blood, and the splinter looked dark and dead. "Is this at all familiar to you?"

"It's a dirty piece of wood."

"That we happened to find inside one of the victims. You left us a physical clue, Risley. One you were unaware of. You made a mistake and we caught you. This tiny sliver will remove all doubt as to your guilt or innocence."

"It won't fit," Risley said, staring at it. "It can't."

Dubric lay the sliver against the razor and it nestled against the worn wood, fitting perfectly into one end of the open strip. He stood straight and stared into Risley's eyes. "The hair and wood belong to you, Risley; my Far-Sight glass has left us no doubt. We have gathered substantial circumstantial evidence against you. All I needed was one scrap of hard proof to link you directly to this mess, even a single hair stuck to a bloody package or a sliver of wood found inside a dead girl's chest. For those, Lord Romlin, and for the murder of eleven innocent souls, I will see you hanged."

* * *

Nella had chewed her fingernails to the quick worrying over the muffled noises coming from behind the locked door. Risley and Dubric grumbled and argued, but she couldn't understand what they said, nor was she certain she wanted to. All the while, Dari sat beside her, quivering and staring at Dubric's office.

The door burst open without warning and Dari let out a startled scream, but Nella took a deep breath and stood, trying to accept the impossible. Lars and Dien shoved Risley toward her, and she swallowed her horror and tried to look into his eyes.

Spattered with filth and his wrists shackled together, Risley gasped at the sight of her. He smoothed his frown and his fingers clenched. "We may have to delay our jaunt to the minstrel," he said, forcing an assured smile. "I'm sorry, love, but circumstance . . ." Lars pushed him forward again as his voice trailed off.

She rushed to him, her hands shaking, and whispered, "Look at me. Please."

Dubric said, "Miss Nella, he is not worth your time. Not anymore."

"Let me decide that," she said, moving closer to Risley, searching his face, his manner, for any hint of guilt or innocence. "Please. Just look at me."

His eyes found hers and he blinked back terrified tears. They were his familiar eyes, gentle and warm even through the haze of confusion. She saw no guilt or admittance there, only shock and pleading innocence being overwhelmed by incomprehension.

"Oh, Risley," she said, touching his face. "Have they hurt you?"

He shook his head. "No. They've actually been rather gentle, considering what they believe." He paused, looking deep within her eyes, and said, "But I didn't do it. I swear."

"Of course not," she said, plastering a smile on her face. "You were with me, all night last night. It's a wonder I was able to work at all, us being awake all night romping like we were."

He chuckled at her attempt and kissed her palm. "Don't lie for me, love. I've already told them I never touched you." He reached up and stroked her hair, the chains jangling and cold.

"Enough of this," Dien said, knocking Risley aside. "Get your ass moving."

Risley straightened his back and said, "Give me one damned minute with her. For Goddess's sake, I may never see her again. Guilty or not, one minute won't make a bit of difference."

Lars shrugged, Dien glowered, and at last Dubric nodded. They stepped back, giving Risley and Nella a pocket of space.

Risley raised his hands, lifting one elbow high, and she slipped beneath his chains and into his arms, ignoring the filthy splatters on his clothes. "Shh, love," he whispered into her hair as he held her close and eased her trembling. "Everything will be all right."

She nodded against his chest, knowing he was trying to encourage himself as much as her. "What happened?"

His lips on her brow were warm and gentle. "They've got evidence against me, love, real, inarguable evidence, but I don't know how. It's impossible. They will hang me for this, and after seeing what they've found I can't blame them." His voice hitched and he kissed her brow again. "I know in my heart I haven't harmed anyone, but they'll hang me anyway. They'll have to."

His hands on her back shuddered as they pressed her against him. "None of that matters now. You need to move on, forget about me. Please."

"No," she said, looking up at him. "I can't. I won't."

"You need to," he said. "I'm no good for you now."

"You've always been good for me," she replied, stretching within his arms.

She kissed him. For a moment he resisted, but the moment crumbled and he crushed her in his desperate embrace.

"Oh, Nella," he whispered into her mouth as he took a breath and kissed her again.

Someone tugged at her. She tried to cling to Risley, but hands wrenched her away, yanking her from his embrace and scraping her back with his shackles.

"Don't you hurt her," Risley snarled, fighting against Lars's and Dien's grip. "So help me, you harm one hair on her head and you'll pay."

"She will be safe," Dubric said from behind her, his voice flat and cold. "Now that you are no longer a concern."

"Please! Don't do this!" she cried, struggling to break free of Dubric's hard grip.

As Dien and Lars shoved him to the hall, Risley looked back at her and said, "I love you. Remember I love you."

Then he was gone.

* * *

Risley said little beyond a single, quietly stated insistence of his innocence as they descended to the gaol. *At least he is not a wailer or a pleader,* Dubric thought.

Nor did Risley resist, other than a slight hesitation at his first step into the gaol. They prodded him forward and he walked amid them without comment, ignoring the catcalls and taunts from the few prisoners. The gaol reeked of piss and puke and mold, and the filthy unwashed bodies of drunks and derelicts. Dubric had always considered it to be a horrid place to spend one's last days, but certainly better than being eviscerated and left to freeze and bleed to death in the courtyard.

Inek sat on his cot and snarled, but said nothing. The eight who had attacked Dubric the night Celese and Rianne died remained behind bars, since none had shown the least bit of remorse. Gaelin and Allin had become oozing hags after a couple of days sleeping in filthy straw, and their once beautiful red hair hung limp and stringy and damp. Gaelin threw a handful of feces at them as they walked past.

"String him up quick now, you old bastard!" she screeched, but they continued on without giving her another glance.

Roaches scuttled away as they stomped through the putrid straw and sawdust on the floor between the cells. Dank water drizzled down the stone walls, leaving green and fuzzy mold plenty of opportunity to flourish. Light filtered dimly through tin lanterns, giving the hall a ghastly, ethereal gloom.

They passed through a set of heavy doors to another hall. It was less noxious than the cells Dubric routinely assigned to drunks and troublemakers, and all four breathed a little easier. Still filthy and vermin-infested, the hall continued into the dark, far past the reach of the single lantern.

Risley squinted into the dark. "Where are you taking me?"

"This is far enough," Dubric replied. "I do not want you out front. Your arrest will create a large-enough circus as it is."

Dien pulled keys from his pocket and unlatched a thick, barred door, then pulled it open. Partly natural cave and partly carved and stacked stone, the cell loomed dark and dreadful, with a loose pile of moldering straw along the back and a slimy puddle near the middle. A toad hopped from beside the puddle to the shadows, blinking as if the dim light hurt its eyes.

"So this is it?"

"'Fraid so," Dien muttered, unlocking Risley's wrists while Dubric and Lars kept him at sword point. "You get a pan of water and two feedings a day, one morning and one evening, but don't expect anything fancy."

Risley rubbed his wrists. "Remains from the servants' table? There's always someone lower than someone else. Someone to accept the refuse and spoilage."

Dubric frowned. "This is not the time, or place, to revisit the inequities between the classes."

Risley sighed. "I suppose not." Squaring his shoulders, he walked into the cell. Without looking back, he said, "Lars, watch over her. Keep her safe, because you've captured the wrong man."

Lars drew a shaky breath and closed the door. "Part of me hopes you're right, Ris, but evidence doesn't lie."

"Then may the Goddess have mercy on my soul." Risley walked to the far side of his cell and sat with his back to them.

After locking the door, Dubric turned away and his men followed, leaving the stink of desperation behind.

*　*　*

"I . . . I have to find a way to help him," Nella said, wiping at her eyes and staggering to her feet.

"But how?" Dari asked. "He said himself that the evidence—"

"I don't care. I have to do something." She pulled a kerchief from her pocket and blew her nose. "He wouldn't turn his back on me. He would move mountains and seas—"

"He killed people! Killed Plien! How can you want to help him after all he's done?"

Nella started toward the door then stopped, her shoulders sagging for a moment. "Because he saved my life in Pyrinn and would do so again without hesitating. Because he treats me like a person instead of a servant. Because he shared a piece of pie with me." She paused and straightened her back. "Because I love him." Turning back to look at Dari, she added, "And I believe he is innocent. I will do everything in my power to keep him alive."

Leaving Dari standing dumbfounded in Dubric's office, she strode into the hall, blanching at the curious glances from passersby.

"Hope they string him up by his guts," a man said from behind her, but Nella didn't bother to look.

"Not so hoity-toity now, are ye?" a sweaty scullery maid said, trying to trip her.

"I heard Dubric found 'im sharpening 'is knife. That true?"

"'Knife'? I heard he used an axe."

"Betcha 'e raped 'em before he kilt 'em. Only reason 'e let 'is whore live a'tall were 'cause they were boppin' ever' night."

Nella pushed through, her mouth set tight and her heart determined, and she soon found herself free of the crowd.

Where do I go? What do I do? she thought, pausing to look around her. *His grandfather?* She looked up the main stairs. *He hates commoners. He'll never listen. Who can I trust? Who can help me?*

She paced near the stairs, her thoughts churning, until a pair of nuns walked past, chattering about an upcoming festival to aid an orphanage. *Friar Bonne!*

She had taken but two steps toward the rectory hall when she heard someone calling her name.

"Miss Nella!" the herald said, rushing to her with his hand fluttering over his heart. "Thank goodness you're not harmed. I'd heard you'd spent the night in that beast's lair and then when Dubric hauled him off just this evening, I had feared the worst!"

She forced a smile. "I'm fine, Mister Beckwith. Honest."

"I'm just relieved you're safe," he said, patting her on the arm. "Especially after he bashed me on the head this very morn. However did you survive your ordeal?"

She fell still, staring at him, and reminded herself to close her mouth. *Goddess, how much more of this can I endure?* "He hit you on the head?"

Beckwith blinked in astonishment, showing her the blood-smeared bandage peeking from beneath his plumed hat. "This morning, when I was on patrol." He turned back, concerned. "When he killed Olibe Meiks and that milkmaid. Didn't you know? I thought that's how Dubric apprehended him. And then, when Dubric questioned me about the razors, I was certain he'd been caught."

Nella took a shaky step back and fell, biting her tongue.

"Oh, goodness gracious!" he said, rushing to her aid. "I'm dreadfully sorry, Miss Nella. I assumed you knew."

He grasped her hands and helped her stand, fussing over her and insisting she use his lacy kerchief to sop the blood from her tongue. "Perhaps you should rest for a moment or two."

"No, I'm fine, really," she said, trying to return the

damp and stained hankie. "It's just been a shock, that's all."

He glanced at the smear of blood and spit glistening against the brilliant white, and held up his hand to stop her. "You keep it, Miss Nella," he said, forcing his grimace into a tolerant smile. "I have several." He patted her on the arm, then turned and hurried away.

* * *

Dubric entered his offices with Lars and Dien on his heels. "Otlee!" he hollered, striding through.

"I'm here, sir." Otlee came to the inner office door with paperwork clenched in his hands and an ink smear on his cheek. "But we have another problem, and it's a dilly."

Lovely. "What sort of problem?"

"Fultin said Brushgar insists you visit him in his suite. Immediately. Or else."

"Count on the rumor mill to kick us in the gut," Lars muttered.

Dubric said, "Hopefully Nigel will listen to reason."

Dien muttered, "Always a first time, sir. Want me to come along?"

"No," Dubric said, "placating our lord is my responsibility." He took a breath and looked to his men to deliver his instructions. "Although our quarry is captured, we still have much to do." Brushing past Otlee, he hurried to his desk and fished a golden token from a drawer.

"Otlee, I need you to scour the library, legal files, even accounting records, for anyone, noble or common, who has had a history of complaining about our leadership and how they could do better. I want their name, rank, lineage, occupation, grievance . . . anything you can get for me. Risley must not slip away by insisting someone with a grievance against authority is to blame." He placed the golden token in Otlee's palm. "This will allow you access to every volume, paper, and file, even the ones that supposedly don't exist."

"Yessir." Otlee stared at the token as if it were magical.

Ruffling the lad's hair, Dubric said, "No unwarranted browsing. You're not there to find new reading material."

Otlee closed his fingers around the token and put it in his pocket. "Yes, sir. I'll find what you need, sir."

Dubric looked to Lars next. "Discover who has access to Lord Brushgar's china, no matter how high that list goes, and what's missing. I need to know how Risley got that plate."

"Yes, sir."

"And me?" Dien asked.

"I want Risley touted as a suspect, not a convicted criminal. Keep the patrols going and keep them on their toes. Allay fears and suspicion as best you can. We cannot afford to allow our alertness to slip."

"I'll see to it, sir."

Dubric nodded his approval. "I estimate we have two or three days at best before word of Risley's arrest reaches Haenpar. We must have every potential bit of evidence collected and confirmed by that time or all the guilt in the known lands will not bring justice. He is too well-known, and his family too powerful, to leave this a Faldorrahn matter if we make the slightest mistake or leave the thinnest thread untied."

He gathered a pack stuffed full of bags, envelopes, and slips of paper. "And I will search Risley's suite after I convince Lord Brushgar of its necessity, removing floorboards and dismantling the walls, if I must. Does anyone have any questions?"

"No, sir," they said, finishing their notes.

Dubric hefted the evidence pack and left, his men dispersing behind him.

CHAPTER

15

Ignoring the curious glances from passersby, Dubric knocked on Lord Brushgar's door, then entered, closing it behind him. Every curtain had been drawn and the shadows grew long and looming. He smelled no scent of perfume today, and felt thankful not to have the lady of the castle staring at him. The eleven following him were bad enough. "Milord?" he called.

"You may enter," Brushgar said from somewhere deep within.

Dubric searched the suite, finally locating Brushgar in one of the many sitting rooms. "Good evening, sir," he said.

"'Good evening,' my backside," Brushgar grumbled. Wearing his nightshirt, he reclined upon a long pillowed bench with quilts and blankets tucked all around him. A book lay upon his lap and a platter of morsels sat beside a pitcher and goblet on a low table. Despite his bulk, he looked frail and thin beneath the bundles of blankets, like a melting drift of snow before the spring rains washed the last remnants away. He glowered at Dubric and took off his spectacles. "Is there a reason you've arrested my grandson after I instructed you to find another culprit?"

"All our evidence leads to him, milord. Evidence I

cannot disregard or deny. Even evidence you tried to hide."

Brushgar tossed the spectacles on the table and leaned forward, his eyes glittering with urgent determination. "Horse piss! You persist in persecuting my grandson for crimes I told you he did not commit! I have had enough of such lunacy. Release him this instant."

The ghosts cavorted, ogling at the opulent surroundings. Dubric rubbed his eyes, but they declined to leave. "I will not, milord. I refuse to let the murderer of eleven innocent souls walk freely from my gaol. Ensuring your people's safety, sir, is my job here. Yours is to endure the facts as life presents them. Risley murdered those girls."

Brushgar reddened. "He did no such thing. Release him."

"No."

"You insolent fool! I give you an order, a direct, uncompromising order, and you refuse?"

Two of the ghosts, Elli and Fytte, bounced on the pillows beside Brushgar's feet. Celese tried to pick up an intricate mechanism from a shelf, but her hand passed through it. Pouting, she tried again and again. The rest wandered aimlessly or annoyed the ghost beside them.

"I have proof," Dubric said. "Proof of his cutting open ten young women and stealing their kidneys to eat them. I cannot and will not allow such a beast loose from my gaol to prey unchecked upon the land. Rabid animals must be captured and killed, and that is precisely what I will do. Your family loyalty be damned."

Brushgar snarled, spittle forming at the corners of his mouth. "The monster you speak of is not my grandson! It is some wretch, a transient, perhaps, or a drunk, and you will discover the truth of it immediately. I don't give a damn who you choose to be guilty, but you will not publicly accuse Risley. You will not bring him before Council; you will not prosecute him, incarcerate him, or hang him! You will release him this instant and send him home to his family. *That* is your duty, because I have decreed it so." Brushgar reached for his spectacles and leaned back onto his pillows. "I refuse to accept it or hear of it again. It is no longer an issue. As far as I am concerned, as far as *you* are concerned, he is innocent. That is an order."

"I cannot do that, sir. I refuse."

"You what?"

"He killed eleven people. Eleven of *your* people, and your people know this. They will not be persuaded by you waxing poetic over your grandson's innocence. They demand justice and justice must be provided. If you choose to lose your entire province to this madness, that is your choice, but I will continue to do my duty to Faldorrah, politics be damned.

"If you insist on denying justice to your people, then you must be the one to see it done. You must be the one to tell them that you value the life of a brutal murderer over the lives of the innocents he slaughtered. Until you have the wherewithal to do that yourself, *sir,* continue to busy yourself with your posturing accountants and your soft bed and your sweet wines while I maintain order and peace."

Brushgar stared at him for a long time without saying a word. "Are you finished?" he grumbled at last.

"Yes, my lord."

Brushgar picked up his book. "Then get the peg out."

* * *

Nella flew into the temple with ice gnawing in the pit of her belly. "Friar Bonne!" she called out to the shadows and the lone lamp shining upon the Brushgar family tapestry. "Please, Friar, I need your help."

She heard nothing but her own uncertain heartbeat slamming in her ears. Stumbling, she staggered forward, toward the light, and fell to her knees. Four tiny candles lay melted in a row upon the floor before the tapestry. A hand spade lay with them, Malanna's holy light shining upon its grimy surface much as her moon shone upon the land.

Tears stung Nella's eyes as she touched the gardener's tool. Olibe Meiks had died, and had left a family behind. His wife and three children had offered prayers and a symbol of his life to the Goddess, asking for strength. She wiped at her eyes, looking at the lamp and its lovely white light.

Her hand shaking, she traced the Goddess's mark on her chest and lowered her head, praying for Olibe Meiks, his family, and the dead girls. Her supplication finished, she drew Malanna's holy symbol on her chest again, then looked to the tapestry, choking back her tears. "He couldn't have done this. Please, Goddess, in all of your mercy, I beg of you. Please. Not Risley."

Crafted of white and silver threads, the silk tapestry shone in the lamplight. Embroidered with religious symbols and the Brushgar family line for centuries untold, it hung from the altar but did not touch the floor. She had never seen the tapestry up close before, and the individual threads sparkled like the gossamer wings of dragonflies in the sunshine. Risley's name was embroidered near the bottom of the list of names. Helpless, she reached out to touch his silvered threads. The fabric shimmered against her hand while his name felt warm and cool at the same time. Somehow just touching it soothed her.

"I wish I had an offering," she whispered, "but I have nothing. Nothing but my faith in him." Her heart clenched and she lifted her hand from the cloth. "And my love."

"That is more than any mortal man dare ask for," Friar Bonne said from behind her.

She startled, lurching to her feet. "Friar! I am so sorry. I didn't hear you." She glanced at the tapestry and reddened. "I shouldn't have touched it, I know, but I—"

"That's quite all right, child," he said, slipping from the dark like a portly ghost. "You've done no harm, and your intentions are most admirable." He smiled, motioning her to him. "Come, sit with me a while. We have much to talk about, I fear."

She let him lead her to a pew.

"I think I need your help," she said, sitting beside him. "Or maybe I just need someone to talk to. I don't know what else to do. I don't even know what to think anymore."

"I am your most humble servant," he said, bowing his head. "Now tell me what brings you here. Worship isn't for three evenings yet."

Her voice cracking, she told her tale from Mirri's fateful illness to Dubric dragging Risley away. "He looked me in the eye and said he didn't kill anyone," she said, crushing the bloody kerchief in her fist. "Goddess forgive me, but I believe him."

Friar Bonne stared forward for a long time, frowning. "You poor child," he said at last. "These developments must tear you apart inside. I had heard rumors of Risley's possible involvement, but I never suspected that he would be capable of such brutality." He looked at Nella gravely. "Dubric must have definitive evidence against him."

She winced, biting her lip. "It looks bad, I know

that, Friar, but you didn't see his eyes. He's innocent. At least my heart says he is, but what if I'm wrong? What if he is guilty? I don't even know why Dubric decided to accuse him. No one will tell me anything and I just don't know what to do."

He squeezed her shoulders gently, like a father comforting a treasured daughter. "Men are not always what we expect them to be, especially to the young women they lure close. I've known Dubric for the entirety of my life. While we have never seen eye-to-eye on religious matters, he has proven time and time again to be of the utmost character, even in the face of great adversity. He would not accuse an innocent man of such terrible crimes."

She balled her fists and slammed them against her thighs. "But I know Risley. In the depths of my soul, I still trust him. Dubric has to have made a mistake."

"While he is as mortal and fallible as anyone, I've never known Dubric to make an error in judgment, especially concerning someone's life. I wish I could be more encouraging." He paused and grasped her hands. "I'm sorry. You're not here to understand why Dubric has deemed Risley guilty, you've come looking for help." He straightened his back and offered her a sad smile. "You've never faltered in your service to Malanna, and I shall not stumble in my service to you. What would you like me to do?"

She laughed harshly and tugged at her hair. "I don't know. I don't even know what I'm supposed to do, or think, or feel. I want to curl into a ball and cry, but I can't. I just can't. I can't desert him; I have to be strong, but . . ." She stood and started pacing, muttering under her breath.

"It will sort itself out, Miss Nella," Bonne said softly. "You must have faith in Malanna's plan."

She nodded, lowering her head. "I know. But I can't just stand back and let Dubric execute Risley for murder, can I?"

"You must do whatever you must, and trust that it is meant to be, just as, at this moment, Risley is meant to be in the gaol."

"But Dubric intends to execute him. That can't be in Malanna's plan." She paced before the altar, muttering. "Is there any possible way to get Risley away from here?"

"I can't see how. We certainly can't sneak into Dubric's gaol and spirit him away."

"But he's the King's grandson. His father's Lord of Haenpar. Surely they could do something?"

"I suppose they could," he sighed. "I have little faith that their involvement would sway Dubric, but I am honored to contact them in your stead to inform them of Risley's incarceration."

"Thank you," Nella cried, hugging him. "Thank you and thank the Goddess!" Beaming, she asked, "Is there something, anything, I can do in the meantime to help?"

Bonne looked at the ceiling for a moment, then said, "You could remain his friend and not desert him, I suppose. Surely he feels utterly alone, and you could do much to lessen that."

"Yes, I can do that. I am forever in your debt, Friar. Thank you. And thank you for listening." She gave him an appreciative smile then hurried away, feeling a faint song of hope in her heart.

* * *

Dubric opened Risley's cracked and battered door, then paused, wavering. The chill of the ghosts pulled at him, rattling in his head like a bucket of frozen stones.

For King's sake, why won't they leave me be? Pushing past the icy burden, he stepped through the portal and frowned.

Ransacked and very, very dark.

Taking a moment to light a wall sconce, he sighed and rubbed his eyes, kicking a chair against the wall. *Damn! I should have left Lars here to secure the premises. Another set of clues compromised.* He walked through the suite, lighting lamps and sconces until shadows clung to the corners and recesses beneath overturned furniture. Books littered the floor like slaughtered soldiers on a battlefield and clothes lay strewn about. He knelt beside a crushed decanter and frowned at the spilt wine.

Everything he looked at seemed tainted by death and blood. His ghosts languished or wandered at their preference, their mutilated bodies oozing spectral drips and sludge.

He moved aside a broken table. "Why will you not leave me alone? I have captured him. Surely you can stop tormenting me?"

Ennea leered in his face and Meiks maintained his angry scowl, but the rest paid him no heed. Rubbing his eyes in a desperate attempt at a reprieve, he walked through each and every room, surveying the destruction. The crowd had been justifiably angry, but they could have stolen a key bit of evidence, ruined even the most blatant clue, all in the madness of relief.

He reached the last room and paused. Unlike the others, this door stood closed and, despite the filthy boot marks on its polished surface, the frame remained unbroken. *Risley's office?* he thought, rummaging through his pockets. *Was it as he had left it? Do I dare hope?*

He fished out a ring of keys and considered the lock.

"Brass," he muttered, flipping through his master keys, "circular entry . . ."

The third key clicked in the chamber and the door eased open without a creak. Putting the keys away, he entered, peering into the shadows. A lamp sat on the desk. He took a moment to light it, then set his evidence pack upon the floor.

Doodles flittered across the surface of a scorch-speckled blotter beneath an assortment of delicate tools. Many drawings resembled Nella, but a few were detailed sketches of a lightweight structure Dubric did not recognize. One of these, an intricately woven curve, was partially obscured by a dark smear of blood.

After noting the blotter and its oddities, Dubric looked around the room. Organized clutter packed a wall of oak shelves with books, boxes, and trinkets, and papers and packets lay in haphazard piles on a long table. A partially repaired saddle lay in one corner and a box of antique armor lay in another.

The controlled chaos of a man with diverse interests, Dubric noted, then sat in Risley's chair. The top left-side drawer of the desk contained an unremarkable assortment of writing implements and papers, the next held color-coded tubes for the messenger birds, a bridle, assorted tools, and notes . . . Again, nothing unusual.

As he reached for the third and deepest drawer he paused. Smeared blood stained the handle. After noting the placement of the blood, he opened the drawer.

A convoluted apparatus stood inside, with blood dulling the steel surface of the support spine. Shimmering in the lamplight, a box of silver wire and etched strips lay askew beside it with a small alchemist's burner beneath. He lifted the apparatus and set it upon the desk, trying to decide what it was.

Clamps held lengths of silver wire and exquisitely

etched strips, weaving and twisting them in a repetitive pattern much like the drawings on the blotter. Delicate and uniquely lovely, the resulting silver strand seemed to sparkle with life of its own as it curved gently toward a circle.

What is he making? Dubric thought, reaching for his notebook. *What does this have to do with the dead girls?*

He paused, listening. Someone in the suite gasped and he heard a *thud* as the outer door closed. Leaving the apparatus on Risley's desk, he hurried to investigate.

Nella looked up as he approached. "Oh, it's you," she muttered, disgust and sorrow flavoring her voice with an angry tang he had never heard from her before. She gathered up an armload of books and began standing them on shelves near the door.

"What are you doing here?" he asked. "I thought this matter had been settled."

"I came to get a book and a few of his things," she said, not looking at him. "I may not be able to get Risley released or absolved, but I can visit him, read to him, and ease his last days, even if you've ruined his life." She finished with the armload of books and turned, scowling as she snatched ripped shirts from overturned furniture and the floor. "But I never expected that you'd destroy everything he owns, as well. You should be ashamed."

Still gathering ruined shirts, she brushed past him and continued down the hall, muttering and picking up clothes.

"A mob created this mess," he said, following her. "Not I."

Nella continued to gather clothing. She paused, frowning at a pile of rumpled towels, then dropped the clothes on a chair. Her back to Dubric, she began folding the towels, snapping each one before folding it.

The ghosts leered at her, treating her as a curiosity. As she snapped the towels through Elli's legs, Fytte laughed and stuck out her gruesome tongue. Dubric walked into Risley's office again, disgusted with the image. "You are wasting your time caring for him, Miss Nella. Hopefully you will realize it soon."

He had barely sat in the chair when he heard her approach. "I am allowed to take him clothes and a bit to eat, aren't I? Perhaps read to him? Even if it is a waste of my time?"

"Prisoners are allowed visitors. As long as you do not attempt to free him, I foresee no problems."

She gasped, the towels falling with a *thwupp* to the floor. "Oh, Goddess, no," she said, her voice wavering like a leaf in the wind.

He stood, snatching up his notebook. "What is it? What do you see?"

Tears running down her cheeks, she stared at Risley's desk. She swallowed then looked up at Dubric with pained and tortured eyes. "He never told me. If only I had known."

"Known what, Miss Nella? What is it?"

She glanced at the desk, then turned her head away. "That bracelet. It's usually made of grasses, not metal, but it's the same, don't you see? The pattern, the . . . Oh, Goddess, no!"

A bracelet! Why didn't I see? Dropping his notebook on the desk, he grasped her shoulders and shook her gently, drawing her eyes to his again. "What about the bracelet? What does it mean?"

Shaking, she said, "It's a Pyrinnian marriage token. If he had told me . . . If I had known . . . Maybe I could truthfully vouch for him. Maybe he would have been with me." Her eyes filled with tears. "Don't you see? Maybe he would have been in bed with me, and maybe he wouldn't be a prisoner now."

"Miss Nella," he said softly, "would you have wanted to be in bed with him if he were the killer?"

She lurched away from Dubric and stumbled down the hall. Blindly, she fell into a chair, covering her face with her hands. "It's all my fault!"

"Miss Nella," he said, touching her shoulder, "you cannot blame yourself. Risley killed those people, not you."

"How can you be sure of that? How can you be sure of anything? Damn it!" She slammed her fists on the padded chair arms. "This can't be happening, it just can't. Not like this, not to Risley. Not now that he knows I love him."

"They are not related incidences, Miss Nella. It is not fair or right to accept responsibility for choices Risley has made. They are his to bear."

She shrugged off his touch and turned away. "Please, just leave me alone."

Not knowing what else to say to her, he returned to Risley's office, gently closing the door behind him. He finished searching the desk and office but found nothing more of interest besides a carefully packed box of gold-etched dishes and cutlery. He stared into the box for a long moment, frowning.

While every bit as exquisite as Lord Brushgar's finest china, the engraved pattern bore no resemblance to the Brushgar mark. The matching teapot and plain pie pan stacked in the box spoke of a far different tale. Pie for two. No more, no less. Risley had shared a pie with Nella, as he had admitted under questioning, in a desperate effort to court her.

Then he had quietly proclaimed his innocence. Again.

Dubric traced the woven silver bracelet with his finger and considered the possibilities it presented. Had Risley worked on it late at night when he could not sleep, weaving it a bit at a time and wistfully drawing images of his intended as he thought of their future together? Even allow her to sleep innocently in his bed without touching her? The image in his mind's eye seemed so wholesome, so honest and pure, so damned *honorable*, it made him frown. Could a man like that brutally slaughter ten young women?

Could Risley be telling the truth?

Evidence does not lie, Dubric thought, pounding his fist on Risley's desk, trying to refute the doubt stinging his mouth. *I have proof. Irrefutable proof.*

All around him the ghosts refused to leave. After a long while he gathered up his empty evidence pack and left, locking the door behind him. Nella had already gone.

* * *

Her legs shaking, Nella descended the east-tower stairs, clutching the battered knapsack she'd found. It contained a complete change of clothes for Risley, a comb, a wool blanket, and a book. She'd pilfered an apple and a hunk of roast pork from the kitchen, sneaking through during the madness of the evening meal. Her own stomach growling, she continued down the stairs until she reached the lowest level.

The stones and air reeked of urine and rot and vomit. She coughed, wondering how Risley had coped with the stench. Across from the tower stairs a thickly

barred door stood closed and she walked to it, crushing
the pack against her chest.

An ancient brass knocking ring with a ram's head
hung before her eyes. She bit her lip and knocked, stepping quickly back as the door opened.

A tall, barrel-chested man stood before her, gnawing on a curved length of rib bone. "Bringing goodies
fer a pris'ner, eh?" he said, shrugging. "Let's see what
ye have, missy."

"All right," she said, holding out the pack.

He rummaged through then handed it back to her.
"Can't argue with the food and clothes, missy, but the
book can't stay. Ye can leave it wit me if ye want."

"I'll read to him and bring it back out. Is that all
right?"

"Yup." He backed away from the door and motioned
her through.

The door swung closed behind them with a *clang*
and a *thud* and she jumped, choking back a squeal. The
air outside the door smelled like paradise compared to
inside the gaol and something scuttled over her foot.
Terrified, she followed her guide down a short hall and
hoped nothing would bite her.

"I ain't ne'er seen ye here b'fore, missy, so here's the
lowdown on the rules. Only approved items goes inta
the cells. I catch ye sneakin' in so much as a toothpick,
I toss yer purty arse inna cell down the black hall and I
don't tell Dubric nothin' fer three days." He turned his
head and winked. "No food er water, and in the dark,
lots can happen in three days. Ye get me?"

"Yessir," she said, looking rapidly around and anx-
iously imagining the shadows eating her up and spitting out her bones.

"Fair 'nuff, then," he said, selecting a key from his
ring. "Yer lucky t'day, missy. Alla the pris'ners 'cept one

is right up front. We had a couple down the dark hall, but they done died, phase'r so ago." He smiled at her and his eyes twinkled. "A nice gal like yerself ain't got no business down the dark hall." He opened the door and she followed, closing her eyes at the filth and squalor.

"Here ye be, then, missy. Don'tcha be reachin' into no cells, ye hear? These here pris'ners is dangerous and I don't wanna see ye hurt."

She nodded and stepped forward while he sat in a chair near the door and continued to chew the rib.

Whistles, lewd comments, and rough-voiced propositions assaulted her ears and eyes. Most of the prisoners were men, and they leered at her through doors of barred iron, beckoning her to come close so they could peek into her knapsack. Mister Inek propositioned her, pointing to the front of his filthy pants. She raised her chin and continued on, wincing at the roaches and mice scurrying from her path.

She neared the door on the far end and turned, her heart pounding. "He's not here!" she called out to the guard.

"I feared that," he said, setting his rib on the chair as he stood. "Ye look too sweet fer the likes of these, but the one ye've come fer ain't no better, missy. Ye do know what he's done, don't ye?"

Nodding, she clutched the pack against her chest. "I know." Hesitating, she met the guard's eyes. "He's down that dark hall, isn't he?"

"Yup. I don't use'ly go down the dark hall 'cept at feedin' time, but I can go wit ye, if yer too feared to go alone." He flipped through his keys and selected one. "The murderin' bastard can't get loose, I guarantee ye that. So ye'll be safe enough, iff'n ye mind the rules."

"I . . . I'll be fine," she said, swallowing.

He unlocked the door and it creaked open, urging her into the dark. Thick, heavy doors lined both sides of the hall, with narrow-barred windows near the top and flat open slots along the bottom. A single lantern dimly glowed not far ahead, illuminating a grayed floor of straw, then nothingness eased on forever, black and bottomless like a pit beneath a rotting crypt.

"How far in is he?" she asked.

"Dunno, missy. Dubric ne'er said, and I don't wanna go look till mornin'. Ye pound on this here door when yer ready to come back out. Sure ye'll be all right?"

She staggered forward, doing her best to ignore her fear and the overpowering stench of death. She heard the key turn in the lock and she took a shaky step toward the light, then another.

"Who's there?" Risley's voice echoed down the dark hall.

She stumbled toward the voice. "Risley! Where are you?"

"Nella? For Goddess's sake, what are you doing down here?" She heard movement somewhere near the light and she hurried, seeing fingers reach out through a window.

"I couldn't just leave you to die," she said, rushing to him.

He grasped her offered hand, squeezing it, and bringing it close to his face. She felt his breath on her fingers as he kissed them. "Oh, love, you can't be down here. Thank you," he kissed her palm, "oh, Goddess, thank you, but you shouldn't. You can't." He reluctantly released her and said, "As much as I want you to stay, you need to go."

"No." Her hands shaking, she opened the pack and

handed him the clothes and comb. "I'm not going to desert you. I brought food, too, and a blanket."

He accepted the clothes and they disappeared through the small window. The blanket followed. "Thank you, love, but I'm going to hang in a few days at most. You need to go. Please."

She looked at him, into his worried eyes and said, "I can't leave you. I just can't. Everyone tells me you're guilty, that there's proof, but I won't believe it. Not about you."

"You had better believe, because I'm going to hang for it." He rubbed his forehead and said, "I saw some of Dubric's evidence, and I'd believe my guilt, too. But I honestly can't remember ever doing the things they said I've done. For Goddess's sake, Nella, Dubric thinks I stole those girls' kidneys and ate them!"

His face disappeared as he slumped against the door. "What kind of monster does those things? He's so certain it's me, but why can't I remember? I can't fathom doing something so vile, so repulsive . . . and yet . . . and yet somehow I have."

He stood again and glared at her. "You have to go. Now. Before I hurt you, too."

"No," she said, reaching up to touch him. "I will not leave you. Guilty or innocent, I will not leave you. I promise."

She handed him the food and fished the book from the pack, opening to the first page. "I've got a bell, bell and a half until I have to be back at my room, and I found this book in your suite. *The Candle in the Window* by Dunclaire. I hope it's all right."

"It's fine, love," he said, his voice catching. "Thank you." Both leaning against their side of the door, she read and he listened, the scuttling of vermin filling the gaps.

* * *

Awaiting dawn and gripping a cup of tea in his hands, Dubric sat in his suite and stared out the window. At his insistence, patrols had maintained their schedule throughout the night, and Dien had not knocked on his door with urgent news or a new crisis. Lars and Otlee had been sent to bed. Every so often he would sip his tea and look at the ghosts.

Eleven were far too many and he did not want more. Fytte sat on his bed and watched him as she combed her fingers through her curly hair. Elli and Ennea seemed to be comparing head wounds. Celese wandered aimlessly, as if looking for something she could not find. She walked through walls, into his wardrobe, and through his bed. Rianne, the egg maid whose murder Lars had interrupted, pulled off an arm, looked at it, reattached it, and pulled it off again. Earlier she had been doing the same thing with her head. The other five girls were still thankfully boring. Olibe Meiks, however, stared at Dubric with disgust. A spectral pitchfork had appeared in his hands during the night, and Dubric did not want to think about what would happen once Olibe started moving.

But the night was almost over and no one else had died. Yet. He was not about to get his hopes up again, especially since a thread of doubt tugged at his mind. Risley had proclaimed his innocence in a steadfast and certain manner, and had shown no weakening of his resolve. He had not screamed or whimpered or begged, merely calmly insisted that he had killed no one, while all along demanding that Nella remain under guard, as if he truly feared for her safety.

What if the lad told the truth? What if he was innocent? Was that even possible? Did the silver bracelet give credence to another theory or was it additional evidence of his obsession and pent-up frustrations?

Dubric took a breath and tried to not second-guess himself. If Risley was innocent, the facts should sort themselves out soon enough with the real killer still loose.

He sighed and turned away from his ghosts. His heart troubled, he sipped his tea and waited for sunlight.

CHAPTER
16

✝

I've gathered a preliminary list," Lars said as he walked through the open door into Dubric's office. "It's a short one."

Dubric grabbed a slipping piece of paper as he glanced up from a statement the gaol keeper had given Otlee. A young woman had visited Risley that morning and the night before, bringing food, clothes, and a book with her. The gaol keeper worried that she had placed herself in danger by visiting him.

Keeping Risley and Nella from flirting had become the least of his worries.

Elli and Fytte were now trying to upset the stacks of notes and books on his shelves. Occasionally they succeeded, with scattered papers mutely proclaiming their achievements. He worried over what would happen once they could move objects of more substance. Would they throw furniture like they threw Rianne's arm?

Lars said nothing as he closed the door. He picked up the few loose sheets and an overturned logbook and returned them to their proper place. Giving Dubric a concerned look, he sat in his chair while Fytte sent another sheet fluttering to the floor.

Dubric clasped his hands over his desk and watched

the boy instead of the falling paper. "What have you found?"

Lars glanced at the sheet on the floor, sighed, then opened his notebook. "The dishes in question were last used at the Council luncheon, held before last spring's festival. Would you like a re-account of attendees?"

Dubric shook his head. The Council that spring had merely consisted of himself, Lord Brushgar, Friar Bonne, Kyl Romlin, and the Duke of Jhalin. No others. They had ruled on the merits of perhaps half a dozen cases of theft, support for two illegitimate children, and a handful of grievances and misunderstandings. Winters tended to cause squabbles and a spring Council was a standard occurrence.

Lars watched a clipped packet of testimonies slide off the shelf and fall to the floor. "Sir? Can you make them stop?"

"No. They pay me no heed."

Agitated, Lars tapped his fingers on the arm of his chair as he returned his attention to his notes. "All of the dishes from the luncheon were washed and dried by Thallia and Fionne. Both are currently employed, and they filled out the proper inventory forms when they finished their chore. Pitta initialed them. No dishes were noted as broken or missing at that time."

He glanced at Dubric again, and went on, "There are standing orders that once each moon the dishes are washed and recounted. Again, this duty has consistently fallen to Thallia and Fionne. I asked Pitta why, and she said these two women, both in their forties, by the way, had the steadiest hands in the kitchen. Evidently, the dishes are quite fragile. Each moon, a page has been assigned to watch them and ensure no thefts occur while the dishes were in the kitchen."

Dubric nodded. One teaspoon alone was worth at least five crown if melted down, and security protocols must be followed when working with valuables. "Go on."

"The inventories have been promptly initialed and filed each moon. The last was three phases five days ago. As of that day, all of the dishes and silverware were accounted for."

Dubric noted Lars's information. The dishes were due to be counted again in two days' time. "Have the counts been accurate?"

"I believe so, sir, but I have not spoken to Thallia and Fionne yet. They're in the midst of washing the finer morning dishes and did not wish to delegate the task to younger maids. I am trying to be accommodating and have requested a private meeting with each of them between three and four bell this afternoon."

Thoughtful yet timely. A good compromise. He smiled. "Nice job. Did you do a recount today?"

"Yes, sir. Pitta, Moergan, and I closed off the valuables storeroom and inventoried the entire cabinet. We are missing two dinner plates, one small bread plate, two full sets of gold eating utensils, a single serving spoon, and a small meat knife."

Dubric paused in his note taking. Lars had listed over a hundred crowns' worth of gold and china. "Are you certain?"

Lars produced two sheets of paper and handed both to Dubric. "I thought Pitta would faint, sir, when we counted them the first time, so we counted again. Both counts are there, and both are identical. The other sheet is last moon's official inventory."

He looked over the numbers and frowned, slamming his hand on a paper as Fytte tried to snatch it away. Tiring of her little game, she huffed off to sulk in a corner. "Who has access?"

"Only you and Pitta have keys to the cabinet, sir."

Dubric met Lars's gaze. "Has Pitta's key gone missing?"

"No, sir. She had them handy in her pocket and insisted they had never left her possession. The cabinet actually takes two keys, sir. Plus a third for the storage-room door."

Dubric clasped his hands together and watched the curious gleam in Lars's eyes. "You think it was me? You think I concocted that plate of gore?"

"No, sir. While it is theoretically possible you may have stolen dishes from the cupboard, I am certain you have not been murdering servant girls."

"Thank you for that vote of support," Dubric muttered as he picked up the papers again. He sighed and compared inventory numbers on the two pages. "Please fetch Pitta. Since Otlee is busy with research, you will take notes of her interrogation."

Lars got up and nodded. Without a glance back, he left Dubric's office.

Dubric grumbled at his ghosts, then folded the two inventory sheets and placed them in his notebook.

* * *

"I did not take them. I swear!" Pitta said. She looked back and forth between Lars and Dubric. Her earnest face was blotchy from crying, and her thick, ruddy hands clutched and pulled nervously at her apron.

"Someone took them," Dubric said. "You and I have the only keys, and I certainly did not."

"I swear, it was not me. All were there last moon

when the girls cleaned them. We three counted them together when we put them away. They were all there, and I locked the cabinet."

The two scullery maids, Fytte and the girl the lackeys had found—Dubric could not at that moment recall her name—stood on each side of Pitta and made faces at her as she wailed. Elli and the laundress had pulled Rianne's head off and were tossing it around her in a gruesome game of keep-away. Dubric hoped one would drop the nasty thing and it would slip through the floor so they could continue their game downstairs in the gaol.

He pulled his attention off the ghosts and back to Pitta's terrified face. "Have you loaned your keys to anyone, for even a moment, this past moon?"

Her denial came frantic and loud. "No, sir. I have two sets of keys, the common set and the specials. I've never loaned the specials. Not to anyone. Ever. Not once in all my summers as kitchen master."

"How about your husband? Has Lander ever used them? Carried them for you?"

"No, sir. Absolutely not! I lock them every night in my trinket box and unlock them every morning before work. That key I wear around my neck." She pulled a ribbon with a tiny brass key from beneath her grease-spattered uniform. "I take every possible precaution I can to ensure that I keep the specials safe."

"What about your eldest son? He is what, fourteen, fifteen summers now? Could he have taken them?"

She shook her head with even more gusto. "The children do not touch my things without permission, sir. Besides, they're all visiting my mother. Been there for almost two phases now. Before that, Telek apprenticed dawn to dusk with the blacksmith every day since the summer solstice. He's been too tired to eat, let alone get into mischief. Like I said, sir, I've always locked away my special keys. I don't think the children have ever seen them, let alone touched them."

Dubric leaned forward. Was she protecting the boy, as mothers were prone to do? "If your son is apprenticed to the blacksmith, why did he visit your mother?"

Pitta looked at Lars, her eyes flicking over the pen he clutched in his hand. Her lip quivered and she slowly turned her worried gaze back to Dubric. "Do you have to write this down, sir? Please, can't this part just be between us?"

Dubric wanted to bang his head on his desk. He forced his voice to remain calm. "All testimonies are private. What you say will not leave this room."

"But it will be written. For others to read."

"For me to read," Dubric said.

Pitta looked at the pen. "I never took the dishes, Lander never took the dishes, and Telek never took the dishes, so I guess this will never end up as evidence at Council." She took a single deep breath and looked at Dubric. "I had the children, all of them, visit my mother for at least a moon."

Red, blotchy embarrassment flared up from her neckline, and she sucked in another breath while Dubric waited. "Tis my marriage, you see," she said. "We have the seven children and all, but it's never been easy and we've grown apart these past summers, ever since Lander became a herald. He has a certain image to maintain, meeting all the visitors like he does, and he's come to like it."

She snuffled in a handkerchief and dabbed at her eyes. "I grew bigger after every baby, and I know Lander looks at the younger, thinner girls. And why wouldn't he? Look at me, Dubric! Greasy and filthy, big as a barn and covered in cooking mess, while he's so handsome and particular about his dress and bearing. He's discovered silks and minstrels and educated discussions, but I'm just boring old pig slop. The ugly old sow he married before he knew any different.

"We've had nary a moment to ourselves and I didn't know what else to do. He's been drawing away from me, looking at the young pretties, but I thought maybe if we were alone for a while we could find each other again. Maybe he could love me again instead of giving me a cold kiss then rolling away every night.

"That's why I sent the kids to visit Nana."

She bawled in her hands while Lars looked at Dubric and waggled the pen.

Dubric shook his head and watched Lars lay the pen onto the paper. The boy was almost as red as Pitta and the ghosts had turned to watch the show. From capital theft to marital trouble, in less time than it took to draw a breath. How did he get himself into these situations? "I am certain everything will turn out all right," he said in what he hoped was a soothing voice. "You two have been married for what, sixteen summers? You can surely work out any troubles."

Pitta nodded and blew her nose, loudly, into her already drenched handkerchief. "You would think so, but it's been tougher than I thought. I'd planned on having a romantic dinner or two each phase, take walks and all. Spend time together. But it's hard to be romantic while these murders are going on, and now you think I've stolen the lord's dishes. We've barely spoken to each other since this started. I don't know how it can get any worse."

Before Pitta could blow her nose again, a knock rattled the door. Dien peeked in. "We've searched their rooms as you've requested, sir. No dishes, no murder weapon, no—"

The sharp slash of Dubric's hand stopped Dien's report. Pitta took one look at Dien and wailed.

What ghosts could leave did leave, and Dubric did not blame them.

* * *

"You shouldn't go," Dari said.

Nella fluffed a pillow, standing it pertly on the bed. "I have to."

Dari smoothed the coverlet. "You're still in the pigsty for pilfering that broom, and if Helgith finds out you've snuck off to the gaol again, I don't know what she's going to do. Why you thought you needed to snatch a broom is beyond me, but she's furious!"

"I did not 'pilfer' a broom. I borrowed it, and I brought it back."

Dari stared at her. "In all the time I've known you, you have never, ever 'borrowed' anything without asking first."

Nella shrugged and gathered up the used sheets. "The answer would have been 'no,' so I didn't ask."

"Can you hear the words you're saying?"

Nella paused, her shoulders and head sagging. "Don't, Dari. Please. I know I'm breaking rules, but I have to. No one will help me, but I have to help Risley, and it's so horrid down there. Just awful. The least I can do is sweep the nastiness from his door or spend time talking with him after all he's done for me."

She looked at Dari, her lip trembling. "They're going to kill him, in a phase, maybe less, he thinks. I . . ." She swallowed, wiping at her eyes with the back of her hand. "I will stand by him. I will remain his friend. I will bring him food and sweep the damned floor.

Helgith can punish me all she wants; just visiting him is more punishment than she can possibly conceive of. I can come back here, but he's trapped down there! He's locked in a slimy, stinking box, and he can't get out for even a moment to make beds or fold towels or get in trouble."

Nella straightened her back and said, "I'll buy the damned broom if I have to. Reimburse the kitchen for the food. It doesn't really matter, because the man I love is going to die and there's not a damned thing I can do to stop it. And I'm not even sure if he's guilty or innocent or anything!"

Struggling to regain her composure, she carried the sheets to the hall and threw them in the laundry cart. The rest of her friends and coworkers gave her concerned glances but said nothing.

She ignored their worries as best she could and gathered an armload of towels, carrying them into Lady Jespert's suite.

Dari stood in the middle of the room, frowning with concern. "I'm sorry," she said, hugging Nella. "I know how much you care about him. I should be more understanding."

"Thanks for caring about me," Nella said, her shoulders shaking. "Really. You're a good friend." Before she could stop herself, she started crying, dampening Dari's uniform with her fear and her shame.

The other girls worked on, leaving Nella to cry in peace.

17

Dubric looked up at the knock on his office door. Ten ghosts cavorted around the room, trying to cause trouble. Olibe Meiks, the eleventh, had wandered away and Dubric had not seen him since, even though his oppressive ache remained as an endless reminder.

"Sir?" Otlee asked, clutching an accounting ledger to his chest as he peeked in the door. "Do you have a moment?"

Dubric set aside his pen and looked through Elli to see the page. She sat on the edge of his desk, her backside squarely on his notebook, and she contemplated Dubric with cool orneriness. When he had inadvertently set his notebook there that morning, she had pounced upon the opportunity to cause trouble, as had the other ghosts. Three of the girls had commandeered the chairs and had spent most of the morning passing Rianne's foot between them. Two fought over who would get to play with Otlee. Dubric wished they would all go follow Olibe Meiks and leave him alone.

"What is it, Otlee?"

"I know you're not supposed to be disturbed unless it's an emergency, sir, but you have a visitor."

"Who is it?"

"Hulda Meiks, sir. She's rather insistent and refuses to leave."

Dubric sighed, wishing Elli would get off his desk. "Send her in, then."

A moment later, Hulda strode in with a baby in her arms. Two children followed her; a girl of perhaps five summers and a boy of three or so. Olibe Meiks stood behind them, the pitchfork clutched in his hands. His eyes glowed with rage. Every living member of the family had a blotchy face and tear-streaked cheeks. Hulda said softly, "Stay out there, darlings. With the boy."

"Yes, Mama," the girl answered and grasped her brother's hand. As soon as they were clear, Otlee closed the door. Olibe stepped through.

Hulda stared at Dubric as she cradled the baby. "Did you see my children? My babies?"

Dubric tried to watch Hulda, but Olibe's hands kept shifting on the handle of that pitchfork. A most worrisome situation. "Yes, ma'am. They are beautiful children."

"My babies lost their daddy because of you," she said. "And look at me when I'm talkin' to you."

Dubric turned his head toward the woman. "Yes, ma'am."

She leaned forward. "Goddess, you're polite now. Not like the night you banged on our door and demanded my husband guard the castle. You sure didn't call me 'ma'am' then. You didn't give us a chance to say 'no.'"

"Your husband was a good man, and our first choice. He would not have said 'no.'"

"He wouldn't have left his wife a widow and his children orphans, either. You gave him no choice."

"We have listed you and your family with the widows and orphans of war. Your husband served in an official capacity and you shall receive full wage payment and relief from taxation, as if he had been in the army."

"I don't want your filthy money. I want my husband back!"

The pitchfork moved, but Dubric forced his eyes to remain on Hulda.

She laughed viciously. "Now you're quiet. Since you sent Olibe to his death you've asked that we have patience. Patience and understanding, while you twiddle your thumbs up your ass. You've tossed the bastard that killed my Olibe into the gaol where he still lives and breathes, despite his terrible deeds. You have no intention of punishing him, do you? He is of your kind, after all. A High Noble. A *Royal*. You never punish one another, only those lower than you."

Dubric took a slow and measured breath. "There is a chance, however slim, that it may not be Lord Risley who has done this. I have to be absolutely certain before I execute an innocent man."

"Horse piss. Tis him and we all know it. No one died last night, did they? But he left his little whore runnin' loose, and I hope he breaks free to get her. Truly I do. I hope he cuts her into pieces, then comes after you."

"Missus Meiks, you do not know what you are saying."

"I know what I'm saying. You've made my children orphans and left me a widow. Then you arranged for your precious Lord Romlin to skip away without losin' his life for his crimes. I hope he cuts you up and pisses on your guts. Leaves you lying dead in the mud and snow like he did my Olibe. If he doesn't do it, I'll do it myself."

"I can throw you in gaol for threats like that."

She tossed her head back and her eyes shone with vile glee. "Try. I know of thirty men ready to hang you and Lord Romlin today. Throwin' a grievin' widow into your stinkin' gaol will be the last mistake you'll ever make."

"Your grief has clouded your mind, madam. Perhaps you should leave now, before you cross the line and I do throw you in gaol."

"My mind is perfectly clear. I hope you die a painful death and rot for eternity in the seven hells," she snapped, then spat in his eye.

Dubric started to stand as the anger flashed within him—no one had ever spat on him and not regretted it—but Olibe Meiks moved quickly to protect his wife, and threw the pitchfork.

The pain flared exquisite and fiery, and Dubric nearly screamed. The force of the blow knocked him off his feet and shoved him back into the chair, which skidded backward, slamming against the wall, the back of it cracking. Dubric's ghosts all watched with deadly interest.

Hulda Meiks had already turned to leave and did not notice. She yanked the door open and stomped through, slamming it behind her. Olibe looked at Dubric for a moment. He mouthed something to the other ghosts that Dubric did not understand, then followed his wife.

"Oh, peg!" Dubric gasped through the pain. His hands slid over his belly. He felt nothing but the cloth of his shirt and his heart slamming beneath his ribs, but he saw the pitchfork. The tines had buried in his abdomen, leaving less than the thickness of a finger between the cross piece and his flesh. He sucked in one painful breath after another, and try as he might, he could not move from the chair. *It is not real,* he told himself. *It cannot be.*

Of all of his ghosts, he had never known one to harm a person, never seen one truly interact with the real world. But only one other ghost had ever remained long enough to move about. She certainly would never harm anyone, although he suspected she had been able to move objects for a long, long time.

He struggled to remain conscious through the pain. There had to be something he could do. Something, for King's sake! *Otlee. He could help. He could pull this thing away.*

He took a breath to call the boy's name, then paused. How could Otlee pull a pitchfork he could neither see nor feel? How could anyone? How could the horrid thing remain even after Olibe had gone?

He looked to his ghosts. "Please," he said. "One of you, please help me."

Nine looked at him and laughed. Elli alone nodded. Darling Elli Cunliffe, the orphan he had bounced on his knee and given sweets to. She had been a beautiful child; a skipping delight of blue eyes, blonde hair, and laughter. She turned around on his desk and crawled toward him. Her dead eyes flickering as if snow still fell upon them, she smiled sweetly, reached out, grasped the handle of the pitchfork, then yanked it downward.

This time Dubric did scream. It felt as if his insides were being dragged across broken glass. The handle vibrated like a bell and his eyes rolled white even as Otlee burst in.

"Sir!" He ran through the door and skidded to a stop as Dubric raised a hand to slow him.

Dubric gasped and swallowed a scream as Elli

pulled the horrid thing upward. He had to get the boy out before the ghosts tried to harm him, as well. "Otlee," he choked out, his voice breaking. "I need you to go to the stable. Ask Flavin if he has had any more grain stolen this moon."

Otlee ran to his side. "But, sir. You screamed! You look ill, sir. Wouldn't it be wiser for me to fetch a physician?"

"No! Get to the stable. Now. That is an order."

"But, sir!" Fytte and Ennea stood behind him, their fingers lifting his hair. Otlee did not seem to notice, but both flashed wicked grins. They could *touch* him. Fytte licked her finger.

What did Olibe tell them? he thought, panting through the pain. *What has he done?* "Go. And hurry!"

Otlee hesitated, then ran through Ennea and Fytte.

Celese closed the door and beamed at Dubric. He felt cold dead fingers glide over his bald head, yank on his ears. Was it Plien? Ennea? Cheyna? All three? Elli climbed onto his lap and reached again for the pitchfork. She felt cold, like ice, and her eyes glittered as she yanked the handle.

* * *

He did not know how long he screamed. He only knew his throat hurt, and his head and mouth felt as if they had been burned by ice. But suddenly the cold and much of the pain lifted away. He gasped for breath as he opened his eyes.

The ten huddled together in the far corner with dead eyes that were wide and afraid. They stared at something on his left. He smelled perfume on the air, and for once he welcomed it.

His head rolled painfully on the creaking bones of his neck and he smiled. "Brinna." He had first seen her ghost over thirty summers before, and she had long since come and gone of her own accord. But she had never truly left, for he had never caught her killer. She had remained the lady of the castle even in death, as she had been in life. Sweet, sweet Brinna Brushgar.

Brinna nodded, saying something he could not catch.

"I do not understand," he said around the blistering pain in his belly.

She smiled and placed a finger on his lips. Like the other ghosts, her touch felt cool, but unlike the others, she was gentle. She pointed to the pitchfork and turned her eyes to the ten girls.

"No, it was not them. It was another. Olibe Meiks. A gardener."

She nodded sadly and curled her arms as if holding a baby.

He almost cried as he thought about Brinna and babies. She had held her infant son, Stev, when she had died. When they both had died. Stev had not lived to his first moonrise, and the church insisted he had not received his soul. Although he had been murdered in his mother's arms, his ghost was forever gone. Brinna often checked on sleeping babies and watched over children at play, perhaps because of the one she had lost. "Yes, he has children. His wife blames me."

She shook her head and frowned, wiping a tear from her eye.

"Yes, it is sad." He took a ragged breath. "Do you know who has been doing this to our castle?"

She shook her head, and "no" was unmistakable on her lips.

He glanced to his ghosts. "Do they know who killed them?"

Brinna looked at the ghosts and he saw his own

question on her lips. She soon turned back to him and shook her head.

He started to nod his disappointment, but Brinna's attention had drifted to the girls.

She said something, her eyes narrowing, and she spoke again. A moment later she returned her glowing gaze to him. She smiled softly, tilted her head, and pointed to the pitchfork.

"Do you think you can remove it?"

She nodded and pointed at him, contorting her face in anguish and pain.

"It hurts now. Removing it cannot be worse."

Smiling, she moved to stand between his knees. She grasped the handle and he sucked in a harsh breath as the pitchfork shifted.

He took a few deep breaths and said, "On the count of three." When Brinna nodded and tightened her grip, he said, "One. Two—"

The pain ripped through him and he screamed again. As darkness engulfed his mind he thought, *She remembered the old trick, after all these summers. Pull on two.*

CHAPTER
18

✝

Otlee had no intention of going to the stable. He pounded on Dien's door until Sarea snatched it open.

She held a sleeping baby in her arms and whispered harshly, "What do you want? Don't you know we're trying to sleep, for Goddess's sake?"

Otlee bobbed a quick bow. "I am truly sorry, ma'am, but there is an emergency."

She sighed. "I should have known. Dubric never lets him have a full day's rest. Come on in. I'll get him up for you."

As soon as Otlee stepped inside, she closed the door and handed him the baby. "I'll be back in a moment. Easier to wake him if I have full use of my hands."

"Yes, ma'am," Otlee said, shifting the baby in his arms and bouncing her gently while he waited, praying that Missus Saworth hurry.

She did. A growl rumbled through the suite and Dien staggered through an open door, filling the portal as he tied a robe around him. "What's happened now?" he said around a yawn.

Otlee hoped he did not sound as panicked as he felt. "It's Dubric. Something's wrong. He's in pain. Sick. I'm not sure." Otlee held the baby toward her mother. "But it's bad. He screamed, Dien. Dubric screamed."

Sarea hurried over to take the baby while Dien said, "Give me time to get my pants on."

* * *

They found him on the floor of his office. He lay unconscious beside his overturned chair, and his skin was cool and pale. One ear bled, and Otlee grimaced as Dien turned Dubric's head. Despite first appearances, the blood had not come from inside the ear. The lobe had been ripped off.

"Goddess, what happened?" Otlee asked. "Is he alive?" Something cold glided along his cheek and he jumped away.

Dien touched Dubric's neck with his fingertips. "He's alive. Fetch a physician. Rolle, if you can, not that blabbering Halld."

Feeling as though someone was dragging icicles through his hair, Otlee turned and ran through the door, a whimper escaping his throat.

* * *

"I can carry him," Dien said.

Rolle stood and looked at Otlee. "Run ahead and turn down his bed. We'll have more luck keeping him in his own suite than the infirmary."

Otlee stood in the doorway, the closest he had come since fetching Rolle. "Yes, sir," he said and hurried away.

Dien glanced at the boy but said nothing. Something didn't feel right, that was for certain. Whatever it was, it had spooked Otlee. The boy had looked at death many times over the past few days; surely it was something other than Dubric's illness bothering him. And why the peg did the office smell like perfume? "What in the seven hells happened?" he asked the physician.

"Considering his age, the murders, and how hard he has been pushing himself, he has probably suffered an ictus of the heart, or perhaps apoplexy."

"Bull piss. Not Dubric."

Rolle shrugged. "The strain has ruptured his blood vessels, leaving a row of welts across his abdomen. I am greatly relieved that they burst there and not on his head or near his heart. Believe me or not, that is up to you, but if he doesn't get some rest, this will happen again, and next time it may kill him."

Lars ran in, his face flushed. "Otlee said— Oh, Goddess!"

Dien lifted Dubric's limp body. "Gather up his notebook and pencil. We're taking him to his rooms."

Lars grabbed Dubric's things. "I'll run up the east tower. Maybe I can get the hall clear."

"Good idea," Dien said. "We should try to keep this quiet."

As Lars sprinted from the office, Dien settled Dubric in his arms. "Will he make it?"

Rolle packed up his instruments. "He should. I'll bring some lily of the valley to calm his heart, and some laudanum to soothe his nerves. I can do no more. But he'll have to settle down, not get so worked up."

Dien nodded. "He'll settle down, if I have to sit on the old bastard myself."

* * *

Dubric awoke to see the ceiling above his bed and to feel a rat chewing on his ear. Grunting, he slapped the rat and snatched his hand back from its bite. "What the—?" he started, but saw Rolle holding a shining needle.

Rolle sighed. "Now look at that. Only two stitches to go and you've ruined my knot."

"Sir!" Otlee said from the other side.

Dien stood at the foot of the bed, as did Lars. Both looked alternately relieved and worried.

Dubric shoved Rolle away as he sat up. "Leave it alone. What happened?"

Otlee looked at Dien on one side; Rolle frowned on the other.

Dien said, "You collapsed."

Of course I collapsed. "Let me up. We have much to do and I have wasted enough time."

"You're not going anywhere," Dien said. Beside him, Lars nodded. Eleven ghosts stood behind them; Brinna and the ten. The ten huddled together while Brinna watched them.

Dubric stared at Dien and Lars. His abdomen hurt, there was no denying that, but it was like a dream of pain. Not real. The ceaseless throbbing of his aching head brought more agony and he had survived it for days. "There is nothing wrong with me."

Dien opened his notebook. "Otlee informed me that Hulda Meiks insisted on seeing you, and right after she left you screamed. That true?"

"Yes and no. Now let me up."

"You are hereby ordered to stay abed," Rolle said. "You're not getting up." The needle moved close again.

"Watch me," Dubric replied as he batted Rolle's hand away.

"Lars and I will handle whatever happens today," Dien said. "Does Hulda Meiks have something to do with this?"

"There is nothing wrong with me. Dammit, Rolle, leave my ear alone."

Rolle cleared his throat. "You have an open wound and I don't want it to get infected."

"'Open wound'? What open—?" Dubric touched his ear and winced. His attention focused suddenly on Dien. "What happened?"

"You'll have to tell me. So far you've been a pretty shitty witness."

Behind Dien, Fytte snapped her teeth together, then slunk back as Brinna said something.

She bit me! Dubric thought, but he said, "How bad is my ear? What am I doing here?"

"Most of the lobe is missing," Rolle said. "I'd suggest you let me stitch up what's left before you lose the whole thing to infection or rot. Beyond that, I'd say you had an episode. Apoplexy, perhaps, or a problem with your heart. They're not uncommon in men your age. You're under too much strain and are bursting blood vessels."

Dubric's heart was fine and he knew it. "Sew the damned thing up, then get out of here," he said. "I do not need to be under a physician's care, for King's sake."

"You're staying right frigging here," Dien said. "I'll bribe half the damned staff into holding you here, if I have to."

Lars nodded. "We can handle things for a few days."

Dubric winced as Rolle shoved the needle through his ear. "I tell you, there is nothing wrong with me."

All three members of his staff contemplated him with disbelief plainly written on their faces.

* * *

Bells later, Dubric looked up as Otlee hurried in. "I've requested a fresh pot of tea, sir."

Dubric flipped a page of his notebook. Lazing around was going to drive him mad. "How many men do we have scheduled to patrol tonight?"

"I'm not supposed to talk work with you," Otlee said. "You're supposed to rest. Do you need anything?"

"Yes. Fetch me my pants."

"Sorry, sir. Dien forbade me to."

That damn Dien had stolen every pair of trousers, every long tunic, robe, or cloak Dubric owned. Faced with the option of indecency, not to mention flaunting his bony knees, Dubric had remained in his suite, even if he had not remained in bed. He sat at his table and had papers strung all around, as well as a box of blood-ied clothing. The welts on his belly no longer hurt, Brinna kept the ghosts corralled in the corner, and even his ear had stopped its wretched throbbing. Dammit, he had work to do, and only Otlee to run his errands.

"Tell Dien he is fired."

"I already did, sir. He thanked me and laughed."

Dubric grunted and flipped through his notebook again while Otlee watched him expectantly. The ghosts watched him, too. Insanity loomed around the corner. He could feel it. If he could only get rid of the ghosts and the boy, at least he could think, for King's sake.

Otlee found a chair and sat while Dubric pored through his notes. Some time later, a knock rattled the door and Otlee jumped up to answer it.

Lander Beckwith stood there, a note clutched in his hands. He looked at Otlee and squinted at Dubric. "Dubric has a message," he said to Otlee.

Otlee accepted the message and nodded his thanks. Before Beckwith could say anything, Otlee closed the door.

Dubric sipped his tea and held out his hand. "I do get to read my messages, do I not?"

Otlee shrugged and dropped the sealed note in Dubric's hand.

The green wax seal broke with a slight snap. "Tunek on a pony," he whispered as he read. "That damned bastard!"

"Sir?" Otlee said.

"Get Dien. Tell him it is an emergency. And tell him to bring my damned pants!"

"But, sir, what happened?"

He slammed his book closed and stood, bony knees and all. "It is from Haenpar. We have been threatened with war if I do not release Risley."

"Oh, peg!" Otlee said, then turned and ran for the door.

* * *

Lars sorted scattered papers in Dubric's office, while Dien righted furniture and tried to repair Dubric's broken chair.

"Looks like a stampede came through here," Dien muttered as he brushed off his hands and stood.

Lars said nothing and Dien turned to look at him.

"Rats steal your tongue, pup?"

"No," he said without looking up. Guilt twisted in his gut. He had a pretty good idea what had come through the office, and it wasn't a stampede. Dubric had a riot all of his own. A ghostly riot. "Just trying to make sense of these papers."

Dien pulled a hammer from one of the cabinets. He

knelt beside the broken chair again. "Have you ever smelled perfume in here?"

Lars glanced in the corner where Dubric had once pointed at the ghosts. "Not that I can recall."

Dien set aside the hammer. He turned to look at Lars and said, "Spill it, pup."

Lars started filing. "Nothing to spill."

"Uh-huh. And you expect me to believe that?"

Lars glanced up, then looked away. He had been ordered to keep the ghosts a secret. No one could know, not even Dien.

Dien said, "You've stared into the corners about a thousand times since we came in here, and you're filing testimonies under inventory. Something's on your mind."

"It's nothing, all right?"

Dien sat on the floor facing Lars, his wrists on his knees. "Is it Jesscea?"

Lars looked up, startled. Jesscea was Dien's second eldest daughter, thirteen summers old and pretty with thick dark hair and pale green eyes. Moergan, Trumble, and several of the other senior pages talked about her sometimes, about how she'd be of courting age soon, but he'd never . . . "No! Why would you think that?"

"A man worries about his daughters. And when a lad such as yourself clams up when the man happens to—"

"I have never, ever, had an improper thought about Jesscea."

"But you're coming of that age. She is, too."

Lars swallowed. "Ar-are you asking me to court your daughter?"

Dien took a deep rumbling breath and shook his head. "What I'm saying is that I'm not so old I don't remember what it's like to be young. You're a good lad. She could do much worse."

Lars blushed. "I hadn't thought about anything like that. Honest. I don't have time to think about things like that."

Dien leaned forward. "I know. You're focused on your work. But a lad your age should be noticing girls, spilling some oats now and then. Not spending all his time filing papers and running errands."

"It's my job, and I have to do my job." Lars raised his eyes. "Everything else can wait."

"Do you really believe that? Has your quest for perfection—"

"I am not questing for perfection," Lars muttered, resuming his filing.

Dien stood. "Fine. Deny it. Shit, you're no different than Dubric, holding everything inside. It's gonna eat you whole, like it has him. He chose to be that way, but you . . ." He shoved the broken chair upright and picked up the hammer. He knelt again and hammered the wood as he hammered his words. "I should order you to get drunk, you know. Order you to gamble, or take up smoking, or get laid. Force you to roughhouse or play a game of pick ball with the other lads. Dammit, boy, you're like a son to me—"

"At least I'm like a son to someone," Lars muttered, the papers rattling in his hands.

Dien snapped his head around and his gaze gleamed piercing and hot. "Pup, listen to me. I don't know what beast crawled up your father's ass, but you're—"

Lars stood. "I'm what? A disappointment? A total slop for brains? Worthless? Useless? Ignorant? Better off dead?"

"Does he say that piss to you?"

"He doesn't say a single pegging word to me!" Lars reddened and his hands balled into fists. "He hasn't spoken to me for almost six summers, even when he's here with Kyl Romlin. Not one blasted word! It's like I don't exist."

Dien said softly, "I'm sorry. I didn't know."

"Fine. Forget you ever did, all right? Just forget the whole thing."

"I'm not going to forget," Dien said. "When he sent you here you were what, nine summers?"

Lars nodded and lowered his eyes. He had left Haenpar on his ninth birthday and had never been back. "Time to grow up," his father had said. "Dubric will make a man out of you." They were the last words his father had ever spoken to him. Upon arriving in Faldorrah he had worked long, hard hours as a junior page, been promoted rapidly, even chosen for Dubric's personal staff. At first he'd sent letters home every phase or so—addressed to his father—but his father never replied and finally Lars had given up. His mother wrote occasionally; he received a letter from her every moon or two, but never his father. Not once in nearly six summers. No matter what commendation he received, what promotion, what accomplishment, no matter how perfect his marks, Bostra Hargrove, Castellan of Haenpar, had never shown the slightest bit of interest in his son.

"That's just the way it is," Lars finally said without rubbing at his leaking eyes. "We'd better get back to work."

"You listen to me, pup—" Dien started, but Otlee burst through the door.

* * *

This is impossible! Lars thought, trotting down the hall with Dubric's pants clenched in his hands. *No one except Nella has visited Risley, and she's searched every time she leaves. If not her, who told the Romlins?*

He rounded a corner and skidded to a stop. A pair of maids were chatting with the herald, giggling at his awkward flirtations.

What luck, Lars thought. *Beckwith delivered the message to Dubric. Maybe he knows something.* "May I speak with you a moment, please?" he called out, moving forward again.

Beckwith turned, grinning. "Of course, young *Master* Hargrove. What service may I provide?"

Lars sidled close to Beckwith and the maids gave him a curious yet mildly annoyed glance. "This is a private conversation, ladies," he said, calmly waiting for them to depart.

One put her hand on her hip and the other frowned, but they left. The first looked over her shoulder and said, "See you later then, Lander. Have fun with the boy."

Beckwith watched them go, sighing, then returned his attention to Lars. He looked Lars over top to bottom and sneered. "Is there a particular reason you're carrying a pair of trousers about in public? It is most unseemly. Surely you are old enough to control your bladder without carrying around spare clothing."

Lars felt his smile freeze upon his face. *Bladder control, my arse. You're just miffed because I chased off the girls.* "No, there's no particular reason. You delivered a message to Dubric a short time ago. Who gave it to you?"

Beckwith contemplated him, and one eyebrow raised in an arc that mimicked the feather curving from his hat. "I do not see how that is any of your concern. Messages are private matters, after all, and our castellan's correspondence deserves discreet handling. I was not aware he'd made you his secretary."

"I am his page," Lars said, wondering if Dien would receive this level of asinine behavior. "And despite what you may think, I am authorized to throw people who refuse to answer my questions in gaol, especially those with snobbish attitudes who have information I require. So, *Mister* Beckwith, I suggest you tell me what I need to know or I may be forced to inform your wife of your incarceration along with your animated conversation with those two maids." He smiled brightly and added, "All in the interest of our continuing investigation, of course."

Beckwith's gray eyes grew cold but his sneer never faded. He stared at Lars for a long moment. "Of course," he said at last, licking his dry lips. "The message was brought to the castle by a man in gray robes. I did not see his face and he did not speak, but he rode a large horse. A warhorse, if I am not mistaken."

Lars resisted his urge to take notes. "Did you notice anything about his horse?"

"No," Beckwith said, staring at Lars. "Are you finished with me?"

"You may go."

Gesturing grandly with his hat, Beckwith bowed with a flourish until his immaculately combed blond head nearly reached the level of Lars's knees. He backed away, bowing again and again, while nearby people snickered.

Arrogant idiot, Lars thought, then he continued to Dubric's suite.

* * *

"'. . . whereupon Garian looked into the faire poise that was Liria's countenance. How may well he guide this girl into the nadir of the abyss, yet how may well he abscond her? He felt a love for her that had not breathed life for aeons long past. Her tresses were reminiscent of the rays of the setting sun, her skin silky as a tranquil mere. She moved with the elegance of breeze, and her tone was the soundest instrument.

"'"I cannot consent your leave, by foot or by heart," Garian spoke at long last . . .'"

Nella paused, yawning, and turned the page.

Risley squeezed her hand. "You should go to bed, love," he said. "Get some rest."

Her backside felt cold and her neck and eyes ached. "I'd rather stay here."

"Go to bed, love," he said, releasing her hand and standing. "I'll be all right."

Sighing, she stood and popped her back, pulling her hand from the slot along the bottom of his door. She had swept the length of floor before his cell clean of straw and muck, but the cold dampness, and the encroaching bugs, made her shudder. She could return to normalcy and dry the seat of her dress and wash her hands whenever she wanted. Risley had no such luxury.

"Is there anything you'd like me to bring tomorrow?" she asked, smiling at his partially obscured face.

"No, you're doing too much already." He grasped her hand and held it to his lips, kissing her fingers. "Goodnight, love. Sweet dreams."

"You, too," she replied. With one last glance, she tucked the book under her arm and walked to the door.

She pounded, three firm taps, and the guard pulled it open.

He looked at her grimy hand and damp dress. "Now, missy, ye sure yer all right? He didn't hurt ye none?"

"I'm fine, really," she said. "Mister? . . ." She waited, hoping he'd respond, but he didn't. He had never told her his name and it felt odd to not know it.

He frowned, stepping aside to motion her through

the door, then closed and locked it. "Dubric said to let ye do this, but it worries me greatly, missy. That it does. He's kilt purty girls like you. Nearly a dozen, I hear."

"I know." She sagged against the door and sniffled back a sob. "He won't hurt me, but if he does, it will be my own fault."

"Oh, missy, don't ye be cryin'," the gaol keeper said. He wrapped his arm over her shoulder and led her through the gaol. "I never meant to make ye cry."

"I'm all right," she said, offering him a hesitant smile. "Can I keep the book down here again tonight?"

"'Course ye can," he said. Taking it gently from her hands, he put it on a shelf in his room. "Be right here by the door when ye come tomorrow."

She nodded her thanks and wiped her nose. Her hands shaking and her head held high, she left the gaol and hurried up the stairs. She wondered if Risley would live through tomorrow, for the gallows in the north courtyard were nearly completed.

* * *

Pants in hand, Lars entered Dubric's suite. "I ran into Beckwith on the way here. The note came from a gray-robed man on a gray-covered warhorse."

Dien frowned at Lars. "We know who it's from, pup."

Lars's face fell and he handed Dubric the pants. "Oh. Well, who's it from?"

Dien checked the sword at his hip. "Never you mind. You and Otlee stay here."

"What? Why?"

His knobby knees respectfully covered again, Dubric said, "Because we said so." He grabbed his sharpest sword and strapped it to his hip. "If we do not come back, Otlee knows what to do." Looking at Dien instead of Lars's bewilderment, Dubric asked, "Are you ready to go?"

Dien clenched a fist, pushing on the fingers to pop his knuckles. "Yes, sir."

"Then let us get this madness over with."

"No," Lars said, gritting his teeth, his hands balling into fists. "Why can Otlee know but not me? Who the heck is it?"

"No one you need to worry about just yet, pup," Dien said, patting Lars on the shoulder. "Let us deal with it first."

Dubric felt a flash of sympathy for Lars's confusion and anger, but the lad had no business being where they intended to go, let alone seeing who they were going to see. "We will be back within a bell or so," he said, clasping on his cloak. "You will know soon enough." Without looking back, he left the suite and Dien followed behind him.

Flavin held two horses ready at the main doors and both men mounted, reigning the beasts around in the courtyard. South they flew, through the gate and down the merchants' road to the village, while gritty snow fell stinging from the sky.

They reigned in at the Dancing Sheep. The air near the alehouse was filled with golden light and golden music.

After tying his horse, Dien popped his knuckles again. "Don't you worry, sir. I'm sober. I won't kill the bastard."

Dubric clenched his teeth. "Business or personal first?"

"Personal." Dien shoved through the door while

countless eyes turned to look at him. "Marlee!" he shouted over the bard's music. "Pour me and the boss a cider tonight, willya?"

The bar matron laughed, tipping her pipe toward him. "Sarea keeping you on a short chain?"

"Yep, and I'm a damn lucky man," he said, lumbering through the crowded room with Dubric walking in his wake.

They spotted their quarry, a compact man in nondescript gray robes, standing in the back corner and smoking. The man nodded their way, then disappeared out the back door.

Dubric and Dien followed.

* * *

Bostra emptied his pipe and slipped into the shadows near the privy. "Thanks for coming so quickly. We're hoping this negotiation will be mutually—"

Pain shot through his mouth and he found himself on the wet, freezing ground, his pipe landing Goddess knew where. *What the peg?*

Dien took a single step forward, yanking off his sword belt. "Get your ass up. You've got about two blinks before my patience runs dry and I decide to kill you." He threw his sword to Dubric and balled both massive hands into fists.

Dubric calmly walked back into the Dancing Sheep, closing the door behind him.

Bostra shifted his jaw around. He tasted blood and it felt like several teeth had been knocked loose. "What are you—?"

"Get up."

Bostra clenched his aching teeth and stood slowly, watching Dien. "Do I get to know why you've decided to assault me?"

"Because you're a goat-raping bastard," Dien whispered.

Bostra tried to block the blow and deliver one of his own, but Dien was amazingly fast for a man of such bulk. Bostra barely stood upright before he found himself in the muck again.

"Damn it, Dien! What's this about?" he snapped as he spat out a mouthful of blood.

"Get up. Only two down. I still have four more to go."

Bostra wiped his mouth with the back of his hand. "The seven hells, I will." Watching Dien, he reached for his dagger.

"Suits me," Dien said, snatching Bostra from the ground as if he weighed no more than a mug of ale.

Goddess, he is fast, was all Bostra had time to think before the backhand sent him flying against the side of the privy. The dagger clattered away.

"Halfway there," Dien muttered, moving close. He kicked the dagger and it skittered into the dark. "I should have known you'd try to cheat. After what you did."

Bostra shoved himself to his hands and knees. His vision faded to nothing, flickered, faded, then came back again. He panted and turned his head, hoping it stayed attached to his neck. "What in the hells did I do?"

Dien cracked his knuckles. "It figures you've gone soft. Never met an archer who was worth his spit in a fight, but you being a castellan and all, I thought you'd put up more of a ruckus. Guess you disappoint me again."

"Are you going to tell me what I did or not?" Bostra asked, spitting blood again. He ran his tongue over his teeth and so far they all seemed to be attached. His eyes rolled to Dien. "We've been friends for what, fifteen, twenty summers? Can you at least tell me *why* you want to beat the living daylights out of me? For Goddess's sake, I came here to avert a war!"

Dien's eyes narrowed. "Get up. I've still got three to go."

Bostra took in a breath, let it out, and took in another. "Tell me what I did."

"Get. Up."

Bostra shook his head and the world swam before his eyes as fluid in his skull sloshed from one side to the other. "What did I do? I've never, ever, done anything to you, or your family—"

Dien stepped forward, snarling. "This has absolutely nothing to do with *my* family, but everything to do with yours." He paused, his hands clenching and unclenching. "I'm not about to kick a man who's down, so I suggest you stand before I drag you to your feet."

Bostra rolled and fell backward, onto his backside, his eyes never leaving Dien. Not that watching him would make much difference. He thought about his family. Jhandra hadn't left Haenpar for summers and Maura tended the sick and poor in southern Lagiern. He frowned. Only one supposed member of his family had been anywhere near Faldorrah. He had been living here for nearly six summers, in fact.

His eyes widened. *Six summers, six blows. Great. The blasted kid.* "What did the boy do? Is he causing trouble?"

Dien shook and dark anger loomed dangerous in his eyes. "Can't even say his name? Your own damned son and you can't even say his name."

"His name's Lars." Taking a breath, he added, "Despite what you think, he's not my son. I washed my hands of him when I—"

Dien growled and grabbed Bostra by the throat, lifting him from the ground.

He fought, struggling against the fingers crushing his larynx, trying desperately to pull himself free, but Dien snarled and threw him aside.

Bostra hit a wood fence and broke through, his body on one side, his legs hanging out the other, and his face in a drift of muddy snow and slush. His balance tottered and spun, making him dizzy. *Goddess*, he thought, spitting out the filthy wetness, *he's going to kill me!*

"That one didn't count." Dien grabbed him by the legs and dragged him out of the fence, over broken wood and muddy snow. "You asked for it all on your own."

"Wait! Wait! I can explain," Bostra coughed out, holding his hands up in warding.

"Explain what?" Dien snarled, flinging Bostra against the alehouse. "All these summers I thought you were a decent man, but then I learn you've tossed aside your own flesh and blood like a wad of used paper." Dien moved forward, balling his fists again. "Get up."

Bostra gasped for breath through his aching head and half-crushed throat, and he blinked in a desperate attempt to clear his vision. "He's not my blood," he muttered. "He's just some kid Jhandra took in."

"So now you're a liar, too. I remember him as a baby!"

Bostra staggered to his feet, his hands held in front of him. He could see, but the world spun and wavered. Dien, however, remained clear and sharp. "Do you want to know what happened, or do you just want to kill me?" He pulled one hand back to wipe at his bleeding mouth, but kept his face turned toward Dien.

"Talk. But make it quick."

Bostra nodded again and his world went black. He heard a bell ringing in his ears and wondered if it was his death knell. He took a breath or two and leaned against the wall before his legs gave out from under him. "After Maura was born, we tried to have another, but it never happened. Jhandra never quickened." He shook his head again, remembering. "I think Maura was three summers, maybe, when Jhandra's monthlies stopped altogether. The physicians said she'd gone barren. She was only twenty-one summers old. She never recovered from the news. A summer or so later she got sick, nearly died, and the surgeon in Waterford . . . he . . ."

Bostra heard Dien mumble something, but he pressed on. "They took out her womb and no one knew. No one but me. Heather kept getting pregnant and each one tore at Jhandra. Heather lost five babies between Risley and Torrent, did you know that? Every one, every loss, made Jhandra worse, but I worried that having a real live baby that close would be worse still. She doted on the staff's newborn children, visited every new mother in town, held every infant she could get her hands on. It drove the other women crazy and we lost more staff those long summers than you can imagine. Babies were all she thought about, all she dreamt about. Nothing else mattered. Not her daughter, not her life, not me. Just babies."

He took a breath and looked toward Dien. The world had stopped its lurching and spinning, but the bells in his head remained. "One spring, I suggested we come here and visit her family. Stay till fall. I thought maybe a change of scenery would help. Do you remember? We had dinner with you and Sarea, back when you still lived in the village."

"Yeah, I remember. Kia was just toddling around and Jhandra played and played with her, carrying her everywhere. It about drove Sarea batty," Dien said softly. "But you left a few days later without saying good-bye. Sarea *still* remembers that."

"Yes. We'd been here no more than a couple of phases or so, and Jhandra comes back from visiting Friar Bonne with a baby. A damn baby! Someone had left him in the temple doorway, an orphan, and she begged me to let her keep him."

"Lars," Dien whispered as if his heart would break.

"Yes. I was hesitant at first. I mean, we had no idea whose child he was. No idea at all. Would they want him back? What if there was something wrong with him? And I also worried over what we would do with a baby. Maura was maybe ten summers, a long way from babyhood, and we were getting too old and set in our ways for the demands of a baby. But Jhandra cooed and awed over him, and she seemed so happy. I thought maybe if she had a baby of her own again I could have my wife back. I was wrong."

Dien took a single step back. Bostra said, "We returned to Haenpar immediately and Jhandra told everyone the child was hers. Wasn't it a *wonderful* surprise? Isn't he a beautiful baby? She became the focus of attention, and I couldn't begrudge her that after she had pined for so long. I think Kyl and Heather suspected the truth, but they've never said a word about it to me. I just went along with her story, not denying but not confirming, even though it was obviously a lie. She had her baby and I hoped our life would settle again.

"I tried to be a father to him. Changed his diddy, bathed him, read him stories. He was a good baby, hardly ever cried, and I don't remember him ever getting sick. I started to like the idea of having a son, but the day he took his first steps, all that changed."

"Go on."

"Jhandra wouldn't let him walk. She had to do everything for him, to keep him a baby. She hand-fed him, doted on him, dressed him like a doll. I told her to let him be. Let him run and play and get dirty. Let him eat the damned dirt if he wanted. Let him grow up, for Goddess's sake. I fought with her over the boy constantly, but she wouldn't listen. He was her baby, after all."

Bostra sighed. "He was always a pleasant child, intelligent, polite, and I know Kyl and Heather did what they could, but I spent so much time fighting with Jhandra over how to raise him, I grew to . . ." he paused, trying to find the best word, the one that wouldn't get him killed. "I grew to resent the boy. He wasn't mine. I didn't want him. And his presence sent my wife further into madness. Every time I looked at him I saw her madness. I still do." He paused and said, "I finally had enough of his eager-to-please whimperings and inability to stand up for himself. He was a boy, not a doll or a plaything. Dubric agreed to accept my wife's sheltered, pampered toy as a page, so I sent him here without telling Jhandra what I'd planned. She almost divorced me for taking her baby away and still hardly speaks to me. But he's better off here, where he can think for himself. Where he's not a mama's boy. Where he can grow up."

"Does Dubric know?"

"No one knows. It would kill Jhandra to be caught in the lie, and I saw no other way to save them. I did the best I could."

Dien moved a step closer again. "But you turned your back on him! You're his father."

"No, I'm not. I don't know who his father is, but it's not me."

A moment later, Bostra landed in the mud again, his vision spinning, his mouth filling with blood.

"There's more to being a father than begetting! He might not be of your blood, but you accepted him as your son. Gave him your name and let him think he was yours. You at least owe him the decency of a kind word or two, and if you were half the man I always thought you were, you owe him a lot more than simple politeness. He's a damn good lad and he deserves better. You just think about that."

Dien turned and stomped into the alehouse, slamming the door behind him.

Bostra shook his head, struggling to stand, but warm hands were there to help him. "Take it slow," Dubric said. "You will survive."

Bostra wiped blood from his mouth. "Why in the seven hells did you let him do that? For Goddess's sake, he could have killed me and you'd have gone to war! Don't you care about Faldorrah?"

"Yes," Dubric said, handing Bostra a clean kerchief. "Of course I do. But sometimes other matters take precedence. You should count yourself lucky. We had decided this particular matter was better discussed by Dien than I."

Dien came through the door, a pair of mugs in his hands. "Here," he said, shoving one at Bostra. "It will lessen the pain so you can talk."

Bostra looked between the two Faldorrahn men. "I think I'd rather you'd talked to me about Lars," he said to Dubric. He took a sip of the cider, winced, spat, then took another.

"Nope," Dien said. "Dubric just wanted to kill you, but I thought my solution might prove more practical, considering our current situation. *And* not leave the lad fatherless."

Watching the two men, Bostra sipped the cider. "I don't like either option." He looked Dien in the eye. "Are we finished?"

Dien sighed, nodding. "You just remember what I told you."

Dubric watched the exchange with glittering eyes but said nothing. Bostra sipped his cider and tried to gauge the old man's demeanor. He shivered at the cold fingers dancing up his spine; something behind Dubric's eyes seemed dead, yet horribly aware.

At last Dubric spoke. "Risley killed eleven people, ten of them young women, and injured three others. One was your son."

"He's damn lucky to be alive," Dien muttered.

"For that," Dubric continued, "I will see him hanged. That is the rule of law you and I are both bound by. Kyl knows this."

Bostra picked a hunk of mud from his robe and flung it into the night. "Lord Kylton Romlin has received word of these absurd accusations against his son and instructed me to offer an . . . arrangement."

"How?" Dubric asked. "Before we discuss transfer requirements, I want to know who told you. A spy in my castle will not improve Lord Risley's chances for survival. War or no war."

"Our priest received a message from your Friar Bonne. Apparently the girl Risley is smitten with— Nella, I believe her name is—asked Bonne to help her aid Risley. Bonne sent the notification in her stead." He took another sip and met Dubric's gaze. "We have no spies in Faldorrah. You have my word."

"What is your offer?" The dead awareness in Dubric's eyes had gone, leaving weariness behind.

Bostra reached inside his robe, retrieved a rumpled

envelope, and presented it to Dubric. "Our most generous offer is twofold."

Dubric opened the envelope and cursed. "A Royal Decree demanding his release."

"Peg!" Dien snarled, slamming his fist against the wall.

Bostra felt the blow shudder the planks and he swallowed, thankful to be alive. "Yes, King Romlin was most upset at his grandson's arrest. We received the decree this very morning."

Dien frowned. "All the way from Waterford? It's a two-phase ride. We tossed Risley's ass in the gaol yesterday."

Bostra shrugged. "We have our ways."

"Powerful frigging magic is what you have," Dien grumbled. "That's no parlor trick. Isn't sorcery supposed to be illegal?"

"The King desires to remain in contact with his family and you expect *me* to tell him it's illegal?"

Dien moved forward, but Dubric's hand on his arm brought the big man to a halt. "What is the second portion of your 'generous offer'?" Dubric asked.

"Survival. We know your army winters away from the castle. Ours doesn't. Lord Romlin himself commands a contingent of more than one thousand men and they're riding for your borders as we speak. If I don't return with Risley, alive, in two days, they'll seize Faldorrah.

"It's your choice, my friends. You can either hand Risley over to us, or we can take him by force."

"Bastard son of a pig-riding whore!" Dien snapped, punching the wall. "What the peg do you expect us to do?"

Dubric folded the Royal Decree and placed it in his notebook. "We have two days?"

Bostra relaxed his official posture and rubbed his aching jaw. "Not exactly. Kyl realizes you may need time to prepare, but he prefers Risley to leave under cover of darkness."

"Tomorrow night, then." Dubric pocketed his notebook again.

Bostra finished his cider. "That's what he hopes, yes. Unofficially, he's willing to give you another day or so, if need be, but don't stretch this out. He doesn't have much maneuvering room."

Bostra pursed his lips and lowered his voice. "Tunkek blames this entire situation on Lord Brushgar; you know how the two despise each other. He's ready to wipe Faldorrah clean, and he doesn't care if Risley is guilty or innocent or anywhere in-between. But I want you to know that as far as Kyl and I are concerned, it's just a convenient excuse to reopen old wounds. We both had a piss of a time convincing Tunkek that we could remove Risley peacefully. We wanted to open a dialogue, find a compromise, perhaps start our own investigation, but Tunkek wouldn't hear of it, insisting that we threaten war."

He paused, looking into his empty mug. "Our hands are tied, too. Considering the political implications, we truly feel releasing Risley to us is the best option, for everyone involved."

Dubric swore under his breath. "He slaughtered ten women! How can you take that back to Haenpar with you? Your people will be in danger. Your wives, your daughters."

"He'll be guarded and under house arrest, locked in his rooms until the trial. You have my word, and Kyl's."

Dubric sagged against the wall. "He is utterly, unavoidably guilty. What is Tunkek going to do when

Risley is brought before Council? Insist they find him innocent or face war, as well?"

"I don't know. At this point I'm just trying to keep the northern territories from being ravaged." Bostra straightened his back, shuddering as he spoke. "If found guilty, Risley's fate has already been decided. It will take perhaps a fortnight for the sages to arrive from Waterford."

"Then what?" Dien asked, paling.

Dubric winced as if an old pain had suddenly flared, and rubbed his eyes. "Then three blessed clerics of Malanna's Holy Church will use their filthy white magic to wipe his mind clean. It is a vicious technique they perfected during the war to control captured Shadow Followers."

"You're pulling my leg!"

"No," Bostra said. "Lord and Lady Romlin decided they'd rather have their son be a living idiot than a dead monster, regardless of political cost."

"If it does not kill him outright," Dubric muttered, pacing. "Surely a quick hanging is kinder than using religious mania to make the boy an imbecile."

"Peg yes!" Dien said. "Has the whole damn family lost their sense?"

"Sometimes I wonder," Bostra said. "How guilty is he, really? Do we have any hope of acquittal?"

"None," Dubric said, revealing the evidence against Risley. "He had topped our suspect list for days, then we found a piece of his razor inside a victim and his hair inside a package he had sent us. A gloating, disgusting bundle of kidneys, hair, and other trophies. We have evidence of exposure to Wraith Rot, as well. An honest Council will have no choice but to hang him."

"That's what we feared. We knew you'd never accuse him unless you were certain," Bostra said. "But you're confident it's Risley's hair and razor?"

"Absolutely. I have a Far-Sight glass. There is no doubt."

Bostra raised an eyebrow. "Not only a sight glass, but a Far-Sight? You tricky bastard! And you accuse us of having illegal magic."

"I said no such thing," Dubric muttered, shrugging toward Dien. "He spoke his own opinion, not mine."

While Dien grinned at him, Bostra said, "If you have any other ideas, I'm willing to hear them. But King Tunkek won't settle for anything less than release."

"Nor will Nigel," Dubric said. "Tell Lord Romlin we agree to his terms, and we will release Risley into your care tomorrow night. Once he is in Haenpar he is no longer my concern, but if he harms one more Faldorrahn, I will execute *you* for his crime."

Bostra's throat clenched, then relaxed again. *What trouble can Risley get into during a day's ride?* "Then we have reached an agreement," he said, offering his hand.

They clasped palms and nodded. Dien turned, opening the door. "Marlee! Gimme three more ciders and a basket of fried boar skins," he hollered over the din. All three went inside.

CHAPTER

19

✝

Nella woke before dawn, feeling dread gnawing at her soul and remembering vague, vaporous dreams of blood and darkness. Numbly pushing her concerns aside, she washed, dressed, and hurried to the great hall to fetch breakfast.

Yesterday a kitchen lackey had brought a cold pan of plain porridge and greasy bacon for Risley's morning meal, and an equally chilly pan of congealed mashed turnips and two-day-old lamb gravy arrived in the evening. Her simple supper offering of slightly bruised fruit, hard bread, and a hunk of cheese looked, and smelled, far more appetizing.

Only the milkmaids and a few morning kitchen workers had begun breakfast, and she walked among them, placing her selections in her apron. A muffin for each of them—one pumpkin and one oatmeal, to give Risley a choice—a handful of prunes, and three nicely browned sausages she carefully wrapped in a napkin. The serving wench gave her a disgusted glare, but Nella paid her little notice. She had a whole bell before work, and she intended to spend all of it with Risley.

Steeling herself for the squalor and stench, she hurried down the east-tower stairs and knocked on the gaol door.

The gaol keeper opened it. "Thought it would be ye, missy," he said, reaching out to touch her shoulder, "but I canna let ye through t'day."

"What? Why?" she asked, feeling tears stinging her eyes. "Have I done something wrong?"

"Oh no, tis not ye!" he said. He seemed to search for the right words, then simply said, "M'lord Dubric came fer him last night. He's gone, missy. I'm so sorry fer ye."

"No!" she said, backing away, her hands flying to cover her mouth. Muffins and prunes and sausages fell at her feet, rolling into the shadows. "He can't be dead! He can't!"

"I'm sorry, missy, truly I am, but tis the way of things here. Those sent to the dark hall don't stay there long, er else they stay there ferever. Either way, it's their last bed. I tried to tell ye.

"Ol' Aghy's seen it all, and I'm sorry, missy, but ye wouldn't listen. And ol' Dubric, he don't listen, neither. Not to me, not to no one but hisself. I asked him to fetch ye, to give ye a chance to say g'bye, but he refused. Can ye forgive me fer my failure?"

She offered a sad smile, touching his arm. "Of course I can, Aghy. Thank you for trying."

Aghy blushed, wiped his nose with his sleeve, and said, "Ye best get goin', missy. This ain't no place fer a purty lady like yerself. Go on now. I gots work to do."

He closed the door and she heard the key turn in the lock. Struggling not to cry, she climbed the stairs, the beat of her heart echoing in the hollowness behind her ribs.

She found herself in the temple, kneeling before the Brushgar family tapestry. She said good-bye to Risley, begging the Goddess to accept him. Friar Bonne stood behind her, his prayer for forgiveness rolling gently over her. When she finished her plea, he held her and let her cry until numb emptiness filled her heart.

Then, swallowing her sorrow, she went to work.

Dari remained unusually quiet, and even Stef gave her a wide berth as they labored through their morning. Time disappeared under a dim haze of loss, until Dari touched her arm.

"Nella?" she said, trying to smile. "Someone wants you."

Bleak nothingness engulfed her in its cold and empty embrace. "Who?"

"I dunno. Some man. Not sure who he is."

Probably Aghy returning Risley's book, Nella thought, taking a breath. She walked to the hall and saw a man in a gray cloak, his face covered by shadows. "You wanted to see me?" she asked, not really caring if he replied or remained silent.

He bowed slightly, offering her a folded note.

It had a seal as blue and bright as the evening sky, and she lifted it from his palm with a shaking hand. He moved, shifting his weight and granting her a glimpse of stylish clothes in a noble cut hiding beneath the robe. "You will not be harmed," he whispered. "I swear on my life to protect you."

Nervously, she broke the seal.

My love,
I must allay your fears. I am not dead, but rescued by your fortitude and by your faith. You have saved my life, and all debts between us are paid, for now and for all time. I leave for Haenpar tonight, love, and I'd like you to join me on our next journey together. I hope you will, and I pray you still love me.
The man before you is my father's castellan,

Bostra Hargrove, and he knows where Dubric has hidden me.

Please come. I love you.
Risley

Her lip trembling, she looked at the robed man standing before her. "You—"

"Do not speak of it, milady," Bostra whispered. "The stones have ears. Will you follow me?"

She folded the note, her hands shaking and rattling the fine paper. "Yes."

He turned and walked away, and she followed him.

They crossed the castle along the second floor, to the west wing, and past the alcove where she and Risley had shared a pie. Bostra knocked on the tower door and Otlee opened it, closing and locking it behind them.

"The tower clear?" Bostra asked, opening his robe. The inside was lined with fine butter-colored silk.

"Yessir. Top to bottom. All doors are locked and secure."

The robe fell away to reveal a tidy, compact man of middle age with a neatly trimmed beard covering a bruised chin. An eye patch and its strap circled his head, but the patch had been flipped up, exposing a blackened eye. "Put this on," he said, turning his robe inside out. "You're going to disappear."

"'Disappear'? I can't just 'disappear.'"

He smiled, showing fine white teeth, and meticulously smoothed his yellow jerkin and black silk pants. "It's a figure of speech. You are now officially in hiding, milady."

"I'm not a lady," she said, drawing the robe around her and raising the hood. "Where's Risley?"

"You have no more patience than he." Bostra laughed gently and ran up the stairs. Nella followed.

"We are officials from Casclia," he said. "I need you to walk beside me and lean close as if we are conferring over an intricate detail of extreme importance."

He reached into a fine leather knapsack beside the door and pulled out a black silk chasuble and a small wooden hand club. He adjusted the chasuble over her shoulders and said, "I want you to hit your leg with this club, a nervous habit of sorts, while you walk. Most people will look at the movement instead of possibly recognizing you."

She gripped the club and tapped her leg in an erratic staccato like her father testing cooling bricks. "Like this?"

"Perfect." He took a step back, adjusted her hood and nodded. "That'll do nicely." He reached into the knapsack again, retrieving a loosely flowing hat with long, bejeweled tails of buttery satin. Placing it upon his head at a jaunty angle, he slung the pack over his shoulder. "Ready for your performance?"

She smiled. "Your eye patch?"

"Oh!" he laughed, flipping it down. "Forgot the damned thing." He gave her an encouraging smile and called out, "Go, Otlee."

Then he opened the door.

* * *

They strode down the hall, quietly discussing a border dispute that hinged upon the definition of a river's location. Rambling incessantly about the rocks on an imagined northern shore, Nella did not glance at Risley's door as they passed it, and no one in the hall seemed to pay them undue notice.

Floor maids curtsied, scurrying out of their way, and a pair of ladies gave Bostra appraising looks, but they walked through the hallway without pause. The herald hurried up the main stairs with a note in hand and his cloak flowing behind him. Gracing them with a friendly nod, he hastened off the way they had come.

Still discussing the same imaginary river, they turned down the short northern hallway that housed titled officials. Without slowing, they walked past Dubric's door.

An accountant shuffled toward them, wringing his hands and muttering, then he wandered away, turning the corner and leaving their sight.

Bostra grasped her arm and turned, guiding her back to Dubric's door. A blink later they slipped inside. She had indeed disappeared.

* * *

Nella had never been in Dubric's suite before, and she had not expected it to be dark, or small. Unlike the bright, rambling rooms of Risley's suite, Dubric appeared to have only two rooms plus a privy chamber, and a lone window facing north. Dim, wine-colored light illuminated the drawn curtains, leaving the room in hazy shadow. A tall oval mirror glowed in the far corner, shining on the old man as he stood beside a table.

Her companion led her to Dubric. "Remain silent," he said in her ear, "before your opportunity for choice is lost."

Dubric motioned her toward him, and said, "You of all people are an innocent in this, Miss Nella, and I cannot allow you to go uninformed into hell."

He smiled at her, kindly yet concerned. "Risley will

be taken to Haenpar tonight whether you go with him or not. He has no choice in the matter. But I cannot in good conscience send you to your possible death without showing you what he has done."

Acrid bile tainted her mouth but she swallowed it away. She noticed he clenched a filthy dress in his hands.

"Show me," he whispered, and the mirror wavered, replacing his reflection with a dead girl in an ale room, lying in a pool of blood. He dropped the dress and picked up another garment. "Show me," he said again. This time the image reflected a milkmaid, facedown in the mud with her back gone.

She tried to turn away, but Bostra held her still, forcing her to see. A scullery maid in the slush with her intestines pulled over her hips. A laundress, eviscerated and nearly beheaded. A horror of meat and barely human extremities scattered in the mud, a dyer bubbling in a vat, another gutted and half-charred. A girl she had never seen, with her back opened and her guts trailing behind her. Plien . . . her insides steaming in the snow, her thighs filleted and her throat slashed.

"Stop it!" Nella cried, scrunching her eyes closed.

Dubric turned, his eyes glittering and determined. "He did these things, Miss Nella. Look at them! Each worse than the one before. He enjoyed it."

"Risley wouldn't do those things! Not him."

"He slaughtered those girls, and if you leave with him he will do the same to you."

The image of Plien remained in the mirror, and Nella turned her head away. "He will not harm me. He loves me."

Dubric dropped the cloth in his hands and Plien's horrid corpse faded away. "I know you love him, Miss Nella, but is his passion for you a symptom of his madness? Does a killer like that understand love? I instructed Aghy to let you do as you wished when you visited Risley in gaol, for I knew he could not truly harm you there. But soon, very soon, he will be able to do as he pleases again. At least for a few days."

Her heart hammered in her throat. "What happens in a few days?"

Bostra released her arms. "After he is found guilty of murder, three sages from Waterford will cleanse Risley's mind."

"Then he'll be fine again? He'll—"

"No, Miss Nella," Dubric said, rubbing his eyes as if they pained him. "Then he will be an infant, less than an infant, in the body of a man."

She took a step back, rabidly shaking her head, and stepped on Bostra's foot. "So you're telling me that if I agree to go with him, at worst he will kill me, and at best his mind will be taken away?" She took one burning breath and another and another as she tried to understand the situation before her.

"Why, then," she said at last, looking between them, "did you make me disappear?"

"Because no one can know Risley lives," Bostra said, "nor that I am here."

"Our people will kill him outright if they knew," Dubric said. "Justice is one thing, murderous mobs are a different matter entirely. I hope you choose to remain here, Miss Nella, but I have watched you for moons and I know how you feel about him. If you remain, we will spirit you through the east tower and return you to your life. But if you go, Miss Nella, if you go, you must be aware of what awaits." He paused and watched her with pity shadowing his face.

She thought of Risley, his face, his touch, his gentle, hungry kiss, and tears welled in her eyes. "Does Risley know?"

"No," Bostra said, "and you must not tell him. He must believe the sages will cure his insanity or he will resist. If he resists, he will certainly die."

"There has been enough death," Dubric said.

Her knees shaking she said, "No matter the danger, I can't leave him. Maybe he will kill me. I think I'd prefer that over watching . . ." she shuddered and her breath fell away, leaving her empty and trembling. "But whatever the future brings, I can't leave him. I won't hurt him like that. I love him too much."

Both men nodded. "That is your choice, milady," Bostra said, leading her away from the mirror. They stood before a closed door while Nella composed herself. "It isn't locked," he said, gently pulling the chasuble from her shoulders. "You seem a fine woman and I am truly sorry we didn't meet under better circumstances."

"Me, too," she said, then she opened the door.

Sunlight sparkled through lace curtains, washing the sitting room with jewels of light. Risley lay asleep on a bed that seemed out of place among the stuffed chairs, bookshelves, and a lifetime of collected trinkets.

Dien stood just inside the room and he smiled encouragingly as Bostra closed the door.

Risley looked so peaceful, snoring softly and sprawled on his belly, that her hesitation melted away. He wasn't a monster; he was Risley, her Risley, and she could never leave him.

She knelt beside the bed and brushed tousled hair from his brow before kissing his cheek. "I'm here," she whispered. "And I love you."

He whispered her name and snuggled into the pillows, moving closer to her, and relaxed beneath her touch. Still stroking his brow she asked softly, "Why is he so tired?"

Dien said, "We pulled him from the gaol around two bell this morning and he hadn't been sleeping. I doubt he'd slept at all."

She whispered his name and kissed his cheek.

Dien shifted his weight and yawned. "Dawn had come by the time we'd agreed on a plan and put it into motion. He's been sleeping ever since."

"Then I won't wake him," she said. Settling into a nearby chair, she watched Risley sleep and wondered if they had any remaining hope.

* * *

Dubric's ghosts examined the bits of ruined clothing on the floor, giggling and nudging one another. Elli picked up a torn and bloody uniform. Grinning, she smacked Rianne with it, knocking her severed arm through the wall beside Bostra.

Startled, Bostra looked up from his tired daze and squinted at Dubric. "Did I just feel a breeze?"

"No," Dubric said, thankful his ghosts' antics were obscured in the dim light. He gathered up a handful of papers, grimacing at Rianne's head rolling across his worktable. "I have paperwork to complete. Would you object to my leaving for a bit?"

"Of course not," Bostra said. "The sooner the paperwork is finished, the sooner we can leave."

Grumbling under his breath, Dubric trudged to his office while his ghosts tormented him.

He found Otlee filing papers the ghosts had strewn about the night before. "I unlocked all the doors like you said, sir. Only one person had asked why the tower was locked and I told them I had to run top to bottom three times as part of an assignment." He beamed. "He believed me, sir."

"That is fine," Dubric replied. "Nice job."

Elli fluffed Otlee's hair and the boy froze, growing instantly pale.

Dubric changed the route to his desk, blocking Elli's cool attentions. "I have been remiss in my duties as a teacher. These past days I have barely given you a moment to read. Here," he reached into his pocket and retrieved his library token, "tell Clintte you have full access in my name. Any book you would like. Even from the restricted section. But I expect a ten-page written report on the material."

"Thank you, sir!" Otlee said. He bobbed a quick bow and left, squealing slightly as Fytte patted his behind.

Once the outer door closed, Dubric snarled, "Do what you must to me, but leave the boy alone."

The ghosts giggled and began pulling books from the shelves.

"Stop it," Dubric hissed, slamming the inner office door, but the ghosts did not seem to hear, or care.

Elli shoved every single thing off his desk. Ennea tossed papers into the air. Plien pulled books from the shelves and dropped them on the floor. Celese took Rianne's head and swung it by the hair at other ghosts, while Rianne bumbled around blindly. Claudette repeatedly tried to trip poor Rianne. Cheyna and the peddler's daughter—her name had been Lirril—huddled together in a corner and had caused no trouble. Nansy, the newest arrival, silently screamed before his desk and gushed blood all over herself. Still barely moving, she seemed utterly oblivious to the chaos around her. Every now and then a piece of her viscera would fall out and splatter on his floor. Grinning, Fytte snatched up the dripping slop and flung it at the walls.

Ten damned ghosts. He wished they would wander away like Olibe Meiks had done. "Why will you not leave me alone?" he asked them. "Why?"

His door opened and Lars said, "Perhaps because they have nowhere to go."

Dubric sighed and nine of his ten ghosts turned to look at Lars. "I thought I sent you to get some rest."

"I can sleep later," he said. "I've noticed since Risley's arrest you have barely spoken with us. In fact, you continually send Otlee and I away."

"Perhaps I do not need your assistance."

"Perhaps these ghosts you see are causing trouble," Lars replied. "Otlee seemed spooked in the hall outside, and I've noticed the air around you is unusually cold. Dien mentioned smelling perfume the other day. Sometimes I smell blood."

Fytte grinned and walked right through Lars.

"What the! . . ." He turned around and his eyes grew wide. "What was that?"

Dubric rubbed his eyes. Nansy faded away, but the rest remained. "That, my dear boy, was Fytte. She seems to be the ringleader. Her and Elli."

Lars nodded slowly and his eyes scanned the whole room. He nudged a book with his toe. "Can I assume they've been making all these messes lately?"

"You can."

"Can I also assume they were the cause of your collapse yesterday?"

"You can."

He looked relieved and took a breath. "All right. May I have your permission to try something?"

"Try whatever you like. They certainly do not listen to me. Why should they listen to you?"

"Because I believe," Lars said. He reached inside his pocket and pulled out a gleaming circlet of silver; a sphere within a sphere. He held it in his palm as if presenting it to the room.

Every ghost retreated from him.

Dubric turned his head away from the circle. "Why did you bring that whore-goddess's bauble here?"

"To see if it would help. What are they doing now?"

"Who cares? Get that thing out of here."

Lars carefully set it on Dubric's desk. "Sorry, sir. If they've attacked you once, they may attack you again, and Otlee and I are tired of cleaning up their messes."

"Get that damned thing out of my office."

"I can't do that, sir. They're afraid of it, aren't they?"

"And what if they are? That thing is no better."

"You may not like to look at Malanna's moon, but it can't harm you. Friar Bonne said—"

"I do not give a rat's ass what frivolity Bonne has put in your head."

"You should. He said your curse has a name. I can't remember what it was called, but he said—"

"You told Bonne about my damned ghosts?"

"No, sir. Not your ghosts. Not specifically. I only told him that while researching the murders I had heard of a person cursed with ghosts and was curious. He said that he, too, had heard of such a thing and the church recommended using Malanna's symbols to keep them at bay." Lars paused and looked at Dubric. "He also said the only way to remove the curse was to return to the church. Perhaps you should consid—"

Dubric slammed his fist on the desk. "Do you think I do not know that? After all these damned summers, all these damned ghosts, do you really believe I have not known about apologizing to that whore-goddess? The bitch can curse me all she wants. She can harm me no more than she already has." He stood and snarled, leaning over his desk. "She gave me the gift of Oriana. Marked us as one soul. I knew the moment I saw her I would love her for the rest of my life and I even thanked the Goddess for my good fortune."

He drew a rattling breath and said, "We had less than six moons together before she was taken away. That damn Goddess did nothing to protect her even though Oriana was of her order. She let my wife, my *pregnant wife,* die in a fire set by Shadow Followers, all because we were involved in that damn war.

"I tried to save her. Did you know that? Siddael and Albin tried to stop me from going in after her, but I could hear her scream in my soul. My Goddess-damned soul! She was still alive, screaming her prayers in the horrid gibberish that haunts my dreams on the rare nights I sleep. She was burning, but she was still alive! Do you have any idea how horrible that was? To see my love burned alive? I grabbed her but her flesh came off in my hands. Her arm, her poor precious arm, ripped off like the leg of a roast chicken, and still the damned Goddess would not let her die!"

"Sir, I knew you lost your wife, but I never—"

"Shut the peg up. You don't know shit. In the end, I killed her. I took my knife and I slit her charred throat. I stopped her suffering. All of it for that bitch-goddess of yours. I wanted the fire to kill me, too, but it didn't. It took me six moons to get on my feet again, one for every moon I spent with Oriana. Six moons in a hospital bed gives you plenty of time to think. Plenty of time to decide."

He reached out and picked up the silver circle, crushing it in his fist as if it were nothing more than a slip of paper. "If you think I will accept Malanna's charity now, you are sadly mistaken." He dropped the wad of metal on the desk and snarled, "She can burn in the seven hells for all I care."

He stomped around the desk. "If seeing ghosts is the price I have to pay for showing my wife mercy, then that is exactly what I shall do. I may not like to look upon them, I may hate them, but I despise that bitch—far more than I hate my ghosts."

"Yes, sir," Lars said.

His hands shaking, Dubric stomped from his office and climbed the stairs back to his room, with the damned ghosts dragging along behind him. *They are mine forever,* he thought, trudging up the stairs and shoving beyond the duty trying to drag him down. "Plague me as you will," he said, "I will not beg for mercy or release." He kicked the third-floor door open and balled his hands as he approached the north hall.

Eleven people dead, a plague upon my land, my people, and my soul. Risley escapes justice only to pay the price of his mind. But that will not suit your damned plots and schemes, will it? Lost in his anger, he ignored the worried glances from the staff as he stomped past. *Nella throws away her life and heart, but you do not care. Lars desperately needs his father, yet neither will seek the other. You leave destruction in your wake, and all the souls you touch, all that sing your praises, the faithful and the kind, receive nothing but pain and torment in return. For this I am supposed to beg your forgiveness? Peg you, bitch! I have seen your forgiveness, felt your pegging mercy. Get out of my life and get out of my head.*

He shoved the door to his suite open, startling Bostra into drawing a sword.

"Go!" he said, stomping through. "Just go and leave me to my demons."

Bostra sheathed his sword. "Goddess, Dubric, you look like you've seen a ghost."

"Get. Out."

Bostra blinked and nodded, glancing over his shoulder as he grabbed the floppy hat. "Risley's still asleep. I checked on them moments ago."

Dubric waved him away, then fell into a chair.

* * *

An eternity later, Dubric looked up, seeing the familiar glimmer of his reflection in the mirror. "Oh, damn," he sighed, standing. He staggered to his dresser, finding Oriana's dagger by its feel, and fell into his chair again. Grimacing, he pulled the dagger from the sheath.

He stared at the silver blade with tears rolling down his cheeks. After all these summers, her loss still felt as if someone had just ripped out a piece of him, laid the wound open, and salted it. The pain would never end, not as long as he lived, all because the wretched Goddess had marked them as one.

Sometimes that hurt far more than the ghosts ever could.

"Show me," he said, and the mirror began to glow.

He wiped the tears from his eyes and smiled at his love. Their union had been both a blessing and a curse. He had known a joy so few could ever understand. A sense of completeness in her presence, the headiness of utter bliss every time he had touched her. But the ache of her loss had never faded, and it remained as fresh in his heart as if she had died moments ago. That, too, was both a blessing and a curse.

She stood in the midst of an endless sea, with water and moonlight glimmering all around her. His despised but still remembered religious teachings insisted she waited for him in the Waters of Life. The Waters of the damned Goddess. Oriana awaited him in heaven, and for that he was truly thankful. She had suffered so before she died, and she suffered no more. The suffering was his alone and rightly so.

More than the guilt of her death and the eternal plague of ghosts tugged at his heart. He said to his sweet Oriana, "I should not have been so rough on Lars. He only tried to help."

She placed a palm against the surface of the glass; in the reflection her other hand seemed to rest on his shoulder. He held his hand against hers and said, "I should apologize."

She nodded. His heart ached to truly talk with her, but lip-reading had proven impossible and heart-wrenching in its frustration. They had stopped trying decades before.

He sighed and traced her fingers with his own. He had always wanted to ask a certain question of her, but had never tried. He was old now, old and tired. Surely his life had neared its end.

He looked deep into his love's eyes, still so sparkling and blue, and asked, his voice cracking, "Will I join you soon? I have waited for so long."

Her lower lip quivered and she seemed to waver for a moment, as if she had trouble standing beside him. Her bright eyes filled with tears and this time he had no trouble understanding her. No trouble at all.

"No, my love," she said. "Not for a long, long time. Your purpose has not yet come."

Dubric could almost feel her consoling touch on his burn-scarred skin and he wished he could hold her just one more time. He covered his face with his hands and wept.

CHAPTER

20

†

Dien shifted his weight. Nella had curled in a chair with a book while Risley slept, and as far as Dien was concerned, the bastard could sleep the whole afternoon away.

He'd always heard no one slept sounder than a guilty man who'd been captured, but Risley's sleep had been far from sound. He had tossed and turned, wrestling with whatever horrors plagued his mind, until the girl had arrived, staggering through the door as if facing the gallows.

She had kissed Risley's cheek, then he slept like an innocent babe, as if he had not a worry in the world. Time crawled by, punctuated by cozy snores and the soft turning of a page.

On the other side of the door, Dubric had gone, then come back again, sending Bostra away, if Dien had heard correctly. He wondered what bug had crawled up Dubric's ass today. He certainly sounded pissy enough for Nella to take notice.

Perhaps a half-bell later Risley stirred and Nella set her book aside, rushing to him. Despite Dien's preference to keep her as far from the bastard as possible, Dubric had insisted she merely be protected from definite harm, not chaperoned. And, with Risley officially under Haenparan protection, Dubric had instructed his staff to remain cordial, yet firm. Dien stoically observed their happy embrace, their longing looks and one quick kiss before he cleared his throat. "Keep it clean," he said.

Laughing, they moved from the bed to a divan and sat, curled together, their heads close and their hands entwined. Their conversation remained whisper-quiet, with occasional giggles, until Dien wondered if he would hurl his breakfast. *Damn, were Sarea and I that disgusting? Yeah, we probably were. Sometimes we still are.*

Their occasional kisses remained thankfully brief, and he allowed their flirtations with only a random grumble to cool their ardor. He reluctantly watched them and wondered when Lars would come to relieve him. His frigging feet were really starting to hurt.

* * *

"Hey, Lars!" Trumble called. "Someone wants to see you."

"Be right there." Lars checked his face in the mirror as he finished washing before guard duty. Running a comb through his damp hair, he hurried from the bath chamber, praying he didn't have bad news waiting for him or a crisis to deal with.

He stopped, staring, the comb clutched in his hand.

His father stood in the chaos of the main room with his hands clasped in front of him.

Of Lars's three roommates, Trumble sat in a chair, scraping mud off his boots and onto the floor. Moergan searched through a pile of dirty laundry for a decent pair of pants to wear and Serian crawled out of bed, mumbling, "You about done in the privy? I gotta take a leak."

Lars nodded dumbly.

Serian broke wind and staggered past him to the privy room, relieving his bladder without bothering to close the door. He rarely closed the door.

"So this is where you live?" Bostra asked, the first words he had spoken in Lars's presence for nearly six summers.

"Yes, sir," Lars replied. He swallowed at the sound of his father's voice. Goddess, it had been so long ago, nearly beyond memory, and yet it still resonated as familiar. As home.

Bostra looked around at the strewn remnants of their frenzied adolescent lives. At the dented practice armor, the grungy clothing, scattered books, stained blankets, and rumpled, unmade beds. Moergan had a pair of girls' underdrawers tacked to the wall above his bed and something rotten stunk in Serian's corner.

Lars felt like he'd been caught in public with his pants around his ankles, but he resisted the urge to try to tidy up. It was too late for that.

"I paged here, too, did you know that?" Bostra asked. "I was about your age when I came here."

"No, I didn't know that," Lars replied, surprised to hear his own voice and astounded by his father's height. *Goddess, I'm taller than he is, by a hand width or more. How did that happen? He was always so big and I so small.*

"My room was down the hall." Bostra chuckled and shook his head. "This brings back so many memories. My roommates and I, we would try to sneak in ale or girls—"

"Dubric won't let us," Lars interrupted.

"I know. He hasn't changed in twenty-five summers.

But you still try, don't you?" Bostra nodded toward the panties on the wall. "Try and sometimes succeed?"

Lars shook his head. "Not me, sir. Dubric doesn't allow it."

The silence stretched before them, a long chasm of lost summers and uncertainty.

Moergan and Trumble looked at each other. "Maybe we should go," Trumble said, glancing at Serian as he staggered from the privy.

Lars held his father's gaze calmly, seeing the disappointment and confusion on his face. He had seen nothing else there, not as far back as he could remember.

"You've never *tried*? Not once?"

"No, sir."

Silence again, somehow both vast and tight.

Moergan yanked on a pair of pants and tossed another pair at Serian. The three left, closing the door behind them while Lars and Bostra faced each other across the room.

Bostra knocked some dirty socks and a broken crossbow off a chair and sat. "Can we talk? For a few minutes?"

"I thought we were talking, sir."

"You're not making this any easier."

"I'm sorry, sir. What would you have me do? I apologize, but I am a bit rushed. I'm supposed to report for duty." Lars put the comb in his pocket and shrugged.

"Are you and Otlee filing papers?"

"No, sir," he said. *I'm replacing Dien after his shift, not that you would care,* he wanted to add, but didn't.

Bostra leaned forward and pulled a pile of armor off a chair. "Then you can spend five minutes talking to . . . to your father." He looked up at Lars. "Please. Just five minutes."

"Dubric is expecting me."

"Dubric will understand." Bostra gestured toward the chair.

Lars sat, knowing darn well Dubric would not understand.

"So," Bostra said, "how have you been?"

"My health has been good, sir."

Bostra frowned. "That's not what I meant." He seemed to struggle with what to say, and his hands clenched and unclenched on his knees.

"I have been fine, sir. Is that better?"

"No." He sighed and leaned forward. "Look, I know I haven't been the best father, and you don't even know me anymore, if you ever did."

"I have no complaints, sir."

"You don't have to keep calling me 'sir.'"

Lars blinked. "But I have always . . ."

"I know. You've always tried to be a good boy. Even when you were little. And I never appreciated you. I know that now, and I wanted to say that I'm sorry." He sighed and said, "I only came to say I'm sorry."

Lars stared. He had no idea what to say or do.

Bostra stood. "I understand if you hate me, sending you away like I did, and leaving you here all alone. But you've done well for yourself and you've made your mother and I both very proud. I thought you might want to know that."

Bostra turned to go while Lars struggled to understand what had happened. Confusion and joy grappled for control as he stared at his father and wondered what to say.

When the door creaked open, however, he leapt to his feet and hurried to the threshold.

"Wait!" he said, scrambling around the chair. "Where are you going?"

"My five minutes are up."

For a few moments, Lars had forgotten about guard duty. He took a breath and nodded, knowing he needed to tend to his work.

Bostra extended his hand. "Thank you for giving me a few minutes."

Lars grasped his hand. "You're welcome, Father."

Both smiled. Bostra said, "Perhaps sometime this spring Dubric can let you come home for a phase or so. I'm sure your mother would love to see you."

Lars grinned. *Home.* "I think I can arrange it."

"I'm sure you can." After one last smile, Bostra turned and walked away.

* * *

Her head resting on Risley's shoulder, Nella startled at the sound of a rap on the door. Lars opened it a heartbeat later, grinning.

"What's got you so chipper?" Dien asked.

"I'll tell you later." Lars laughed, following Dien back to Dubric's main room. He frowned at Risley and Nella, then he and Dien conferred quietly with Dubric, just outside the open door.

"While we have a moment alone," Risley said against her cheek, "I'd like to ask you something."

She turned in his embrace to look into his eyes. Try as she might, she could not conceive of him committing the murders. She just couldn't. "Ask me anything," she said, smiling.

He reached into his pocket, pulling out a C-shaped curve of silver. As he gently placed it on her wrist, he looked deep into her eyes. "I know this isn't the best of circumstances, but will you marry me?"

Her heart thudding, she touched the bracelet. "It's gorgeous," she said, fingering the delicate work.

He chewed his lip, watching her. "It's the right weave, isn't it?"

"Yes, but usually we Pyrinnian women wear bracelets after our wedding day."

He grinned and his nervousness seemed to fade. "We Haenparan men like to give gifts when we ask our beloveds to marry us. I thought a bracelet could be a compromise."

He glanced at the door and the continuing discussion between Dubric and his team. "Do you like it?"

"Very much." The bracelet sparkled in the filtered morning light as he kissed her palm. She closed her eyes, considering her answer, then it rang clearly in her head. Risley was innocent. He could not, would not, have killed those girls. Dubric had made a mistake. No matter what their future held, she had only one answer to give. She leaned forward, her fingers tracing along his cheeks, and said, "Of course I'll marry you. I love you."

"Thank the Goddess," he said, drawing her close and kissing her. "I thought for a moment I'd lost you." His hands in her hair and his breath in her mouth, he leaned back against the cushions and she followed, climbing onto his lap.

She felt no hesitation, no fear, no worry or second thoughts, only the warm encouragement of his hands upon her back.

"I think that's enough," Lars said from behind her.

Risley kissed her one last time before releasing her. "Ah, what I wouldn't give for a few glorious minutes truly alone."

She searched his eyes and smiled. "Oh? Whatever do you mean?" she asked, wishing Lars would wander off again. Time crashed against her, shortening with every breath, and she did not want to lose a moment.

Risley kissed her softly and said, "Wait here."

She nodded and he slipped away, walking to Lars and Dubric. She didn't hear what they discussed, but a short while later the door closed and latched, leaving them alone.

"We've ten minutes," he said. "Let's not waste it."

Ten minutes sounded like an eternity to Nella, and she leapt into his arms.

* * *

Sunlight shimmered through the curtains and he smiled, gently tugging on the laces of her uniform as he kissed her. "I've waited so long for this." He nibbled her shoulder, tasting her sweet, clean flesh.

"So have I. Far too long." Her hand on the back of his neck trembled with her nervousness, but she didn't pull away.

He kissed her again, pulling off his shirt and casting it aside as he pressed her back upon the bed. A shaft of filtered sunlight gilded the pillows in a warm inviting glow and he smiled as he caressed her arms, her breasts, her lips. Her dark eyes glimmered in the sunshine.

A twitch pulled at his smile, but she didn't see. "So small, so slender, so delicate," he said. He took great care and he took his time, drawing her to him, stroking her short brown hair, kissing her succulent throat and her honeyed mouth.

Her touch was both a bliss and a torture, addictive as the finest wine, and he marveled in her presence and her skin. Despite his aching need to finish, he warmed her slowly, savoring every morsel of their touch. Their clothes disappeared, landing with a whisper on the floor as they rolled together. She held his head as he suckled her, her thighs alongside his hips.

"Will it hurt?" she asked him, her voice airy and soft as she moved beneath him.

He shifted her hips, pressing close against her warmth, and her head rolled back with her delight. Her mouth fell open and she gasped his name, arching against him.

"Maybe at first," he whispered against her throat. "But I will be gentle. As gentle as I can."

He kissed her as she pulled him close, her fingers digging into his buttocks with her hunger and need. He felt the cool metal of her bracelet against his back, dragging against his skin like ice beside the fire of her touch, and he smiled. "Shh," he said, nuzzling her neck. "Are you in a hurry?"

"Someone could come," she replied, blushing, her eyes searching his. She reached up to touch his face and raised her head to kiss him, bringing him close.

That's my girl, he thought, shifting her hips again, adjusting the angle as he kissed her, pressing her back, pressing against her. Holding her breast in his left hand, his right brushed the hair from her eyes. He wanted to see her, see her eyes in the sunlight, and he suckled her as he whispered her name and reached beneath her pillow.

She lay warm and quivering beneath him, ready and oh-so-willing. He looked into her eyes, into her soul, and moved forward, stabbing into her hips—and into her throat.

Blood spurted against the wall, curving to his right as she arched beneath him. "Shh," he said, timing his strokes to the rhythm of her blood as he pulled the dagger away. "The pain is done. It's done."

Her eyes grew wild, terrified with their agony and surprise, and clouded with confusion at the realization of what he had done. She flailed against him, trying to cover her throat and trying to get away, but he held her still and watched her eyes.

Blinking, she weakened, her fingertips and toes cooling as the arc from her throat lessened. "Stay warm," he said, thrusting toward his goal, yet never leaving her eyes. "Stay warm, my love. I'm almost done, almost there." She grew limp and he pulled his hand from her mouth, for she no longer had the strength to scream. His left hand free, he grasped the headboard to help his balance. He did not want to crush her.

As he filled her with his seed, her eyes started to grow distant and peaceful. He shuddered inside her, her limp legs alongside his own, her hand twitching on the bed, and he grinned. "All done," he said, kissing her lips and avoiding the blood-drenched sheets. "Now, that wasn't so bad, was it?"

She didn't answer, merely stared at the ceiling above them. Her hand stopped fluttering.

He kissed her again and climbed off, stretching. "An amazing gift! Thank you for sharing it with me." He smiled at her, the one who had cleansed him. Lifting the dagger, he ran a finger down her warm thigh and licked his lips.

He climbed atop her, straddling her chest, and reached down to remove her lovely brown eyes.

Grinning, he slurped one luscious orb, popping it like a grape between his teeth. Chewing happily, he took her nose and ears, as well.

* * *

Certain that his sitting room contained nothing more dangerous than furniture and books, Dubric boxed the last of the evidence against Risley while Lars told him how his father had come—to his rooms, no less—and invited him home for a visit.

Dubric smiled, happy for the lad's exuberance. "It is about time," he said, folding the last bloody dress. "You have not been home once since you came here."

"It's unbelievable!" Lars cheered, wandering away with his nervous energy. "And he talked to me, Dubric. Can you believe it? A genuine conversation!"

Smiling, Dubric tucked the dress away and hefted the box. He walked toward the closet in the corner while Lars chattered away. Without warning, the horrid, familiar ache of a new ghost fell into his head like a block of ice. He gasped, staggering, and the box fell at his feet and burst open. "No," he said, closing his eyes to the naked girl appearing before him. Slender, petite, and dark-haired, she rose limply from a supine position with blood streaming from her throat and her eyes gone. Clinging to the wall with his eyes scrunched shut, he scrambled away, toward the closed door of his sitting room, but she remained in front of him, her hands fluttering.

Oh, Nella, he thought, trying not to look, trying not to see, but he had to move, had to catch the monster while he was still trapped. He braved a glance, so quick it was barely a breath, and her face had disappeared, lost beneath a nest of cuts.

"No, no!" he cried, trying to catch her nose, her ear, her pert chin, but they fell through his hands to splatter on the floor.

"Sir?" Lars asked, helping him stand. "What is it? What's wrong?"

"Nella's ghost!" he rasped, stumbling through the mangled image. "Run!"

"Oh, Goddess!" Lars turned and bolted, leaving Dubric to manage alone.

Dubric saw Lars kick the door open, pulling his sword with a flash of steel. Somewhere in the madness, a woman screamed. He had nearly reached the door, his head throbbing like the tide, when Lars came through again.

"She's fine, sir."

"She's what? But I saw!"

"Dubric?" Nella said from inside. "I'm fine. Really. We both are. Even with Lars scaring us half to death."

Dubric straightened his back and staggered into his sitting room, pushing past the pain in his head.

Risley and Nella stood beside the divan, their hands locked together and her new bracelet gleaming in the sunlight.

"For Goddess's sake, can't I have a few moments of private conversation with my betrothed without having the door broken down? Why in the seven hells did you have Lars barge in here?" Risley asked. "Surely our time isn't up yet."

"I saw . . ." Dubric rubbed his eyes and the pressure lessened for a blessed moment. "I saw her die."

Nella gasped and covered her mouth. Risley drew her close, protecting her against his chest, and his voice grew hard and deadly. "You what? How? Where?"

"A few moments ago," Dubric said, falling into a chair. "But she is still alive."

"Of course she's alive! Goddess, I told you I'd never harm her."

"I know that now," Dubric said as his stomach fell to the floor with dark dread. *He is innocent. All this time, all the evidence, yet he is innocent, and the killer is still loose. By the King, I almost killed Risley!* "I am truly sorry I misjudged you," he gasped, his words strangled.

Risley and Nella sat, their hands still locked together. "What are you saying?" Risley asked.

"I was wrong. Someone else murdered those girls." He drew a shaky breath and looked into Risley's astounded eyes. "All accusations are dropped. You can go home a free man."

"But," Lars burst in while Risley and Nella gasped, dumbfounded, "if it's not Risley, who is it?"

Dubric shoved himself to his feet, following Lars through the door. "I do not know, but he is no longer afraid of broad daylight, and we have to find him before he kills again."

Dubric shook his head. The physical proof—the hair, the splinter of wood—were Risley's, but he was not the killer. What if someone had planted them? Could they have been stolen? Lars had reported that Risley had forgotten to lock his suites. Dubric winced. He had been so sure that he had found the killer's undoing with that tiny sliver of wood; instead it seemed that he had simply fallen into the murderer's schemes.

Otlee burst through the main door with a folder clutched against his chest. "Sir," he called. "I found something."

Startled, Lars and Dubric turned, their hands falling to their swords. "Damn, Otlee," Lars sighed, pinching the bridge of his nose, "you scared the piss out of me."

"Sorry," he said, rushing to them, "but this couldn't wait." He opened the folder and pulled out the killer's letter and a page of notes taken from Risley's office.

Risley and Nella walked through the sitting room door and Otlee frowned, leaning close to Dubric and lowering his voice. "I'm sorry, sir, but I don't think Lord Risley wrote the letter. Look." He pointed to several words and letters common to both pieces. "They're actually written differently. Look at the letter 't' especially."

Dubric squinted at the killer's note, then the sheet taken from Risley's office. While the overall look was indeed quite similar, almost identical, the killer crossed each 't' with a single, straight line, whereas on Risley's notes they were consistently all one piece, loop up, cross over, continue on.

"I'll be damned," Lars said, whistling through his teeth.

"The angle of the end strokes is different, too, but the 't' . . . It's just not the same person, sir. I think he tried to make it look like Risley's handwriting. It is very similar, but it's not the real thing." Otlee shrugged.

"Nice job," Dubric said. "Faced with this, I would have definite doubts, as would any Council in the land." Smiling, he looked to Risley and Nella. "Hard evidence supporting your innocence. Congratulations."

"That's damn good news to hear," Risley said, relieved. "I'll leave you to discuss the case, if you don't mind." Hand in hand, he and Nella disappeared into the sitting room.

Dubric followed with Risley's sword and ledger, interrupting the pair before they became too involved. "We will smuggle you out tonight as originally planned, but in the meantime stay here, out of sight. I will not bother you again until then." He handed Risley his belongings and backed away. "I am truly sorry for this mistake and I hope you both can forgive me." He paused, not sure what else to say, but at last he added, "Carry on."

Leaving Risley and Nella to their privacy, he closed and locked the door behind him.

* * *

"Something's wrong," Dari muttered, helping Stef stretch a sheet across Lady Helline's bed. "Nella hasn't come back."

"Who gives a rat's whisker?" Stef muttered. "She's been nothing but trouble since she came here. You're just griping because Ker asked to not work today, and with Nella sneaking away to mourn Lord Sweetie, I get stuck working with you. Dammit, I hope they replace Plien soon. I dunno how much more of you and Little Miss Perfect I can stand before I snap."

She didn't sneak; someone lured her away. Dari grumbled, "Why don't I do towels instead of Mirri the rest of today? How would that be? Then you won't have to look at me anymore."

"Pfft," Stef said, tying her last corner. "Better you than eye battings and giggles."

Dari worked in silence for a while, wishing she had a snappy retort. Mirri came and went, restocking towels and humming a sappy tune, and she gave Dari a cheerful wave as she carried out the last of the used linen.

Dari smoothed the embroidered coverlet, letting Stef fluff the pillows, and she was about to pronounce the room done when a bloodcurdling scream filled the air.

Stef froze, but Dari ran. "Mirri!" she called, barely hearing her own voice over the next window-rattling wail. Calling Mirri's name again, she skidded through the door.

A handful of other cleaning maids gathered in the hall, their screams and terror adding to the chaos. Dari shoved through, working toward the noise, to see Mirri stumble back from a room while screaming her fool head off.

"What is it?" Dari asked, turning Mirri's face away from whatever terrified her.

Mirri raised a shaking hand, pointed, and fainted dead away.

Dari turned and swallowed her own scream. The suite Mirri had pointed to was one of several un-claimed rooms on The Bitches, which occasionally housed visitors. Policy demanded all suites receive fresh linen every phase, even if no one had slept in the bed or used the bath. As she took a single step forward, Dari doubted this bed would ever be used again.

Blood had soaked the mattress and pooled on the floor like buckets of spilt wine. One arm leaned against the bedpost above a mangled mess of flesh and bones. Blood splattered the walls—scrawled in words, she thought, although she could read little beyond her name—and dripped from a neatly stacked pile of flesh on the bedside table.

Waving off cautions and concerns from the girls behind her, she took another step forward, through the doorway. An armload of towels lay on the floor at her feet, probably dropped by Mirri, and had started to soak up the mess. Despite the horror upon the bed, her eyes continually sought the pitiful arm tied to the bedpost. "No," she whispered, over and over, blink-ing at the simple steel bracelet on the woefully thin wrist.

She reached for the latch and backed away, drag-ging the door with her. It closed with a sharp slam and several girls screamed. "Find Dubric," she said without

looking at them. Banging her head on the door, she
cried and waited for Dubric to arrive.

* * *

The crowd growing silent behind him, Dubric
opened the door. Someone screamed and Otlee cursed.
Remaining in the doorway, Dubric surveyed the scene
with dread gnawing at his vitals.

The latest victim's skin and muscle had been removed from both thighs and her abdomen, leaving one
uncut arm tied to the bedpost. Blood flowed to the floor
like water, still liquid and fresh, while four bright towels sopped the puddle's edge.

He took a step in and checked the inner latch to
find it dripping with gore. "Right-hand print again," he
said, and all three of his men noted the observation. He
turned and tried to take in the scene.

Blood splattered all four walls of the narrow suite,
dripping down the plastered surface like rich red frost-
ing. *Nella make me clean Nella make me perfect Nella
make me kill make me eat,* the walls said, proclaiming
passion and rage intertwined.

"But it is not Risley," he whispered to himself. "Who
else? Who else wants Nella?"

"Sir?" Lars asked from behind Dubric, but Dubric
shrugged him off and strode deeper into the room.

"Otlee, question the girls who found this."

"Yes, sir," the boy said, and the door closed, blocking out the chaos of the crowd.

"The girl's name is Ker," Lars said. "I met her while
guarding Risley. She rarely talked, seemed meek, was
nearly invisible."

"A friend of Nella's?" Dubric asked. He examined
the wounds opening her belly. The blade had torn the

skin, moving up her right hip, across the bottom of her ribs, and down to the void that had once been her left leg in one curved slash. Slicing sideways, the killer had removed her belly skin above her pelvic bone, leaving her pubis and female organs intact and strangely devoid of blood. Unlike the other girls, the leavings glistening in her privates left him no doubt that she had been raped.

Her left arm had been drawn upward to lean against the bedpost, tied securely at the wrist, and her limp hand hung from a bracelet of cold forged steel. It pointed to the pile of thigh meat laid out upon the bedside table. Each slab seemed to have one bite missing.

Tossed beside her like a discarded morsel, the removed portion of her belly lay on the far side of the bed, along with most of her right arm—the skin and muscle stripped from the main bones, yet still attached to her wrists—and one lung. Not bothering to skin or break the ribs, the killer had pulled her chest organs out from below and thrown them aside, leaving the torso an empty husk. Both breasts were bare and covered with bloody smears and streaks, the filthy ardor of a killer's caress.

Only one wound marked her throat, a fatal piercing of the jugular below her jaw on her left side. It had left the nightstand and nearby wall saturated with her life's last blood. Her face was simply gone, every feature and defining mark removed and taken away, while her skull lay crooked and nightmarish under her blood-drenched hair. Her grayed, tiny teeth seemed to scream.

"You are sure this is Ker?" he asked, sketching a diagram of the scene.

"Yessir," Lars said. "I recognize her hair and bracelet."

"Frigging bastard son-of-a-whore," Dien muttered

from the far side of the bed. "Our friend left us another present."

Leaving Ker for the moment, Dubric rounded the bed. He stopped and stared at the horror on the carpet.

Ker's intestines lay piled into a neat and tidy nest, cradling both partially chewed kidneys like eggs from a demonic bird. A pert white sheet of parchment stood amid the gore, held upright between the two kidneys.

Snarling, Dubric snatched the letter away and broke the seal.

> *Marinade not to your liking? Perhaps fresh would suit your whims better, and I promise she is delectably tasty, indeed. Forgive me for my indulgence, my Lord Castellan, but I've grown hungry these past days awaiting my release from the pits to the joy of light.*
>
> *I take what opportunities present themselves, and your politics have set me free. For that, I, and my Nella, thank you.*

Lars knelt beside his knee, lifting delicate strands from the mess. "Three hairs," he said. "Just like Risley's."

"Bastard thought we missed them last time?" Dien asked.

"Perhaps. There is no telling what the beast may have stolen from Risley's rooms, or when he had taken it." Dubric handed Dien the letter. "'Politics have set me free.' How can he know Risley is no longer in the gaol?"

The crowd erupted outside the door, and something hit the wall. They turned as Dari's voice screeched, "Where is she? Damn you, boy, I know damn well Dubric sent that man to fetch Nella and now she's disappeared. Did he feed her to Risley? Is she dead, too? Answer me!"

The door creaked open and Otlee fell through, landing on his back while Dari pummeled him. "He's not dead, is he? He's killed two of my friends. Tell me where he is."

"I can't say anything," Otlee screeched. "No one tells me anything."

The crowd roared, throwing whatever they could land their hands upon and calling for Risley's immediate execution. A voice rumbled from deep within the bedlam, "I saw strangers enter Dubric's suite. I saw them. Risley's alive, did you hear? Risley's alive and they're taking him back to Haenpar."

Silence filled the hall for a heartbeat of time, then chaos erupted, spread, and thundered away, moving to the main stairs.

Dubric yanked Dari off Otlee and snarled, "Yes, he is alive and Nella remains with him. He is also completely innocent of these crimes, of that there is no doubt." Shoving her away, he added, "But you may have just signed her death warrant. We were keeping her safe, for King's sake, keeping her hidden until we took her to safety."

Giving her a last scathing glare, he pulled Otlee to his feet and staggered toward the door with his ghosts dragging behind him.

* * *

Nella snuggled close, safe and warm in her love's embrace. *Haenpar,* she thought, *we're going to Haenpar and we're going to be married.* They sat together on the divan, a blanket covering them from the winter chill, and they talked and kissed and held hands, discussing the coming days. Every so often when they kissed, Risley's hands would wander forward from her waist and back. His touch on her belly and breasts felt like the gentlest spring breeze, and if he didn't linger she pretended she didn't notice. A touch of more than a brief moment or firmer than the flutter of a butterfly's wing would get his hands brushed away, and he'd smile against her mouth.

He had lingered but three times—and Nella wished he would linger again, just for a moment—oh, Goddess, it felt so nice. Then he stopped trying and became more gentlemanly, more reverent, more awed.

And he smiled more.

Curious, she asked him why he smiled and he said, "Because you pushed me away, love. At first I wasn't certain. I barely felt your touch upon my wrist, so I tried again. I hope I didn't scare you." He kissed her, snuggling her close against him. "We have no reason to hurry. I can wait as long as you need me to."

"I'm not scared, not really."

"I know, but after what had happened to your sister, after what you endured in Pyrinn, I'd rather not take the chance." He kissed her nose. "Perhaps we will wait to make love until our wedding night, perhaps we won't. Only time will tell. But I'm honored to take as much time and care as you need." He kissed her then, slow and lingering. "Because I love you, and because you're not ready for me to touch you like a lover."

"Maybe you could just ask?" she said, gazing into his eyes. "Give me a chance to say 'no,' or to say 'yes'? Like you did when you first kissed me?"

One eyebrow rose and he grinned. "All right." He kissed her, holding her close, and whispered against her lips, "May I caress your breasts, my love, just for a moment?"

Trembling but not afraid, she nodded, whispering her answer into his mouth. "Just for a moment, yes."

She felt the warmth of his hand through her dress and they sighed one breath as he gently explored her.

Something outside crashed, and Bostra yelped in surprise. Risley pulled his hand away and lifted his head, listening. Another crash slammed against the wall and Nella gasped. Angry voices filled the air, calling for blood, their ire punctuated by destruction and noise. He left her, covering her before he ran to the locked door. "What is it?" he called over the din. "Bostra?"

The door burst open without warning, knocking him back to skid on his backside across the floor. Furious people fell upon him with a vengeance, screeching and clawing and trying to rip him limb from limb.

"No!" Nella screamed. She flew from the divan, tripping over the blanket, and she struggled to stand. She had not yet regained her footing when a lady hit her across the face with a broken bit of board. She fell again, gasping and spitting blood, and she reached for Risley's struggling arm. "Don't go!" she wailed, crawling forward. "Don't take him from me."

Their hands locked, his flailing from beneath the pummeling assault, hers shuddering from the board's staggering blows on her back, and she collapsed, falling face first to the floor.

As if her grip had held him there, he slipped away, gone with the screaming mob, and the lady stood over her, sneering. "This is all your fault, bitch," she snarled, slamming the board against Nella's head.

Risley disappeared from Nella's sight and everything fell black.

* * *

Dien, Lars, and Otlee ran well ahead, while Dubric struggled to keep up. The ghosts tugged at him, making him stumble in his fatigue and pain, but he remained

near enough to see his men try in vain to halt the ri-
otous spread.

Destruction and madness surged through the halls
and charged up the main stairs. Dubric gasped and
grunted, following the noise toward his suite. A
screaming woman fell down the stairs with her right
arm cut off and spurting blood. He let her fall.
Staggering, he dragged his aching body to the third
floor, only to witness the crowd surging back toward
him.

"Hang him, hang him!" they chanted, knocking
Dubric aside as they passed. He glimpsed Risley in the
midst of the crowd, carried limp and battered. He saw
Bostra fighting at the rear of the crazed group with his
forehead split open. Bostra struggled to reach Risley,
but the crowd heaved him back again and again like a
bad potato. Dien, Lars, and Otlee were nowhere to be
seen.

The ghosts laughed and Elli threw Rianne's severed
arm into the frenzy. Dragging Risley with them, the
crowd thundered down the stairs, growing ever louder
with each passing moment.

Dubric staggered to his feet, using the wall as lever-
age, and he tottered for a moment before taking a step
toward the retreating crowd. *Where is Nella?* he
thought, his vision darkening for a moment. *Surely she
would follow Risley . . .*

He stopped. The rioters knew Risley was in his
suite. Someone had told them. The killer knew Risley
had been released, and the killer had written of politics, hinting he knew about the threat from Haenpar.

"But no one knew Bostra was here," he said aloud in
the empty hallway. "None but us four, Risley, and
Nella." He tried to remember the faces of the patrons
of the Dancing Sheep, but, dammit, Bostra had re-

mained covered, he never showed his face. No one knew, not a single soul outside his little circle. Even the note had been delivered sealed.

He fumbled in his pockets and pulled out the rumpled bit of parchment, wincing at the flecks of green wax that crumbled, falling to dust his boots. Green wax. *Faldorrahn-green*. Not Haenparan-blue.

All his ghosts stopped their cavorting to stare at him.

Beckwith had delivered the note from Bostra. Beckwith, the herald, always ready with a stub of wax to seal—or reseal—a message. He read the note; he knew where to find Risley. Small things, things Dubric had not noticed at the time, suddenly came back to him. Beckwith had heard him argue with Risley the day the package arrived, and had heard Risley's exact phraseology. He could have known what to put in the letter to sound like Risley. Beckwith's wife held the key to the china cabinet and he had free access to Brushgar's papers. Dubric shook his head, trying to clear his thoughts. Risley had denied that he had been given a razor, but Dubric had believed Beckwith's account of the delivery. What if it had been Beckwith who was lying? He hated Risley. Dubric suddenly remembered Lars's report of the scuffle between the two men. Beckwith had had the opportunity to kill Meiks and Nansy, yet had neatly eliminated himself as a suspect with the presence of a head wound, one just like Nella's. But the wound had been in back while Nansy was attacked from the front.

Why did I not see the connections before? How could I have been so blind? Beckwith's own wife testified about him desiring young, pretty women, but I dismissed the connection, seeing only his foppish demeanor and mincing attitudes.

His throat went dry as he thought of the common thread that had led him to Risley. Nella. She cleaned for the Beckwiths; he had often seen the herald tittering over her, wanting her to scrub doilies and polish trinkets or asking about Risley . . . "No!" Dubric howled, staggering toward his suite. "Nella!"

No more ghosts, he pleaded with himself. *Please get there in time, so there will be no more ghosts.*

* * *

Nella blinked away the black haze of pain and tried to raise her throbbing head. She tasted blood, and spat, which made her head swim alarmingly, but she grimaced and opened her eyes anyway. *I have to get to Risley,* she thought, struggling to get her legs beneath her. *I have to save him.*

Someone else was in the room with her; she could sense them, hear their breathing and a low delighted chuckle. A man.

"Dubric?" she asked, crawling forward, still unable to see clearly. The world shimmied and spun, flapping like a flag in a strong wind.

"Not Dubric," the voice rasped. A terrifyingly familiar metallic *click* filled her ears. "Are you ripe yet, little girl? Have I let you marinate long enough? Are you ready for me?"

Squealing, she scuttled away, slamming against the divan and trying desperately to see, to make sense of the wavering view.

No one was there. The room settled to a slow ripple and she rubbed her eyes. The chairs, the bookshelves, the etched glass lamp shattered on the floor. Curtains brightened by a daytime sky. The same room she had spent the last few bells in. Cluttered, ransacked, and perhaps broken, but the same room, and she was alone in it. And yet she wasn't.

"Are you going to answer me, little girl?" he asked, closer this time.

She drew her feet beneath her hips and pressed herself against the divan. "Where are you? Who are you?" She smelled blood, but saw nothing, nothing but the room.

"What's this?" the voice said, and someone grasped her arm and wrenched her to her feet. The bracelet spun on her wrist, turned by his scalding touch. "What a lovely little trinket."

"Risley made it for me," she said, her voice faltering.

He hit her across the mouth and sent her reeling onto the divan. "We shall not speak of him again, little girl. It has taken me many days and much planning, but your Lord Romlin is finally dead."

Cold stinking metal slid across her throat and she shied away. "Why?" she whispered, shoving her voice through her trembling throat. "Why blame all this on him? Why do this to me?"

The thing she could not see hissed and said, "The moment I saw you I wanted you for my own, but Risley already had your heart in his hand when he brought you here. You couldn't see, could you? How I longed for the briefest words, the most innocent touch. All you saw, all you wanted, was that beast who would tire of you and toss you aside like last week's moldy soup. He didn't deserve you, and any man who would leave his rooms open and unlocked was just begging to take the blame for my cleansing."

His blade traced meandering patterns across her throat. "I could remove two obstacles at once, give Dubric a handy and plausible suspect and free you for the taking, all the while preparing myself for our union.

"They were no more than a pox upon the land, with their tainted flesh and lewd ways. But you! Perfect, pristine, and lovely. Risley didn't deserve you."

He laughed and pulled her upright, sitting her on the divan while keeping the blade at her throat. "But I do. I want you. I love you. I made myself virginal again, just for you!"

Her chest heaved and she clenched her fists against the divan cushions. "You killed those innocent women!"

"They were not 'innocent'!" he snarled, the blade moving downward to slice the flesh along her collarbone. "They were vile and filthy whores. All but the last, but I needed her gift to make me ready for you. Can't you see? And you and I, we are meant to be together."

She whimpered, scrunching her eyes closed. "No, please. Don't hurt me."

Lander Beckwith appeared from nowhere, pulling back the hood of his cloak and easing from the empty air like a wraith. Nella screamed, trying to scramble away from the apparition, but she had nowhere to go. Wildly, she searched the room, looking for something to use as a weapon against him, and she noticed Risley's sword leaning in the corner, right where he'd left it. Struggling to control her terror, she swallowed and returned her attention to the ghostly image of Beckwith.

"Shh, my darling. I'm not going to harm you." He knelt before her, grinning and becoming solid as he completely pulled back his hood. Blood smeared his teeth and chin, and had dried upon his hands, turning the edges of his fingernails nearly black. She saw a bit of dark meat between two of his teeth and her stomach roiled. He leered at her and traced the blunt edge of his razor up her thigh. "I've aged you to perfection and you're mine now."

She stifled a scream and stared at him, panting and struggling to remain calm as the razor dragged across her belly.

He pulled the blade away, slowly, and she saw layers upon layers of dried and blackened blood on the blade and the handle, coating but not obscuring Risley's gilded name. The razor looked and smelled like death and damnation. "That's my girl," he said. "I'm not going to hurt you, not if you cooperate."

"That's . . . that's Risley's."

He laughed, licking his lips. "'Risley's'? Goodness, no. He never knew about it, never missed it. It fit my purpose so well and gave me a bit of well-deserved finery. I must admit that I was surprised when Dubric discovered its disappearance, though. The old bastard was smarter than I thought, but not smart enough, was he? He looked right at me yet never saw the truth. No one suspects a lowly messenger, especially one so clean."

She stared at him, her heart thudding a staccato of terror, but she said nothing.

He showed her the razor, closed it and put it away, his eyes never leaving hers. "See? I've put it away. Stand up."

She shook her head, but he grabbed her by the throat and pulled her off the divan. "Never, ever disagree with me. Do you understand?"

She tried to speak but could get no more than a squawk past his grip.

"So pretty, so fine, so mine," he laughed, looking into her eyes. "I've waited a long time to touch you, but at last my plans have reached fruition." He grinned and kissed her, the taste of death filling her mouth as his lips burned against hers. She froze, mewling, and the pressure at her throat faded away.

She fell back, onto the divan, and sucked painful gasps of air through her throat. "How could you have . . . have killed all those people?" she asked, spitting away the rotting taste in her mouth. "You were always such a nice man. I trusted you! We all trusted you! You have a family, for Goddess's sake!"

He laughed, yanking her to her feet again. "Power belongs to those who take it, not to the meek. I am meek no more." He wiped the smear of blood from her collarbone and licked his finger clean. "You, my darling, are luscious enough to eat. Let's have us another kiss, shall we? And then we'll see what other tasty treats our love can find."

She took a step back, her hands balling into fists. "Never. I'll never love you, you filthy, disgusting beast!"

Snarling, he tossed her on the bed and lunged for her. "Mouthy little bitch! And here, after all that I've done, you dare to question me? We're perfect for each other, both of us clean and pure, both of us at the precipice of our destiny. You'll be begging for more before we're through, you'll see. You'll be so happy that you're mine."

Slamming her onto the mattress despite her struggles, he kissed her, his mouth and breath reeking of death. She fought, biting and kicking, until she felt the hated blade against her throat again, then she fell still.

"That arrogant bastard did teach you to like it rough. I should have known he'd steal my prize away." Foamy spittle collected at the corners of his mouth as he clawed up her skirt. "I should have killed him when I had the chance."

"We never!" she screamed. "He's never touched me. Please!"

He shoved her knees apart, pinning her to the bed with his weight on her hips and the razor at her throat, and he grinned, kissing her again. "Then I get the first taste, after all."

Her eyes widened as a shining sword appeared beneath his jaw. "Get off her," Dubric said, "before I save the executioner the trouble of removing your head."

Beckwith laughed and rolled slowly backward until his weight rested on his knees instead of her hips. "Will you?" he asked.

"Are you all right, Miss Nella?" Dubric asked.

Nodding, she scrambled away and pressed herself into the far corner.

"Get up. Slowly," he said to Beckwith, glancing at the blood spattering Beckwith's face and hands. "Drop the razor on the floor. Now."

"Certainly," Beckwith said, then moved in a sudden lurch, swinging his arm beneath Dubric's sword.

Dubric yelped, stumbling back, and Beckwith grinned. He rose from the bed and stood. "My Lord Castellan," he said, moving toward Dubric and reaching for the hood of his cloak, "I do believe you're bleeding."

And then he disappeared.

CHAPTER
21

†

Lars fought near the temple hall, shoving a kitchen lackey face first against the wall. "I said that's enough!" Blood flowed freely down his right arm and he wrenched the offending knife out of the boy's hands. Behind him, an archer named Almund tussled with a pair of scullery maids screaming filthy insults.

"I ain't scared a you," the boy yelped, struggling.

"You ought to be," Lars snapped, pulling the boy off the wall and slamming him into it again. He glanced around. The worst of the riot had moved away, but remnants of anger still brewed in the halls. Men, women, and children ran to and fro, most just trying to get away, but a few continued to cause trouble. One, a leather worker named Earst, swung a flaming torch like a club. Helplessly, Lars watched him light a fleeing privy maid afire.

Earst looked Lars's way, his eyes glowing red in the reflected light of the torch. "I'm gonna see you burn, page," he snarled.

Lars turned, instinctively yanking the lackey in front of him, and the boy's filthy, grease-spattered tunic burst into flames. The boy screamed and Lars shoved him away as Earst pulled the torch back for another swing. Lars threw the lackey's knife and it embedded in Earst's upper chest.

Earst yanked the knife free and snarled, "You'll pay for that."

Lars stumbled back and pulled his sword, but Earst slumped to the floor like a burst sack of flour as his right arm and shoulder separated from the rest of him.

Bacstair the Baker stood there, bloody sword clenched in his blood-spattered hands. "Where's my son?" he asked, stepping over the body. "Where's my Otlee?"

Lars tilted his head toward the temple and tried to ignore the throbbing pain in his shoulder as he desperately patted out the lackey's fire. "Sounding the alarm."

Bacstair nodded and ran past, slamming the sword into whoever or whatever got in his way. Almund clonked the two scullery maids together and both finally fell limp. Near the north-hall entrance, Dien flipped a nobleman headfirst against the wall, then shoved aside a caterwauling seamstress.

The lackey's fire out, Lars clenched his sword in his hands and ran forward to help Dien and the archers. He smelled smoke and hoped it was just the privy maid or the lackey.

Where's Dubric? Where's my father? he thought, pressing through the chaos.

"Lars! Behind you," he heard Otlee scream.

Even as he elbowed away a screeching window maid, Lars turned, sword in hand, shallowly slicing open the belly of a weaver wielding a pair of brass candlesticks. Before the weaver slumped to the floor, he turned the sword and clubbed the maid's head with it. She dutifully fell at his feet and he stepped over her without a second thought.

Just ahead of him, Dien struggled with four swine-herders. Lars hamstrung one and grabbed another by the collar, yanking him aside, toward Bacstair and Otlee.

Dien snarled and ducked, flipping one over his back as he reached for the next.

"You all right, pup?" Dien asked, drawing a breath before knocking a swineherder against the wall hard enough to crack his skull.

"I'll live," Lars said. The throbbing pain in his shoulder had all but disappeared, but so had much of the strength in that arm. His blasted sword arm. He stepped over the man on the floor and a swineherder howled as Bacstair cleaved off his hand.

Perfume tickled Lars's nose and he sneezed. It seemed so close, like a great aunt suffocating him in a hug, but he stood in a pocket of relative quiet. Something cool grasped his free hand and started to lead him forward. He felt like he was fading into the welcoming chill, like stepping into a pool of cloudy water, and he saw a hazy shape of a woman, a lady, beckoning him to hurry. Bluish and nearly transparent, she looked to him with great sadness and riveting urgency.

One of Dubric's ghosts? Goddess, how can I see her? How can I feel her? Who is she? What does she want with me?

"Lars!" Dien said, shaking him. The big man held his face and peered into his eyes while madness careened around them. "You get bashed on the head? That arm wound worse than it looks?"

Startled, Lars blinked as the haziness surrounding him vanished, but he still felt the gentle pull on his left hand. "No, I'm fine, really."

The ghost shimmered at the edge of his vision, like a

flickering play of light on water, yet floating in the air. He could not see her, not in any true sense, but her touch flowed up his arm, soaking into him, freezing his heart and the blood coursing in his veins.

"You must come!" a voice inside him seemed to say. "Now. For Dubric. Please!"

The coolness tugged within his chest and he lurched to the side, gasping through a tickle of perfume in the air. She appeared solid before him for a moment, her glowing eyes filled with urgency and pain, and she touched his cheek, mouthing words he could not understand. The chill in his blood faded with her image, then he felt the gentle tug on his hand again. "I think there's something wrong with Dubric. I can't explain it, but I have to go."

"What the peg?" Dien smacked a nobleman aside and started following Lars, but a group of milkmaids wrestling over a tapestry blocked his way.

"Lars, don't! It's too dangerous!"

"I have to," he yelled over the din as the ghost dragged him toward the stairs. "I'll be careful."

Dien's reply was lost to the chaos, but Lars paused on the stairs to see Otlee pulling a laborer off Dien's back and Bacstair shoving a cleaning maid aside. He started back down to help them, but the ghost pulled him up the stairs, refusing to release her grip upon his hand.

* * *

"Get behind me!" Dubric yelled, swinging his sword toward a recently fallen chair. Beckwith had disappeared into thin air as if he never existed, leaving no more than the stink of spilt blood to mark his passage.

Nella sidled toward him, clinging to the wall, but the bed heaved downward then sprung up again. She squealed, jumping away, then suddenly rose from the floor and slammed into the wall. She hung there, gasping for breath, her eyes wild and terrified. Blood smeared across her throat and she squeezed her eyes closed, turning her face away.

"*Tsk, tsk,* my Lord Castellan," he heard Beckwith say. "This morsel is mine. She stays with me."

Afraid to move for fear of harming Nella, Dubric watched, horrified, as the line of smeared blood moved downward, plucking a button from the front of her uniform. Nella gasped and her eyes opened. Without warning, her knee shot upward, then she fell suddenly to the floor.

"Don't you touch me," she screamed, clawing her way upright and scrambling for a wooden chair. "Kill me if you must, you bastard, but *do not touch me!*"

She swung downward and Beckwith howled. The chair, an antique that had belonged to Dubric's grandfather, shattered like old porcelain.

As Nella swung again with the chair's severed back, Dubric rushed forward to help her. With a cry of defiance, she scrambled away, toward the far corner, then skidded to a halt.

Dubric froze, hearing the unmistakable sound of a sword being drawn.

The broken chair shifted and Beckwith laughed. "Looking for this, little girl?"

She turned, slowly, and backed away, shaking her head. "Please," she whispered. "Not Risley's sword, please don't kill me with his sword."

Where is he? Dubric thought. He moved forward, searching the room for the slightest hint of movement, of noise, of the scent of death.

"All right," Beckwith tittered as pain exploded in Dubric's sword arm and he slammed against the wall.

"Dubric!" Nella screamed, staggering toward him.

"Oh, peg! Goddess-damned son-of-a-whore," he yelped. Risley's sword had skewered the muscle of his upper right arm, pinning him to the wall, but he could not reach the hilt with his left hand. Agony ripped from his shoulder to his wrist and his own sword clattered as it fell, skittering away from his feet. He smelled hot, rancid breath and laughter burned his ears.

"My dear Castellan," Beckwith chortled in his ear, "I am so glad that you've decided to remain as witness to my latest endeavors. Although I'm delighted to allow you the pleasure of watching, I have no intention of sharing her with you." Dubric heard a hard metallic *click* beside his ear. "She's all mine."

"Nella, run!" Dubric begged. He turned his face away from the razor against his cheek and found himself staring at his ghosts.

No longer causing trouble, they stood frightened, mouths agape, and stared at Beckwith. Fytte seemed to say something, and she backed away, pointing and shaking her head. *What are they looking at? Why suddenly now?*

Nella mewled Dubric's name and he rolled his eyes to look to her. By the King, she seemed miles away as she stumbled farther from Beckwith's dark laughter.

"No!" Nella squealed, falling to her backside as her feet shot out from under her. Dubric watched her try to scuttle away, but she flipped onto her back and her legs lurched apart.

"What happened to the quiet, compliant girl I used to know?" Beckwith muttered. "After all I've done, you dare to disappoint me? You owe me this; you owe me your love."

Wishing his ghosts would do something to help instead of remaining rooted near the door, Dubric tried to relax his muscle enough to move the sword, but the pain kept his bicep tense and howling in agony. And he could not reach the damned hilt!

Nella bucked and fought her attacker, one hand spurting blood from a crosswise gash. "I paid my debt and I'm free. I don't owe anyone anything." She clawed the air and turned, lurching to the side, and her knee shot up again.

Beckwith howled.

Nella scrambled away, climbing over the bed and leaving a trail of blood splatters and handprints on the blankets. Both hands and forearms sported defensive cuts, and the slash across her collarbone had drenched the bodice of her dress.

She had almost made it, nearly reached the relative safety of Dubric's side of the room, when she squealed and fell face first to the floor, pulled back by one foot across the bed.

"No!" she screamed, grabbing anything she could, reaching for Dubric, but moving backward despite everything she tried.

The blankets lumped up behind her knees, as Dubric continued to struggle against the sword. Desperate, Nella grabbed a bedpost and hung on, screaming as blood burst from the back of her leg in a spattering shower. "No! I won't go," she cried, kicking.

She lifted from the bed by her feet and she thrashed before she was flung away, against the wall, on the far side of the bed. She slumped to the floor, twitching and bleeding. Again Beckwith laughed. "Oh yes, you will, little girl. I didn't do all this for nothing."

"Help her!" Dubric yelled at his ghosts, the blade

ripping a larger hole in his arm, then he smelled Brinna's perfume.

"Nella!" Lars hollered from the doorway.

Praise the King. "He is there!" Dubric said, pointing with his free hand. "The other side of the bed. Help her!"

Grunting, Lars pulled the sword from Dubric's arm. "Who?"

Dubric tried to take a step forward but fell back against the wall, grabbing his tortured bicep. "Beckwith!"

Lars settled Risley's sword in his hand. He nodded, taking a deep breath. "Then I'll aim high." His back straight and his head held high, Lars strode toward the blood-splattered corner, then fell backward as a shallow gash appeared on his belly.

Brinna had yanked him back, and she turned, yelling something at the ghosts.

Dubric stumbled forward, dizzy, and weakly fell to his knees.

Blood reddening his shirt, Lars rolled and heaved with his legs. Something heavy crashed against the bookshelves, knocking them over. Lars shoved himself upright, leaning sideways with his sword dragging on the floor while his free hand pressed against his belly. "Wanna try that again, little man?"

"No, Lars. No!" Dubric cried, scrambling toward him. He felt a rush of cold like a harsh winter breeze, which knocked him onto his face near the shifting pile of books.

The underside of blood-splattered boots materialized in front of his nose, peeking from beneath a tattered wool cloak. Dubric raised his eyes and looked into Beckwith's sneering face. Elli had snatched off his hood, but she cowered away, watching the black and bloody razor, as Beckwith struggled to find stable footing among the scattered books. Every ghost stared at Beckwith's blade, their eyes huge and terrified. *By the King! The ghosts do not fear him, they fear his razor. Not the man, but the thing that killed them!*

Glancing at Lars's hesitant approach, Beckwith kicked Dubric in the face then rolled away, disappearing under the cloak again.

Dubric howled, the ache in his arm lost under the bright agony of a broken nose. Books skittered beside him and he tried to crawl away, but he felt a slash open his upper arm, his back, his side.

Lars leapt to stand over him, swinging his sword, and Beckwith yelped. Books scattered in all directions as he slipped away, some slamming into Dubric's face.

Lars panted, dripping blood on Dubric. "Can you stand, sir?"

"Go! Save Nella. Save yourself," Dubric said, crawling to his sword.

"I hit him, sir. It's not impossible."

Dubric grasped his sword and swung toward movement he felt more than saw. The sword shuddered in his hands, hitting bone, and Beckwith howled. "Get Nella!" Dubric ordered. "Get her and get out of here!"

He saw Lars stumble toward the far side of the bed, and a trail of blood splatters followed. Dubric lunged on his hands and knees, tackling the air above the dripping blood, and they tumbled across the room, hitting a bureau.

The razor skittered away, under the bed. Every ghost watched it go.

Cold air rushed past Dubric. Screaming, Beckwith kicked him again and again, knocking him aside, but the ghosts swarmed, ripping and tearing Beckwith with their teeth and nails.

"What the piss?" he cried, trying to get away, but the ghosts had him and would not let him go. "There's nothing there. Nothing!"

"There is more than you think," Dubric said, gathering his feet beneath him. An ear, a ripped off finger, and bits of clothing flew through the air. Staggering upright, Dubric left Beckwith to the wraiths he had created.

They lifted him, wrenching him around and tearing gashes in his clothes and flesh. Rianne, always the butt of jokes and torture, leered at him, snatching at his scalp and peeling strips of his face away.

"What magic is this?" Beckwith screamed. "What demons have you set upon me?" He crashed and stumbled, tossed around the room like a child's toy.

"You set them upon *me*," Dubric muttered. He staggered around the bed despite the pain from his injuries and the weakness threatening his legs. "But you are welcome to them."

Lars knelt with Nella and he looked up. "I think she'll be all right, sir," he said. "Her breathing's strong and I've got most of her wounds bound. Maybe she just hit her head."

"Let us hope so." Putting his sword away, Dubric knelt beside Lars. "Nella?" he said, patting her face. "Wake up. I need to get you out of here."

She batted him away, squealing. "No. No!"

"Shh," he said, trying to catch her hands. Behind him the chaos continued, punctuated by screams and crashes. "It is all right, Miss Nella. We need to get you to safety."

Panting, she braved a glance. "Dubric? Lars?

Goddess, you're hurt!" Pushing his hands aside, she leaned forward to help. Just starting to examine Lars's belly, she glanced up and screamed.

Hot, wet fingers encircled Dubric's throat, pulling him backward. He struggled, his lungs starved for air, and tried to reach for his sword.

Lars stood, protecting Nella. "Let him go!"

"I'm taking one of you with me," Beckwith said, and Dubric felt hot breath and hot blood on his cheek. "I'll rip his throat out with my teeth, if I have to."

Dubric struggled to see Beckwith, but saw only raw meat and dripping skin. From the corner of his eye he saw a flash of white, then he and his captor tumbled backward, onto the bed. Beckwith's fingers clenched into his throat and Dubric's vision wavered, turning gray and black. He blinked, struggling for a breath. Lars stood above him, pulling his sword from the thrashing beast beneath.

"Die, you bastard," Lars said, slicing downward.

One last heave and clench, then the vise at Dubric's throat lessened and fell away. He slid down from the bed to his knees, gasping through his crushed throat while his head swam with sudden lightness. The pounding ache behind his eyes had disappeared.

Nella scrambled to him, calling his name and catching him as he fell into her arms. *They are gone*, he thought, slipping into the empty void. *The ghosts found their justice. Praise the King.*

* * *

"You're sure he's dead?" Nella asked.

"I'm sure," Lars replied, bandaging Dubric's injuries. "I cleaved his chest open. What was left of it, anyway."

Nella held Dubric in her arms and rocked him while tears rolled down her cheeks. "How can I ever repay you both? All you've given for me."

Lars cut off the ends of the makeshift bandage before tearing another strip off the bedsheet. He flexed his fingers, trying to shake away the tingle he had felt when holding Risley's sword. "Marry Risley and have half a dozen kids or so. Name one after Dubric. He'll be thrilled."

She smiled sadly and stroked Dubric's bald head. "I think I can do that." Still comforting the unconscious man in her arms, she asked, "What happened? How can I explain what I saw?"

Lars frowned, tossing answers through his mind. "I don't think you need to explain it, Miss Nella. Beckwith got what he deserved. We lived. He died. Justice is served."

"But something tore him apart, something angry and vicious. For Goddess's sake, his face has been ripped away, leaving only blood and mess and one eye! How can I be sure whatever did that is gone?"

Lars smiled. "Because justice has been served, Miss Nella, and she's a harsh mistress. Beckwith didn't realize it until it was too late, but her scales are balanced again. I promise."

A crash filled the air and Lars stood, drawing his sword, then sagged with relief as Risley burst through the door.

Bruises and welts marked his skin, his clothes hung in tatters, and he only wore one shoe, but he scrambled over broken furniture without heed to his injuries. "Oh, Goddess," he croaked, stumbling. "Nella!"

"She's right here, Ris," Lars said. "She'll be all right."

"Risley!"

"I'm here, love," he coughed out, rounding the foot of the bed. "Are you all right? What happened?" He winced as he spoke and his voice cracked.

Putting his sword away, Lars stepped aside to make room.

They embraced over Dubric and Risley looked at the man bleeding on her lap, then the man bleeding on the bed. "Who is he?" he coughed, kneeling beside Nella and holding her close as he checked her injuries.

"Beckwith," Lars sighed.

Risley cleared his throat, rubbing it, before speaking to Nella. "What happened to you?" He swallowed, wincing as he rubbed his throat again. "You're bleeding. Are you all right?" Shaking his head and struggling to breathe, he coughed then forced out, "And what in the seven hells happened to him? For Goddess's sake, he's shredded."

"Justice is a harsh mistress," Nella whispered, still stroking Dubric's brow. "And I'll be fine." Her fingers paused and she gasped. "What happened to your neck? Oh, Risley!"

He coughed, nearly choking. "They tried to hang me, but Bostra cut the rope, and Dien . . ." Risley swallowed, grimacing, then cleared his throat ". . . he opened a path through the mob. The archers and some other men there were trying to help. The crowd wanted to kill me! But all I could think about was getting back to you." He coughed again, his face reddening for a moment as he choked. His eyes watered as he sucked in a breath, then another, panting and leaning his forehead against Nella's shoulder. "Thank the Goddess you're all right."

While Nella worried over Risley, Dubric's eyes flickered and he shuddered awake, looking at his three companions as if he'd never seen such miracles before. "They're gone?"

Lars nodded and helped him stand. "Yes, sir, I do believe so." Once Dubric was on his feet, Lars smoothed his bloody shirt and bowed slightly. "The murderer is dead, sir. The lady is saved. What would you have me do?"

Dubric laughed. "Get me out of here and find someone to clean this mess up." He paused, looking Lars over. "And get that gash stitched. I do not need to purchase you yet another uniform."

"Of course, sir," he said.

Supporting one another as best they could, the four stumbled from Dubric's suite, leaving death behind.

* * *

The moon had risen, shining its slender grin among the sparkling stars, as Dubric followed Risley and Nella from the castle. The wound through his bicep ached, but the shallow gash on his side itched. He struggled not to bump his broken nose when he covered a yawn with his hand.

Bostra stood beside a carriage, the bandage on his head gleaming in the moonlight. He bowed as they approached. "Your carriage awaits, milord, milady," he said, opening the door. "And we have a long ride ahead."

Nella looked from Risley to the grand horses to Risley again, then she turned to smile upon Dubric and his men coming down the steps behind him. For a brief moment she looked so beautiful, like his beloved Oriana had in moonlight, that his heart clenched.

"How can I ever repay you?" she asked. "You saved our lives."

"We have no life debt here, Miss Nella," Dubric said. "Surely you know that."   •

She smiled, nodding, her hand leaving Risley's. "I know." She hugged him, kissing his scarred cheek. "Thank you, Dubric. Thank you."

He blustered and Nella slipped away to hug Lars.

Dubric's heart had barely settled before Risley said his good-byes and helped Nella into the carriage. Bostra lingered a moment before following the couple and closing the door behind him. The driver clucked to the horses and the carriage rolled away, shimmering in the moonlight like reflections on water.

"And there they go," Dubric sighed. "May they have a happy life together."

Lars scratched his belly. "I think they will, sir."

"Sir?" Otlee asked. "Shall we start clearing the mess and begin preliminary paperwork?"

Dien laughed, turning and holding his lantern to illuminate the stairs. "It'll wait till morning, lad. Never you worry. We've finished what we need to and now it's time for an ale."

Dubric yawned. "Followed by a full night of sleep. Paperwork can wait until the morrow."

The others started up the stairs but Dubric paused, squinting at a patch of snow along the southern wall. A tiny crocus peeked through, its petals reaching upward. By morning it would be in full bloom. He knelt beside it, pushing snow away from the blossom.

"What do you see, sir?" Lars asked, coming back down the stairs.

"Spring," he said, standing. His head felt light and clear, as did his heart. The ghosts had found justice and spring's harbingers had come. Praise the King. The dying days of winter had finally ended.

Lars looked at the flower and chuckled, shaking his head. "Aye to that, sir. I'm ready for a little warmth."

As am I. Dubric draped his arm over his page's shoulders. "Let us get that ale, shall we?"

"Yes, sir!"

Together they walked into the castle, leaving the night to the moon and the coming spring.

ABOUT THE AUTHOR

Tamara Siler Jones lives in a refurbished farmhouse in her native Iowa, USA, with her husband, daughter, and menagerie of pets. A creator by nature, Tamara worked as a graphic designer until Dubric's ghosts forced her to chronicle their demises. She enjoys making quilts, watching horror flicks, and baking sweet concoctions whenever possible. Visit her website at www.tamarasilerjones.com for more information and slave monkeys.

*Can't wait for more gruesome,
spine-tingling mystery?*

*Don't miss the next chilling
adventure with Dubric Byerly . . .*

THREADS
OF
MALICE

Coming in fall 2005 from Bantam Spectra

THREADS OF MALICE

Coming in fall 2005

B raoin saw strings.

They streamed from somewhere above, dangling before his eyes. Black and shining in reflected firelight, they rustled in the slightest breeze yet hung ever before him, just out of reach.

Not that he could move his hands to try and touch them. He felt like immovable sludge, thick and heavy and still. He lay on his belly, his head balanced upright on his chin, while his muscles remained lax and uncooperative. He blinked and time strung away from him, fading to a dark river.

When he dragged his eyes open again the black strings had disappeared and his view had shifted.

His head rested on its side and he stared at his right hand—at least it looked like his right hand, with paint on his knuckles as he remembered—but it slumped upon a board like a dead slab of meat. Beyond it he saw only darkness. He took a breath, determined to stay awake, and tried to move his fingers. One finger, the smallest, twitched, but the rest remained still.

Goddess, I've never been this drunk, he thought, letting his eyes fall closed again. He remembered eating supper with Faythe and her father but he'd had to leave before sunset, had to get home early because . . .

The dark! His eyes bolted open. His paint-stained right hand and his bare wrist and forearm lay still; there was no reaction when he tried to move his fingers. He could not lift his head, nor move his legs, which somehow hung free beneath his hips. His upper body lay chest down on a hard, scratchy surface; his arms were bare and his back and shoulders felt cold. Braoin could tell from the breeze on his toes and testicles that he no longer wore his boots, or his pants.

Desperate to move, he forced a twitch through his dead fingers then a spasm gripped his hand, flipping it off the board like a fish out of a bucket.

"Waking, eh," a man's voice said from the dark. "Was afeared of that. Quit yer kicking if ye know what's good for ye."

* * *

Dubric Byerly slouched behind his desk and tapped a pencil on a slip of paper. He knew what he wanted to write, but what politics permitted him to write was a different matter entirely.

"The boy merely wants a short visit," he muttered. "Why must it be such a difficult request?"

He had spent the past two bells sequestered in his office contemplating the same thin slip of paper. He remained determined to convince Castellan Hargrove of Haenpar to let his son come home. Somehow.

At sixty-eight summers of age, he had been Castellan of Faldorrah for nearly forty-six summers. In all that time he could not recall having to walk such a fine razor between common sense and the needs of one boy.

He knew Lars wanted to go home; it was all the lad had spoken of in the moon since his father's reluctant offer, but there had been no confirmation or encouragement of the visit from Haenpar. Not that Dubric had expected there to be. Six summers before, Castellan and Lady Hargrove had sent Lars into Dubric's care, insisting he be made a page. Not once in all that time had Castellan Hargrove enquired as to his son's welfare, nor expressed polite interest in his life. Lars had been banished, penniless and barely literate, on his ninth birthing day. With his fifteenth soon approaching, Dubric could barely believe that the lad wanted to go home, or that his parents would let him.

Sighing and rubbing the back of his bald head with a burn-scarred hand, Dubric took another sip of tea.

The door burst open and Dubric looked up as Lars ran into the office. Gawky as any lad on the cusp of manhood, Lars's cheeks were flushed an urgent purple and his straw-colored hair was unkempt and wind-blown like a tousled halo. He smelled of mud and horse manure.

"Sir! We've received a messenger from the northern reach."

"What is it?" Dubric asked, standing, his plea to Lars's father forgotten for the time being.

Lars held Dubric's gaze. "A murder, sir, at least I believe that's what he's saying. I do know he rode all night and he's terrified."

Not again, Dubric thought. *Can we have no peace?* Gathering his cloak, he followed Lars from the office.

By the time they reached the stables, Dubric had slopped a fair share of mud upon his boots and trousers. Flavin, the stable master, waited outside the door, crushing his hat in his hands. "The lad's nigh about spent," he said, "and his horse . . . I'll do what I can, but I ain't holding out hope, sir. Plow horses ain't a meant to run like that. I've got Goudin walking her, but I don't dare tend her further 'til she cools."

Dubric nodded grimly and Lars opened the stable door for him.

Dubric's squire, Dien, knelt near an open stall door,

holding a filthy, bleeding boy as the lad splattered Dien's boots and the straw on the ground with tendrils of vomit. Dien cradled the boy as if his hulking presence could protect the lad from whatever horrors he had come to tell.

Dubric hurried toward them with Lars close behind. "What happened?"

"Not sure yet, sir," Dien said, patting the boy gently on the back as the retching eased. "Eachann bashed his head and he's not making much sense. Someone died, best as I can tell, from the northern reach. Beyond that, your guess is as good as mine. He's insisting he talk to you."

The stable door opened again and Otlee, Dubric's youngest page, ran through, the physician Rolle following him.

"Fetch him a drink," Dubric said to Otlee, "at least to get the foulness from his mouth."

"Yessir!" Otlee bobbed a quick bow and ran through the door again, his hair shining coppery red in the morning sunlight.

Dubric approached the boy slowly, leaving Rolle plenty of room to work. "How old are you, son?"

The boy winced at the physician's touch. "Thirteen summers, m'lord, give 'er take. Never paid much 'tention."

"And your name is Eachann?"

"Yessir, I—" He grimaced, lurching away from the physician. "Hells! Ye ain't gotta kill me, I'm a'ready half there!"

Dubric offered a consoling smile. "You were saying?"

"Geese, m'lord. I tends 'em." The physician touched Eachann's bleeding shoulder and the boy yelped again.

Dubric rubbed his forehead. "Blast it, Rolle, must you torment him so?"

The physician grasped the boy's chin, holding him still while he moved a finger in front of the boy's eyes. "Besides a variety of contusions, he has a dislocated shoulder, a broken elbow . . ." the finger dropped and Rolle leaned close to look into his patient's eyes, "and a concussion, apparently." He stood, sighing. "I do believe he will survive questioning, but please, get him bathed and into a warm bed as soon as possible. You have no business keeping him here in a stable."

Rolle gathered his things. "Send a runner to inform me when he's settled so I can set the arm and give him something for the pain. Until then, I leave him to your care."

"Thank you," Dubric said as Rolle walked past.

Eachann winced as he cradled his broken arm and looked at Dubric. "Yer him, ain't ye? Lord Dubric hisself."

"So they tell me. What brings a battered goose farmer to my castle?"

Eachann looked up at Dien before returning his pained gaze to Dubric. "The dark, m'lord. T'was the dark."

"That's the same thing he's been telling me," Dien said, drawing his cloak higher over the boy's shoulders. "I think the fall rattled his brain."

Dubric knelt before them, his knee beside a steaming puddle of vomit. "Why the dark, Eachann? What happened in the dark?"

"It took another one," Eachann said. "This time it was one I knew."

Dubric watched the boy's fingers clench into the fine wool of Dien's cloak, tearing it. "What scared you? And why brave the dark to come here?"

"Another gone, and yesterday they found him, dead, spit up'n the river near Barrorise. My pa said someone hadta ride, I hadta ride, hadta get to the castle, to tell Lord Dubric about the dark. No matter how scared I was, I hadta tell."

"You said another. How many have been taken by the dark?"

Eachann shuddered. "I dunno. Some. Lots. I hear stories 'bout the dark, how it's taking us, but it ain't never took no one I knew, nor spit him back b'fore."

Dubric rocked back, resting his weight on his heels. "Who?"

"Neighbor. Missus Maeve's boy. Name's Braoin."

Dien paled, holding Eachann closer. "No. Oh Goddess, no."

Dubric looked at Dien. "You know this Braoin?"

Dien smoothed the boy's blood-stiffened hair. "Yes, sir. He's my wife's cousin, her aunt's son. Good lad, never one to cause trouble. Sarea and the girls are up there visiting."

Dubric stood, gently taking Eachann from Dien. "Lars, gather my things, find Otlee, and get ready to ride. Dien, tell Rolle I am taking Eachann to my suite. Meet me here in half a bell."

His two most trusted men nodded their acceptance and followed Dubric from the stable. As he helped the boy to the castle, the wind picked up. The air smelled like rain.

* * *

Gray sky had begun to darken by the time four grim riders crossed into the reach. Spattered with mud and drenched from the incessant drizzle, they rode into the village of Stemlow and drew their mounts to the golden warmth of a tavern.

"Otlee, bring the map," Dubric said as he tied his horse.

He entered the tavern first, his nose wrinkling at the stench of dung-laced tobacco. Farmers and laborers looked up as he entered, their suspicious glances taking in his official garments and ready sword. The lone barmaid, a thin woman with a pox-scarred face, slopped a drink over her hand as she stared at him, and the barkeep paled before returning to his ales.

Most of the patrons turned away when Dien's dark bulk filled the doorway. "Guess they don't get many travelers," Dien muttered.

"Likely not," Dubric said, pulling back the hood of his cloak. "If memory serves, this village is little more than a mark on the map." He spotted an empty table far from the welcome heat of the fire and led his men to it, maneuvering between groups of grumbling men.

They had no more than grasped their chairs when the barmaid appeared with a pitcher of ale and four tankards. "Tea for the boy," Dubric said, "and four bowls of whatever is hot."

"Rabbit an dumplins, m'lord," she said. He nodded and she scurried off, leaving them in peace.

"Let us see where we are." Dubric accepted the map from Otlee and spread it upon the table. "Your family is in Tormod?"

"A couple of miles north, sir," Dien said. "At Sarea's parents' farm. But her aunt Maeve lives in Falliet."

Dubric tapped both points on the map, Tormod almost due north along a road curving slightly to the northeast, Falliet closer but northwest. "We cannot reach both tonight," he said. "The road through Falliet pulls too far west, surely two bells extra ride."

"Yes, sir." Dien sipped his ale and frowned at the map. "Nearly three with two of the rivers forded along that route. The road through Barrorise and its bridge give a far quicker ride. To Tormod, at least."

Lars wiped ale foam from his lips with the back of his hand. "So what do we do?"

"We separate." Dubric rolled the map and returned it to Otlee. "Dien must see to his family whereas I must investigate the disappearance."

The barmaid set a mug of hot tea before Otlee. "Beggin' yer pardon, m'lord, but I overheard ye talkin'. The younguns maybe oughta stay here if they can. It ain't safe up north."

Dubric noted her thin, worn hands, ragged apron and earnest worry. "You have heard of the disappearance in Falliet?"

"Pah," she said, rocking back and rubbing her arms as if she felt a sudden chill. "Tain't just Falliet, but most all the reach. Us'n Bendas are the only ones to not lose younguns, far as I know. We hear the stories, m'lord, and keep 'em dear."

Dubric took a sip of ale, grateful for the warmth filling his belly. "What sort of stories?"

"Tis the towns along the rivers sufferin' so, m'lord. Somethin's happenin' with the dark and the water. Younguns disappear in the rain or headin' to the well, and Goddess knows ain't no child allowed to go fishin' no more, even in broad daylight. Atro the peddler came through here a phase er two back, said he saw the dark reach out an' take a boy, an' the boy ne'er even screamed. Was there, then he was gone. Taint safe fer yer boys, m'lord. Not on a rainy night like this."

Lars calmly regarded her over his mug of ale and said nothing. Otlee held the map-case in his thin, ink-stained hands and said, "I'm not afraid of the dark."

"Mayhap ye oughta be," the barmaid said. "Yer just a lil' feller, bout the size of my Guin, an he knows to be afeared." She sighed and glanced over her shoulder to the bar. Waving an affirmation, she turned back to Dubric. "We don't use'ly let rooms, m'lord, but I can tell Earl to give ye one, iff'n ye want. His daughter done got hitched last moon an' her old room's still empty. Be tight sleepin', but the younguns'd be safe."

Dien drained his ale as the woman trotted away. "You and the lads can stay here till morning, sir, but I have to get to my family. If the shit up north is so bad they know about it in this piss-pot village, I need to protect my girls."

"I'll go with you," Lars said, his cheeks turning pink. He took a long drink and set his tankard on the table.

Dien frowned at him and shook his head. "Maybe you'd better stay here. We don't know what we're up against yet."

The barmaid appeared again, placing bowls of stewed rabbit and a trencher of bread on the table before hurrying away. Ever hungry, Lars reached for a bowl and started in. "Heck, I'm not afraid of any kidnapper, and maybe two swords are better than one, especially for protecting your family."

"I can protect my own family, pup," Dien said, scowling into his bowl of stew. "Besides, Dubric will need you. You're better off helping him."

Otlee smiled conspiratorially at Lars. "We don't both need to go with Dubric. I can do most everything myself. It's mostly just taking notes."

Dien picked at his food. "Maybe neither of you should go, not if children are being taken. I've half a mind to send you both back to the castle."

Dubric let them argue, their voices fading to nothing as he ate. *Missing children suggest slavers. Mines? Textiles? Why only the reach? What is the connection with water? And what about the one found dead? An escapee, or something else?* His thoughts paused and the spoon in his hand trembled.

He knew what awaited him on the dark road ahead, and he knew he had no choice but to face it. It was his curse to bear, and a burden he would not shirk, no matter the cost.

He took a sip of ale, washing the tang of dread and disgust from his mouth. His boys had nothing to fear from slavers. "No one is staying behind. Otlee, you ride with me. Lars, you ride with Dien. We are leaving as soon as we finish dinner."

The matter settled, the others resumed eating and left Dubric to dwell upon his worries. He sighed. His eyes were beginning to ache already.

* * *

In a night turning rapidly colder, they crossed an unnamed creek without incident and bade each other farewell at the crossroads. Dien and Lars cantered to the east while Dubric and Otlee continued north. The drizzle became speckled with sleet, stinging Dubric's hands and stiffening his knuckles until he could no longer feel the reins.

Otlee rode beside him, silent and watchful, one hand guiding his horse and the other on the hilt of his shortsword.

Dubric unclenched one hand, opening and closing his pained fingers to loosen them. "I truly do not believe there is anything to fear. We likely face a small band of slavers who take children to work mines or for other unskilled labor."

"I know, sir. I'm just cold." Otlee turned, his face barely visible from beneath his cloak. "Is there an inn in Falliet? I hate to think we'll have to make camp in this."

"As do I," Dubric said. "Never you worry. Whether there is an inn or not, we will sleep somewhere warm and dry. You have my word."

Otlee drew his cloak tighter across his narrow shoulders. "Thank you, sir."

They rode on in silence for a time, with only the rain and mud-muffled steps of the horses marring the night. Farms stood well back from the road, warm lights from their windows twinkling through the rain. They saw livestock and stone fences and an occasional clump of trees, but no other riders, no people at all.

Not that I could blame them, Dubric thought, flexing his fingers again. *It is truly a miserable night.*

Suddenly he felt a pain in his head like ice falling behind his eyes. He gasped at its familiar and hated chill, clenching desperately for his horse's mane before he fell from the saddle. A score or more ghosts slid from the wet dark all around him, blocking the road and reaching for his cloak, his horse, his soul. All young, all male, they wailed silently and grasped at him in vain, some dripping spectral blood onto the muddy road. Their glowing green touch passed through his arms and legs, leaving only icy trails behind. *So many,* he thought, struggling to breathe past the pain quickly filling his head. *And all boys. By the King, what have I dragged the lads into? Slavers would not kill so many boys.*

His horse shied, lurching to a sudden halt and rearing back. One ghost reached for its bridle and it backed away, snorting.

"Sir!" Otlee called from beyond the glowing green horrors. Try as he might, Dubric could not see the lad past the chaos of the ghosts.

A small ghost the color of mid-summer swamp water hobbled to Dubric, pushing past taller, older boys. Twisted and lame, he stared into Dubric's eyes, demanding retribution, demanding vengeance. He reached for the saddle, his frigid fingers grazing along the leather to clench against Dubric's ankle.

"No!" Dubric hollered, lurching away and kicking at the specter climbing up him. The boy fell to the mud and faded away, as did most of the others, leaving just two ghosts blocking the road.

One of the remaining pair moved. A wiry lad of perhaps fifteen, he paced across the road and seemed oblivious to Dubric's presence. Glowing green sludge oozed from a flattened gash behind his right temple, and dripped from his crushed and mangled ear. The other, slenderly built, with a shadow of beard sprouting upon his chin, remained rooted where he stood. He wore not a stitch of clothes and stood with his hands clenched beside his hips, silently screaming. Sludge dribbled down the inside of one leg and pooled at his feet.

"Sir?"

Dubric blinked, shaking his pounding head.

"Sir!"

Dubric felt a tug at his arm. *Boys, all boys. What have I done? Lars! Otlee! No, please no.* Cold, wet fingers wrapped around his wrist, demanding he turn to look, insisting he pay them notice, while the two boys before him bled in an endless stream of glowing gore.

Snarling, he wrenched his hand away and lashed out, striking at the apparition that dared to cling to him, but he hit wet flesh and drenched woolen cloak, not the icy mist of a ghost.

Otlee yelped and fell away, disappearing into the dark.

Panting, Dubric blinked, wiping his eyes with a shaking hand as his horse danced away. *By the King, what have I done?* "Otlee?"

No answer, only the rain and the sleet and the ghosts bleeding onto the mud.

"Otlee!" Dubric scrambled from his horse and he fell to his knees, cursing the Goddess for plaguing him, cursing her again for his mistake. All the while his head throbbed and glowing green wisps tugged at the edges of his vision.

He crawled toward Otlee's horse, to the still form beneath its feet. Dubric's fingers clenched in the frigid mud, pulling him forward despite the shards of pain in his arthritic knuckles.

Otlee's charger, dark and dripping wet, stood over the boy and bared its teeth, stomping once beside the lad's head.

"I'm sorry, I'm sorry," Dubric said, crawling. "I never meant to strike the lad. Please, for King's sake, let me tend him."

Steam puffed from the beast's nose, and the same hoof pawed at the road. *So cold, so wet, and I promised the lad, I swore for King's sake, that he would have a warm, dry bed, not this damned mud!* Dubric reached toward Otlee then quickly yanked his hand away, just beyond snapping teeth.

"I did not mean to harm him! Damn you, beast, let me see to my page!" He pounded the mud with his fists, each slam sending pain through his aching head and stiff hands. "Please! I will beg if I have to!"

The horse snorted again, puffing moist heat over Dubric's face. The hood of his cloak had fallen back and icy water dripped down his spine, chilling him to the core. "Please. If he lies there long, he could freeze to death. He could die! Please!"

A burst of warm air, then another, and the pawing hoof stopped, falling still a step beyond Otlee's head.

Dubric inched forward, watching the horse as he reached for Otlee, and the beast's head dropped, warming the side of his face with another snort.

"Do not die, lad," he said, maneuvering between muddy hooves. "That is a direct order. Do not disobey me, you hear?"

His hands shaking, he felt along the back of Otlee's neck—all the vertebrae remained in place, praise the King—before rolling the boy onto his back.

Otlee gasped at the movement, moaning, and drew his legs toward his chest. Dubric felt steamy breath warm the back of his neck, and he hurried to check Otlee for injuries. All his bones felt straight and strong—but with no fat to keep him warm—and his heart beat a steady rhythm of blood through his veins.

When Dubric's fingers slipped behind Otlee's head he paused, his heart clenching. Gently, he touched the warm and tacky swelling again, feeling the damage with his fingers, and Otlee moaned in reply.

"Stay with me," Dubric said, lifting Otlee as he crawled out from beneath the horse. "We cannot be far from Falliet. I will find help and you will be all right. I swear on my life, you will be all right."

Otlee lay limp and unmoving in his arms as Dubric staggered to his feet. Wrapping his own cloak around Otlee, he climbed onto the saddle with Otlee cradled in his arms.

His horse shied as it moved through the remaining ghosts, but Dubric gripped the reins in one stiff hand and continued on, ignoring the chill soaking through him. Otlee's horse followed. As did the ghosts.

* * *

Side by side, Dien and Lars crossed the bridge over the Casclian River at Barrorise and continued north along the road following the Tormod River.

Just past the bridge, Dien reined his gelding in and dismounted. "Do you see that, pup?"

Lars heeled his mare backward then slid off the saddle. "I don't see anything but rain and mud."

"Then you need to look closer." Dien led his horse to the edge of the road and knelt.

Lars stood beside him. "It is a bit wide for a fishing path."

A wide swath of dead grass and weeds had been trampled flat in a careening path to the riverbank and rainwater flowed down through a pair of deep gouges in the mud. Dien stood, squinting, and pulled his sword. "Let's take a look."

Lars peered down to the river. "It's probably nothing."

Descending, Dien grabbed a sapling to keep from slipping in the mud. "Didn't that boy this morning say they found Braoin's body just north of Barrorise?"

The bank sloped down in a treacherous, slick path and Lars turned to inch down sideways. "You think they found him down here?"

Dien reached the bottom and looked up at Lars. "Someone dragged this tangle onto the bank. It didn't get here on its own."

Lars leapt the last few feet, landing in the rocks beside Dien. A pile of branches and brambles lay high upon the bank, a strip of cloth hanging forlornly to one broken branch. "Somebody tore their shirt," Lars said, pulling it free.

"Maybe it was Bray's." Dien squinted at the red and black diamond pattern. "I don't recognize it, but that doesn't mean a lot."

Lars reached into his pocket for a cotton evidence bag—Dubric insisted they carry basic supplies at all times. "Probably someone else's, but it won't hurt to keep it." The scrap of cloth tucked away, Lars walked along the bank, surveying the rocks and mud. "Between the rain, the river, and the dark, we're not going to see much."

Dien stretched, looking up to the sky. "No, I suppose not." Rain clouds moved overhead, sliced with glints of moonlight. "And what was here is probably washed away."

Lars crouched at the river's edge and reached into the frigid water. "Not everything." Something was standing in the water, breaking through the surface and sparkling in a moonlit circle against the black. He pulled a bottle from the muck and stood, tossing it to Dien. "Someone have a celebration?"

"Or a wake," Dien said, tilting it in the moonlight. "Whiskey. And the label's still fresh. It hasn't been in the river long. Less than a bell, I'd say."

Lars rinsed the mud from his hands before standing again. "Eachann came to the castle this morning, after riding all night. The body was found, what, yesterday?"

Dien nodded. "Yep, if not the day before. Give me another sack. Someone came down here tonight."

"In the rain," Lars said, tossing Dien a white cotton bag. He reached for a bush on the bank and started to hoist himself up. "I'm going to check the road."

"Be careful. I'm right behind you."

Lars nodded and continued to climb. He scrambled to the road and walked several steps in both directions, looking for tracks or more broken weeds, but the rain had nearly smoothed the mud. He heard Dien climbing the bank. "Cart tracks, I think," Lars called out, "but it's hard to tell. If so, they're heading north. There's nothing south of the horses."

"You sure about that, pup?" Dien asked, packing the bottle in his saddlebags. Grasping the horses' reins, he led them to Lars.

"Not sure at all," Lars replied, kneeling beside a curve softly gouged into the grasses. "Everything's washed away. But I think he turned around here. Look."

While the rain had leveled the road, the gouge in the grassy edge remained, open to the mud like a wound.

Lars pointed up the road to a sprawling manor house with windows brightly lit by lamps. "Who lives there? Would they have seen anything?"

Dien scowled and tossed Lars his reins. "That's Sir Haconry's estate. He doesn't see anything except . . ." Grimacing, Dien shook his head and mounted his horse. "Never mind. Promise me you'll stay clear of him. No matter what."

"Sure," Lars said, climbing onto his horse. "Whatever you say. I won't go near the place."

* * *

His head pounding like the tide against the stones of Waterford Bay, Dubric reached the village of Falliet only to discover that it made Stemlow look like a teeming city. Two shops, a church, and a handful of homes clustered around a cleared scrap of land and a wider stretch of road.

Dubric guided his horse to the closest building, a shop with a house attached to the back. Light shone from within, warm and welcoming, and he sighed with relief. Even the poorest fire would be better than this freezing rain.

Cradling Otlee close, he slid from his horse and stomped to the door, leaving the horses standing untied in the mud. Both ghosts followed, but he grit his chattering teeth and kept his back to them.

With Otlee balanced against his shoulder, he banged on the door with his free hand. "Open this door in the name of Lord Brushgar and the province of Faldorrah!"

Hurried footsteps, then the door eased open, bringing with it a rush of light and heated air.

A woman motioned him in with a candle in her hand and a hopeful look upon her finely-boned face. "Thank the Goddess," she said. "Eachann found help. Please, please come in. You must be freezing."

Dubric brushed past her, hoping his teeth did not chatter nor cold tremble his words. "I need a light, a basin of clean water, bandages, and a bed, and I need them immediately."

"Why?" she asked, closing the door. "Has something—" Gasping, she rushed to him and peeled back the drenched cloak. "Here, this way," she said, leading him past racks of fabric and clothing to an open door.

Dubric's host beckoned him from the shop into her home, a tidy dwelling with upholstered chairs and pillows and woven rugs. She led him farther in, beyond a small but immaculate kitchen to a closed door. "It's my son's room, but he won't mind," she said, pausing long enough to light a lamp near the door. "Take what you need. I'll fetch the water and bandages."

"Thank you." Dubric pulled the quilted coverlet back and lay Otlee upon the bed, removing the sodden cloaks as gently as he could with his shaking hands. "Your linens," he muttered at the smear of blood on the pristine pillowcase.

"Never you mind about that now," the woman said. She appeared at his elbow with a basin of steaming water and a clean rag. "Here, let me get that." She dampened the rag and wiped Otlee's face, rinsed the mud from the cloth, then began to clean the wound. "I've got a good selection of men's garments in the shop and another kettle of water warming. Help yourself to them before you catch your death. I'll tend your son until you return."

Dubric swallowed his guilt and choked out, "He . . . he is not my son."

She paused, glancing at Dubric for a moment before returning to Otlee. "I'll tend him anyway. Go on now. You're doing no one any good dripping all over my floor."

"Mama?" Otlee murmured, his eyelids flickering.

"Not your mama," she whispered, caressing his brow. "Lay still now. You're going to be fine."

Dubric staggered to his feet, slogging through incredible cold threatening to overtake him.

Otlee winced, pushing the woman away without opening his eyes. "It hurts."

She dampened the rag again and shooed Dubric toward the door. "I know, darling, but we'll make it all better. You'll see. Shh, now, and let me tend it." She stroked Otlee's cheek with one hand while mopping the wound with the other, whispering soothing words all the while.

Dubric lurched to the hall to find the pair of ghosts waiting for him. He closed his eyes and stumbled through them, his teeth chattering. Shivering and dragging the ghosts behind, he made his way back to the fabric shop. He grabbed a beautifully woven wool blanket and tugged it over his shoulders, but it did little to ease his chill.

His vision glazed over but he blinked the haze away, reaching for a rack of trousers, then tunics. He leaned in a corner, his fingers struggling to undo the buttons of his shirt. They were cold, stiff, and frozen, filled with arthritic pain, and incredibly uncooperative. The ghosts continued to stare at him, but he turned his head, his teeth clattering through a muttered curse. He had released one button and nearly had another free when his legs buckled. He fell to the floor, shaking with cold and staring at the still ghost's bare feet. After a moment, they shimmered and faded with Dubric into the dark.